Glory and the Lightning

TAYLOR CALDWELL

Glory and the Lightning

COLLINS   St James's Place, London

1975

William Collins Sons & Co Ltd
London · Glasgow · Sydney · Auckland
Toronto · Johannesburg

First published in Great Britain 1975
© 1974 by Taylor Caldwell

ISBN 0 00 222250-7

Set in Monotype Perpetua
Made and Printed in Great Britain by
William Collins Sons & Co Ltd Glasgow

For my dear friends,
William Everett Stancell and 'Bob' Curran
of *The Buffalo Evening News*

FOREWORD

I am refraining in this book from giving a complete bibliography, for all the students of Greece and Pericles know them too well, and have read them as carefully as I have read them.

From childhood I have been fascinated by Greece, and particularly Athens, but not by the endless wars and skirmishes of the period of Pericles. Wars, though sometimes interesting, especially when they are fought for freedom and the dignity of man, tend to repeat themselves throughout history, and not always for virtuous reasons.

The glory that was Greece was not the glory of the people of Athens but of their few sons, who, against the most terrible opposition and persecution, fought to make her the wonder of the world. It was in Greece that the first movement was made to control and limit the power of government, to give the people a voice in that government and to encourage them to vote and express their opinions. That later they were only too happy, for a little security, to surrender their right to free speech and inhibit their government when it became oppressive is the sad lesson of history which has repeated itself over and over since the days of Pericles.

As Aristotle said, 'That nation which will not learn from the past is doomed to repeat it.' We have seen that over and over in history, and again are about to repeat the doom.

This is the story of men who made Athens glorious and who made her history, rather than the story of tedious wars and oppressive government, though, to make the heroes relevant and in context, it is necessary to show how their own government, conceived under the noble laws of Solon, became despotic, and how the heroes fought that government and sometimes – but rarely – succeeded.

If the story sounds familiar, it is because it is indeed

familiar. A little study of present history will also show how ominous and pervasive of tyranny our present world is at this exact moment. If we do not learn from the past we will be doomed to repeat it.

Taylor Caldwell

'THE GLORY THAT WAS GREECE'

The genius of a nation strikes but once in its history. It is its glory and its immortality in the annals of men. It is aristocratic, discriminating, radiant and selective, and abjures all that is mediocre, plebeian and mundane. It is regnant. It is spiritual. It is the flame emanating from the core of the Universe, which is the generation of life. It is the lightning which sets fire to the small spirits of men, and raises them above the field and the plough, the house and the hayfield, in a sudden revelation of grandeur. It is, above all, masculine, for the aristocracy of the soul is purely masculine and never feminine, which is concerned only with petty matters and insistent trivialities. It transcends the humbleness of daily living and stands even the least important of men upon Olympus for a brief hour. It is never democratic, for democracy is a destructive thing, conspired in the inferior minds of envious men.

'If that nation which would survive in glory would cultivate only the masculine principle its name in history will be written in gold and blaze through the centuries.'

Zeno of Elea

PART ONE

Aspasia

'She was not only the most beautiful of women but a woman of mind and character and charm and tenderness, and the women of Athens owe much to her.'

Socrates

CHAPTER I

Acilia, the beautiful young mother, was visiting her child, Aspasia, in Thargelia's school for courtesans.

'She is like Aphrodite, newly risen in pearl from the sea,' she said to Thargelia. 'Who knows her fate? Her father desired to expose her. I am glad that I rescued her and brought her to you. Is not her hair like gold, her eyes like autumn leaves and her flesh like nacre? Who could destroy such? Alas, her father would kill her even now if he knew she lived, for what man is proud of begetting a female?'

'She is extremely intelligent,' said Thargelia in a tone of consolation. 'She has a mind that scintillates, throwing off myriad lights like a prism. She will become a magnificent courtesan, even more than you were, my little one.'

The mother moved restively. 'I should prefer her to be married to a distinguished man. If my child's father, Axtochus, my lover, could see her now and hear her converse, young as she is, he might take her into his house with me and his other concubines. But I do not wish her to become a courtesan.'

Thargelia pondered. 'You brought Aspasia to me,' she said, 'when she was but a few days old, fleeing with her from the house of your lover, at night, after you had concealed her from the sight of her father. It was from my house that Axtochus chose you for his own, and he has been faithful to you, in his fashion, more than he has been faithful to his wives and other concubines. You are happy, Acilia, for I see happiness in the sleekness of your skin, the shimmer of your hair, and in the glitter of your jewels. Would you be so happy as an immured wife, under the law, neglected by your husband, relegated to the women's quarters, sighing alone, while some concubine lay with your husband?'

Acilia thought. 'No,' she admitted. 'But every mother desires safety and honour for her daughters, and where can safety and honour be assured for a woman except in a distinguished marriage?'

'Bah,' said Thargelia with a shrug. 'It is only fools who yearn for safety. I disagree that marriage is the only haven for women. Property and education and jewellery and power over a man are much more to be desired. Men rarely tire of an engaging concubine, but they inevitably tire of their wives. Concubines know how to amuse a man, and, at the end, that is a woman's true function. We teach our maidens here that a woman's destiny is to amuse, entertain, serve, console and love a man, and for these gifts any man will pay a fortune, and even lay down his life.'

They sat in the portico of the pillared house of courtesans, overlooking the Gulf of Latmic, near the mouth of the Meander river. The scent of jasmine was rising. Women were singing in the house and strumming lutes and harps, and for an instant Acilia's face was filled with memories and longings.

Aspasia was leaning against her mother's knee and contentedly eating a pastry stuffed with poppy seeds and honey and citron peel. Acilia smiled down into her daughter's large, light brown eyes, which were filled with mysterious liquid lights and shifting sparkles and shadowed and starred with golden lashes of enormous sweep and length. The child's hair hung far down her back and seemed to be a mass of soft gilt threads. Her features were delicate and hinted of increasing maturity, though she was but six years old. When she smiled, as she did now, there was an endearing charm about her. She is far more beautiful than I was, thought Acilia with pride. Alas, the destiny of woman is full of sorrow, whether mistress or wife or concubine or slave. Should we not have a higher destiny than this?

Thargelia saw the mother's changing and melancholy expression, and she said, 'I have trained many children and maidens, but Aspasia is more than them all. Though very young she is already a philosopher. Her appearance is enchanting. Her mind will command the attention and the respect of even the most dissolute men. I predict a marvellous future for her. She has fate in her eyes, profound and immeasurable.'

'Women must change this world of men,' said Acilia, suddenly, and put her hand in protection on her child's shining head.

Thargelia shrugged. 'Would it be to our advantage? Men are now our adorers and our slaves. Let us not long for equality with them! We would lose our privileges and gain nothing but coarseness, anxiety, toil and disrespect.'

She laughed. 'Let men continue to protect us and we will continue to rule them from our beds and with our blandishments. He who sits on a throne is never at peace or at rest. But she who is the voice behind the throne, however concealed, has all the advantages of power, and all the prerogatives, and can sleep tranquilly of a night.'

'So long as she is young and beautiful,' said Acilia, sighing.

Thargelia was vexed. 'It was one of your faults, dear little one, that you were always sighing even when most happy. Youth? Clever and noble men may proclaim that they prefer green fruit. But they are ruled by women who are not young but remain dazzling, as any woman can remain if she desires. It is only the dull failed man who seeks his own futile youth in the youth of a woman, and thinks of a woman as merely a thing, like a slave.'

The young Aspasia was sipping her own small goblet of wine, but she looked up at her mother over the rim and her eyes were wise and merry and full of understanding. She is six years old, thought Acilia with some uneasiness, but she was never young!

Thargelia, watching with her astute eyes, said, 'I have had a soothsayer for Aspasia. He predicts that she will glow like the moon over her country and have great men in her power, and everywhere she will be the inspiration of poets.'

'Soothsayers!' said Acilia with indulgence. Nevertheless, she was flattered and pleased. She laid a purse of gold coins on the ivory and lemonwood table. 'Nothing must be denied my daughter. I trust you, Thargelia, for I have had reason to trust you. You are wiser than I. Do with Aspasia as you will, for I see you love her.'

'Aspasia and I understand each other,' Thargelia said, with affection, 'for all we have our moments of rebellion. There are no uncertainties in her mind, no doubts, no hesitations. She will have what she wills, as a woman, and her will is already formidable.'

CHAPTER II

Thargelia sat with her choicest maidens – all chosen for both their beauty and their intelligence – in the outdoor portico facing the west.

She had aged but little over the fourteen years since Aspasia had been delivered by her mother to this house. 'A woman must not frown; it creates wrinkles on the brow and between the eyes, and gentlemen detest wrinkles. Nor must she laugh too much; that induces furrows about her mouth. A merry face, yes, always. But never one which resembles the masks of the theatre, with too much emotion and emphasis. A soft smile, with a regard to curvature, a twinkling of the eyes, as you have been taught, a gentle inclination of the head – these are desirable and do not age a woman. They enhance her charm. Gestures, too, must never be too emphatic. It annoys gentlemen, for they do not like vigorous women, except in their kitchens and in their beds. A woman must always imply; she must never assert. I repeat these admonitions, my treasures, so that you will be successful and rich and endlessly amusing and seductive.'

There were eight among her choice maidens, and among them was her favourite, Aspasia. She controlled the diet of her maidens sedulously, and as vigilantly as she preserved their virginity, which would be delivered to the richest and most eminent bidder, and for a very high price to Thargelia herself. But the maidens were not virginal in their minds and their hearts. 'Even green fruit must prophesy ripeness and deliciousness, my treasures.' She wished a sheen on her maidens, so she encouraged love among them – with discretion so that they would later be lovers of men and not lovers of women. In truth, if a maiden became too ardent over a sister neophyte Thargelia would remove her to another building where she could be trained to be a pleasure to some rich widow or dissatisfied wealthy matron.

All the maidens found little leisure in the school for courtesans. They attended classes presided over by female and male teachers of the best mentality, where they learned – not the arts of a household, which were the province of illiterate ladies intended for marriage by their parents – but the arts of politics, philosophy, exquisitely perfect language, rhetoric, music, dancing, the arrangement of garments, the nuances of perfumes, seduction, conversation, history, gentle athletics to preserve the figure and enhance it, a smattering of medical lore, mathematics – 'One must deal with bankers later' – artistic placing of furniture, selection of fabrics most flattering, graceful movements, hairdressing, charming sophistries, penmanship, the keeping of books, literature, poetry, sculpture, painting, science, but, above all else, how to please and entrance a man and all the arts of love, including perversions.

The maidens were taught delicacy. 'There is nothing more abhorrent than a coarse lewd woman,' said Thargelia and the other teachers. 'Never must an indecent word cross your lips or a lascivious jest, not even in passion. You must keep in mind that you are great ladies, of taste and discrimination and learning. You must always be in control of your emotions, and never utter a hasty harsh reproach, no matter how provoked. Pleasantness is most desirable.'

Once Aspasia said in her soft voice: 'We are, then, only toys for the pleasure of men who may be inferior to us.'

Thargelia smiled at her, for it was impossible to be irritable with Aspasia. 'Say, better, that we are jewels, precious jewels. How is a jewel preserved? In fine cloth, guarded and cherished, valued above all things, adored, proudly displayed. We are not utensils of the kitchen. They serve their purpose, and are used by wives, whose husbands give us gold and gems and lay their heads on our knees and worship us. Do they worship their wives? They flee from them.'

As she sat with her maidens this sunset Thargelia rejoiced in their beauty, and especially in Aspasia's, for the promise of the maid's childhood had not been false. Aspasia was taller than the other girls, and Thargelia could not recall any of her earlier maidens who could compare with her, nor even her present companions. Amidst all that loveliness of black and brown and russet and fair locks, of brilliant eyes and rosy cheeks and white throats and young creamy bosoms, of dimples and curved red lips and alabaster chins and springlike bodies, Aspasia was a girlish Aphrodite among mere mortals. They diminished, for all their loveliness, in her presence, as bronze dims before gold, and they became, despite their choice and unusual grace and sensuous charms, mere milkmaids before a queen. They all wore the plain white peplos which announced their virginity, and with silver girdles of modest design, but the peplos became radiant upon Aspasia's perfect body, hinting of sensuality and incomparable delights. Her nose was of the classic Grecian shape, worshipped by sculptors, and her mouth, deep red and soft, was without flaw, neither too generous nor too small, and when she smiled dimples twinkled about it, enchantingly. Her eyes were unusually large, set in fine pale violet shadows and surrounded by thick golden lashes, and were of an arresting colour, like light brown wine and luminous.

All this, at the age of fourteen, and a virgin, was enough to drive men out of their senses, Thargelia would think with pleasure, but beautiful though Aspasia was her intellect surpassed it. Thargelia had sometimes regretfully observed that unusual beauty was sometimes accompanied by lesser intelligence, but this was not so with Aspasia. She was not only accomplished in music, and had a voice of strong sweetness and range and feeling, but she was a superb dancer whose movements were at once carnal and innocent. Her conversation was not by rote or mere memory from her teacher's lessons, and sparkling and witty, but excelled in subtlety and intimations and a naughty impudence which aroused laughter even among the sullen and the most grave. She observed everything and her comments were inventive and full of perception, and often startlingly wise and deeply thoughtful. She outwitted her teachers in an exercise in rhetoric, and could declaim movingly on almost any subject, and she had a gaiety which aroused gaiety where sadness lived before. Thargelia feared at times that there was a power not of the flesh but of the mind in Aspasia, and that Aspasia's thoughts were not always feminine. Alluring beyond description though she was, and an ecstasy to the eye, her remarks were sometimes too sharp and pungent, too scornful of pretence. For this reason Aspasia's teachers endeavoured to teach her self-control more than they taught the other girls, and though she was acquiescent and listened carefully there would appear a shining and shifting glint in her eyes, humorously defiant.

The tutors for the maidens were usually erudite females, some of them former courtesans themselves, and learned, but Thargelia also employed male teachers who were of a respectable age and of no prepossessing appearance, for one must guard virgins.

A year ago the tutors had solemnly approached Thargelia, saying, 'The maiden, Aspasia, is of an intricate mind, and excessively talented. She desires to know all things, and not superficially. Discourses on medicine, mathematics, and art engross her, and her questions are incisive and controversial, and she will not be satisfied with idle answers. In short, she will demand to know all that we know, and will not accept cursory instructions. She has the mind of a man, which may be unfortunate.'

'I have suspected this,' said Thargelia, not without pride. 'But what human brain can contain all knowledge? Still, if one is talented one is gifted freely by the gods, who pour down upon the chosen one a full lavishness of mental treasures, just as when a beautiful woman is created she is perfection in all ways. Truly, Aspasia is formidable in talent as well as in loveliness. She wishes to encompass all things. But in what is she most proficient?'

An elderly sage said, stroking his grey beard, 'She is fascinated with Solon, the founder of democracy, and all his laws.' He hesitated and then continued, 'She wishes to know why Greece does not follow the laws of Solon, as laid down over a hundred years ago. We have explained that the Athenians were too capricious and too inconstant a people to demand that their rulers obey an unchangeable Constitution, for they suspected what they considered inflexibility, even in perfect laws.'

'Our Aspasia, then, is a politician as well as an artist and a mathematician,' said Thargelia, smiling.

'Lady,' said a woman tutor, 'is it not our custom to discover the talent of each maiden, and train her therein, that she may be the perfect companion of a man of that bent and occupation?'

'True,' said Thargelia. 'But our Aspasia is Protean, and her talents are equally enormous. She has myriad eyes, all developed. Would you say, then, that she is most proficient in politics, mathematics, art, science?'

'She is also engrossed with medicine,' said the physician, 'and is most dexterous and inventive in potions. She is constantly in the infirmia and often I conjecture if Apollo was not her father.'

22

Thargelia laughed. 'I am assured that that is not so. But it is a pretty concept, for does she not shine like the sun? What a maiden this is! Only a mighty Persian satrap would be worthy of her. Do not discourage her. Answer her deeply and with candour, respecting her intelligence. She was born in Miletus, and not in Greece, where women and their intelligence are despised. It is true that we are now under Grecian dominance but she is a daughter of Asia Minor.'

She smiled at the uneasy tutors. 'The gods must indeed be her guardians, for had she been born in Greece she would have been confined to the gynaikeia (women's quarters) and would have been forbidden the meanest learning. Give to Aspasia all that is in your power, and do not fear that you will fatigue her. The mind has no boundaries.'

She contemplated the price that Aspasia would bring, but still she was as proud as if she, herself, had been Aspasia's mother. The damsel was a prodigious gem, deserving of polishing and of a setting that would reveal all her colours and her glory. A jewel like this, and a virgin in addition, was worthy of even more than a Persian satrap. An emperor was more to be desired.

CHAPTER III

The physician, a lively man of middle age was, like Aspasia and Thargelia, an Ionian of Miletus. His name was Echion. He had never been a slave, but had been born free and of a prosperous family who manufactured silver and gold ornaments, and he had attended an Egyptian school of medicine. He was broad and fat and muscular, with a round red face and eyes like glittering blue stones, yet mirthful, and he was bald and had a rosy dome rising above his thick black eyebrows, and several fatty chins which testified to a good digestion and an excellent appetite. He affected short tunics in many hearty colours, and they revealed legs of an admirable shape for all their bulk. He was one of Thargelia's lovers, and she paid him well and did not underestimate his talents in bed or in the schoolroom. She loved his lustful mouth which was almost always smiling, for he had perfect teeth of which he was proud. He was not so proud of his nose, which Thargelia fondly called a turnip, and his nostrils were filled with virile black hairs.

He was quite content to instruct the maidens of the school for the hetairai, and if he yearned after any of them he was prudent enough to confine himself to an apparently paternal touch on the shoulder or arm or cheek. He was also very lazy in spite of his vigorous appearance, and preferred the luxurious life in this house to any medical practice in the city, for such practice could be arduous and held few rewards in money or esteem. He had his own small marble house on the grounds of the school, from which Thargelia summoned him when she was in the mood to be amused and treated roughly in bed. He was amiable and shrewd and a fine physician, and had much wit and, to the respect of many, his knowledge of medicine was astounding and his potions magical.

Above all the other beautiful maidens Aspasia enchanted him, though she was less than a docile pupil and provoked him into controversy. He preferred her disagreeable dissents, sharp remarks and questions, and disputations to the meek acceptances of the other girls. He saw little slavish respect in her great brown eyes, and knew that she listened avidly not only to learn but to pounce upon him if he showed doubt. But when she honestly admired him and leaned forward so as not to waste a single word his gratification was immense. He felt, to his own amusement, that he had received an accolade from a colleague and not a mere chit.

'She is, in all truth, possessed of the soul of a physician,' he would say to Thargelia. 'I marvel at her prodigious talents. It has been said that the beauteous woman has the soul of an ape, but it has been my experience that those endowed by the gods with intelligence are also agreeable to the eye.'

'She is worthy of an emperor,' Thargelia would repeat.

'Or of Apollo, himself,' he would reply. 'But let us hope that Zeus, in whom I do not believe, does not discover her and bear her off in a shower of gold. Or impregnate her as he did Leda, though a woman who lays an egg might be an interesting spectacle to a physician.'

'You are no Zeus,' Thargelia said on one occasion, with an affectionate but warning smile. 'Let us remember that.'

'But you are a veritable Hera, my adored one,' he replied with gallantry, and Thargelia laughed and shook her finger at him. 'It is said, in the city, that you are tireless,' she remarked.

'But, my divinity, that is only rumour. Am I not faithful to you?'

'No,' said Thargelia. 'But you amuse and satisfy me and I enjoy your conversation, and that is my contentment.' She looked momentarily troubled. 'There are times when I fear that Aspasia will not be the happiest of companions to a man, for men do not cherish a dagger tongue in a woman. She is rebellious and not too supple of character. I advise and rebuke her often.'

'There are men who prefer a woman of fire to a complaisant woman in their arms. Who would not prefer to subdue a spirited horse rather than a donkey, or a listless mare? You have a treasure in your house, Thargelia.'

'Whom I guard,' she replied.

So Echion, though he lusted after Aspasia, who was healthy and wondrous in appearance and intellectual, was ever decorous with his pupil. He luxuriated in his pleasant life, and not even an Aspasia would ever threaten it however much he desired her. But he had his fantasies, which had to satisfy him.

The artist-teacher, Tmolus – named after a mountain – rejoiced in Aspasia, his best pupil and a docile and eager one. Unlike most Greeks, he did not denigrate the minds of women. Without women, could art exist? No, he would tell himself. Women were the supreme art of the gods. Tmolus had seen that Aspasia agreed with him. Once she had said to him, 'Tmolus, you are truly a philosopher,' and he understood. He had received her comment as an accolade, even though she was only a maiden and he an old man.

He was small and slight of body, and bent and grey, but his eyes were vividly alive and filled with unquenched youth and joy in living, for he found, as did Aspasia, all things beautiful, even a warted toad or a lichened stone or a weed. Ugliness did not revolt him, for he believed all things intrinsically lovely. 'A withered crone with no teeth, with whitened hair, with crippled hands, has an innate glory,' he would say. 'Does she not live and have being? So, she is beautiful. Her life and her thoughts have moulded her. Have they been hideous? But – they too have mystery, and therefore their own charm. When we learn that nothing is boring, nothing too mean or despicable, we can have serenity for serenity is the soul of art.'

Beautiful male and female slaves posed for the hetairai for their lessons in painting and sculpture and mosaics. The bodies were carefully chosen for their grace and youth. Though Thargelia instructed the teacher that he should emphasize the attributes of alluring sexual differences, and expose the male slaves to the utmost scrutiny of her virgins, and discourse on their attributes and endowments, Tmolus preferred that these matters be discussed in the frame of artistry. 'There is no coyness or libidinous aspects to Art,' he would say. 'That which is exquisite is above tittering and filthiness. The evil is not in the object but in the viewer. We bring to art all our falsities and degradation, but in themselves the objects are neither lewd nor meretricious. In short, what we view can be interpreted innocently and with admiration, or debauched. It is in ourselves.'

Today, Tmolus had a new model for his maidens.

The young girl, nude and gleaming like amber, was of some twelve years, innocently unaware of her nakedness. Her long black hair touched breasts still budlike and she had little pubic hair. She looked with curiosity at the maidens who trooped in, but it was a childlike curiosity, vacant and only vaguely aware. She stood with one elbow leaning on a half pedestal of marble and moved restlessly. Her name was Cleo. Slender and delicate, she was being considered by Thargelia as a candidate for the hetairai, for she was quick of thought and beguiling, when it concerned herself. Thargelia had recently received her as a hand-maiden, and she was reputed not only to be the child of a beautiful courtesan but of a man of some importance in Miletus.

Cleo looked more closely at the maidens who assembled at their stations for clay moulding and painting and mosaics, considering them somewhat elderly. Then her eyes fixed themselves on Aspasia, who seemed to bring a lambent light into the room. Immediately, she was filled with childish adoration, as one is transfixed at the sight of a nymph. Drawn by the girl's intent gaze, Aspasia looked intently at her and she was touched with admiration. She was like a statue of the young Eros, and resembled spring. As always, Aspasia felt sadness and frustration that she was unable to mould in an exceptional manner and that never could she re-create in perfection what she saw.

Tmolus, who loved Aspasia, saw her longing face and he thought: Why cannot she understand that one cannot be excellent in all things? But he understood that it is the nature of genius to desire nothing but perfection, so he did not rebuke Aspasia for her air of desperation when she attempted to mould in clay or chisel in marble, or when she dashed a brush to the floor when working at her easel. She despised herself in this room. Yet she could not have enough of being in it.

The next class was in rhetoric, in which Aspasia excelled. Here she could forget her humiliation in Tmolus' room. Her voice, resonant and firm and exceedingly musical, moved her teacher to wonder and tears. It was a voice without the coyness of a woman's. The other maidens would listen, enthralled, even if they barely understood the subject. Aspasia's eyes would take on an unusual brilliance and her gestures had more than grace. When she quoted a passage from Homer the room seemed filled with the glory of the Gemini and Achilles and Apollo and Hercules and Odysseus. She has a Syren's voice, the teacher would think. She will be able to lure men to good and evil. Helen of Troy must have possessed such, for beauty is not enough to enthrall men.

After this class came dancing and music and instructions on the lyre and flute. Here, too, Aspasia excelled, though she considered dancing of no particular importance. But music enchanted her. She could, even now, manipulate the musical instruments so that they appeared to have an extra dimension and depth, and struck the heart with emotion.

Her lessons in theology were no felicitous occasions. But she held her tongue, knowing the punishments inflicted by the Ecclesia on anyone suspected of heresy or dissent against the prevailing religion. Her face would flash, however, and her eyes become scornful at some pious pedantry. The teacher would reduce the grandeur of the gods to mere mortality, he believing that degrading the inexplicable and the majesty to low human understanding and status and familiarity made them more comprehensible.

Aspasia always felt embattled when she went to her class in politics and history, and her teacher detested her for her arguments and controversies. 'Who writes history?' she had asked him once. 'Mere mortals, who make their own interpretations, according to their whims and subjective opinions, of what has transpired. History is easily distorted. As for politics, it is an exercise in hysteria.' But the subjects engrossed her as well as angered her. It was said that if Helen of Troy's nose had been longer or her eyes less luminous Troy would never have been burned, nor would her husband have desired her to the death, nor would Paris have abducted her. On such trivialities did the affairs of men founder! She found both politics and history endlessly amusing, for the light they shone on the vagaries of human nature. 'They should be the province of comedians,' she once remarked, 'but certainly should not be regarded as objective and immutable truth.' At one time she had even said that history was made by madmen, and wars were the ultimate madness, a remark that did not endear her to her teacher.

'Is not everything made by man and the result of man?' he had asked her, to which Aspasia said, 'No. There are imponderables beyond the knowledge and the understanding of man.' The teacher complained she was a mere chit, and a woman, and so therefore of no importance, and her opinions of no consequence. The maidens, who did not love Aspasia for her beauty and superiority to them, would titter. At least Aspasia dispensed with the ennui of teaching with her arguments, and for that they were grateful.

The teacher, Aeneas, was a Greek. Therefore he expounded frequently on the defeat of the Persians at Thermopylae. 'I am not superstitious,' he would say, 'but I believe in the Fates. Athens, and all of Greece, was preserved by some mysterious intervention. It seemed impossible that Xerxes could be defeated by us, we contentious Greeks, who suspected and even hated each other and were constantly quarrelling and envious – men from the sallow mountains, the hot cliffs and passes, the fishing villages, the small towns even smaller than Athens, which is itself small and insignificant. Outnumbered by at least a score or more to one – and the immediate invaders but the first wave of a sea of soldiers and sailors – the Greeks had met the foe on their sacred land and waters and had driven him ignominiously away. This little land, all burning silver dust and mountains, all furious green torrents and crags and small green valleys and brilliant purple seas and miserable villages and stony roads and powdery fields and ardent blue skies, had stubbornly refused to be conquered and held slave to the mighty Xerxes and preferred, in all truth, liberty or death.'

Aspasia admired the poetry of his words, but she had said, 'Solon declared that all men should be free. But we have slaves. Is not a slave a man?'

The teacher had glared at her. 'We believe a slave to be a thing, not a man. The gods ordained his fate. The gods ordained freedom for men. If a man is not born free, then he is not truly human.'

'There is something wrong with your syllogism,' Aspasia said.

'Enlighten me!' said the teacher with wrath.

'Solon was a great and wise man,' said Aspasia. 'He desired to establish a republic, but Athens has declined into a democracy. Therein is a great tragedy in government. But no matter. When Solon declared that all men should be free, and free from inquisitive and interfering government, he did not divide mankind into those born free and those who were born slave. Again, he demanded that slavery be abolished, so he did not consider a slave a mere thing, but a man.'

The teacher had then ignored this chit, had drawn another breath and continued with his history lesson.

Few of the maidens understood the controversy, but all were pleased by Aspasia's composure and Aeneas' wild anger. It relieved the monotony of dull lectures.

It was now sunset and the class was dismissed. The western sky was a vivid and burning gold, seething with light, and the sea and the land below it lay in mute purple and shifting shadows. The leaves of the myrtle were plated with gilt, and the cypresses stood pointing in blackness against the sky and the palms were tremulous in the soft evening wind. From the earth there rose a scent of jasmine and roses and cooling stone and water, and the fountains threw up frail arms touched with gold and lilac.

Wandering in the garden before the evening meal Aspasia came on Cleo, who was sitting by a pool trembling with golden reflections. The young girl wore a short tunic the colour of silver and her black hair was rolled on her nape. She looked at Aspasia shyly, and rose. Aspasia gazed at the pool in which iridescent fish swam idly, and then at Cleo.

'Tell me,' she said, 'what is your heart's desire, Cleo?'

The girl looked at her with wide eyes. Then she tittered. 'I should like to be a hetaira like you, Lady.'

'I have heard that you will be. Will that satisfy you?'

The girl was bewildered. 'But it is the most desirable of all things, Lady.'

Aspasia sighed. She, herself, was a fool to expect anything but this reply, for Cleo knew nothing. Why am I always looking for intelligence in mankind, in which it rarely exists? she said to herself.

She was conscious, as she increasingly was, these days, of a restlessness of spirit and a strong rising of something she could not as yet name. There was a loneliness in her, she who had never been lonely before, a longing without a form, an itch, a heat which was both profoundly physical and as profoundly spiritual.

She stood watching the sunset and the wind lifted her hair and when it fell upon her shoulders it was like an embrace, and she sighed. Her yearning grew until it was like a vast hunger in her, but for what she yearned she did not as yet know. She was soon to be enlightened, and disastrously.

CHAPTER IV

The athletics tutor for the maidens suddenly died and Thargelia went to the slave market for a suitable replacement. She came upon a male slave of remarkable beauty, all red pouting lips and smiles and mirthful blue eyes. He also had a mass of auburn curls and muscles beyond description and the body of a young god. He was as sleek as oil and as burnished as bronze and had

31

engaging manners and a felicity of tongue and a gleeful and gladsome countenance.

What a treasure, thought Thargelia, with a warmth in her loins she had not experienced for a long time. She had tired, in this past year, of Echion and other of her mature lovers, who appeared to be suffering the fatigue of their middle years, while she, herself, was never fatigued by love. Sometimes they fell asleep in her arms, leaving her sleepless and distraught, and without satisfaction.

However, she was a prudent woman and inquired why such a morsel of perfection was offered for sale, even though the price was high. The answer was that his master had discovered that Thalias was too interested in the young sons of the household and so desired to sell him. Thargelia wondered why the master had not availed himself of such implied pleasures, then dismissed the thought. Would it not be possible for such a seductress as herself to educate him in the arts of normal affections? In any event, Thalias would be a safe athletics teacher for her guarded maidens.

What Thargelia did not know was that the report on Thalias was untrue. The young slave had availed himself of the charms of both the master's wife and his daughters, who had wept when he was taken away. He had also seduced all the women slaves, who wailed for days on his departure. Three were already pregnant. Thalias was a man of prowess, who was tirelessly erotic and potent. The master had thought of having him castrated, but his natural masculine nature revolted at this, fortunately for Thalias. As a castrated male Thalias would have no value except in an Oriental bazaar, and among effetes, and he was too valuable for this. So the master arranged for his sale – at a very high price – and discreetly kept the slave's proclivities to himself. Let the buyer beware.

Thargelia studied his athletic young body thoughtfully, both as the mistress of the courtesans and as a woman. She took him aside and questioned him. Her maidens must not develop muscles, for muscles on a woman were disgusting to men of discrimination. The athletics must be limited and intended only to round and firm a young female body. Thalias listened to this acutely, and his eyes began to shine at the prospect, and being intelligent he held his tongue though his mouth watered. A veritable bower of beauties! He hoped they were also judicious. He told Thargelia fervently that he knew exactly what she desired, and Thargelia wryly remarked to herself that she anticipated that she could give him other desires, for herself. After all, she was most expert and had often turned the lovers of men into the lovers of women. She looked at his throat, and at the muscles of his chest and his arms, and licked her lips. However, being cautious, she required that she examine him without his loincloth, to be certain that she would not be cheated. The inspection was all she could have desired. Thalias watched this inspection and understood perfectly. He would happily oblige the lady, then go on to more luscious conquests. He was naturally of a cheerful nature, and accommodating, and he knew how to please women and make them ecstatic and his slaves. His former mistress had been a splendid teacher, and ardent, and her husband had a hetaira, and she had hungered. What Thalias did not know about women was insignificant.

Thargelia bought him. She bore him home in her own curtained litter and fondled him. He pretended to be modest and retiring but a certain phenomenon elated Thargelia, and she joyously deluded herself that her arts had aroused him as no woman had aroused him before, and that, therefore, after this, he would be her slave in her bed. She took him to bed at once in her house, and he shyly told her that she was the first woman who had made him aware of feminity, and that he doubted that any other could so awaken him. He performed excellently, and Thargelia sighed deeply with rapturous joy and contentment, and had his bed moved to her door. For a woman as astute as Thargelia this was amazing, but her female nature deceived her. She could not have enough of the young man, and her face bloomed and she felt young again and desirable. Thalias also enjoyed himself. When the curtains were drawn and the chamber scented, he hardly saw Thargelia's wrinkles, for she had an exquisite and youthful body and she also knew the arts of love and had peculiar appetites which he satisfied. In the meantime, Thalias surveyed the maidens he taught and enjoyed them in anticipation, particularly Aspasia.

Thargelia was candid with the young ladies, who listened to her with demurely cast-down eyes. Thalias, she said, was not interested in women, so they need not practise their arts upon him, however innocently. She also hinted that he was not quite a man. The girls listened, not believing a single word, for slaves gossiped and they had heard rumours of Thargelia's blissful cries in the night, and her vows of devotion. Moreover, Thalias wore a most complacent expression. It was evident that Thargelia could hardly bear him out of her sight, and would stroke his arm and his cheek even when she was among the maidens, and that her eyes would moisten with remembered exercises. She had gained an air of youth and vitality and sparkle and energy. The maidens noted this and pondered, and looked at Thalias under their lowered eyelashes.

As for Aspasia, who loved beauty, she found him physically entrancing. His youth appealed to her, who saw no other young men. She studied his body, his face, his chest. She conversed with him briefly at recess during the athletics lessons and the lessons with the bow and the arrow. She thought him intelligent to some extent, but he could not meet her mind and he could stare at subtleties. However, he was a beautiful animal in her opinion, and his touch, when he directed her at the bow, caused a sharp thrill to run along her nerves.

What Thargelia did not know was that despite Aspasia's fondness for her she was in enormous interior conflict, and in furious silent revolt. So Aspasia both loved and hated her mentor, and at times was even afflicted with a wrath for nameless revenge. There was also the fact that her body, usually controlled and contained, was experiencing the pangs of adolescence and desire. Sometimes, at night, she imagined Thalias in her bed and would sweat, both to her disgust and her awakening passion, and her hands would fumble helplessly in the air and touch her body. The violet shadows increased under her eyes and made her more alluring and delectable. Thargelia, not knowing the reason, was elated. Aspasia's virginity would bring a tremendous price. There were Oriental potentates rich beyond imagining who would be infatuated with this wonderful maiden. Thargelia sent out delicate messages to the East. In the meantime Aspasia thought of Thalias increasingly, for his flesh bedazzled her, to her distraction, and so her thoughts were in conflicting disarray, between corruption and intellect.

The child, Cleo, was accepted into the school of the hetairai, and was given the chamber next to Aspasia's. This was not to Aspasia's liking, for she had discovered that Cleo adored her as well as admired her, and she noticed that the younger girl had begun to copy all her manners and gestures and even the intonations of her voice, imitating a certain way Aspasia had of inclining her head with soft mockery and enlarging her eyes with amusement and touching her lower lip with her thumb. Cleo's big black eyes glimmered with strange lights when she looked at Aspasia. She had a pert appearance, most engaging, and a pouting pink mouth, which trembled when Aspasia spoke to her. She deferred slavishly to Aspasia, who found such sedulous attention irritating. When Cleo would touch her timidly her flesh would shiver, for girls did not attract her, and Cleo was not of notable intelligence in spite of a natural shrewdness. Others, more ruthless than Aspasia, would have taken advantage of this adoration. But Aspasia would have disdained to be so base.

Once Cleo crept behind her as she sat thinking alone in the gardens in the shade of a mass of cypress trees, and Cleo lifted a lock of her hair and kissed it. Revolted, Aspasia rose and struck the girl silently across the cheek and left her. Cleo fell to the ground in a paroxysm of grief and desire and tore up handfuls of the grass and writhed, and wept. Glancing back over her shoulder Aspasia saw this and made a mouth of disgust and aversion, for she was not innocent in her mind. She thought of reporting these things to Thargelia, but she had a strain of compassion in her heart and did not want Cleo sent to the dormitory where such girls were rigorously trained to give pleasure to women. For she had guessed that Cleo was attached to herself alone, and she hoped that the child would recover from this aberration.

When thinking of Thalias, Aspasia would also think of Cleo, but not with the same designs. For some time she shrank at the thought of exploiting the slavish younger girl in her own behalf. But as her desire for Thalias increased, despite efforts to suppress it, she gave Cleo more and more thought. The girl would do anything she would ask of her.

Aspasia knew that she did not love Thalias; it was impossible for her to love where her mind could not rest also. But now she lusted for him with increasing desire. She would gaze at his strong sun-browned arms and her loins would thrill and become hot and tense. She imagined his body on hers and would almost faint at the prospect and she would arch her back and shudder. She remembered that Thargelia had taught that a woman should feel no such response to a man, for then all was lost and she might love him, to her calamity.

One day Aspasia sought out Cleo and smiled at her with all her sensual and bewitching charm. Cleo, surprised at this condenscension, was devastated and began to tremble and tears filled her eyes. Aspasia led her aside to the shade of a grove of green myrtle trees, hidden from the others, and she touched Cleo – though her own flesh winced – on the cheek and the throat. Cleo's eyes misted. She gazed at Aspasia as one would gaze humbly at a goddess and could not believe this strange and sudden tenderness from one who had been avoiding her. When Aspasia bent her head and kissed her gently on the lips the younger girl swayed, and Aspasia, making a wry mouth to herself and feeling subtly ashamed, caught her and held her against her own body.

She whispered in Cleo's ear. 'Some night, my love, when our guardians have left us, you will come to me.' Cleo trembled and timidly kissed Aspasia's throat. It was a child's kiss. What if she should permanently debauch Cleo's nature? Aspasia paused in herself and then she thought of Thalias. She conversed in her own mind. Were not all the maidens taught the arts of love, without shame? Let Thargelia bear the consequences.

After their athletics lessons in the afternoon, and their baths in perfumed oils and their massages, the maidens retired to their chambers to sleep. But before this retirement Aspasia became particularly provocative to Thalias one day, and the young man's thoughts became dizzy and he looked at her with a half-opened mouth and his face swelled and flushed deeply and he shivered. Aspasia smiled with all the arts she had been taught, and her eyes were ravishing. She leaned briefly against his shoulder, and let him see the swell of her young bosom. He closed his eyes and he shivered again, and seeing that they were alone he touched her breast and sweat drenched his countenance and his eyes became doglike both with passion and love. She permitted his hand to wander, and her own body responded with an ardour and a fire she had not even imagined before. Her eyelids dropped, her full red mouth moistened and her breasts swelled. She had an almost uncontrollable desire to draw him down to the green earth below them, but some maidens were approaching, laughing, with a teacher. She feigned to be interested in the adjustment of an arrow, aware of a cooling sweat along her brow. The sun blinded her and she felt that nothing existed but the middle of her palpitating body, which had become heavy, and at once languid and quickening. The imminence of Thalias was maddening, and there was suddenly nothing else in her world but her desire.

She whispered, 'Tonight?'

He could not believe it. But he whispered almost inaudibly, 'I share the chamber with Thargelia. In this garden then, in that grove of myrtles, under the moon, at midnight? Oh, my adorable one! It is not possible that you love me! Oh, by Castor and Pollux, that I might possess you even once – I would die of the joy!'

'Live. Do not die,' said Aspasia. The other maidens were chattering like a veritable swarm of swallows. 'You are Adonis,' she said, and when his hand touched her intimately she felt as if she was bursting into flame and could hardly walk to leave him.

A little later she drew Cleo apart and said to her, 'My love, I am devoted to Artemis, the goddess of the moon, the eternally virgin, and tonight the moon is full and I would worship her in silence in the gardens. I fear I cannot give myself to any man, but be as Artemis, removed from the embraces of men. I must invoke her for her assistance. Therefore, my dear, arrange your bed so any of our guardians, passing in the night with their lanterns, believe you sleep there, then lie in my bed with your head covered so that they do not see the darkness of your hair. Murmur softly, as if restive in the dim light, as I do. Sigh deeply, as I do. They will be deceived. You will do this little service for me, dearest lovely child? Your reward will be commensurate.'

Cleo's eyes were as adoring as those of Thalias, and as abject, and Aspasia felt chilled. She would keep her promise and give pleasure to this little one, after her own pleasure, and would restrain her aversion. She had been taught that one pays for everything in this life, and she intended to repay, however repugnant to herself or damaging to Cleo. She said, 'Swear by the thunderbolts of Zeus that never will you betray me.'

Cleo swore, in her child's light voice, and Aspasia was

satisfied. She gently removed Cleo's little hand, which nestled against her breast and left her. Aspasia had a very lively conscience, but she was learning that when a woman desires a man she has no conscience at all and only awareness of her appetites.

She lay, rigid and trembling and sweating, on her narrow couch in her chamber, to which there was no door – it was only a cubiculum – until the guards had shone the lantern dimly in upon her bed, and she murmured restively as if slightly disturbed. The lantern light retreated down the hall, wavering on white walls, then dying. She smiled to herself. Her window was open, high on the wall, and the moon, pure argent light, flooded over her feet, and there was a passionate scent of jasmine in the warm air and the fragrance of grass and the aromatic odour of pines and cypresses. Somewhere a nightingale trilled poignantly and an owl answered in dolorous accents. Hot stone exuded its own peculiar arid but exciting scent, and now the roses sent forth their perfume.

The guards would not make their rounds again for an hour, and by that time she would have returned. She waited a little, then silently rose from her bed and went to the chamber of Cleo. The young girl's eyes shimmered in the moonlight, as brilliant as black opals and as variable, and she rose at once and embraced Aspasia, and the older maid felt the heat of the child's body through her shift. She endured the embrace; she kissed the innocent brow, then disentangled herself, murmuring softly and even consolingly.

Aspasia had wrapped herself in a dark cloak. She stole from her chamber, where Cleo now lay with covered hair, and moved like a moth down the hall. At a distance she could see the torches beyond the atrium, thrust into the walls, and the light of a far lamp, which smelled of ambergris. There was no sound at all except for the nightingale and the wind and the owl and the sea and the soft rustling of leaves.

A guard, a man, passed through the atrium, his sword in his hand, and Aspasia shrank against the wall, holding her breath.

She waited until the sound of his sandals had died on stone, and then she fled as silently as the wing of a bird through the atrium and out into the night. Her bare feet were immediately wet with dew and she could smell the grass, and she sped lightly over the warm and glittering earth. The moon stood at the apex of the sky, full and swelling, like an enormous plate of light against the blackness of the heavens. Avoiding all open places Aspasia bent double in the sharp darknesses, hardly breathing, and listening for an alarm or a movement. Her heart was thrumming and her body was trembling. She had covered her bright hair with the hood of her cloak and had dropped it over her face, so that she appeared part of the shadows themselves.

She reached the grove of myrtles, panting softly and quickly. The tops of the trees were blazing with moonlight, and, as the leaves stirred, they gleamed as if plated with shining and restless silver and their voices were as the movement of gentle silk. Beyond the gardens and the grass the sea heaved slowly, a plain of white light nearly motionless. The columns of the house behind Aspasia were lucent as alabaster, splashed by the ruddy light of an occasional torch which shifted over them like the shadow of burning leaves. The torches hissed a little and crackled and the odour of resin mingled with the fragrance of earth and flowers.

She paused in the deep shadow of the myrtles. There was still no sound of anyone abroad this night except herself and the guard. She crept deeper into the shade. She dared not call. Had Thalias been detained by his mistress? Had he been unable to slide from her bed? Then Aspasia felt the strong grip of a man's hand on her arm, and she started and almost cried out. Instantly a hot firm mouth was on hers; arms encircled her like arms of iron, and she sank to the grass in the embrace of Thalias and his breath was in her throat and his tongue pierced between her lips.

She was suddenly terrified of the unknown, though her flesh was singing a fierce and joyous song it had never sung before, like all the drums and the lutes in the whole universe, sweeter than life itself and as overwhelming and strange and a little terrible. Feebly she tried to thrust Thalias from her, but he held her with one hard muscular arm and with his other hand he lifted her shift and then his lips were on her virgin breast and a rapturous languor overcame her and she lay still.

The crushed grass exhaled; the nightingale sang more poignantly, the plangent fountains splashed and then became the confused roar of a cataract, spilling fragrances, and the whispering myrtles, dancing with light, were a chamber of pleasure. There was the stammering moan of love in one of Aspasia's ears, the rising gasp of a man's passion, and she could not move, weighted down by a man's body upon hers, aware of the crispness of a man's hair against her cheek and the inexorable and rigid thrust between her soft thighs. The night swooned in its own melody.

Once there was the quick cry of a startled girl, swiftly silenced by demanding lips, and the ground appeared to rise and fall like the sea itself under Aspasia's body, moved to ecstasy, a fainting ecstasy which momentarily darkened the girl's consciouness. She felt herself not only in her own flesh but part of the flesh of the whole world, writhing in almost intolerable bliss. She gave herself up to joy, incoherently murmurous, and weeping in the embrace which was both mutual and hotly entangled.

Somewhere there was a man's moan, a rapid groaning growing more tumultuous, and a savage and triumphant delight seized Aspasia, the delight of the conquered and yet the conqueror, and suddenly all was fire and shuddering transports beyond description.

CHAPTER V

When Aspasia crept into the house she remembered her erotic promise to Cleo. Her flesh was still throbbing and her heart shaking and the thought of Cleo sickened her. Resolutely, however, she ran silently down the hall to her chamber, and, to her joy, she discovered that the child was sleeping heavily, her hand under her cheek. But she was in Aspasia's bed, and Aspasia paused, thinking. Finally she went to Cleo's chamber and lay down on the bed. Exhausted with delight, she fell instantly asleep, but not before covering her hair.

Before dawn she awakened, and went to her chamber and aroused Cleo. She whispered, 'Do not speak. You have slept the night through, my dear one, and must return to your own chamber at once, for soon we will be called to arise.'

Cleo's eyes filled with disappointed tears, and Aspasia suffered her embraces and caresses for a brief moment, then again whispering a warning she removed the girl's arms and forced her gently to leave, nodding promises for the future. She had hardly composed herself in her own bed when the guardians arrived to wake the maidens to another day.

She was in her mathematics class when she received a summons from Thargelia. This was most unusual, and the girl paled with apprehension. Following the slave, she came to Thargelia's chamber, to find the mistress of the hetairai in a cold rage. Never had she worn such a countenance before, pallid and tightened, her eyes glinting, and Aspasia thought, All is lost. I have been discovered. But, at Thargelia's silent gesture, she seated herself and folded her hands on her knee. If Thargelia had not been in such anger she would have been curious as to the reason for Aspasia's whiteness and the fear in her eyes.

42

The mistress said abruptly, 'Did aught disturb you in the night, Aspasia?'

She is tormenting me, the girl said to herself. She wet her lips and mutely shook her head. While Thargelia stared at her implacably she prepared to speak and finally could do so. 'I sleep very well, Thargelia. Little awakens me.'

Thargelia played with her jewelled necklace and continued to stare at the girl. She said, 'You are not one to betray a companion. I have discerned that before. But this is very serious. Did you not hear any furtive footsteps in the night or see a passing figure?'

Aspasia returned her stare and some of the fear left her. 'Nothing. I saw and heard nothing.'

'You saw none of your companions in the hall?'

'None. I slept through the night.'

Thargelia did not remove her hard gaze. 'One of the guardians looked into the chamber of Cleo, and discovered her absence. Very quietly, so as not to alarm others, the guardians searched the house, including the latrines. Cleo was not to be found. The guards outside and in the portico had seen no one. But one of some superstition swore that he had glimpsed a maiden in the moonlight, but when he pursued she vanished, and he is of the opinion that he had seen a nymph. He could not discern her features, but he swears that her face reflected the moon, and now he is convinced that he saw Artemis, herself.' At this Thargelia's mouth writhed in scorn and fresh fury.

'Oh, gods,' thought Aspasia with new fear. Cleo! If she kept silent she would suffer terrible punishment, and be sent to work in the meanest of occupations. She was only a child, and therefore, in dread of such punishment she doubtless would tell the truth. Both probabilities were equally appalling. Aspasia said, in a shaking voice, 'I have remembered something. Cleo, who is still a thoughtless child, came into my bed, whispering she had had a nightmare, and she was afraid. She remained for a while with me, while I comforted her.'

43

Thargelia considered, while Aspasia gazed at her with strained eyes. Thargelia then said, 'You are a poor liar, Aspasia, and it is possible you have never lied before. Why should you protect such as Cleo? I have seen no affection in you for the girl. Yet you admitted her to your bed! A child, you say. She is but two years younger than yourself, and you are nubile. I will question her.'

'She is about to pose again for Tmolus, Thargelia. It would not be well to interrupt his class.'

Seeing that Thargelia was still studying her with reflection Aspasia continued: 'Perhaps Cleo was restless, and the moon is full. Perhaps she was heated in the night – after she left me – and roamed in the gardens, as a child roams who cannot sleep.'

Thargelia said, 'Have you discerned any predilection on her part for any particular young male slave?'

'We have few here, and most are younger even than Cleo, and the others are of no great beauty and work in the gardens all day. No, Cleo has not looked at them with any attention.' She had a thought and then said boldly, 'Why do you not have Echion examine her to confirm, or deny, her virginity?'

Thargelia pursed her lips. 'That is an excellent suggestion. However, I mistrust Echion. He might destroy her virginity, himself, with his ruthless fingers, if not worse.'

'Then, Thargelia, you must watch him, yourself.'

Thargelia played with her necklace. 'That, too, is a good suggestion. I will have that done. Echion is in the city and will return tomorrow morning. In the meantime, do not alarm Cleo, Aspasia. She might run away.'

She dismissed Aspasia. Aspasia did not return to her class, for she was too overwhelmed by this calamity. Instead, she went to her small chamber. She sat on her bed in the silent dormitory and began to think with despair. The situation called for extreme decision. She could not let Cleo suffer for her own wantonness. Even if she, herself, confessed – and she trembled at the thought – Cleo would also be punished for her part

44

in the escapade. Enough. There must be instant action.

She now considered Thalias for the first time. Discovery would entail the most drastic punishment a slave can receive: castration. She did not love him, but he had become her victim. She no longer remembered her ecstasies in his arms, and only determined that he must not suffer for her own abandon. She knelt by her bed and pulled out her small bronze chest of treasures from beneath it. The last gift of her dead young mother was still here, a purse of gold coins. She weighed it in her hand. It was very heavy.

Now she must seek out Thalias, who, before he was called to teach the maidens, spent his time gossiping with the other slaves in the kitchens. There was no one she could trust to send for him. But she must face the danger. She left her bedroom and wandered out to the gardens and to the spot where the maidens practised archery under Thalias' direction. She found her bow and quiver and with apparent desultoriness shot at the target, and then expostulated aloud as if overcome with her own lack of skill. The gardeners covertly watched her and admired her beauty and the posture of her young body. Seeing this, she threw down her bow with exasperation, turned, tossed back her hair, and appeared to think. She let her eyes wander to an old gardener nearby, and she summoned him imperatively. He came at once.

She said, 'I am about to engage in a competition with other of the maidens, and I am a poor archer, and this shames me. Summon Thalias — that lazy and ever hungry slave — from the kitchen. He must help me at once.'

The gardener bowed and touched his breast. He was stupid as well as old and Aspasia had chosen him well. She picked up her bow again, and though she was usually accurate and skilful she pretended that her missings of the target were in spite of her efforts. She sank on the grass dolefully, shaking her head, and fretfully pulling at the grass.

Thalias was suddenly at her elbow, his eyes ardent with memories. After furtively glancing at him she put her finger

45

to her lips and he was immediately still. She rose and said loudly, 'You must help me! I am worse today, with the bow, than ever before.'

As he was moderately intelligent he became tense and acutely aware, and his cheeks paled. It was not approved that a maiden should see an instructor alone, and so he was aware that he was in danger. He helped Aspasia to her feet and whispered in her ear, as he bent to brush her clothing free of grass, 'What is it, my adored one?'

'Silence,' she said. She took the bow from his hand and fitted an arrow in it. 'Become an actor,' she murmured. 'You are bored by my lack of dexterity. You will put your hand on mine as I draw the bow. You will lean against me from behind. You will reproach me loudly. Now.'

The gardeners watched with amusement as the proud young hetaira was reproached by the slave, Thalias, for her clumsiness. They saw his vexation, for Thalias was by nature an actor. None but Aspasia saw his paleness and his trembling hands nor saw the fright in his eyes. She no longer desired him. She only knew that he must be saved. She pushed the purse of gold into his hand, and immediately he dropped it into the pouch at his girdle without even an exclamation.

She whispered, 'Do not ask me any questions. But you must flee at once. Do not wait for the night, when the guards are most attentive and pursue even shadows. Stroll down the road idly. They will not suspect, for are you not the pampered darling of Thargelia? I can only tell you that you are in the most desperate danger, and must not delay even another hour. You have much gold. Go to the harbour and take the first ship leaving the port, no matter its destination. You have not been branded as a slave, and gold answers all questions. Be at ease and haughty. In the city purchase a chest and fill it with garments, and induce a beggar to carry it for you to the vessel. It will be thought he is your slave.'

His face was contorted with terror. She pushed his arm.

46

'Array yourself in your finest tunic and sandals, and a cloak. Go at once. There is not a moment to be lost.'

'We have been discovered,' he said through his dry lips.

'Yes,' she said with wild impatience.

Then he said, 'But what of you, my sweet nymph?'

In spite of the extremity of her own fear she was touched, and she gazed at him. 'Naught will be inflicted on me if you have fled,' she answered.

With an oath he took the bow from her hands and threw it on the ground and the gardeners were more amused. He walked from her as if deeply outraged, muttering to himself. Aspasia looked after him with an air of anger and mortification. Then she stamped her foot and ran back into the house, shaking her hair off her neck and shoulders. It was a cloud of gold in the sunlight.

She returned to her chamber and again sank on her bed. She covered her face with her hands. She did not believe in the gods but she prayed to Aphrodite for Thalias' and Cleo's preservation. She had seduced both. They must not suffer for her. Cleo was in less danger now, and would be subjected only to Echion's rough examinations, which would reveal her virginity. Aspasia sighed out of the extremity of her emotions.

Later, after she had forced herself to attend her classes, she went to the gardens to join the other maidens who were chattering with excitement. Thalias had not appeared. One of the girls wished to run for the overseer of the hall to inform him. Aspasia, knowing that every moment was precious, said with contempt, 'He is a mighty eater and drinker. No doubt he is lying in his chamber, drunk.'

'Or in Thargelia's arms,' one of the girls said, slyly.

The others tittered. 'Then, of a surety, we must not disturb him,' said Aspasia. 'Come, let us practise our archery.'

She had authority, and the girls obeyed her. Cleo was among them, with her innocent child's face. Seeing her, Aspasia was newly distressed. Nothing must hurt this little one.

47

The overseer of the hall, wandering out to the portico to watch the delectable sight of the young hetairai romping, noticed the absence of Thalias. He came to the maidens and asked, 'Where is that rascal of a Thalias?'

'Thalias?' Aspasia asked, as if in wonder. 'Was he not here a moment ago?'

To her dismay one of the maidens answered, 'He has not been here at all.'

'Then he is with Thargelia,' said Aspasia. 'Come. Let us toss and catch the ball.'

The overseer became enchanted by all this young grace and the joyous laughter of the girls. He watched for a long time. He caught glimpses of their round young legs as they ran and as their long tunics lifted, and he saw delightful young bosoms heaving. He was certain that not even in Arcadia were the nymphs so beauteous and so perfect in face and form. He kept licking his lips as he watched. Then he remembered that Thalias had never been absent before. He went back to the house and Aspasia saw him go with anxiety.

When the maidens returned to the house they found everything in confusion. Slaves excitedly ran everywhere, and the house was filled with vehement babbling. Thargelia stood with the overseer of the hall in the atrium. Discerning Aspasia, her favourite, she exclaimed, 'Have you seen Thalias?'

Aspasia halted and seemed to think, frowning. 'But an hour ago,' she said. The other maidens raised a chorus of fluting voices declared he had not been seen at all today.

'Where did you see him, Aspasia?' asked the mistress, and Aspasia knew she had made a foolish mistake. She put her finger to her lips and considered. 'It was after history class. He passed us in the hall.'

'No!' cried the maidens, shaking their hair.

'Yes,' said Aspasia. 'He seemed intent on some errand and did not speak.'

'I have heard,' said Thargelia, 'that he gave you a lesson in archery this morning.'

'He did. I requested it.'

Thargelia's eyes narrowed. 'You, who are so proficient with the bow, Aspasia? You desired a lesson alone?'

'I desire to excel in all things. I am yet no Amazon.'

Thargelia continued to regard her. 'He has not been seen since one of the overseers saw him walking idly along the road to the city.'

Aspasia shrugged. 'He will return.'

'Perhaps,' said Thargelia, still watching. 'He has no money. He has only jewelled trinkets which I have given him. They are gone.' She pursed her lips. 'I have sent slaves to the port, but none had seen him there. Nevertheless, he has run away.'

'Alas,' said Aspasia. 'But I do not believe it. Why should he flee?'

'That is the question,' said Thargelia in a grim voice. Her eyes went to Cleo, who returned her regard innocently and Thargelia made a gesture of frustration. But she was a clever woman. Her gaze reverted to Aspasia. She bit her lip. The maiden had been very evasive.

Runaway slaves were not usual in Miletus, for all the punishments were dire and often resulted in death. But Thalias had been an indulged slave and the lover of Thargelia, who had adored him, and he had been given many privileges. Thargelia did not appear in the dining hall that night, and the maidens chattered discreetly among themselves, and laughed and winked. They knew that a wide search was being conducted for Thalias, and in the city itself, where officials had been informed. Thalias had been caught up into the air and had disappeared like a cloud of mist. Aspasia, listening, began to feel relieved. A gentleman, with a slave and a chest, richly attired, and arrogant of demeanour, would not be suspected as a fleeing slave. Moreover, Miletus was a busy port and multitudes of passengers boarded the vessels for many destinations.

Thargelia was beside herself. She loved Thalias, and he had been treated, in her house, as a free man, given gifts and

49

tenderness and had dined with Thargelia and had slept in her bed. At no time had he appeared restive. Therefore, thought Thargelia, something extraordinary had occurred. Slaves like Thalias did not flee from delights and pamperings and all that they desired. He had shown his contentment and happiness. He was one who lived for the hour, and all his hours in this house had been filled with pleasure. He had been all laughter and gaiety and had come eagerly to Thargelia's bed. It was not possible that he had been seized by a desire for liberty – not such a man as Thalias! Thargelia was an authority on the ways of humanity, and so she knew that Thalias had not fled for freedom but from fear. Of what had he been afraid? There was but one answer: He had feared discovery.

Suddenly she thought of Aspasia, who had been so indifferent and had hastened to assure Thargelia that Thalias had not fled, and had seemed intent on persuading Thargelia that she had encountered Thalias in the hall. Thargelia felt a deep grief. Aspasia had never attempted to deceive her before. Why had she engaged in deception today?

The answer was terrible and devastating.

Thargelia began to think of what the guardians and the guards had reported of the night before, and she almost wept. Aspasia! Aspasia, who was the bright jewel of this house, loved and protected, with a great destiny – it was not possible. But Thargelia knew that all things were possible in this world.

Later, she discreetly sent a slave to summon Cleo to her. In the meantime she bathed her eyes in water of roses and composed herself. Cleo entered the chamber shyly, looking about her, for she had never been here before.

'Come, child,' said Thargelia, touched unwillingly at the sight of this little one hardly out of childhood and in appearance as fresh as an almond blossom. The girl approached her timidly and lifted her dark eyes questioningly. All at once Thargelia knew with bitter certainty that Cleo had never left the house the night before. She said, in a voice she tried to make kind,

50

'Cleo, you must answer me in truth or I shall be very displeased with you and my displeasure is not to be despised. Did you sleep well last night?'

Cleo looked at her and then suddenly her face was deeply flushed and Thargelia had a momentary hope that it had been Cleo who had gone to Thalias under the moon and not Aspasia. Cleo was nodding now, unable to speak.

Her hope made Thargelia say almost tenderly, 'Do not be afraid. I want only the truth. Did you leave this house at any time after you retired for the night?'

The girl shook her head with quick denial, and Thargelia knew that she was not lying and her own heart was again filled with grief, and also with formidable anger.

'I have heard from the guardians that your bed was empty at midnight, and that a maiden was seen in the gardens.' She looked at Cleo and now her eyes had changed and had become relentless. Her hands clenched on her embroidered knees. 'Was it you?'

Cleo uttered a faint dying cry and then dropped on her knees before the mistress of the courtesans, and she beat her forehead on the floor in abject terror. 'Was it you? Ah, you shake your hidden head. Where were you last night, Cleo?'

The girl whispered, 'In Aspasia's bed.'

Thargelia breathed deeply, and hope lived with her again. Was it possible that Aspasia had not deceived her after all and had told her the truth?

'Why?' she asked of Cleo. She had a disgusting thought concerning Aspasia and Cleo, then rejected it. She looked down at the trembling child who had begun to weep, her shoulders and back heaving. 'Cleo,' said Thargelia, 'there is nothing reprehensible in that you crept into Aspasia's bed, for consolation or because of an evil dream.'

Cleo crouched in stillness for a moment, then she sat up abruptly on her heels, throwing back her hair and her round wet face was bright with sudden relief and her eyes shone with the joy of one who had been delivered out of danger. 'Yes, yes, Lady, that is what I did, and Aspasia comforted me!'

Thargelia studied her for a long moment and her experience told her that the child was lying. She clapped her hands for a servant and a slave woman moved aside a curtain and entered the chamber. 'Summon Aspasia to me at once,' she said. The slave bowed and retreated. Thargelia gave her attention to Cleo again. The girl was as white as new bone, even to her lips, and she stared at Thargelia with dread. She is as one who gazes upon a Gorgon, thought Thargelia, so fixedly does she gaze at me and with so intense a horror and fear. Thargelia could not bear the sight, for she was not a cruel woman. Cleo had been used by Aspasia without regard for the mortal fright Cleo was now enduring. Thargelia looked aside. All was silent in the chamber, except for the raucous parrot and the music and singing in the portico which had invaded the room. Thargelia did not know what emotion was the most overwhelming, her grief or the hot hatred she felt for Aspasia, who had not only deceived her wantonly but had seduced Thalias. She had no doubt that the seduction had taken place, for Aspasia was no soft maiden and Thalias was too cautious to make an overt approach. Now Thargelia hated him also and was filled with humiliation. Had he been in this house she would have ordered him flogged to death, or tortured to the same end. She vowed to find him if it cost her all her fortune. She would post a reward in all of Miletus, and at the port.

The curtain was moved aside and Aspasia entered, her face calm but rigid. She had dressed her hair in the Greek fashion, bound up in ribbons, and Thargelia, looking at her, was conscious, with tremendous fury, of the maiden's extraordinary beauty and youth and grace and regal air. These had seduced Thalias. Thargelia felt old and withered and undone and repulsive, and this increased her wrath. She was like a harpy in the presence of a nymph, a harpy who must buy love and not receive it ardently, and in truth.

Aspasia bowed, and then saw Thargelia's face and the child

kneeling on the floor, and her heart clenched with terror. I am undone, she thought. But she was proud. In her stately fashion she approached Thargelia closer and looked down in silence into those eyes raised to hers, and she saw that Thargelia's eyes were vivid with hatred. I am to die, she said to herself. She had never been a slave, but this would not protect her from Thargelia's vengeance, for Thargelia knew too many powerful men in Miletus who were in her debt.

Thargelia saw and savoured her favourite's helplessness, and she gloated and even smiled. The smile was hideous. What would this beauty be like after long flogging and torture? She envisioned Aspasia covered with blood, that exquisite body reduced to bleeding tatters, that face obliterated, those wondrous eyes blind with agony and death. She, Thargelia, would be avenged and by a lift of her hand. She longed for the moments of destruction. She would watch in rapture. She felt no compassion for this maiden who had so humiliated and betrayed her.

Aspasia looked again at Cleo and she was sick with pity and regret. Cleo gazed up into Aspasia's eyes, imploring help, and then her little hand reached desperately for Aspasia's tunic and clung to it, winding her fingers in it. Contrition seized Aspasia so that her own eyes filled with tears. She would probably die, but nothing must harm this child. The very sight of the childish body, the faith in the round face, the small feet peering from beneath her tunic, the abjectness of her posture, moved Aspasia enormously. She said, as softly as a mother speaks to her little one, 'Speak, Cleo. Tell the Lady Thargelia what transpired last night.'

Cleo hesitated and Aspasia could not bear the sight of her countenance, for she saw that Cleo was not only afraid for herself but for her friend. 'Speak,' she repeated, 'and all will be well.'

Reassured, but not looking away from the one she adored, Cleo spoke in a half whisper. 'You said, Aspasia, that you wished to worship Artemis under the moon. So you requested me to lie in your bed, with my dark hair covered, and arrange my bed clothes so it would seem I lay in my own. You then left me, and I fell asleep. You awakened me before dawn and I returned to my bed.'

Ah, the sweet one is prudent even at her age, thought Aspasia. She will not repeat my promises of vileness to her. She placed her hand on Cleo's bent head and looked at Thargelia. 'That is all,' she said. 'The girl is innocent of any wrong. If wrong there had been it was my doing, and my indiscretion. But I desired to look upon the moon. I was restless.'

'You are often restless, Aspasia,' said Thargelia, and laughed aloud in derision. Then she paused and regarded the girl with renewed love and hatred. Her intuition told her that she had heard the truth, and also lies. She looked down at Cleo. 'You may leave us, child. I am no longer angry with you, for you have been victim and not transgressor. Go to your bed.'

Cleo stood up slowly, wiping her tears with the palms of her hands, like an infant. Her lips quivered. She looked at Thargelia and then at Aspasia, and Aspasia smiled with reassurance, bent and kissed the girl then pushed her towards the curtain. Cleo fled, scampering, her feet slapping on rug and marble.

'Are you not ashamed,' said Thargelia, 'that you corrupted that child?'

'I did not corrupt her,' Aspasia replied. 'She told you the truth. As I have told you the truth.'

'All of the truth, Aspasia?'

Aspasia could only say, 'Cleo and I have told you the truth.'

'You lie,' said Thargelia, calmly. 'What of Thalias? You met him in the moonlight and for a purpose that I know. Do you deny this?'

Aspasia shut her eyes for a moment. Before she could speak Thargelia said, 'He left me at midnight. He thought I slept. He did not return for some time. I believed he had

54

gone to the latrines, or had strolled in the gardens, for the night was hot and the moon high.' This was not true, but Thargelia was determined to know the whole of her mortification.

'You seduced my slave, Aspasia,' said Thargelia. 'He is young, and foolish, and you have been taught arts. Because of your infamy he will die, and painfully, and I will force you to be present to see what you have done.'

Aspasia could not control herself. 'He has been found?' she cried in a loud voice.

Thargelia did not answer for a moment, and then she said, 'Yes. He attempted to board a vessel in the harbour, and was taken into custody. I heard but a short time ago. He will be delivered to this house in the morning. Prepare yourself for an interesting spectacle, Aspasia. Thalias is strong, but he will shriek for mercy and death. I can assure you of that, though he is a man.'

Aspasia was young and so still possessed considerable credulity. Moreover, Thargelia had never lied to her before. She looked about her wildly, as if seeking succour. She was filled with despair. Then she sank to her knees before Thargelia and clasped her hands convulsively.

'Spare him,' she said. 'I alone am guilty. I seduced him because the heat of my desire was too much for me and had to be relieved. Any man would have sufficed. As you have said of Cleo, he, too, was my victim. You have taught us that men are seized with irrepressible passions which they cannot control, and that any woman to them then is desirable. I have also been taught the arts of seduction, and he is not experienced as I am, and not intelligent. It was a moment's madness to him only. He is not guilty. He is only a man.'

Thargelia's face twisted until it was extremely ugly, and the cosmetics on her face increased her wrinkles. Her dyed golden hair was a travesty. She saw her beloved Thalias in those round white arms; she saw him kissing that adorable breast. She saw him enter that body, and could hear his gaspings. They would be more delirious than in her own bed, for he had been embracing youth and divine loveliness. All that the girl was had been tended since her birth, and she had had a glorious destiny, which was now lost. Pain seized Thargelia then, pain for herself, pain for Thalias and even pain for this wanton, Aspasia, whom she had loved like an only daughter, and whose prospects had been destroyed. Thargelia rarely had wept in all her life but now she was taken with a desperate desire to weep. She controlled herself.

'How did Thalias flee?' she asked.

'I gave him the last of my mother's money.' Then courage returned to Aspasia. 'I told him to flee. I am not sorry, except that he will suffer for it. I wish he had escaped to safety! I should have that to remember with joy.'

'Do not mourn,' said Thargelia, with answering passion and fresh mortification. 'He has not been taken, as yet. When he is I will send him only to the fields, for his punishment, in chains so that he cannot run again. Does that comfort you?'

Aspasia stood up and for the first time she regarded the mistress with loathing. 'Then you have lied to me,' she said. 'And I trusted you.'

Thargelia mocked her. ' "Then you have lied to me, and I trusted you." Go to your bed, Aspasia. I will consider your fate tonight. I assure you it will not be a happy one. I may send you into the kitchens or the fields. I may have you flogged to death, or your beauty destroyed forever. You will know in the morning.'

Aspasia knew that she had nothing to lose now. 'I am not a slave,' she said. 'I was born free and am free. You can do nothing unlawful against a free woman, no matter your wrath. In the eyes of the laws of Miletus I have done little wrong, nothing to merit extreme punishment.'

Thargelia looked at the girl with contempt. 'Do you think the law in Miletus will be concerned with the fate I mete out to a mere chit in my care, who has induced a slave to flee – a capital crime in itself? Ponder on that, insolent one.'

'Let me go, tonight,' said Aspasia. 'We will see each other no more.'

'Where will you go, you fool? On foot, with only the peplos on your body, and no money? Or would you sell yourself into slavery, which is all you deserve? Or become a public whore?'

'I know not what I shall do,' said Aspasia. 'It is enough for me to go. I have long been rebellious of the fate you have designed for me. At least I will escape that, and with joy.'

Thargelia considered. She said, 'The fate you so despise was a fate of power and wealth and comfort and adoration and cosseting, the mistress of a selected and distinguished man. You would prefer the streets of Miletus and its noisome alleys and squalid dwellings, and the encounters with brutes of the ports and the slaughterhouses and the manufactories and the sea – for a handful of drachmas or a little bread and wine?'

Aspasia could not speak for a moment. Then she said, 'I would be free to make my own fate, to live or to die.'

'You speak like one born an imbecile,' said Thargelia. 'Go to your chamber. You have not interested me. I may set you, penniless and without even a cloak, on the streets of Miletus tomorrow. There you may use the arts you have been taught for a crust of bread.'

She made an imperious gesture of dismissal, and Aspasia, still holding high her incomparable head, retired. Thargelia threw herself upon the bed and gave herself up to weeping, for her own anguish, for Thalias and Aspasia.

CHAPTER VI

Thargelia's eyes were swollen and red in the morning, when she consulted Echion, who listened with deep interest to the story she had told him. His mouth watered and he had to keep swallowing and his eyes had glistened. He wanted to say to Thargelia, 'Give me the maiden, as a servant in my small house, or the tender of my garden, or my cook.' But discretion warned him. So he shrugged.

He said, 'Having lost her virginity she is now worthless.'

Thargelia thought. She said, 'We know the arts of deception so that even a wanton can simulate virginity.'

'With the aid of a chicken's blood,' laughed Echion, 'and some clever simulations and cries of pain.'

'It is true that men are fools and believe what they wish to believe,' said Thargelia. 'They always believe women, which is not perspicacious of them. They think women are too stupid to deceive effectually.'

'Ah,' said Echion, with an arch look. He added, 'The maiden is young and helpless. You can do with her what you will.'

Being a cynic, he did not know that Thargelia had spent the night in pain pondering this very matter and that she had been desperately seeking for a way not to destroy Aspasia, but to save her. But it must be done with expedition. She could not remain in this house, under Thargelia's eye, to be a reminder of betrayal and shame. So this morning she had sent a slave to discover what foreign men of distinction had come from the vessels on affairs in Miletus, or on their way to Greece. The slave had not as yet returned.

'There is a possibility that she is still a virgin,' said Echion, as if seriously considering. 'After all, it is not easy to violate a virgin, and the man was a slave and may have been frightened, or, at the last, she may have struggled. Let me examine her in discreet privacy.'

Thargelia narrowed her eyes at him. 'I am certain she is no longer a virgin. I am experienced in these things,' She laughed abruptly. 'If Aspasia were still virgin she would not be after leaving you, Echion. Let us understand each other.' They laughed together.

There had been many Greek and Ionian men who had been allowed to glimpse Aspasia in this house, without her knowledge. They also trusted Thargelia. To give them a violated hetaira, when they desired only a virgin, would be reprehensible and dangerous. (Many had ardently desired Aspasia and had offered Thargelia the most enormous sums, but she had been too loath, like a mother, to part with the girl as yet, and Aspasia had not completed her schooling.) Worst of all, Aspasia had been deflowered by a mean slave, a thing, and that was unpardonable.

Thargelia gave orders that Aspasia was to be enlightened in the art of simulating virginity, at once and with all dispatch. Even foreign men, men from the East, were entitled to a kind deception, for they were notable for riches and extolled virginity more even than did the Ionians and the Greeks.

Aspasia at first resisted the information and the instructions. Then, as she was not a fool, she acceded. She was still pale and listless and full of pain for herself, and even for Thargelia, who had been as a mother to her. To her joy, however, she was permitted to resume her classes, for Thargelia wanted no scandal in her house, and Aspasia saw that little Cleo was not to be punished in any manner. For that Aspasia was deeply grateful, and she loved Thargelia again, if with reluctance and resentment. She, herself, was not to be punished severe- ly, it would seem, though she understood that she could not long remain in this house, her home, suddenly dear to her. She wondered about her fate, and shrank from the unknown.

The slave Thargelia had sent to the port returned in a state of excitement. A Persian gentleman, accompanied by a rich retinue, had arrived that morning, and was now the guest of a famous man in Miletus, one Cadmus, who had long desired Aspasia. Thargelia was both elated and troubled. She could not offend Cadmus, but the Persian gentleman, Al Taliph, must be engaged. It was reputed that he was enormously wealthy, so Aspasia would bring a great prize. Cadmus, though rich, could not meet the price, as he had discovered to his regret a few months ago. Thargelia did not love the Persians, but a satrap like Al Taliph could be endured.

Thargelia thought of Cleo. Once Cadmus had complained – the object being a reduction in price – that Aspasia was no longer young, being fifteen years of age, and so the price should be lowered. He preferred little girls and little boys. So Thargelia wrote a message to her dear friend, Cadmus, informing him that she had a young girl in her house, only twelve years old, though in fact Cleo was thirteen. She described Cleo, so like an almond blossom in the spring. The girl, she wrote, had not yet reached puberty, and that would be most desirable to Cadmus. Then, as if it were an afterthought, she invited Cadmus to bring his foreign guest to her house for dinner and revelry and music. Her dinners were famous, her maidens gifted in dance and song. Cadmus had always infinitely enjoyed these occasions and had always brought Thargelia lavish gifts in gratitude. He already had two of her hetairai in his house, as well as an assortment of beautiful female slaves. Yes, he would adore Cleo, in her innocence and virginity and, thought Thargelia, her stupidity. She had not as yet been taught all the subtle arts of seduction, but that would only enhance her in the eyes of Cadmus.

Certain that Cadmus would eagerly accept her invitation, she prepared her house, for the invitation was for this night. She sent orders to both Cleo and Aspasia that they must retire to their chambers for sleep, and then must elaborately array and dress themselves and perfume and oil their bodies.

The windows were opened to the warm night, the green curtains undrawn, and so the rattle of palm trees and the sighing of sycamores and oaks and myrtle and cypresses, and the surging of the ever-present sea, could be heard clearly.

Thargelia greeted her guests in the atrium. She was attired in crimson and yellow with an enormous Egyptian necklace falling over her bosom, and she exhaled exotic perfumes with every movement of her slender body. Jewels glittered in her dyed yellow hair and on her arms and fingers. She was splendid and even heroic, and her white teeth flashed and her eyes glinted amiably. 'Welcome to my poor house,' she said to Cadmus and the Persian satrap, Al Taliph, and bowed deeply.

'It is hardly a poor house, dear Thargelia,' said Cadmus, who had a voice like a squeaking mouse and effeminate gestures. He looked about him with pride and then at Al Taliph and was pleased that the other was visibly impressed. What! Had he expected a mean brothel? thought Cadmus. We may not be as opulent as Persia, but we are not peasants in Miletus! They repaired to the dining hall where the girls were already singing and playing and posturing in a slow dance at a farther wall. Al Taliph and Cadmus sat on a soft couch covered with brocaded silk, and Thargelia seated herself in an ivory chair opposite them. Two chairs awaited Cleo and Aspasia. Slaves, dressed like fauns, poured whisky into small glasses and wine into the goblets, and Cadmus offered a libation to the gods. Al Taliph looked about him curiously. This house of courtesans was far more lavish than the house of Cadmus, who was himself a rich man, and everything was in the most perfect taste. If the damsel to be presented to him was as fair as her surroundings and as exquisite, then she was greatly to be desired. Al Taliph, a man not in the least garrulous, listened smiling to the light chatter of his hostess and Cadmus, and sipped his whisky and listened to the music and idly watched the slow dance of the maidens in the distance.

He would have been pleased to have had all of them in his harem, especially those of white skin and light hair. His favourite concubine was from the island of Cos, and she had hair the colour of silver touched with gold and eyes as blue as the legendary blue rose. But, alas, there were few such treasures as his favourite and he doubted that Thargelia's hetairai could compare with her, though, as promised by Cadmus, they were more seductive.

Thargelia knew that Cadmus still lusted for Aspasia, though she, at fifteen, was too old for him. So Thargelia said, 'My dear Cadmus, I have a jewel for you, as I wrote you today, a mere infant, but like spring just budding into flower, and not yet a woman. Her name is Cleo and she was not born of slaves or mere peasants, but of a distinguished father and his adorable concubine. I warn you, however,' she added with a coquettish smile, 'that her price is high.'

'Your prices are always high,' grumbled Cadmus, motioning to a slave to refill his glass with whisky. 'But then, the maidens are exceptional.'

The hall was permeated with swooning fragrances. The cheeks of the guests began to be flushed both with warmth and whisky. They sat contentedly on the soft couch and smiled with anticipation.

Thargelia summoned Cleo and Aspasia to join her and to be seated one on each side of her. She looked at Al Taliph and liked his appearance. She hoped he would be kind to Aspasia, and she sighed, remembering that the Persians had an even greater contempt for women than did the Greeks.

The maidens struck up a more lively and louder melody at a gesture from Thargelia, and Aspasia and Cleo entered.

CHAPTER VII

Al Taliph, the satrap from Persia, looked at Aspasia as she silently walked to the table with averted eyes, and he thought, Ah, she is far more entrancing than my Narcissa, that lily from Cos, and she is also much younger. He could not believe that any woman could be so fair and so bewitching, and of such perfection of face and form. He stirred on the couch and his face became delicately lustful. As for Cadmus, after a first desiring glance at Aspasia, his eye was caught by the pristine charm of Cleo, who had a young boy's body and an infant's face, and who retained the tender awkwardness of childhood. He imagined her in his bed at once, this little virgin. No matter Thargelia's price, he must have this girl, and tonight. He would be gentle with her deflowering, for roughness might kill her, and then his money would be lost.

Cleo ate the unusual dishes with open and delighted pleasure. When Cadmus' hand would steal under her peplos she merely pushed it away so as not to be disturbed in her enjoyment. To her it had no more significance than a vexation. She was too engrossed to consider herself his mistress as yet. He rubbed the palm of his hand over her breasts and said to Thargelia with satisfaction, 'She is like a boy, still.' Thargelia frowned. 'I beg of you, Cadmus, not to annoy the child.'

Aspasia shuddered in herself that such a man was to be given Cleo, the immature little bird. He will crush her to death, she thought, with the weight of his body. He will tear those frail limbs asunder. Ah, if I had but gold I would flee with this child and hide her. Gold answers all things. Without it we are helpless and the gods are deaf to our importunities, despite the pieties of philosophers. She saw Cadmus' hand fondling one of the budlike breasts of Cleo and Aspasia wished to kill him. Cleo irritably slapped his hand away and gave herself up to the voluptuous delights of the table. Her round face was rosy with wine.

Aspasia had never learned resignation but she was beginning to learn it now. There was nothing she could do to help Cleo, so she gave her full attention to Al Taliph, to whom she would be presented. She was not a slave, but Thargelia under the law was her guardian and she the ward of Thargelia and what Thargelia willed for her would be legal and accepted. Thargelia desired Al Taliph to take her, Aspasia, and she must obey her guardian.

Al Taliph was not the man she had feared would resemble Cadmus. He was middle-aged, possible thirty-five years old, and tall and slender, almost bony. He was magnificently arrayed in the Oriental fashion, and he wore a robe of intricate design in scarlet, blue, green, yellow, violet and gold, all in a pattern that had no beginning and no end. It was made of the finest silk, and glistened. His narrow waist was clasped by a girdle that resembled a living snake, with a jewelled head and an open mouth. A similar but smaller snake clasped his thin and sun-baked throat, and there were even smaller snakes on his arms and wrists. A short mantle of cloth of gold covered his shoulders, which were broad if thin. His sandals were of gold also, and the thong was in the form of a gemmed viper. There were many rings on his long dark hands, fabulous rings that glittered blindingly, and several of them were of the snake design also. He wore ear-rings, looped gold.

On his head he bore the first turban Aspasia had ever seen, of cloth of gold sprinkled with jewels. It was like a crown, high and wide, and gave him a look of majesty, lifting above his fine spare ears and his broad dark brow, which was also high and as unlined as brown marble.

But it was his face that engaged Aspasia's attention. Like his body his countenance was narrow and very attenuated, if nearly as black as an Ethiopian's. He had strange eyes which at one moment appeared brown and at another grey, and they were almost as large as Aspasia's, and glimmered and shone and changed with his thoughts. He had long black and silken lashes, and his eyebrows were like the wings of a bird, swooping upwards to his forehead; giving him a barbaric expression, and a delicately cruel one. His nose was short but beaked. His mouth was extremely mobile and satirical, and only faintly coloured with red cosmetics. He had the hidden sneering air of the Persian aristocracy, and his whole face was subtle and occult beyond the comprehension of the western people. She thought, Here is a man who reveals nothing of his thoughts or passions, and rules himself.

Those, she remembered from her lessons, who were in command of themselves were inevitably powerful and potent, beyond the hysteria and disastrous emotions of lesser men. Al Taliph, she thought with growing respect, would never permit vulgar vehemences in himself.

Al Taliph had several wives and a huge harem. A man went to other men for intellectual understanding. He looked at Aspasia, to ponder again, with conflicting thoughts, on her intelligence or her lack of intelligence. Could anything of consequence come from that adorable mouth? If so, it would be infinitely exciting.

He spoke to her for the first time and his voice, Aspasia thought, was not coarse and loud like Cadmus' but low and quiet and pleasing to the ear, almost like the sound of the sea. 'I have heard that in this house the women are taught many things which other Ionian and Grecian women are not, and that their minds are respected.'

'Yes, it is true,' said Aspasia, and out of her bitterness she spoke loudly and clearly and the Persian was surprised at the resonance and fascination of her voice, though he deplored the strength of it. Women in Persia had soft whispering voices and when they spoke they meekly bent their heads and let their lashes fall. But Aspasia looked at him straightly, and he saw her eyes and marvelled, for liquid lights increased and shifted in them, as if they contained crystal waters in themselves. 'But that does not help us. We are despised.' In Persia men did not address women as they addressed men; they kept their eyes averted so as not to contaminate them by looking too long at a woman. However, he found himself, to his amused vexation, returning her regard. Then his gaze wandered once more over her body, at the swelling young breast, at the dainty waist and virginal hips.

'Tell me,' he said, 'would you like to live in my country?'

She shrugged. 'Does in matter where I live? I have no choice.' Then she added, 'Are you going to Greece, sire?'

He coughed slightly as if she had asked him a bold and embarrassing question. 'In the midst of all these wars and turbulences, Aspasia? I doubt I would live long in Greece, if I were discovered. I do my affairs from this sanctuary in Miletus, where I meet with Greek merchants, lapidaries, manufacturers, weapon-makers, dealers in oils and excellent works of art, and many other things. Here we are pragmatic men and not enemies. Merchants are not emotional; it is gold, only,' and he rubbed the fingers of his right hand together. 'Is that not sensible?'

There was a sudden exclamation from Thargelia of annoyance mingled with drunken mirth. Cadmus had dexterously divested Cleo of her peplos and had swung the child on to his knees. He began to explore her little tawny body with rough hard fingers and Cleo started to cry. Without thinking Aspasia sprang from her chair and put her arms about Cleo, seeking to lift her from the huge knees on which she struggled in fear. Cadmus' hand reached out swiftly and he caught Aspasia by one of her breasts and squeezed it, laughing up in her face with a salacious light in his eyes. She cried out, strove to push away that gripping hand, but he held her breast tighter and his thumb rubbed her nipple painfully.

Later Al Taliph thought that he himself had behaved in a ridiculous fashion, for what was a woman and especially such as the hetairai? Aspasia, he was to think, had been presumptuous and forward in attempting to rescue that worthless little creature who had taken the fancy of a man, and who should

66

have been grateful for it. It was probably Aspasia's cry which caused him to rise quickly, for he had already, in his mind, declared her his and it was intolerable to see another man touch his property.

So Aspasia saw a long lean hand dart like a striking snake at Cadmus' hand, which held her breast, and Cadmus uttered a short howl of pain and released the girl. Cleo fell from his knees and sprawled on the soft carpet and whimpered like a puppy.

Cadmus grasped his wrist and shrieked like a woman, half-rising. He looked up at Al Taliph's smiling face and he shouted, 'You have broken my wrist, may the Furies seize you!'

Al Taliph spoke gently. 'I do not think it is broken, though I struck it with the side of my palm, a Persian lesson from Cathay. Had I struck your throat so you would now be dead, my friend.' He shook his head as if in reproof of his own impetuousness.

Aspasia fell on her knees beside the wailing Cleo and held her in her arms against her breast and she regarded Cadmus fiercely. Thargelia, amazed, stood up and was no longer drunk. She was filled with dismay. Never had this happened in her house before, no matter how intoxicated her clients. But above all she feared that this episode would result in the two men rejecting her hetairai for boldness, on Aspasia's part, and Cleo's absurd objections to Cadmus' caresses. She exclaimed to Cadmus, 'I will send for unguents at once!' To Al Taliph, standing near her, she said, 'I am humiliated at the actions of Aspasia. But she has the effrontery of youth. I implore you to forgive her, Cadmus,' and she turned to the other man.

He said, through clenched yellow teeth, still holding his wrist, 'Give her to me and I promise that every morning she will be flogged, as a punishment. What other man would have such a wench?' He looked at Aspasia with mingled hatred and desire, and sharply kicked her in the side with his sandalled foot.

Al Taliph caught his injured wrist and stared down into his

eyes, smiling, and said, 'Do not kick what is mine, dearest of friends.' His voice was soft.

Cadmus shrank. He whimpered with pain, remembering that he had dealings to do with Al Taliph and extremely profitable ones, and he was jeopardizing them. He swallowed his hatred, and said, 'Shall men quarrel for such as these? No. I am ashamed.'

Cleo was clinging to Aspasia, weeping into the older girl's shoulder, and Aspasia was filled with despair. Thargelia's bosom rose on a deep breath of relief. She said to Cadmus, 'You will take Cleo with you tonight?'

He scowled at her, biting one of his thick lips and his eyes narrowed shrewdly. 'I have discerned that she is close to puberty. Her price must be lowered, for in less than a year she will be worthless to me.'

'She is not a slave,' said Thargelia, suddenly touched with pity at the sight of the two girls sitting on the carpet. More-over, Cadmus had dared spurn her darling, Aspasia, with his foot as if she were a canine bitch. The singing and dancing and playing maidens and the serving slaves had become still and silent, watching. 'Cleo,' Thargelia continued in a cold voice, 'was born free and is still free. When you have had your pleasure and your fill of her return her to me.' She looked inflexibly at Cadmus who began to fear that never again would he be invited to this house of joys and luxuries.

'You will also treat the child with care and gentleness,' said Thargelia. 'If ill comes to her, Cadmus, not all your wealth will protect you from my wrath and the justice of the authorities.'

'You are insolent,' he muttered. His wrist was swelling and he was in pain, and he rubbed the wrist with the fingers of his other hand. 'Am I a heathen barbarian, a murderer? The girl will be treated well in my house.'

Thargelia clapped her hands and two male slaves came obediently to her, and she said, 'A bowl of hot water and unguents and linen.' Al Taliph had returned to his chair. He was taken by a deep tenderness for Aspasia, and was so astonished by this unique emotion for a woman that he almost burst out laughing in ridicule of himself. Yet, when he looked down into her eyes and saw the suffering in them he was moved in an unfamiliar fashion, for he was not a man of pity and mercy was almost unknown to him.

He touched her shoulder lightly, bending down to do so, and she lifted her head and regarded him in silence. She saw his swarthy face and something curiously arcane in his subtle eyes.

I do not fear him, Aspasia thought in wonder. I will go with him and gladly, for I feel in my heart that he is not as other men. She said, 'I pray you to take Cleo also.' But he shook his head and removed his hand and turned away in grave rebuke.

'She is not mine to take,' he replied, and glanced at Cadmus, whose wrist was being bound up by Echion, himself. Though Aspasia was again filled with despair she understood. Al Taliph was a man of honour.

CHAPTER VIII

Kurda, the master of the eunuchs, and a eunuch himself, stared after the golden-haired woman with hatred. For three years now she, a detestable female, had ruled this household, this palace, with more power than a lawful queen, with certainly more power than the four noble wives of the lord – the ruler of the province. Not for this creature the confines of the harem, where lived two hundred young concubines and slaves! Not for her the cymbals and the flutes and the zithers and the dance, to please the lord, Al Taliph, during his weary relaxation after affairs of state!

Kurda stood at the bronze gates leading into the hall of the palace and watched Aspasia's queenly and stately passage across the blue and white tiles of the courtyard, which was lighted by the ardent sun. She is not even young, he thought, with malevolence. It is said that she is eighteen years old, a withered leaf. She was as old as the oldest wife of the lord, who had already given birth to five children, all sons – for which the lady was honoured. She was far older than the concubines of the harem, most of whom were not over fourteen years, for women began to fade at that age and the lord could not endure old women. Yet, he endured and suffered this one! Incredible! Shameful! Had she cast a western spell on him, to so derange his wits?

The multitudinous women of the palace unceasingly teased and even lightly tormented Kurda, and his eunuchs, but they feared him also, for at his will he could order whippings and other punishment for the women of the harem. Only the princesses – the wives of Al Taliph – and especial favourites – were safe from his malice and his detestation of their sex. But this western woman, who was neither princess nor true concubine, and not even a slave, pretended to be unaware of his very existence, he whose trousers were of silver or cloth of gold and embroidered with scarlet and blue and yellow and purple, with a vest equally magnificent and a turban even more so, and whose girdle was of gold studded with gems and who wore a curved sword of magnificent workmanship. He might have been a leashed jackal, for all her attention.

Ah, but she was growing old! It would not be long before she was banished to the lower stratum of the harem, to tend children and wash the feet of new favourites and oil their young bodies and serve them. Then he, Kurda, would have his revenge. He would order her flogged at sunrise every day until she died of it, and then he would have her body thrown to the pariah dogs who infested the mountains. None would mourn her. She was feared and hated not only by the noble wives but by the entire harem, who would rejoice in her final fate, this insolent and impertinent one who not only dis-

70

dained Kurda but the wives, also, and the other concubines.

The master of the eunuchs was an immensely tall and immensely fat man, with a huge belly and a great pallid face, as smooth as an infant's buttocks. His tiny black eyes were sunken in his facial flesh; he had a nose like a mushroom, a fat sullen mouth pouting like a peevish child's, and a number of chins so full that they concealed his neck. His whole appearance was gross, even grotesque, and when he spoke Aspasia could hardly refrain from smiling, so high and thin and girlish was his voice. But she knew at once how dangerous he was, how full of vindictiveness and malignance. She had heard that all eunuchs were like such as he, detesting women, murderous, lustful for the infliction of torture as other men were lustful for girls. But surely Kurda surpassed all his brothers in these attributes. She knew that though he hated all the other women in the palace, even the princesses he served so sedulously and guarded with such ardour, he hated her more than all others. At first she had been inclined to pity him, believing he mourned his mutilated state, but she soon learned that he was proud of it, accepting it as a superior endowment. His big belly, naked and hairless, protruded from between the sides of his patterned vest, and his navel was tinted rose, which Aspasia thought particularly obscene.

Once she had asked herself idly. Why does he loathe me more than the other women, and why does he fix his eyes upon me with such a desire to kill? It did not come to her for some time that this was because he had a woman's love for Al Taliph, and he had learned that the satrap loved Aspasia as he had never loved any other woman. Worse than all else, however, Aspasia was treated like an empress in this house, and never was she banished to that part where the women lived but sat at feasts with the satrap and his guests at the table, bold, shameless, conversing as men converse, and held all in fascinated attention. The guests did not disdain her or regard her as worthless, as they did even their own wives and daughters, and this inflamed the jealous Kurda. They gazed upon her like men under the spell of a golden moon set upon a mountain top.

Again, it was the privilege of the master of the eunuchs to strike a recalcitrant young concubine or slave girl who became mutinous in the harem, or punish her in some other corrective fashion, which did not mar her skin or bruise or truly injure her. Kurda understood that from the moment Aspasia entered this palace she was beyond his corrections and that he must speak to her with even more respect than he did Al Taliph's wives. How this was he did not know; hence his hatred and resentment of her, this alien barbarian woman.

Watching her with fury today, as he always watched her, Kurda saw her looking ahead into the hypnotizing vista of the high blue and white pointed arches which led from the court-yard like the myriad diminishing reflections in a mirror. They seemed to extend into infinity, growing smaller with distance, one within another, an illusion of endlessness.

She was not unhappy. She had a tutor who sedulously taught her the language of Persia and the customs and she endeavoured to learn, the better to please Al Taliph. She was endlessly curious, endlessly engrossed. She had access to Al Taliph's libraries and those areas exclusive to him, filled with art which at once repelled and captivated her.

She believed that he loved her, if only as a novelty. Once she said to him, 'Will you discard me when I am old, in a few years?' He had gazed at her with that amused tenderness which she sometimes found infuriating. 'Lily of Shalimar,' he had replied, 'you will never grow old.' He would then tell her of Egypt and India, their customs and religions, and her mind was diverted and she was eager to learn. He said, 'That is the attribute of those who are eternally young – they learn, their souls are ardent, their eyes, seeking, never fade, their bodies are never bent. My mother was such.' That was the first and the last time that he ever spoke of his mother.

He asked her, 'Are you lonely, my love?' When she

72

answered that she had never truly known loneliness he had nodded as if deeply gratified and content. She had received priceless gifts from him, jewels and gold, and knew that she could leave him at any time she willed. But she did not want to leave. There were occasions when she felt the exhilaration of happiness.

On this early morning Aspasia, unattended, walked through the palace from her gorgeous chamber to the harem. She wore the eastern dress and not the tunic or peplos of Greece. The robe was blue, a colour Al Taliph preferred for it warned against evil spirits, tight and revealing over shoulders and breast and waist and belly, then unfolding into flares and pleats bordered with gold embroidery. She did not wear a headdress and her hair floated behind her in a pale bright cloud, and embraced her hips and thighs. Her arms were partially bare and clasped by many gemmed bracelets, and her sandals were also gemmed over white arches and painted toes. Her strong yet delicate face was set, even fixed, and her eyes, the colour of topaz wine, were very sober. The eunuchs everywhere, and the guards, stared after her, the guards furtively desiring her and even the eunuchs feeling a faint stir in their mutilated loins. They all believed she was an evil spirit, for what human woman possessed such divine beauty, such grace, such fluid movements of hidden limbs, such whiteness and scarlet and gilt? Her very regality was a wonder, and foreign, and intimidating. They believed that she did not even eat, for she was not plump; demons did not eat human food. They dined on unmentionable abominations. It was rumoured that she conversed like a man at the table with their lord, and that alone frightened the inhabitants of the palace, who whispered that she was not truly a woman but a demonic masculine apparition. So, she was unclean, and dangerous. Each man, eunuch and guard, made the sign against the evil eye when she appeared.

She passed through gleaming white halls whose arched doorways blew with blue or red or yellow silk curtains, and whose floors were strewn with colourful Persian carpets. Silken couches and Chinese tables lined the walls, and immense vases filled with flowers. Through the grilled archways facing the gardens there came the passionate smell of blossoms and water and resin, and the cries of parrots and the screams of peacocks and the quacking of ducks and the songs of the gardeners. Everywhere there were dancing reflections from fountains and sunlight, striking on floor and fretted stone walls and on mosaic like strenuous paintings. There was the music of zithers and harps at a distance, and the far sound of women's smothered laughter or the slap of some hurrying slave's foot-steps on marble.

It was still very early, yet the palace hummed with life and movement, and the presence of many people. Aspasia came to the bronze double doorway which led to the harem, and which was guarded by six enormous eunuchs, hairless, fat, naked to the waist, arrayed in magnificent trousers and with turbans on their heads, their hands holding bared swords. They wore golden chains about their thick necks and gold bracelets were clasped on their vast upper arms. Their shoes, of gilt leather, were turned up sharply at the toes. They eyed Aspasia without favour, and their eyes, sunken in fat, were sullen if respectful. She noticed that they made the sign against the evil eye, and she smiled and her beautiful white teeth sparkled. But she had to wait until the eunuchs opened the carved metal doors for her, and they did not hasten.

She entered the large room where the women of the harem disported themselves. Here it was dimmer, the light shaded by carved ebony screens from Cathay, the rugs thicker, one upon another, the walls hung with silken curtains, the floor scattered with heaped cushions of every hue, the divans soft and luxurious, the multitude of small brass tables from India covered with baskets and bowls of fruit and sweetmeats and cakes, the brazen urns redolent of wine even this early, and everywhere flowers on table and on floor so that the air here, hotter than in the halls, made the head swim with scent and musk and airlessness for all many slaves waved fans of ostrich plumes continually. There was also an odour of perfumed sweat, sickening to western senses. The overpowering luxury never failed to displease Aspasia, who thought it wanton and stale and deadening. It reeked of woman flesh, indolent and dissipated and oiled and sultry, and sensual. Aspasia thought of it as a voluptuous kennel of coddled bitches, constantly in heat and delivering litters. There had been a certain atmosphere of controlled and elegant austerity in the house of Thargelia, a civilized restraint, for all it had been sybaritic too.

She found the harem depraved with a spiritual depravity unknown in Miletus or Greece. She often thought that over-elaboration, the overly intricate and embroidered, the overly suffused with animal comforts, the too opulent, were not only decadent and cloying but hinted of dissolution and decay. Possessing the western mind she was revolted by redundance, by detail heaped on detail, as one is with exhaustive carnality – surfeited. She was never to come to terms with the eastern mind, the excessively ornate. In some peculiar fashion it wearied and oppressed her. She was aware of the hostility with which she was greeted.

The harem, as usual, was filled with women and babble and noise and clashing music and laughter. Some little naked children raced about, complaining and stuffing their mouths or flinging themselves upon their mothers with petulant cries and demands, or fighting. A few small monkeys swung from curtains and screeched, and a few cats yowled and leaped upon tables to devour the dainties there, and parrots shrieked from gilt cages. The hot dimmed air seemed to Aspasia the very atmosphere of Hades, reeking. There was a fetid smell, a sickening odour of overripe fruit, dates, figs, citrons and melons, all rotting away in beautifully painted and enamelled Chinese bowls. Even the flowers had a sickly effluvium.

The fat oiled women, clad in rich trousers and tight bodices, reclined on cushions as bloated as themselves, or on soft divans, unveiled, languorous, smiling, gossiping, laughing, playing with the children or upbraiding slaves who were rough with their hairbrushes and combs, applying odoriferous cosmetics and perfumes, reddening their lips, scratching their hair or their voluptuous bodies, chattering, murmuring lewdly or slapping the more obstreperous children who were too exigent. The ostrich fans waved but could give no coolness nor for long banished the swarms of insistent flies which bit and polluted the sweetmeats and fruit. The music jangled on Aspasia's ear, for it seemed discordant to her and without coherence.

For a long time now Aspasia had endeavoured to teach the younger concubines the skills of reading and writing and the appreciation of art, and even, unfortunate girl! philosophy. At first the young girls had appeared interested and had even learned a little. Then their natural indolence overcame them and they asked her, in their light pouting voices, of what use this would all be to them. She had replied, 'It is your right as a human being to learn about the world and to comprehend it.' At this the older women had laughed immoderately and had said, 'It is enough for women to understand men.' Aspasia reluctantly acknowledged, from her teachings at Thargelia's school, that that knowledge was the most important in the world, but there was also the question of a woman's mind and soul. When she would tell the women this they would stare at her risibly and shrug, as at the intrusion of barbaric ideas. They had everything a man could give them, and what more did they need or desire? Too, who had said that a woman had a mind and soul apart from men? They had never heard such absurdities. In the meantime, life was enjoyable and for that purpose were they not created? In the face of this mocking argument, this bland and superior amusement, this contempt for her 'barbarian' ideas, she could only fume and despair.

Still, she persisted. Today, as she entered, to the familiar humming babble and broad and ridiculing smiles and the stuffing of mouths and the clamour of tambourine and zither and harp and flute and lyre, and the screaming of children, she saw, to her vague alarm, that Kurda was stationed here instead of the usual eunuchs. He stood half-hidden against a drapery and Aspasia unconsciously shrank, for all she despised him. His eyes gleamed like the eyes of a wild animal in the dusk. She could only ignore him; and the sight of his deliberately bared sword.

She waited until there was a comparative silence, trying to avoid noticing the smiling repudiation in the women's eyes, their overt envious scorn of her, their awaiting her next words and gestures as one awaits the antics of a comedian.

She said, 'You have often remarked, ladies, that I am the favourite of our lord, the noble Al Taliph, and it has made you resentful and unhappy. Did you ever ask why he preferred me to you?'

They ruminated on that, exchanging sly glances. Then one of the wives, seated aside on a divan, said, 'You make him laugh, and he needs laughter, as a king needs a fool to entertain him. We serve his deepest needs and passions, as you do not. What! You have never even borne him a child! Therefore he has not regarded you as a woman but as a jester, a tumbler, a dancing girl of no importance.' She spoke out of malice, for she knew that Aspasia was treated as a queen in this house.

'I speak to his soul and his mind,' said Aspasia, standing among them. Her face was proud and pale.

The women burst out laughing, throwing their heads on each other's shoulders, slapping each other's hands, feigning exhaustion of laughter, sprawling on their many coloured cushions, and exhaling sighs of exquisite titillation. The slaves laughed also, and the children screamed with delight, not knowing why. The whole harem moved in a tumult of derisive joy. Kurda grinned at this evil woman. Only here did she find her proper position as a rejected slave.

One of the wives said, 'Last night my lord called me to his bed and was pleased by my ministrations and I slept at his feet until dawn, and then he kindly rewarded me with a gift and a smile. Where were you last night, O Aspasia of Miletus?'

'This morning,' said a concubine of about thirteen, 'my lord summoned me for unusual pleasures and I gratified him and he said I was delicious. Where were you this morning, Lady?'

I was in his libraries, reading, thought Aspasia. Nevertheless, she was filled with angry humiliation, for all that she knew of Al Taliph and his harem. He never spoke of these women to her and in her fashion she had thought them of no consequence to him.

'I am about to bear his third child,' said the second wife. 'Is your belly swollen, O Aspasia of Miletus, you his favourite?'

It is absurd to feel betrayal, thought Aspasia. I am a hetaira. I am his chief concubine. Why, then, should I feel degraded?

'He was weary when he came dusty from the city yesterday,' said the third wife. 'Did he summon you to his green marble bath, there to anoint him and massage him and clamber on his body for pleasure? Did he then slide into his pool and invite you to engage in more acts of love and tender consolations? Did you disport with him like a dolphin, a female dolphin pursued by her mate? Did you then enfold him in soft garments, give him wine while he reclined and sing to him softly until he slept? Where were you, O Aspasia, learned one?' She added: 'I am again with child by him.'

I was pondering on Hesiod, thought Aspasia, and she was mortified. Never had Al Taliph asked these things of her as he asked his wives and concubines. She was formally summoned to his bed when he desired her, and then fondled and loved, but in no other way was she asked to serve him out of her woman's heart. After the love-making he would discuss poetry and politics and art and science with her, and philosophy, while her head faced his on the pillow, and then he would sleep. She forgot that his arm would still embrace her as a treasure. Now she only thought of his disporting with his wives and his slaves, and laughing, and a terrible sorrow overcame her which she had come to fear was the sorrow of love.

Then her pride came to her rescue. She was an Ionian woman, and she had been educated and trained and was a human being, not a mere thing such as these women. It was a poor consolation, but she clung to it. Let him disport himself with these animals she had tried to raise to the status of humanity. She had his mind and respect – she hoped – and could entertain him with epigrams and stories and philosophies, and was that not the better part? She paused, doubtful.

She then noticed two little naked girls disporting themselves among the other children, and they were strangers to her. They were not more than seven years old, pretty olive-coloured little girls far from puberty, and as hairless except for their flowing black hair as young pigs. Slaves kept catching them to massage their small bodies with scented oils and to comb and dress their long hair and weave pearls among it and brush it. Their infant bodies were smooth and vulnerable, their private parts closed and tender. Their only ornaments were ear-rings of pearl and enamel. The childish eyes were smeared with kohl, their plump cheeks coloured with unguents, their voices keen and babyish. They ran from ministrations and shrilled with the other children, until caught again. One was eating pomegranates with gusto, her chin running with scarlet. The other hugged a doll to her breastless chest, and kissed it lavishly and jingled its bells, holding it up for admiration. They were as newborn as lambs, and Aspasia was touched.

'I have never seen these little ones before,' she said. 'Who is the mother of these twin children?'

The women tittered, overcome with laughter. Then one of the wives said, 'Our lord purchased them in the slave market yesterday, as a gift to a great merchant tonight, from Damascus.'

Aspasia was appalled, and she thought of Cleo, who, at

thirteen and still not nubile, had been given to Cadmus. She said, 'As hand-maidens, until they are of a proper age?'

The women were even more hilarious, rocking on their fat buttocks. 'No,' said one, 'as concubines.'

Aspasia disbelieved. 'They will die,' she said.

The eldest wife said with superiority over this barbarian: 'They have been introduced today to phallic instruments of ivory.'

For the first time Aspasia noticed small tricklings of blood on the children's round thighs. She put her hands to her cheeks and shuddered. The slaves, seeing her gaze, wiped away the blood indifferently, then smeared unguents on the parts. The children winced and whimpered, then ran off to play.

Aspasia turned to the four wives of Taliph. 'Are not your maternal hearts in revolt against this desecration and deflowering and torture of children? Is it not abominable to you, you who are mothers of children, yourselves?'

They looked at her with fresh derision and wonder. 'Is this not for what a woman was born, to give pleasure to men?' Thus spoke the oldest wife.

Then Aspasia realized fully, and for the first time, that the eastern concept of women was accepted by females, not denied, not rebelled against, but serenely recognized as their fate, against which it was unbelievable to protest, unthinkable to revolt.

The oldest wife, who did not detest Aspasia as much as the others did, said to her almost gently, 'Why would you destroy our happiness?'

Aspasia made a wide gesture with her white arms. 'Is this happiness, to you?'

'Yes,' said the wife. 'What more could be given? Alas for you, poor foreign woman, your mind is beset by turbulent demons.'

'I will protest this monstrous torture of little ones to my lord, tonight, and remove them from this noxious harem,' said Aspasia, and left the room, her heart thudding with anger

and sickness. She was followed by the high tinkling laughter of
the women, and she felt unclean.

CHAPTER IX

Aspasia had been summoned to attend the banquet given
by Al Taliph for some illustrious guests. She was bathed and
anointed and perfumed by her slaves, her long glistening hair
brushed with fragrant lotions. Seething with rebellion and
horror at what she had learned today in the harem she refused
to wear eastern garments, and chose a white Greek tunic
bordered with silver, and a full toga of the finest Egyptian linen
the colour of a faint hyacinth petal. She dressed her hair
herself, binding it up in Greek fashion with ribbons of silver,
and the tunic and toga revealed her white neck which was
embraced by pearls. She put no armlets on her arms nor rings
upon her fingers. She would not use more colour upon her rosy
lips nor cheeks. When she stood up before her polished mirror
she was as untouched as Athene Parthenos, the virgin goddess
of wisdom, and the slaves were intimidated. Her aspect was
austere and remote. Her brown eyes had dangerous glints in
them. She intended to rebuke Al Taliph in every gesture
and intonation of her voice. She would confront him with
western principles and her abhorrences, and, in his bed, she
would rebuke him coldly. Though she was supposed to conceal her hair under a light veil she now rejected it. She was a
woman of learning and consequence and she was again determined so to impress Al Taliph. She was his companion and not
a compliant slave, concubine or wife. She could leave him
at her will. She considered the wealth he had given her. With
sickness in her heart, she reflected on leaving him, and almost
wept.

She decided to recline upon a divan in her chamber to rest

and compose her mind before appearing in the dining hall. For once the sound of wind and tree and the scent of the gardens and the cries of the birds did not calm her. They were a hot discord, mocking. She understood fully now that eastern women had no more regard for human life than did their lords, or perhaps even less. The fate of those little girls was no more deplored than the fate of a fly or a locust or a rat.

She began to doze in the languid heat of the day despite herself. She suddenly started awake at a touch on her shoulder. A female slave said to her, 'Lady, the lord Al Taliph wishes to see you at once in his chamber.'

This was most unusual. He never desired to see her this early. She rose, arranged her garments and went to the satrap's chamber. A eunuch stood at the entrance to the chamber and he stared at her and then with insolent slowness he opened the door. She entered, bowing as customary. Al Taliph, whose chamber was royal and filled with treasures and perfumes, sat at a distance on a divan. He was splendidly clad in scarlet trousers and a silk shirt as white as snow and a vest of blue woven with gems. His turbaned head was majestic, his swarthy face unreadable. His whole posture was contained yet alert, as a panther, lying in shade, is alert. He did not respond to Aspasia's greeting. He merely observed her without expression. Then for the first time she saw Kurda near him, Kurda with a whip in his hand, Kurda gloating and grinning, his fat jowls gleaming.

'Lord,' said Aspasia, her first start at the presence of Kurda subsiding.

'Stand before me,' said Al Taliph in a voice she had never heard from him before. It was not angry or emotional nor raised. It was merely indifferent, as one who speaks to a slave. Aspasia halted. Was this cold and remote man the man who had held her in his arms and kissed her hands and called her his lily of the Shalimar, his rose of India, his moonlit blossom? For the first time she felt a thrill of apprehension and dismay. She glanced at Kurda again, and saw his hateful triumph. She raised her head proudly, and waited. Al Taliph continued to regard her as if she were a slave beyond his notice who had finally intruded her presence impertinently upon him.

'I have indulged you,' he said. 'I have heard for some time that you have been vexing the women of my household with wild exhortations and fulminations against authority and the customs of our country. I did not protest. I even thought you would amuse them or awaken them to some liveliness that might entertain me. But they have finally appealed to me to bar you from their presence as a disturbing and unpleasant trespass. You have, they say, attempted to incite them against my pleasure and my comfort. They can no longer endure your blatant western barbarities and from them I have now delivered my women. Never again must you visit them unless you can control your tongue and be one with them.'

Aspasia forgot her fear and her face coloured deeply. 'I am no barbarian, lord. I am a free woman, not a slave, not an unlettered concubine, not a fat and mindless wife whose sole joy is in eating and languishing on cushions and serving you at her will.'

He inclined his head. 'What are you?' he asked.

She felt her heart jump. 'I am your companion, at your pleasure, to converse with you, at your will. I am freeborn, and have been educated, and my mind has been admired.'

He lifted the lid of a box of sweetmeats, drew out a honeyed date and ate it slowly, watching her. Then he said, 'What are these things to me, you bought woman of Miletus? I paid an enormous price to your mistress, Thargelia, for the alleged delights of your company. You no longer please me.'

She was suddenly sick and dazed and something enormously sentient in her heart quailed. She felt tears in her eyes. But she lifted her head proudly. 'Then,' she said, 'I will depart and no longer fatigue you with my presence nor bore you with my disputations. If you paid an enormous price for me I will return it.'

83

'From the gifts I gave you,' he said, in that same low and terrible voice.

She was silent. She felt as if she were dying both of shame and something else she could not comprehend.

'You are not even young any longer,' he continued. 'You are eighteen years old. I dismissed my Narcissa, and she was younger than you, seventeen, but she had become too old for me. Why, then, do I suffer you, the disturber of my peace, the turmoil of my women, the disorder of my household?'

Kurda gave a muffled chuckle of joy and victory, and Aspasia heard but did not look at him. The whole intensity of her eyes was fixed on Al Taliph, as she stood before him like a white goddess, the colour gone from her lips and cheeks.

'If I did these things which displease you, lord,' she said, 'it was because I could no longer bear to see my sex degraded, my womanhood shamed, my very existence made less than the existence of a dog.'

He raised his sharp black eyebrows. 'I have done so to you?'

'No,' she said. 'But you have done this to the women of your harem, and in their ignominy I have seen my own, however kind you have been to me.'

He said, very slowly, as if with distaste, 'You have learned that women are not considered truly human in civilized countries. Yet, you have set your face against this absolute truth. Are you not presumptuous, because I indulged you? You have not been treated in this house like a woman of the harem. I have proffered you honours which are unbelievable in my country; I have accepted you almost as an equal. For that you have not been grateful. You have tried to incite rebellion in my house, among creatures less valuable than a good horse.'

'Some are mothers of your children!' cried Aspasia, goaded at the thought. 'Or are your children less than the dust also, because they proceeded from "a good horse" or a dog?'

'Your father considered you less worthy to live than a donkey,' said Al Taliph. 'Your mother rescued you and gave you to Thargelia; otherwise you would have perished as an infant. Are your men of more compassion and gentleness than I?'

At this, Aspasia was silent for a moment. Finally she said, 'If there was one thing for which I was born it is to elevate the stature of my sisters, and to deliver them from dishonour, to make them recognize that they are human also, with human prerogatives. Twice that was so, under the laws of Solon, and in the Homeric period. It is said that the women of Israel are honoured by their men and respected by their sons.'

'You are indeed learned – in the wrong things,' said Al Taliph and now he smiled and the smile was more threatening than his voice. 'You are my companion, you say – my bought companion. Do you not know that in the eyes of our laws you are only an animal? Yet, if you wish, I will have pity and release you, and you may go where you will. But without the gifts I have given you.'

Aspasia was suddenly reminded of what Thargelia had threatened her with nearly four years ago, and she was filled with such despair that she instantly thought of suicide. There was no other deliverance. It was evident to her now that Al Taliph had wearied of her, though only two nights ago he had actually kissed one of the white arches of her feet, and, in passion, had declared that she was the moon of his delight and dearer to his heart than all his possessions and his position. But what a man swore in lust, Thargelia had taught her maidens, was not to be taken seriously, but only exploited at that moment before desire had become cool, or before it was satisfied.

Part of her mind contemplated her desperate condition but her heart was crushed with misery and longing and her white lips parted as if in agony. She said, 'Do with me what you will. It is no longer of significance to me.'

He studied her as if probing her soul. He idly played with the golden tassel of his girdle. At last he said, 'I have heard that you pronounced some wild words upon discovering the women I have designated as a gift for my friend from Damascus tonight.'

'They are infants, not women!' she cried.

'They are animals,' he replied. 'Would you have demurred so at a gift of twin lambs or a young colt?'

'They are human,' she said.

He shrugged. 'I have not discerned it. Aspasia, you have known for a long time that in the east human life is very cheap; it is worthless. It is not of any importance unless it is well-born, and even then, if female, it is not considered of any consequence. But an Arabian steed – ah, there is beauty and value. *There* is something admirable and to be cherished.'

Kurda thought with hot impatience, Why does he even converse with this creature, as if she possessed a mind and an intellect?

Aspasia sighed with broken-hearted exhaustion. She repeated, 'Do with me as you will.'

'That I intend,' he answered and held out his hand to Kurda. The eunuch responded swiftly and gave Al Taliph the whip he held. Al Taliph took it and idly slapped his knee with it and it made a sharp and crackling noise in the room. Aspasia could not believe what she saw. She glanced at Kurda with an appalled look and started.

'No,' said Al Taliph, 'I do not intend Kurda to flog you though for less I would command him to flog even my favourite wife. I do not intend for him to witness your punishment either. Kurda, leave us.'

The eunuch was bitterly disappointed. He wanted to see this final crushing of the foreign creature, her absolute humiliation. He hesitated. Al Taliph raised his voice and said emphatically, 'Begone, slave.' Kurda bowed, and backed away and left the room and slowly closed the door behind him. Aspasia drew a deep and sobbing breath, seeing to the last his taunting and hating face.

Al Taliph rose and loomed above her. He said. 'Remove your garments to your waist.'

86

Aspasia glanced with terror at the thin but lethal whip. Never had she been struck before except once when receiving a mild slap from the impatient Thargelia. Despite her efforts her flesh quailed with mingled dread and shame. She looked up into Al Taliph's face for some sign of mercy, but there was none. It was incredible to her that those metallic lips had lain upon her own, that that hand had caressed her breast and fondled her body and given her delight. It was this incredulity rather than pride which held her still and mute.

With an oath he seized her hair with one hand and with the other, which held the whip, he stripped and tore the tunic and toga from her shoulders and forced her to her knees. He flung her forward so that she lay prone. But instantly she raised herself to her knees and clasped her hands to her breast and lifted her head in silent repudiation.

'As you will,' he said. 'It will be your last decision in this house.'

He lifted the whip and it sang through the air and struck her across her shoulders and then her back. It was as if a hot knife had seared her. But she did not tremble; she did not utter a sound. She pressed her lips together and stared into the distance. The whip lifted and fell, whistling, and each stroke was of renewed fire and ferocity. Pain almost overwhelmed her; her tender white flesh quivered but did not shrink. Her hands protected her breasts from the curling weapon, but the sides of her palms were scorched. Then her whole back was in flames, in torment almost more than she could endure. Still the lash rose and fell with a steady hissing, and it was the only sound in the chamber. She did not cry, attempt to escape, or moan. She was like a marble image receiving blows it could not feel. Once she thought she would faint, but from that last indignity she held herself, nor did she groan for mercy.

At last he was done and he threw the whip from him with a sound like detestation. She pushed herself to her feet, her whole body in torment. She could feel a trickling of blood between her shoulder blades. Calmly, then, not looking at him, she attempted to cover her nakedness with the remnants of her torn clothing.

Then his hands were suddenly on her, and he was kissing the welts on her back and the broken flesh with a passion she had never known him to display before, even at the most ecstatic moments. He was uttering gasping words, incoherent, almost moaning. Dazed, she endured it. He brought a brazen bowl of water and a jar of unguents and dressed her wounds and soothed the swollen welts. His hands were as tender as a woman's.

'Ah, that you did this to me!' he cried.

Sick and dizzy and only half-conscious, she closed her eyes. Then she was in his arms and he was holding her against his breast and kissing her face, brow, cheek and lips and throat, and she could hear the thundering of his heart against hers. Without her own will her arms lifted and she put them about his neck and began to weep, and did not know why the pain in her breast, more awful than the pain in her flesh, subsided, leaving an anguished sweetness behind it.

CHAPTER X

Though Aspasia was overcome by her emotions as she traversed the long blue and white halls to her own chamber she was aware of a peculiar pent silent in the palace, and understood that her humiliation at the hands of Al Taliph had flown through all corridors and rooms like a bird, and that, without her hearing a sound, all were maliciously gleeful and triumphant. Her body smarted unbearably, in spite of the unguents, and she held her torn garments about her and lifted her head, conscious of unseen and gloating eyes behind fretwork and curtain. Her hair hung about her in disorder, and she threw it back from her burning shoulders.

Calmly enough she told the slaves that she had decided on other dress, and they brought forth an eastern robe of scarlet and gold. She permitted the maidens to bathe her again and anoint her bruises and welts with unguents. She had not been relieved from attending the banquet given by Al Taliph. She perfumed herself with attar of jasmine and wore an Egyptian necklace of large stones and golden fringes and wound strands of pearls through her hair. She was deathly pale, the natural vermilion of her complexion and lips absent. She applied herself to the paint-pots and clasped her waist with a gilded girdle, which blazed.

She thought, I must leave him, and the next moment she said to herself, That I cannot do, for it may be that I love him while I hate him also. She could not understand her own conflicting agitations, at once infuriated and then composed, at once full of hatred and resentment, and then melting. She wanted to weep again but her eyelids had become dry and aching. Then something emerged from her chaotic thoughts.

When she left this place she would go to Athens and establish a school like Thargelia's, but not with its lustful teachings. It would be an academe for girls of intelligence and gifts so that never would they be mere concubines with a smattering of learning to intrigue powerful men. The young ladies would be taught professions – Then Aspasia thought, warily: To what end, when women are so despised even in civilized Attica and their minds and souls deprecated? She had another thought, and it was exhilarating. An educated and learned woman, in the company of similar sisters, could be a force again in Greece, could come to terms – and not through lust – with the men with whom they associated. The power of their minds would be greater than the power of their beauty, for beauty was evanescent but the spirit grew in stature if nourished. It was said that in Egypt royal women had enormous influence on their Pharaoh husbands and in matters of state, and that well-born girls were almost as expertly educated as their brothers. It was not even denied women to be rulers of Egypt. In Greece there were priestesses, and in Egypt also, and in the latter country the goddess Isis was adored even more than Horus and Osiris, and she had special priests to attend her altars. Women were not considered unclean in Egypt and if they had private quarters it was at their own wish and husbands and sons could not invade except by special permission.

If this was possible in other countries it could again be possible in Greece. As for Persia – Aspasia shrugged, then winced with pain. She put the matter far back in her consciousness and, serene as an eastern goddess, and as haughty, she made her way to the banquet hall to join Al Taliph, who had just summoned her. The halls and corridors were now lighted by lamps and torches thrust into walls and the yellow and crimson shadows flickered over white and blue floors and on draperies of many colours. The gardens were now dark but the nightingales had begun to sing. Pots of incense smouldered in all the corners of the halls and the warm air was heavy with it, overcoming even the delicate scent of flowers in the huge Chinese vases.

A eunuch held aside the curtains to the dining hall for her and she saw his smirk, only half-hidden. She entered the hall, which was large, its marble floor almost completely covered by Persian carpets of endless colours and patterns. The walls were alive with mosaics, and elaborate patterns of flowers and trees and hideous monsters, all lavishly painted. Al Taliph sat in his alcove on a divan heaped with cushions, so that he half-reclined in the small enclosure. The other guests sat cross-legged on vast cushions of silk on the floor, with very low individual brass tables before them laden with gilt wine vessels and Chinese plates and spoons and knives, in the eastern manner. At a distance there were musicians, all men, softly playing on flute and zither and harp. Large brazen lamps hung from the domed and frescoed ceiling, burning perfumed oils and throwing shifting light over the guests. Slaves were hurrying on muted feet with platters and jugs of wine.

Al Taliph was gorgeously arrayed in cloth of gold with a sash of red silk, embroidered heavily, and with gold tassels. He wore a headcloth of cloth of gold also, held by knots of jewelled cord. Never had he appeared so darkly handsome to Aspasia, nor so desirable, for all the fresh hatred she felt for him and the sick longing in her heart. He was conversing with his guests and did not halt at her entrance, but languidly summoned her to his divan in the recess with a wave of his hand. She made her way in silence to the divan and was permitted, as usual, to sit at his feet. For an instant she was dimly conscious of hearing a man gasp, then appear to choke. But as Al Taliph's guests were invariably astonished at her beauty it was of no immediate significance to her.

There were several men present, all resplendent in their robes and turbans, eating and drinking with flattering voracity, and listening to their host. Aspasia hardly saw them. She was not permitted to speak unless addressed by Al Taliph, or his guests. She sat silently at his feet, her hands clasped in her lap. Occasionally, as if caressing a favoured dog, Al Taliph would idly stroke her bare arm or shoulder or throat, or lift a lock of her hair, then would let the lock fall carelessly. For the first time her cheeks became hot and flushed at this treatment, but she did not shrink. It would only surprise and anger him, and she had come to fear his anger.

Al Taliph was not only governor of his province he was also a very rich and astute merchant. He owned many bazaars in the city and also in other cities, fleets of vessels, caravans, a bank and countless olive groves, fields, orchards and meadows and multitudes of sheep and cattle and goats. He was invested in prosperous manufactories and was the possessor of jewellery and curio shops in profusion, including priceless objects of art. It was alleged he was a stern usurer in addition to all else, but never had he been accused of looting his province as did other governors, and his judgements though severe, were invariably honourable. Not only was he received with respect at the court of Artaxerxes, the emperor, but was famous in Samarkand, Persepolis, Naksh-i-Rustam, Kerman and Kashan, and in Damascus. All these things did Aspasia know, and she felt his power and both resented and adored it.

Surely, she thought to herself as she sat at his feet and listened to the laughter and conversation – in multiple tongues – of the men, the glory and the lightning of the human soul should not be suppressed in women.

She glanced at the guests, whom she had never seen before, but from their appearance she guessed that two were Babylonians, one was a Mede, two were Egyptians, three were Syrians, four were dark-skinned Arabians, two were Indians, one was a Greek, and the last, a young man with lascivious eyes and auburn curls – Her heart lifted in horror and panic and a dazed terror. She was gazing at Thalias, and in return he was gazing at her with the same appalled emotions, which she did not at first discern.

Al Taliph never introduced Aspasia to his guests, nor them to her. Her position was recognized at once: She was not a slave, she was something more than a favourite concubine, she was not a wife, for she was permitted to leave the women's quarters and allowed to speak when addressed. As the guests were invariably rich men of some learning and intelligence and travel, many remembered the hetairai of which they had heard or had seen for themselves, and not an inconsiderable number respected a hetaira for both her beauty and her intellect. They were women apart from both harems and prosaic marriages, and frequently they had power. So if some were offended by the presence of a woman at Al Taliph's dinners, the others were pleased to look upon Aspasia and even to listen to her conversation, and Al Taliph was often envied for possessing such a treasure.

He was an intuitive man, as well as subtle, and though he treated Aspasia when among his guests with none of the tender consideration and attentiveness he displayed to her in private, his awareness of her presence, the imminence of her body, her very breathing, was singularly acute. He knew when she suffered ennui, when she was distressed, weary or uninterested during these dinners in his dining hall. Her dignity and calm in spite of these things were admirable to him, and he thrilled with pride in her. Therefore, he now knew that she was deeply disturbed, that her flesh had become rigid, that something had assaulted her emotions, and that, mysteriously, she was frightened.

He continued to speak with one of the Egyptians, but he sharply glanced at her through the corner of his eye, and he wondered. She had not as yet been addressed; he had not spoken to her, himself. Was she in pain? It was true that her pallor made the vermilion cosmetics on her cheeks and lips too vivid, but there were no contractures of brow or chin which would indicate physical suffering. He had been conversing in the Egyptian language with one of his guests, a tongue with which she was not familiar, so she could have taken no offence though the conversation was delicately lewd. (Above all things Aspasia was never lewd.) She had not been suddenly seized by illness, for she was remarkably healthy. He saw her staring as at a basilisk at one of the guests, and then he saw her look away. A faint shudder ran through her and Al Taliph perceived this.

At whom had she been gazing? His eye studied all his guests, one by one, while he continued to talk and smile and eat the small portions of spiced and peppered lamb and artichokes on his plate. He even sipped a little wine. Had she recognized one of these men, his fellow merchants? That was impossible, for none were displaying any of the alarm she was so manifestly feeling, and all were attentive to their tables or exchanging little comments with a neighbour. Aspasia had seen but two or three of these guests before; the others were strangers. Yet, one had terrified her. How was that possible? It was true that two or three were old and gross at the table, but Aspasia was accustomed to this because of similar guests in the past.

His curiosity became keener. She was sitting now with decorously downcast eyes, her hands folded on her knee. He knew she was exercising all the discipline she had been taught, all the control. Then, to his surprise, she was smiling a little, her red lips curving.

For Aspasia was thinking: Thalias dare not betray me, for he is a runaway slave, for all his fine blue Grecian tunic and his wonderfully draped toga and his jewellery and fragrance. He is more frightened than I was, a few moments ago, for should I speak he would be seized and returned to Miletus for punishment, and he knows that surely. Now that her fear had subsided she was inclined to compassion for him, and she conjectured how he had come to this magnificence and position as an honoured guest of Al Taliph. She had observed how handsome he was, how engaging in manner, how refined in gesture, and how obviously rich. She had not as yet heard his voice, did not know the name under which he lurked. She remembered that he had always been shrewd and intelligent and swift in answer to another's moods, and then, remembering his concern for her before he had fled Thargelia's house, she felt some suddenly amused affection for him. She desired, above all things, to convey to him that he was in no danger from her.

She is no longer afraid, thought Al Taliph. Aspasia drank from her silver goblet and then lifted a pungent morsel in her spoon and ate it. Her colour had returned. Her hand was not trembling. Feeling that Al Taliph was studying her too closely she turned her head and smiled faintly at him, and her brown eyes were bland. For some involved and feminine reason she felt a vague triumph over him as if saying in herself, that man before you took from me the virginity you believed you deprived me of, my lord. I did not come to your bed immaculate. I lay with him within a grove of myrtles one hot summer night, when the leaves dripped moonlight on the dark earth, and he introduced me to joy. His kisses were the first I had ever known; his arms embraced me as

94

strongly as ever yours did, and for an hour I loved him.

Her thoughts delighted her. She had never been so beautiful, and now her mouth dimpled with mischief.

Seeing this, Al Taliph frowned. He had never deceived himself that he knew all there was to know about Aspasia. Aspasia was full of mysteries to him, and that was why he found her forever entrancing. She withheld something from him, and he was always in chase and never did he seize upon her inmost thoughts.

Seeing her secret smile as she tranquilly ate and drank, he remembered that the hetairai had been rigorously taught all arts, and especially the arts of alluring deceptions. Was she trying to deceive him that his punishment of her was of no consequence to her, and that she felt herself the victor? He frowned again.

Thalias was scrutinizing her no less intently. Finally, as he was no fool, he began to understand that Aspasia would never betray him, as he would never, he said to himself with virtue, betray her. They had memories of one joyful night. Aspasia glanced up serenely and their eyes met and she smiled briefly then averted her gaze. Al Taliph saw that smile, but Aspasia frequently smiled in this manner at his guests and he saw no significance in it. She was trained to be silently amiable and charming.

Thalias, immeasurably relieved, felt all his not inconsiderable courage returning to him. He addressed his host with great courtesy and respect. 'It is said, lord, that we have, throughout the world, entered upon a period of peace and enlightenment. Is your noble Emperor in agreement with this?'

'There will be peace,' said Al Taliph, 'only when all the world, my dear Damos, becomes one vast market place.' He smiled cynically. 'I never discuss wars, which are tedious. Wars interrupt the natural discourse between nations, for they diminish and constrict the markets of the world, and impoverish them. War has no victors but only victims, whether conqueror or conquered. But the market place is the only peaceful ground where all men can meet, argue, cheat, lie, purchase the pleasurable, exhibit simple honest greed without shame, arrange caravans and commerce, engage in sincere and vivacious conversation – except with customers – and disputations with rival merchants, plan expeditions, display novelties and beauteous objects from far countries, thus increasing understanding and admiration for that which is strange and felicitous, and so enhancing knowledge of one's fellow men. Even the hot uglinesses of the market place are a warmth to the spirit.'

He paused to eat of a melon, a handful of cherries and some plums. A sudden cool gust of air came through the arches of the hall, for the year was drawing to a close and only the days now held scalding heat. Aspasia thought, So, our Thalias is now Damos, and where is his home, and why is he here in this house? Her sympathy for him and her affection increased, even as she listened to the conversation, which was now in Greek.

Al Taliph continued: 'Commerce is the one activity in which customs and cultures from all over the world are regarded with amity, and therefore the market place is our only hope for peace. Merchants have the greatest respect for each other, for they deal in tangibles and realities. You, my dear Damos, and all our friends here tonight are merchants, and do we not converse in a common tongue? We compete, but we do not kill each other. That is left for ambitious governments and professional soldiers and such lesser beings. Tell me, Damos, have you not discovered that the roads of Persia, and all the caravan routes from your Damascus through Persia, are safe from robbers? You will see that even governments have the greatest regard for us merchants.'

So, thought Aspasia, with kind inner mirth, our Thalias is a merchant from Damascus. Al Taliph was absently stroking her neck, and the other merchants, having drunk from their goblets, watched with interest and concealed envy.

Now Al Taliph looked at Aspasia, and his large and brilliant eyes smiled upon her. He said in his remarkably rich voice, 'Tell me, my love, what you think of this conversation?'

Thalias was the only man present who did not raise eyebrows in surprise at this question asked of a woman, however beautiful. Aspasia smiled at Al Taliph in return, with an acid sweetness that was very significant to him. 'I am thinking of what a Greek philosopher has written of such as you, my lord, who pretend to be a mere simple merchant. "We must look about under every stone, lest an orator bite us." '

Some gasped at this impudence, but Al Taliph pretended to wince, and laughed. He lifted her hand and pressed his lips to it. 'Ah,' he said, 'to be praised by such lips for my eloquence is more intoxicating than wine.' He raised his own goblet and held it to her mouth, and she drank and then inclined her head.

He added, tweaking her ear, 'Let me, in turn, quote from Euripides: "A woman should be good for everything at home, but abroad good for nothing." '

The guests laughed with appreciation, and Aspasia continued her acerbic if charming smile while she flushed.

'Permit me, my lord,' she said, 'to reply to you from what Herodotus has remarked of your nation: "They are accustomed to deliberate on matters of the highest importance only when drunk. Whatever else they discuss when sober is always a second time examined after they have been drinking." My lord, are you drunk or sober?'

All the guests sat as motionless as statues, holding their breath at this unpardonable insult to their host. But Al Taliph only laughed again, and laid his hand on Aspasia's shoulder. He addressed his guests: 'You will observe that my pretty thing can quote from the philosophers – as a parrot repeats words without understanding them. Nevertheless, you have discovered that her remarks are astonishingly pertinent and her banter swift. So here is the puzzle: Have I been a good teacher?' He put his hands over his face in mock horror. 'Or, can she truly think?' He shook his head and shuddered. 'From such, the gods deliver us!' The guests burst into laughter, Aspasia stared fully at him, a deliberate affront, and she was filled with such anger that she began to rise without permission to leave the hall. She was as white as bleached linen and her eyes were like the flashing of knife blades. The guests saw this. (Only Thalias thought, My poor Aspasia.)

As aware of her as always, without actually looking at her, Al Taliph darted his hand from his face and pressed it strongly on her thigh with such force and command that she sank down again on the divan. Her mortification was complete. She was certain now that she hated him. The slaves poured more wine, and pastries were brought and peaches the colour of dawn. Al Taliph looked at Thalias, but Aspasia, as acute as himself, understood he was addressing her, for she recognized that certain tone of voice. She waited, her heart tumultuous, for calamity.

'Damos of Damascus, and Greece itself, I have a gift for you, for you and I have done profitable affairs together though never were you in this house before.' He clapped his hands and a eunuch came running from an archway. Al Taliph said, 'Bring to me the little maidens I purchased but two days ago.'

Aspasia sickened. She thought of the small girls she had seen in the harem but this day. She closed her eyes briefly. Al Taliph said, 'They are rare treasures, my dear Damos, and I chose them myself, thinking of you. For do not we all prefer the young and untouched?'

Thalias murmured in assent. 'I promise you,' said his host, 'that they are mindless and can only babble pleasingly, and is that not to be desired, in a female, above all things?'

Thalias smiled uneasily, not glancing at Aspasia, who was now gazing at him fiercely. The guests repeated as one man, with smiles at each other, 'Above all things!'

The little girl children were brought in together, and they held each other's hands tightly for protection, and it was obvious that they were frightened and had just been aroused from sleep. White linen tunics clung to their diminutive bodies, and their tiny feet were bare. But their fine sleep-dampened hair had been combed hastily and was tied with white silken cords so that their faces could be seen with all their appealing infanthood, their innocent vulnerability and bewilderment. They blinked in the light of the lamps. The guests murmured approvingly and a number with desire.

Their lips were the lips of babyhood, and without artifice, and their small olive-tinted arms and legs and complexions shone with perfumed oil and their defenceless throats were clasped with pearls as lustrous as themselves. Aspasia's eyes filled with tears and her mouth shook.

Al Taliph drew them to him as gently as a father, and then he lifted their tunics so that their hairless children's bodies and private parts could be seen clearly. He admired them elaborately. 'They are twins,' he said, 'and as healthy as new-born lambs, without blemish or stain or the touch, so far, of a man's hands. Will they not grace your bed, Damos? It will be ten years – before they are too old for your taste. In the meantime, they are delightful as little boys, and do not you Greeks prefer such?'

Thalias was more uneasy than before. His cheeks coloured. Now he felt the force of Aspasia's stare and he looked quickly at her.

She did the unpardonable: She spoke without first being addressed. She said, 'They are slaves, and too young and help-less to run away. Who would succour them? Who would hide and comfort them – or give them gold?'

Thalias paled. He heard and understood the explicit threat in her raised clear voice, and he knew that she was prepared to destroy herself, and him, for the sake of these children. Moreover, he had no lust for such little ones and he was not depraved. He hesitated in confusion. He dared not refuse a gift from his host, and he wet his lips. He could feel Aspasia's wild and terrible challenge though she did not speak again. As for Al Taliph he ignored her as if she had not spoken at all. The guests were incredulous at his sufferance of this forward woman.

Thalias said, 'I am deeply touched, lord, for your kindness and condescension.' He paused. The guests nodded and moistened their own mouths.

Thalias continued: 'My wife has given me one son, and longs for a female child or two. I will give these children to her, for she can bear no more, and she brought me an excellent dowry and has been most dutiful in all her ways.'

Al Taliph's smile became fixed, and the guests exchanged glances of amazement. But Thalias' smile was brave.

'My wife,' he went on, 'is a lady of much virtue and the only offspring of her parents, and she was nurtured and tended and educated. One can understand this, for her people were brought out from Babylon by a leader of the name of Abraham and they now live in the land of Israel. They have a certain respect for women. Permit me, in my wife's name, to thank you, lord, and if it will not offend you I shall request her to send you a grateful message.'

Al Taliph spoke with gravity, inclining his head. 'They are yours, my dear friend, to do with as you will.' He looked suddenly at Aspasia, saw the tears in her eyes and her trembling smile and he touched her knee with a caressing hand, and left that hand there. She sighed. She bent her head so that she would not weep openly. She pressed her knee, without volition, against Al Taliph's fingers, in an involuntary caress of her own. I have been forgiven, he thought, and laughed inwardly at himself. Yet, he was pleased.

He said, 'The message from your lady will be received by me with pleasure. Let them be daughters to her, these little ones.'

Later he summoned Aspasia to his bed and kissed the wounds he had inflicted on her, and she turned impulsively to him and laid her head on his breast and did not know why, in her turmoil of thoughts, she felt happiness and desire and a dangerous emotion she refused to examine.

He said, 'Had you, today, asked me for those children as handmaidens for yourself, my empress, I should have given them to you at once. No, do not speak,' and he laid his lips on hers and drew her down beside him.

CHAPTER XI

Al Taliph was about to go to Damascus with one of his caravans, and he had invited Thalias to accompany him and permit Thalias' overseer to guide his own caravan to the city. Thalias had heard of the splendour and foods and wines and girls who accompanied Al Taliph on these expeditions and eagerly accepted, thinking of huge Persian tents and luxuries, and of the dancing and singing women. He also thought of Aspasia and wondered if she accompanied her lord.

The satrap was still away this afternoon, just before sunset, and Thalias, who was always bored when not engaged in some activity, wandered out into the garden, chewing a handful of ripe dates. He found the palace oppressive with all its halls and fountains and its eastern air. He did not like Damascus, either, but he lived there on his business and with his wife – he had only one – and often longed for Miletus, or for Greece which he could visit at will, and in particular, Athens. As yet he had not dared to go to Miletus, where he had been born, for he might be recognized as a runaway slave and seized. In Greece, however, he found refreshment from the hot turgidity of the east, and it was good to speak his own tongue among fellow merchants, who admired and respected him, and to enjoy, as he said, honest food.

He did not look at Kurda who appeared not to see him, for the eunuch was staring fixedly at someone in the garden, and

Thalias looked with interest in that direction. There, in the shade of a group of date palms sat Aspasia on a marble bench whose arms were carved in the shape of Persian tigers. She was a young and lonely girl, engaged with her thoughts. Thalias' heart tingled with pleasure, for often he remembered Aspasia even in the arms of his wife, and had loved her. She was gazing at a fishpond but did not seem to see it. He went quickly across the path towards her, the gravel grating under his elegant shoes.

She lifted her head and looked at him absently, then her face changed. Kurda stiffened at the doors. Surely even the barbarian understood that no male guest approached a woman this openly, and in the absence of his host or the absence of slaves and attendants! But Thalias, acquainted though he was with the east, forgot everything in his desire to speak alone to Aspasia. She watched him approach, then glanced with alarm at Kurda, who had left the doors and was now standing on the low steps leading to the gardens, his fat face avid. She did not stir, but when Thalias, smiling like the sun, was almost upon her she said in a very low voice, 'This is most indiscreet, Thalias. Yonder eunuch is master of the other eunuchs, and he wishes to destroy me. He watches me constantly for something dangerous to report to Al Taliph.'

Thalias halted, his smile disappearing. 'Do not look at him,' whispered Aspasia. 'No, do not sit beside me.' She rose, then indicated that he should seat himself, and he did, and she stood before him. 'Let us pretend that we are strangers, and that you wish to amuse yourself for a moment with my company, and that you disdain me.'

'Aspasia,' he said, with sadness.

She was moved at his tone. She tried to smile. 'I am not unhappy,' she said. 'There are hours and even days when I am very happy and content.'

She assumed a humble attitude, and Thalias shook his head slightly. He said, 'Alas, I am only a slave after all, and I have never forgotten you nor what you are in truth.'

'What am I?' she said, with sudden bitterness. 'I am the hired concubine of my lord, little more than a whore. Yet, I am without discontent.' She half-turned from him and stared at one of the bronze statues and he followed her eyes and said, 'They are monstrous, are they not, and do they not resemble the east?'

'Tell me of Greece, and Athens, which I have never seen,' she said.

'Ah, Athens!' he exclaimed, and she put her finger warningly to her lips. He dropped his voice. 'It is foaming like the sea with thoughts and movements and great men! Have you heard of Pericles, the famed son of Xanthippus? The father many years ago was a power in Athens and its politics; he defeated the remnants of Xerxes' fleet at Mycale. Xanthippus was a heroic man, and his wife was Agariste, the niece of Cleisthenes, she was the mother of Pericles. Her family was connected with the former Tyrants of Sicyon and she was also of the family of the Alcmaeonidae. Surely, you have heard of the illustrious Pericles?'

'Pericles?' repeated Aspasia. She thought. 'Ah, I believe that my lord has mentioned him with humour, for the Persians still believe the Greeks to be barbarians in spite of their victories over Xerxes. Is he not a politician?'

'He is more.' Then Thalias added, 'But Al Taliph quotes the Grecian philosophers with ease, so he can hardly believe Greece to be barbaric.'

Aspasia said, 'He believes that only Persia is entirely civilized, though he admits that Greek philosophers are now commanding attention throughout the world. He speaks to me little of modern history or the movements of nations. They bore him. He prefers things only of the mind,' and her smile was bitter again as she remembered Al Taliph's harem. 'His library is constantly replenished with the works of many philosophers, and he is convinced that the Persian ones are more subtle and mature, and certainly more profound. I am permitted to sit in his library and read what I will.'

'You are as confined here as when you were a maiden in the house of Thargelia,' said Thalias, with pity.

'In a greater measure,' said Aspasia. 'I go only to the market place. I have no companions, no friends. Ah, do not look so compassionate, my Thalias. I have told you I am often happy.'

'Yes, he is a man of mind,' said Thalias, who was fascinated by Al Taliph. 'But he is also a merchant, and very rich and discerning. Why does he not speak to you of what he sees and hears in the cities his caravans visit?'

'I am only a woman,' said Aspasia, but she smiled. 'But still, he converses with me on all things which do not concern the immediate present. We have very erudite conversations, when we are alone,' and her smile was wry. 'Tell me of this famous Pericles.'

Pride was in Thalias' voice as he said, 'He is a statesman, and more, and is married to the daughter of a noble house and has two sons, and is very rich. He was educated by Zeno of Elea, who taught him the power of dialectic, and by that most famed astronomer, Anaxagoras. So his eloquence can turn marble into flesh. He can even move that damnable Ecclesia. He helped to prosecute Cimon on a charge of bribery, after Cimon's Thasian campaign. He also attacked the Areopagus two years ago, and though his colleague, Ephialtes, has been given the credit of renouncing the Spartan alliance and the League with Thessaly and Argos, these were indeed the labour of Pericles, who deferred to his elder and allowed him to be celebrated for these acts. Pericles is a man of honour and discretion and tolerance.'

'Alas,' said Aspasia, 'all these are but names to me. I have become an ignorant woman.'

'Alas,' Thalias echoed her. 'I will continue. When Ephialtes was assassinated Pericles inherited the highest position in the State. He has not abandoned the dream of Ephialtes of making the citizens of Athens self-governing, and he is constantly challenging the Ecclesia, for he is not only bold but he is brave.' Thalias looked at Aspasia reflectively.

'Pericles has a hetaira as a companion. Would that you were she, most beauteous Aspasia.'

She laughed a little.

Thalias continued. 'Pericles has a noble mind and is irked by the rule of the Ecclesia and its religious intolerance. It is said that he has confided to friends that Athens is in need of a rejuvenation of mind and soul. Many agree with him, but at the present it is not adding to his popularity. But he is like Zeus, not afraid to hurl thunderbolts, for he is Olympian of character and is famous for his composed bearing and his godlike dignity. He is also very handsome and proud.' Thalias hesitated. 'It is said his head is deformed and that is why he wears a towering helmet on almost every occasion, but that could be a slander.'

Aspasia was silent and melancholy resumed its shadow on her face. Seeing this, the naturally warm-hearted Thalias said with impulsiveness, 'Ah, that I could help you as you helped me, Aspasia!'

She made herself smile again. 'I was not entirely generous, my dear Thalias. But you have not told me how you fared when you fled Miletus.'

'I took the first vessel, and after long journeys I arrived in Damascus. I became the friend of an elderly merchant, who had no sons. He was from the land of Israel and I married his daughter.' He paused, and smiled widely. 'I adopted their religion and I –' He paused again and Aspasia laughed aloud, and he laughed also. 'I was duly circumcised and though I am still regarded with some suspicion by my father-in-law, who is very devout, he has no cause to complain. I also had considerable of the gold you gave me and I used it wisely and invested it with Ephraim. I am not unknown in Damascus,' and he dropped his merry eyes in a parody of humility, and Aspasia again laughed.

'I am happy that you are so successful,' she said.

He stood up and would have taken her hand but she shook her head with another warning. 'It is best to leave me now,

Thalias-Damos, and may the gods be with you.' She glanced at Kurda, who was still standing on the steps, his hands on his hips and his legs spread apart in a virile attitude. He was staring with even more avidity at the girl and the young man at a distance and was still trying to hear what they had been saying. But their voices had remained low.

Thalias said, 'May the gods – and also Jehovah – be with you, Aspasia. It may be that we shall meet again.'

Mindful of Kurda she bowed to him formally and he bowed in return and left her. He passed Kurda with a genial smile but the eunuch scowled at him savagely and did not move, so that Thalias had to step around him. Aspasia resumed her seat on the bench, and she considered all that Thalias had told her and she thought, 'I am immured here like a nymph caught in crystal, or I resemble Dryope, who was changed into a mute tree, and when I would grasp my hair to assure myself that I still live as a woman my hands are filled with leaves.'

Then she laughed a little even as she sighed. 'But the leaves are fragrant and shine like silver, and my fate could be worse.'

Kurda went to Al Taliph, bowed his head almost to his knees and said, 'Lord, the foreign woman has been indiscreet again.'

Al Taliph frowned impatiently. 'Has she been annoying my women despite my commands?'

'Ah, lord, if it were only that! It is much worse.' Kurda assumed the face and posture of a tragedian and Al Taliph suppressed a smile.

'Tell me,' he said.

Kurda hesitated. He knew that Thalias was an honoured guest in this house, so he had prepared his story in advance. He said, 'Your noble friend, lord, Damos, was walking in the garden just before sunset and the foreign woman approached him boldly in an open encounter and spoke with him. He would have left her but she forced him to sit upon a marble seat, and not desiring to give offence to one of your household, lord, he submitted and she stood before him and they conversed together. I tried to hear the conversation but they spoke very quietly.'

Al Taliph's face was inscrutable. 'The women of Miletus are not so immured as ours, and my guest is from Athens where women have greater freedom.'

He dismissed Kurda who was sickened with disappointment. As for Al Taliph, he felt some vexation at Aspasia's indiscretion. Kurda, in spite of his malignance, had found nothing excessively wrong and Al Taliph, knowing Aspasia, did not believe that she had seized upon Damos shamelessly. As for Damos, he had married an Israelite woman and doubtless he was accustomed to a more tolerant attitude with regard to women. Aspasia often refused to wear a veil in the palace or the garden, as did the other women, and he, Al Taliph, had indulged her. She was a beautiful woman and had sat at his feet two nights ago and he had conversed with her before his guests, so Damos had probably guessed that she enjoyed a unique position in the household and had shown her courtesy. Al Taliph tapped his teeth with his finger and sent for Aspasia.

She soon entered his chamber and he held out his hand to her and she came to him at once and was drawn down to his feet. He poured a goblet of wine for her and put it into her hand gently, then kissed her wrist.

'I have heard, my snowy swan, that you have been indiscreet today,' he said.

Aspasia started and he saw this. Her thoughts fastened on Kurda. Had he heard any word in the garden? Had he heard the words of affection and admiration which Thalias had uttered? She held herself from trembling and said, 'How have I offended you, lord?'

'It is not our custom, Aspasia, for women to accost male strangers and to converse with them in secret.'

She forced herself to laugh lightly. 'Oh, that Kurda! He has the mind of a cesspool. And my conversation with – your guest – his name is Damos, is it not? – was concerned only with the children you gave to him, for his wife.'

Al Taliph studied her closely. 'And what was the conversation, my adored one?'

She said at once, 'I told him that I prayed that his wife would love the little ones and accept them in her house, as a mother.'

Al Taliph shook his head in amused exasperation. 'You are very tenacious, are you not? You wished to assure yourself that the girls would not serve their original purpose?'

Aspasia knew that her best defence was boldness. She bent over him and kissed him deeply on the mouth. 'Can any woman trust a man?' she asked. 'It is true that I wished to reassure myself. Did I not deserve that at the least, for what you did to me in punishment?' She dropped her robe from her shoulders and back and let him see the healing wounds and then let the robe drop farther so that her beautiful breasts were fully displayed to him. She eyed him artlessly, as if this was an accident and his dark face flushed. He put his hand on her breast and felt the strong beating of her heart, and thought it passion and not fear.

'There are times,' he said, 'when I think you are a veritable child.' He kissed the breast he held and Aspasia closed her eyes with relief, thanking Thargelia in her mind for having taught her wiles and control. 'I forgive your forwardness,' he said, then remembered what he had been considering all the day in the city.

'I must leave for Damascus tomorrow,' he said. 'I will be gone for some time. And it came to me how I would yearn for you, my sweet treasure, and would be wild with impatience to return to your arms. Therefore, I have decided not to deny myself the joy of gazing upon you and receiving your kisses. I shall take you with me.'

Her amazed delight at this gratified him. She pressed his hand tightly to her breast and now she had no need to dissemble. 'Lord,' she said, 'if you have yearned for me in that great city, surrounded though you were by your women, how much more have I yearned for you, left here alone, alas, and dreaming of you in my bed and longing for your return!'

He heard the sincerity in her voice as well as her happiness, and it came to him that this was the first time he had been certain that she was not somewhat deceiving him with taught fervour. He was moved and was ashamed of his pleasure.

'But you will wear a veil at all times,' he said, fondling her. 'I have indulged you here in my house, but that cannot be on the journey nor in Damascus. I desire no one to gaze upon your face and contemplate slaughtering me and carrying you off.'

'Like the bull who bore Europa away?' She laughed, and shook her head. 'I have heard that the women of Damascus are great beauties.'

'No, they are extremely ugly,' he replied. 'The men are handsome and corrupt, and the women are virtuous and an offence to the eye. Their veils, then, are less to conceal their faces than to spare men from looking upon them. Were the men of Damascus to glimpse your countenance they would lose their wits.'

He drew her down beside him on the divan and she thought as she clung to him, Alas, I love him, and this I see to my sorrow. But never shall he know.

CHAPTER XII

Aspasia had never seen a caravan. It was not until she was part of Al Taliph's own caravan that she realized how she had been so closely immured in his palace and how her mind, despite his libraries and the books he bought for her, had become stifled not only with luxury but with monotony and absence of communication with others.

Her excitement, as the caravan set forth long before dawn this cool autumn morning, was so great that her heart thumped and she almost wept for joy. Veiled, wrapped in a warm crimson wool cloak, she was guided outside the walls by Al Taliph who smiled down at her glittering eyes as a father smiles. Torches had been forced into the sockets on the outside walls and they cast red shadows in the morning breeze and on the waiting caravan. Aspasia looked about her eagerly. It seemed to her that a multitude of loaded camels, mules and horses and donkeys extended from the fluttering light of the torches into the darkness and into Infinity on each side. Now she heard the hubbub of men and beasts, the screams of the camels, the neighing of the horses, the complaints of the donkeys, and saw the enormous bustle of preparation. Men in long dark robes and cloaks and with headcloths covering both head and face rushed everywhere, carrying burdens to be hoisted to the packs on the animals, and as they hurried feverishly they chattered and cursed and laughed, and their eyes were alive in the torchlight. They yelled and bellowed as loud as the beasts they tended and dragged or struck. They also stank furiously and even the scent of the gardens behind the gates and the aromatic odour of the wind could not abate the stench of sweat, unwashed hot bodies, damp wool, urine and manure. They had an animal rankness which Aspasia, the fastidious, found offensive. She leaned lightly against the arm and shoulder of Al Taliph, who was alertly watching, surrounded by guards with swords and lances.

Aspasia saw that the camels were linked together in lines of one hundred each, hair ropes attaching the rear of one to the neck of another, and all were heavily laden with merchandise. The leader, whimpering nearby and stamping his huge padded feet restlessly, was ornamented with coloured cloths, fringes and tassels and tinkling bells. An ass, without a burden, was to guide the long strings of camels. He surveyed the scene philosophically, and seeing this and his wise eyes, Aspasia laughed and pointed him out to Al Taliph. 'Ah, yes,' he said, 'he is a very clever creature and has deep thoughts of his own. He has no high opinion of camels, but they trust him.' He left Aspasia, motioned aside his guards and went to the ass. 'Hamshid,' he said, 'I am very proud of you. Again, you will protect us.' The ass acknowledged this compliment with a grave whinny and rubbed his nose against Al Taliph, who patted him tenderly and who then returned to Aspasia. She was laughing behind her veil and her brown eyes with their gilt lashes were alight with mirth.

'Lord,' she said, 'I swear you love beasts more than you love any man or woman.'

He answered her with seriousness. 'Are they not honest and do they not work industriously? I respect them. They could survive without us but we cannot survive without them, and where is our vainglorious intelligence before that truth?'

Aspasia was momentarily abashed. She thought again, with a sigh, of how dull her mind had become, how stifled, how lacking in excitement and conjecture, behind those walls. She determined not to offend Al Taliph, for his displeasure dimmed her spirit and she wished to greet the world again with joy, as one delivered from a prison; tasting, feeling, smelling, touching, seeing, hearing. Moreover, if she pleased her lord he would take her again on other journeys, perhaps even to Greece.

For the first time she saw that he was armed, a long curved sword buckled to his girdle. Like the men about him he was clad in dark wool robes and a heavy cloak, and like them he wore a woollen headcloth secured with rope cords. The rough material covered not only his head but also his face from the nose down, and only his eyes could be seen, changing from grey to brown as the torchlight shifted, and his gaze ranged over the men and the animals. Aspasia had only seen him in elegance and grace, and as an aristocratic satrap. Now he was of the desert, as were his men, and he had the wild leanness of the desert-born, the acquaintance of far places and dangers and hazards and endless sands and storms.

The guards moved aside and Thalias approached, saluting. He, too, was clad as was Al Taliph, but his blue eyes were gay and young above the cloth that covered his face and a lock of auburn hair could be seen over his forehead. He glanced briefly at Aspasia. 'My own caravan, lord,' he said, 'will leave tomorrow. It is very small compared with yours.'

'You need fear no robbers in Persia,' said Al Taliph. 'But you have known that.'

'True, lord, but we will not be always in Persia. I have been robbed before.'

'My dear Damos, you will travel under my protection,' said Al Taliph. 'The banners we carry are royal, and not the boldest robbers between Persia and Damascus will trouble us. Nevertheless, we are armed also, as you will observe, if some savage band ignores our standards or does not recognize them.'

Now that the hour of departure had been reached the noise of man and animal rose to a higher pitch. It was discordant and deafening, yet Aspasia saw that the confusion had become order. The bright amber crescent of the moon was perched on the top of the highest mountain, which was as yet undefined except as a dark cloud against a lighter cloud. But in the east there was a bluish shadow. A group of veiled women approached the guards. Al Taliph nodded towards them and said abruptly to Aspasia, 'Go. Do not be afraid.'

Two of the women carried lanterns and Aspasia joined the silent group, knowing they were five of her own attendants, who would care for her. Al Taliph had not indicated how she would travel. She glanced back at him. He was talking to one of the guards and appeared to have forgotten her, as a creature of no importance to him. She did not speak to the women. They surrounded her and the women with the lanterns led the way past seemingly endless lines of camels, mules, horses and donkeys. The burning torches spluttered and hissed and smelled of hot resin. The men ignored the little group of females, for they were of less value to them than the beasts.

They came upon a train of four long and wide platforms, each drawn by six black horses in silver harness and with plumes on their heads. Every platform supported a large tent of brown wool with closed flaps. The first, and the biggest, led the train and a nomad, carrying a pennant, rode one of the horses. 'This tent is the tent of the lord,' said one of the women, bowing her head in its direction. Even the spokes of the ironclad wheels were inlaid with silver and enamel. The second tent, somewhat smaller, had been assigned to Aspasia and two of her women; the others would sleep in the third tent until called to their duties. Among them, as Aspasia guessed, were a number of slave girls who were dancers and singers and tumblers and music-makers. The fourth also held women.

Aspasia climbed the platform to her tent, accompanied by two of the slave women. The flap was opened, and she entered and was amazed. Soft yellow glass lamps were affixed to walls and the walls themselves were completely covered with hangings of the most luxurious sort – ornamented silk of curious designs depicting colourful flowers, birds, trees and twisted patterns intertwined with gold and silver threads which glistened and sparkled in the lamplight. The floor of the platform was strewn with Persian and Indian rugs no less brilliant with colour, and thick and soft under the foot. There were small brass tables and chests, and the famous crimson and blue Damascene huge cushions to sit and lie and sleep upon, all fringed with gold tassels, and many of them had afghans of wool and silk neatly folded to protect the sleeper or sitter from any desert or mountain chill. The whole tent was pervaded with the scent of sandalwood and nard. Aspasia felt the warmth in the tent and the fragrance was languid and somnolent. She was suddenly aware that she desired sleep, for she had lain for hours in the arms of Al Taliph, quivering with passion and excitement, and had not slept at all. The women removed her veil and cloak and other garments and dressed her in a white shift of linen, and she lay upon a cushion and fell almost instantly asleep, hardly conscious of the fact that an afghan had been placed upon her and that the other women had fallen upon cushions, themselves. The movement of the vehicle was lulling, the scent overpowering. Aspasia slept like one drugged.

But she was awake at dawn, after a short doze. Her women slept and moaned softly, their mouths agape. Aspasia threw a cloak over her shift and opened the flap of the tent and stood in the doorway. Then she was awed, and her old exaltation at the spectacle of beauty returned like a wanderer who had been banished and then had come home, rejoicing, intoxicated.

The caravan was travelling over a plain littered with small and large stones and heavy dust. But the eastern sky was a vast conflagration of palpitating gold and saffron streaked with scarlet and emerald green, and it seemed to extend forever from horizon to horizon. It threw yellow and purple shadows on the ash-coloured ground. Boulders on the barren earth were ignited instant by instant and burned like gigantic cores of fire. There was no sound in that stupendous incandescence of the heavens except for the creaking of wagons and the rattle of harness. Then, at the rim of the world, the edge of the ruby sun began to mount in his panoply of awaiting banners, and the tent of the night, still high in the heavens, and the hue of hyacinths, folded and sank to the west.

Aspasia felt that she was seeing for the first time in her life. She clutched the sides of the fabric doorway and stared and her face was illuminated by the grandeur she gazed upon with distended eyes. Her hair blew about her in the morning wind. Then she heard the pound of horse's hooves and there loomed beside the tent the figure of a horseman black as an iron statue against the wild storm of the sky. The horseman, mounted on a great stallion, was Al Taliph, his face covered with his head-cloth, his eyes set ahead. He did not seem aware of the woman in the doorway.

He resembles a centaur, and is as unearthly, thought Aspasia. He rode beside the tent, silent and supple, tall and lithe. Never had he seemed so remote to Aspasia, so far removed from her, so alien, so strange, so in command of all about him. She felt a pang of fear as well as a thrill of pride. He touched his horse with his whip and the animal soared ahead, almost as if he were flying rather than running, like Pegasus, and both man and beast were gone. A peculiar feeling of loneliness and melancholy came to Aspasia and she returned to her cushions but not to sleep.

The caravan came to a halt. Aspasia rose, and her women rose with her, groaning. She opened the flap and saw that the caravan had stopped at a green oasis blowing with palm trees. Men were beginning to shout and fill pails and large buckets with spring water for the horses and camels. A fine golden dust floated in the warm air, for the sun had now completely risen, and heat touched Aspasia's cheek like a hot hand. She did not know if she were supposed to remain in her tent, or alight. Her women came to her and dressed her and covered her with veil and mantle, then, bowing, they indicated that she should follow them. She emerged from the tent and climbed down beside the women. As she did so she saw that an elderly woman, veiled and in dark clothing, was leading a girl child sternly by the hand. The child's face was uncovered though overlaid with cosmetics against the ardent light, and she was bewildered and frightened. She could have been hardly ten years old. Her robe was white and blue, her hair the colour of brown wine. She pulled back once and the woman jerked her impatiently and said something in a tongue Aspasia did not know, and it was admonishing. The child cried again, a faint whimpering sound, then bowing her head she submitted.

The two approached the tent of Al Taliph, then climbed into it. Two of Al Taliph's men, who shared the tent with him, emerged and jumped to the ground and went to the spring. Aspasia's heart jolted and she was filled with anger and despair. Her women motioned to her to go with them, but she lingered. They patiently waited. Then Aspasia heard a muffled scream of agony within Al Taliph's tent and could barely restrain herself from running to it. She was sickened. The child within the tent screamed again, like a tormented animal, then Aspasia heard the sharp crack of a man's hand against childish flesh and the screams subsided to breathless moans of torment. Al Taliph's voice could now be heard, muttering and gasping and sometimes impatient.

But I always knew, thought Aspasia. Did I not know the fate of the women in the harem, the young girls, the children? Yet, she had not heard helpless cries until now. She was taken by pity and humiliation. Only a few hours ago Al Taliph's dusky body had lain on her white flesh, and she had embraced him and his voice had been loving. He had called her his light of life, his moon, his lily, his swan, his dove. I hate him! she thought with deep rage, and I hate, above all things, what he is doing to that innocent child.

She tried to make her heart cold and still. She saw that her women had heard the sounds within the lord's tent and thought nothing of it. She followed them to the area set aside for the women's rest in the oasis. She was brought ice-cold water. A linen cloth was laid on the cool green grass before her, and upon it was placed a ewer of wine, sliced lamb, fruit, bread and cheese and oily artichokes and a pitcher of foaming goat's milk. All the women, a large company, sat around her in a circle, gossiping to each other. They had removed their veils. A wall of canvas had been erected about them to protect them from the men's gaze. Aspasia, as the favourite of the lord, was isolated but watched and tended. She could not eat. She drank only water. I am ridiculous, she told herself. I knew from the very beginning who and what he was. I knew he was pitiless and ruthless as well as kind and intellectual and full of power. Yet I deluded myself that he was superior to other men in appetites and passions. Had I not been warned by Thargelia? Alas, in this man's arms I was as melting wax and I believed his vows and rejoiced in his embraces! He did not deceive me. I deceived myself, because I desired the deception. However, from this moment on I shall be deceived no longer.

A sense of strength came to her, and even her despair

116

lessened. She began to think. Could she steal away as Thalias had stolen away from Thargelia's house? Could she take with her the gold and the gems Al Taliph had given her, and go to Greece? Alas, she was a woman, and a woman travelling alone was in awful danger. But, I am strong and I was taught self-defence by the athletes in Thargelia's house, and I would not hesitate to kill if necessary. Her thoughts became some-what confused as she realized the predicament of women in the modern world. Then she thought of Thalias. He had vowed to help her if she needed his help. He owed her much and was naturally benevolent, and he had loved her if only for a night.

I must bind Thalias to me, for my use, thought Aspasia. Her women came to her, mutely offering the food on the cloth. She shook her head. If a woman, she thought, becomes as hard and cruel and merciless as a man she may prosper. But at what a price to her womanhood, her woman's soul, her woman's tenderness and softness and compassion!

The vast company was now returning to the caravan in a bellow of noise, and Aspasia rose with her women. She passed the tent of Al Taliph. The flap opened and the elderly woman emerged, leading the little girl by the hand again. The child walked like a wounded and crippled lamb, staggering, bent over, holding her lower body in both her small hands. Aspasia could not control herself. She ran to the girl and enfolded her in her arms, to the astonishment of the women. She pressed the brown head to her breast. She murmured consolations, and the child cried and clung to her as to a mother. Then Al Taliph appeared on the platform, fastening his girdle.

Aspasia looked up at him and he saw her lifted glowing eyes. He saw her disgust and dread. But he said nothing. He did not even shrug. Yes, I am a fool, thought Aspasia. What is this child, or any other woman, to him? She smoothed the child's hair and returned her to her guardian. Al Taliph leapt from the platform and went to his men, and Aspasia watched him go. He did not even have contempt for her, and that was the worst of all. She had entered his world at her own consent, or the consent of Thargelia. She had known from the first that to Al Taliph she was only a woman.

By Castor and by Pollux, Aspasia swore solemnly, I will regain my self-control and never, from this moment on, will a man ever beguile me. I will deceive him as he has deceived other women; a woman is cleverer than a man.

Ah, but surely in this intricate and various world there can truly be love between a man and a woman, and dignity and pride. And I will find such a man, even if I have to wander all the world. She wondered at her pain.

She did not know that Al Taliph loved her, and that to him other women were only a diversion and a necessity, and above all only a novelty. He had seen her revulsion and her disgust, and he was angered. She had spent over three years in his house and had seen many things there, and she remained blind and obdurate and without understanding. They had talked endless hours together, and it had come to nothing. He wanted to go to her and hold her in his arms – he fresh from the sweat and the blood of the nameless child. But Aspasia would not understand, though she was a hetaira. He, too, was filled with pain, as well as anger. She would never comprehend that he loved her, and he dared not try to convince her. Between men and women, even though they spoke the selfsame language, there remained an impassable chasm, hewn from their nature and their very lives.

While her women slept in the heat of the late afternoon Aspasia wrote to Thargelia.

'Greetings to Thargelia, my dearer than mother:

In these years, sweetest of friends, we have exchanged no letters for none would have been permitted to be sent nor any given to me. I have not been unhappy in my situation. In truth, I have had much happiness. But now I find my circumstances untenable, insufferable. I have, in my mind, the thought of establishing a school for young girls in Athens, though not a school for courtesans. Do not laugh, dear friend and mother. I know you will not for always you knew what was in my soul even as a child, and my rebellion against the degradation of women. In Persia the degradation is far worse than in Miletus or Greece. Surely you are aware of this, for do you not know all things? Enough. I am sending this letter through the kind offices of one Damos of Damascus, a rich merchant. I implore you to help one you loved so tenderly when she was an infant in your house. When it is possible I will go to you and my former home, and in the meantime you will seek a house for me in Athens where I may live and establish my school. May Hermes, swift of winged foot and helmet, speed this letter to you and your reply through Damos of Damascus, who lives on the Street called Straight. Never have I forgotten you nor my sisters, and I long to embrace you, to throw myself, as a loved daughter, into your arms there to weep and tell you my story. I commend you to the protection of Athene Parthenos whom you have always worshipped and honoured.'

She was weeping as she signed and sealed the letter, then placed it in her bosom. The next step was most dangerous and her heart thumped with fear at the thought. She looked closely at her women; they still slept. The heat in the tent was almost intolerable though it was nearing sunset. She drew her veil across her face and silently stepped through the flap of the tent and stood upon the platform, glancing fearfully about her and swaying with the motion of the wide platform. The men who drove the horses were half-slumbering on their seats, the pennant one held drooping in the fierce light. Aspasia crept along the side of the tent to the rear and found, as she had hoped, a narrow width of platform, which was covered with thick dust and sand. There she crouched, praying for the appearance of Thalias whom she knew rode at intervals with Al Taliph, and sometimes alone.

She held her veil across her face to protect it from the sun. She heard the sound of an approaching horse and, thanking the gods, she saw that the rider was indeed Thalias and that he was alone. He discerned her sitting on the platform and reined in his horse in astonishment. She threw aside her veil and pressed her lips with her finger, imploring quietness. He bent from his horse and said in a very low voice: 'What is it, Aspasia?'

She stood up, the better to be close to him. The horse's breath was hot and parched against her cheek. She could see his great white teeth. She held up the letter to Thalias and he snatched it quickly. She whispered above the sound of hooves, 'Send it before Damascus, dear Thalias. I have asked that a reply be sent to you in the city.'

He glanced down at the letter. He saw to whom it was addressed and looked afraid. 'Do not fear,' she said. 'I have not betrayed you, my dear Thalias. I have given your new name to Thargelia, and the name of the street where you live in Damascus.' She gazed at him with desperate appeal. 'Help me,' she pleaded, and clasped her hands tightly against her breast. 'Help me as I helped you, for I am in danger.'

He thrust the letter into his robe and his eyes smiled with promise upon the girl. He dug his heels into the horse's side and the animal sprang forward and away.

Al Taliph did not send for her that night, nor the night following, and Aspasia did not know whether to be relieved or to be crushed. She longed for him with a terrible longing, and she knew that this was just the beginning of pain and the darkness of grief and the unforgetting. But her resolution remained.

CHAPTER XIII

The caravan climbed slowly and heavily to the great high plateau, between the valleys of the Tigris and the Indus, a vast basin surrounded by mountains, and fed by the Tigris and Euphrates rivers, and partially divided by a desert.

Once when she saw a narrow river the colour of gold between dark and looming banks and another like a vein of deep purple stained with fire, she could hardly restrain her delight and worship.

She was conscious again of still being young and alive, of having her eyes filled with constantly changing marvels. The fragile hope in her began to increase. This, then, is what men feared in women, she would think : They fear, if released from a man's arms and commands, we would see the world and desire to be part of it, and be not in a state of servitude and a victim of random passion, but a member of humanity itself. So must an exultant slave feel when he discovers that in his heart he is free, despite his chains, and so must a master know fear when he discerns that though he can control the body of his slave he cannot control his spirit.

Her resolution for ultimate and absolute freedom became stronger hour by hour. It was only at midnight, when she slept alone, and the deep silence was about her, that she suffered torments of yearning and her tears wet her silken pillows.

The caravan came upon the ancient city of Damascus early one evening just before sunset. It seemed to Aspasia that the walled city approached the caravan rather than the caravan approaching it over the plain. The walls were golden and gleaming in the light of the descending sun, and piercing above them could be seen the glittering turrets and the tall thin towers and illuminated domes against a sky the colour of heliotrope. Here, then, awaited the 'Market of the Desert,' so named by merchants, and famed for its Wine of Helbon, its delicate woollens, linens, dried fruit, damasks, exquisite and weblike silks of many colours, its Tyrian purples, cushions with golden and silver tassels, leather work of incredible intricacy, gemmed filigree work in gold and silver, enamels, inlaid wood and metals, its marvellous brocades, its incomparable Damascene steel weapons, its works of art in brass and copper, and its covered Street called Straight, wherein dwelt rich merchants and their shops, the banks and the bankers, many markets, fountains, and inns. It ran from the Damascan Gate from east to west, and few there were who had not heard of its wonders, its scenes, its opulences, its wealth, its commerce and its power. Older than the memory or records of man, Damascus had been assulted many times by lustful enemies, Egyptians, Israelites, Assyrians and others, but she survived and was soon to be termed 'immortal.'

It was a fervid city, a dazzling city, exciting and excitable, trembling always with the yellow dust that whirled over it, sometimes incandescent in the sun like golden particles, and pearly under the moon. Here could be heard the tongues of many nations and many races, and every man hurried in spite of the heat, his face thrust forward as if he desired to run and not walk. Veiled women were everywhere, in stalls, selling flowers and sweetmeats and spiced morsels of meat and rice and wine and fabrics and vegetables and fruits and cheeses and ornaments, and their shrill cries and quarrels were louder than the complaints of streams of camels and horses and mules ever-flowing through the streets as caravans came and left. Almost every street held an inn, poor or lavish, for travellers and merchants.

The bronze Gate of Damascus was opened swiftly by guards, who recognized the illustrious banners carried by the caravan of Al Taliph. Above the arch blew gay pennants and on the apex there was a crouching stone statue of an ambiguous creature, half lion, half woman, winged and crowned, with a beautiful and majestic face. Aspasia was enraptured as the caravan slowly passed through the gate, and entered a narrow rising street walled on both sides. On the tops of the walls stood throngs awaiting the cooler air of evening, chewing delicacies from their palms, arguing, laughing, curiously eyeing the caravan, joking, spitting and staring. Aspasia could hear music rising and falling everywhere, music alien to her ears. She had thought the market places of Miletus and Persia unbearably noisy. They were muted compared with the uproar that now assailed her, the sleepless uproar of a city beyond her imagination. When the caravan wound its way through the street men and women in vari-coloured robes took refuge in slits in the walls. As the sun fell to the horizon torches began to sputter from sockets and lanterns began to move restlessly like illimitable stars.

On the Street called Straight the caravan separated itself from the four tents, and the occupants alighted under guard at the entrance to a very large walled inn. They entered a court-yard in which was centred a tiny garden with a fountain. Windows peered down from all four walls, and were crowded with faces inspecting the new arrivals, especially the women, thinking many of them were beauteous slaves to be displayed tomorrow in the slave markets. The turrets and towers and domes began to shine under a soaring moon, as if touched and plated with silver. Aspasia and her women were assigned two handsome chambers in the inn, rich with silks and brocades and divans and fat pillows and cushions, carved Chinese tables and ivoried chairs, the floors soft with rugs of many bright patterns. Aspasia discovered that the windows were barred by beautifully wrought iron in a vinelike shape. A dinner was brought to them of roasted lamb and vegetables simmering in garlic and olive oil, and dates and honey and soft pale bread and wine and assorted cheeses, and sauces and condiments of pungent odour and enticing aromas, and heaped fruits. She dined, listening to the music and the voices and the clamour of the city. Bells began to ring at random until all the air was pervaded with their dulcet or imperative tongues. Gaiety filled her, and excitement, and gratitude and love for Al Taliph who had condescended to give her such gratification. The vessels of oil flickered with light in the chambers, and were sweetly scented, partly to lull the senses and partly to cover the pervasive stench of latrines below.

Aspasia fell asleep on her cushions, after bathing in water redolent of jasmine, and she smiled in her sleep, her golden hair streaming about her. Her happy face had the innocence of a lily, and her women hated her and envied her.

In the morning Aspasia, after dining, was summoned to the chambers of Al Taliph. She was surprised, for he rarely summoned her before evening. She drew her veil across her face and arrayed herself in thin white linen and silver and went, attended by two of her women, to Al Taliph. Near him stood Thalias who bowed at her entry, and Al Taliph smiled. He held out his hand to Aspasia and she sat, as usual, at his feet and looked at Thalias. Then she pushed aside her veil and he saw her face, fresh and curious if a little anxious. Almost imperceptibly he nodded his head. So, the letter had been sent many long days ago and Aspasia sighed.

'It would seem, my white rose, that Damos my friend, has brought his wife to this inn to thank me for the little girls given to her, and to thank you also.' A risible flash passed over his eyes. 'She is in the next chamber, Hephzibah bas Ephraim. Do you desire to see her?'

'If my lord has no objections,' replied Aspasia. Al Taliph laughed lightly and touched her cheek. 'Your lord has no objections,' he said, as if he mocked her. A eunuch opened a door at a little distance and Aspasia rose and left the room, and also her women.

The chamber beyond was evidently used for dining and when Aspasia entered a young woman rose shyly, unveiled, and dressed very soberly, and her manner was both timid and sedate. She had a plain young face that was also appealing, as if she implored kindness. The two little girls sat side by side on cushions and happily devoured handfuls of a sweetmeat of honey and ground almonds, and they were rosy and clean and patient.

Hephzibah had beautiful blue eyes and her partly uncovered hair was soft and brown. She seemed a little abashed at the sight of Aspasia and her pale lips trembled a little. She said, in Aramaic, 'I wished to thank you, Lady, for giving me these small daughters, whom I already cherish, though I saw them first this morning.'

Aspasia was touched. 'It was not I. It was Al Taliph who did so, a gift for you.'

At the mention of that name Hephzibah's face changed, and Aspasia wondered. Hephzibah drew a deep breath and looked aside. 'Yes,' she said. 'That is what my husband told me. He also told me something else.' Now she looked directly at Aspasia. 'Lady,' she said, 'you are not only beautiful but as great of heart as any of the Mothers of Israel.'

Aspasia did not believe that Thalias had spoken of her beauty to Hephzibah, and she smiled gently. 'Damos is fortunate in you, Hephzibah bas Ephraim, and you –' she paused, 'are fortunate in him.'

For another strange and unspoken reason the other woman's eyes glistened with tears. She took Aspasia's hand and kissed it. She whispered, 'I thank you for Damos also.'

Aspasia was alarmed. She glanced over her shoulder but no one stood there. She whispered in reply. 'There are certain things a man should not tell his wife and I am surprised at Damos' indiscretion. Let us not speak of this, now or at any other time.'

'What my husband tells me is ever safe in my bosom,' said Hephzibah and lifted her head. 'But if a man cannot confide in the woman who loves him to whom can he confide?'

When has Al Taliph ever confided in me? thought Aspasia with a pang of sadness. But she looked at the other woman with interest. Here was no woman whose husband despised her femaleness but gave her honour and all his secrets, and it seemed enviable to Aspasia. True, Al Taliph spoke with her always of philosophies and abstruse things, but never had he permitted her to see him as he was. She yearned for a man who would trust her utterly as Damos apparently trusted his wife, and who put his very life into her hands. Truly then, and only then, could a woman be happy and content and proud, and never feel herself deprived or lonely or forgotten.

Hephzibah, though always she had been sheltered and loved and respected, had a woman's intuition and she was seized with confused pity for this beautiful girl who suddenly seemed so bereft and desolate. A bar of sunlight wavered over Aspasia's face, yet it only increased her air of melancholy. Hephzibah turned to the little girls, touched each fondly on the cheek and said, 'This is Ruth, and this is Rachel, my daughters.' The children leaned their heads briefly against her breast then ate another sweetmeat with childish voracity.

'They love you even now,' said Aspasia, and Hephzibah smiled for the first time and her plain young face became radiant. 'I love them dearly,' she replied. 'They will be sisters to my son.'

Now both the women were silent. They could hear the vehicles rattling over the stones of the courtyard and the distant clamour of the city. They listened for a moment, but both were thinking their own thoughts. Aspasia said to herself, 'This woman is happy as I was never happy, and I would change places with her with joy.' Not for Hephzibah wild nights of ecstasy mingled with devastation. Yet not for her fear of ultimate rejection and abandonment, by either divorce or banishing. For the first time in her life Aspasia saw another existence, infinitely gracious and serene and prideful. She saw that Hephzibah's hands showed evidence of toil at the loom and in the kitchen, among servants, Hephzibah singing tranquilly and eagerly awaiting the return of a husband who honoured her. What are all my gems and opulences compared with this? she asked herself, and all my excitements and fevers?

My heart bounds at the sound of Al Taliph's voice and I am joyful when I see his face, but always there is my dread and my fear. But Hephzibah is not tormented so, and she is blessed of the gods. When Thalias arrives home she is enfolded safely in his arms.

Hephzibah was gazing at her again and she discerned Aspasia's pain and she recalled what Damos had told of her, that she was a courtesan and the companion of Al Taliph. According to the Law women like this were frequently stoned to death for adultery or licentiousness. But Hephzibah suddenly wanted to embrace Aspasia and hold her to her breast with the same tenderness she had shown to the children, and to console and weep with her. This further confused her for never before had she seen or encountered a lewd woman, and why she should feel such compassion she did not know.

The young Jewish woman lifted an object wrapped in silk and tied with ribbons and placed it in Aspasia's hands. 'It is a gift I have brought for you, in gratitude, Lady,' she said. 'My husband has declared it will please you, perhaps.'

Aspasia said, 'I must thank you, Hephzibah bas Ephraim.' She began to unwrap the gift, but Hephzibah covered her eyes quickly with her hands and said, 'No, I implore you. It is a graven image, so my husband has told me, and of the heathen. He bought it in the bazaar this morning for your pleasure.'

'You do not know what it is?' asked Aspasia in astonishment. The other woman shook her head and dropped her hands. 'It is not permitted,' she murmured. Aspasia was more astonished than ever. Had Damos bought her something obscene? Her cheeks flushed and seeing this Hephzibah said, 'You must forgive me, but pious Jews do not gaze at graven images, and that is why I sit in my litter in the city with drawn curtains.' She drew a deep breath. 'I believe it is a statuette of a god.'

Aspasia wanted to laugh a little. 'You miss the excitement and the wonders of the city, then?'

'I have my household, and my children, and my women and

127

my parents and my dear husband, my gardens and my roses and my friends. What more can a woman desire, Lady?'

What indeed? thought Aspasia, looking at the wrapped object in her hands. An awkwardness came to them, and there was nothing more to say between a woeful courtesan and a beloved wife. Then Hephzibah, who was rarely demonstrative, put her hands on Aspasia's shoulders and kissed her cheek and Aspasia returned the embrace. In silence then she went to the chamber of Al Taliph.

Thalias was no longer with Al Taliph. The latter said indulgently, 'What is this you bear in your hands, my sweet one?'

But Aspasia said, 'I have seen what it is to be truly a woman.' She began to unwrap the silk. She did not see Al Taliph's dark and ambiguous expression, nor did she see him move a little restlessly on his divan nor did she see the sharp sombreness of his eyes. She said, 'It is a gift from Hephzibah bas Ephraim, but she would not permit me to reveal it before her.'

'Ah,' said Al Taliph and sat up alertly. 'Be certain it is either useful or edible. I know these Jews. If useful, what will you do with it? If edible, it will be delicious.'

The silk fell from the gift and Aspasia's hands enclosed an exquisitely carved and detailed image of a fat and smiling god, of ivory, with a vast belly and with legs folded in a fashion she had observed among the Indus.

'Buddha,' said Al Taliph, and held out his hand for it. He turned it carefully in his fingers and examined it with pleasure. 'This was created by an exceptional artist,' he remarked. 'I have never seen anything so perfect. It must have cost our dear Damos a fortune, for doubtless he purchased it himself, that apostate Jew!' and he laughed.

He glanced at Aspasia and he no longer smiled. He balanced the object on the palm of his hand, the hand dusky against the ivory, which glimmered in the morning light and showed, in the intricacy of its carving, a faint golden glow. 'Buddha,' he repeated. 'The ineffable One. The ultimate in a non-embrace-ment of the world. Sit beside me, my love.' She did so and he said, 'I have heard that if one rubs his belly and prays for what one desires, it will be granted. That is the superstition.'

He held the image in his hands and presented it to Aspasia, who, trying to smile, rubbed the belly of Buddha. Then, without her own volition, she prayed, 'Let him love me as I love him!' She dropped her hand. She said, 'What? Will you not rub him also, lord?'

'I am not superstitious,' he said. Very carefully he placed the Buddha on the table before him and contemplated it. As though speaking to himself only he said, 'The Persians honour all gods, all manifestations of the Deity, Buddha, Lao T'sai, Zoroaster, Mithras, Zeus, Ahuramazda, Ptah, Osiris, Vishnu, and even the vengeful Jehovah of the Jews. We are on the best of terms with them all, for of what concern is it what name men call God? He has illimitable Faces and aspects, and reveals Himself in whatsoever guise He desires. It is enough, it is said, that men love Him.'

He closed his eyes and she saw that he was suddenly weary and she rose and silently left the room, baffled.

Her women were absent and Aspasia felt a sweet freedom, for rare was it that she was alone. She went to the barred window and looked down at the crowded courtyard. Below her Thalias was standing, looking up, evidently expecting her. He smiled like a loving gay brother and kissed his hand to her and nodded. Then he moved away swiftly and Aspasia followed him with her eyes and she was filled with warmth and gratitude. She forgot that he had once been a slave, for in his salutation was all understanding, all reassurance, all kindness, all promise.

Aspasia accompanied Al Taliph to the bazaars of the city and she was like a child in her jubilation and staring excitement. Her eyes were wide and illuminated above her thick veil, seeking to encompass all the colourful movement and watch all things at once. Al Taliph took her to a jeweller and there, in the back room where an unveiled woman could not offend the eyes of men, he bought her a necklace of opals, all blue and rose and pearly fire in their restlessness. He clasped it about her neck himself and she pushed back her hood and her hair fell about her face and the jeweller was entranced. He was a very rich man; he believed Aspasia to be a favourite slave, and he drew Al Taliph respectfully aside and offered a fortune for her. In the meantime she was regarding herself rapturously in a silver mirror. She heard Al Taliph utter a word or two that was half-angry and then half-amused. But the language was unknown to her.

He returned to her and regarded her as if with new eyes. 'Does the bauble please you, my golden hibiscus?' he asked, and fondled both the necklace and her throat. She looked at him ardently and then he lost his smile and gazed at her with a stern earnestness she had seen but few times before and which had always puzzled her. It was as though he were trying to interpret her words or her gestures or her expressions, and was never certain. She said, 'If only I pleased you, lord, as much as this pleases me then indeed I would be happy.' He sighed and turned away.

He bought her embroidered and brocaded silks and jewelled slippers and sandals and carved jade and ivory containers for cosmetics and golden bangles and ear-rings of designs uncommon to her and reaching to her shoulders, yet as light as down. He bought her girdles of flexible gold and fretted silver, also set with gems. She had but to admire and it was hers. A mantle of argus-eyed peacock feathers charmed her, and he flung it over her shoulders and it caressed her. He carefully told her the origin of all these and she exclaimed, 'What a marvellous world is this, where so much beauty is revealed!'

They were to remain for a considerable time in Damascus. The days went by for Aspasia like a repeated dream, changeless. She understood that Al Taliph sold the goods of his caravan and was replacing them with goods for his own shops and market places and bazaars. Very occasionally he invited her to dine with him at noonday. But he seemed increasingly weary and preoccupied, and often he would leave abruptly when a visitor arrived to consult him, and not return. Then she had a choice of sleeping in the afternoon, as most of Damascus slept during that period except for the busy merchants and bankers, or to venture out again with her guards and women for another view of a different part of the city. There is nothing more terrible than idleness, she would think, and I am an idle woman. She would try to read the books Al Taliph bought for her but the philosophies and poems were strange and elusive to her and the allusions cryptic.

She wondered if Hephzibah bas Ephraim had forgotten her, for Al Taliph had humorously mentioned that the Jewish lady would invite her soon to partake of a quiet dinner alone with her. However, no invitation came and Aspasia was filled with disappointed resentment. Doubtless Hephzibah regarded her as unclean and did not desire her house to be polluted by such a woman as herself.

She began to think of the house she would have in Athens, but even that was taking on the semblance of a lost dream. Al Taliph would never let her go until he tired of her, and the air of Damascus made her mind languid and without hope. She existed for the benefit of Al Taliph's pleasure; beyond that she had no existence, but was just a glass bubble aimlessly drifting in any random breeze, catching light and colour though having none of these within itself. Where was the incandescent resolution she had possessed only a few months ago? Her listlessness increased and became animation only in the presence of Al Taliph.

One day she said to him, 'I had hoped to see Hephzibah bas Ephraim again. She has forgotten her promise to me.'

He averted his face and said, 'Damos mentioned that she had been indisposed.' He hesitated, then continued: 'I know you have pleasure in seeing the city, but it is my desire that you do not go forth again from this time on, but remain in your chambers.'

131

She protested. 'But that is my only diversion!'

He looked at her forbiddingly. 'It is my command,' he said and at first would not explain for all the bright anger in her eyes. 'Also,' he said, 'drink not of the water from the well but only wine and eat no fruit but that it is washed and peeled by yourself, with your knife and fingers. Let no water reach your mouth, even for the cleaning of your teeth, and when you bathe close your lips tightly so that no water can enter, nor must it enter your nostrils.'

Now a faint cold alarm came to her. 'What is this of which you speak, lord?'

'There is a rumour that some illness is spreading through the city and the physicians fear it is carried in wells and rivers. That may be a superstition, yet it is wise to be prudent.'

Her alarm grew stronger. 'What of you, Al Taliph? Are you being prudent?'

He shrugged and smiled. 'I must drink and eat what is given me in the houses of my friends and my fellow merchants, but their kitchens are fastidious and so no harm will come to me. This inn has a reputation for cleanliness. But you must remain within.' He hesitated and said inwardly: Lest you come to harm and I would be desolated. He smiled at her again and said, 'Does not a man guard his treasure and are you not mine?'

She answered with acerbity, 'Until I am no longer your treasure but have become tarnished in your eyes.'

Now her life became more restricted than ever before. She was not permitted to go down even to the courtyard, and she saw fright in her women's faces. She heard them whisper; she saw them fingering amulets. Once she said to them with impatience, 'Of what are you afraid?' But they did not answer but only peeped at her furtively, and she knew they feared to give their terror words lest it fall upon them like a Fury, as at a summoning.

The women were much older than herself and fat and repugnant to her eyes, and as none now left the chambers the rooms began to reek with the smell of sweat and increasing incense and rank perfumes. She noticed, from her window, that men went continually through the courtyard, swinging censers or burning fires in the corners and thus filling the air with acrid smoke, and chanting as the women chanted. Perhaps the season for the caravans was ending, for Aspasia saw few and even these were decreasing and often days passed when there were none at all. She, herself, began to feel fear, and longed for news.

At last she could bear it no longer and cried to Al Taliph, 'You must tell me! What is this illness of which you have told me? Would you leave me a prey to fright? It is better to know than to be ignorant.'

He appeared very tired. There were no more bronze lights on his cheeks, she saw with dread, and his nose seemed larger and his subtle mouth tighter. 'Then I will tell you,' he said. 'It is cholera.'

At that fearful word Aspasia shivered and trembled. 'Cholera,' she whispered. 'Are many ill – dead?'

'A fourth of the city is dead,' he replied. 'I thought to spare you the knowledge. The gates of the city are closed. None can leave or come in. Does it make you more at ease to know this?'

But she whispered again, 'Cholera!'

'Even the physicians are dying,' he said.

She put her cold palms to her face and closed her eyes briefly. 'Almost all die, lord.'

'True. I did not wish you to be afraid. You are safe here if you are careful in your food and your drink.'

She exclaimed, as she had exclaimed before, but now with terror, 'What of you, lord?' Her face had turned very white and her eyes enlarged.

'I am careful also,' he said and tried to smile at her. 'I tell you now so that you will understand why we are prisoners here. If not for this we should have departed three weeks ago. It is not my wish to keep you in a dungeon.'

She reached out and seized his hand and she was trembling again. 'Remain with me, lord! Do not go forth again, I implore you.'

He regarded her curiously. 'Do you fear that if I sicken and die you will be helpless here? Do not distress yourself, dear one. My men will convey you home.' His tone was sardonic. 'Your name, sweet blossom, is in my will.'

She withdrew her hand and turned aside her head helplessly. She said, 'Is the family of Damos well?'

'His wife died a month ago.' He threw the words at her as if she had incontinently wounded him and he wished to wound her in return.

She cried out and clenched her hands together. 'Hephzibah bas Ephraim? Gods, what of her children – and Damos?'

'The children sickened, but are recovering. Damos had cholera in his childhood, he has told me.'

Aspasia wept for that loving young woman and covered her face with her hands. When she looked up at last she saw that Al Taliph had left her. Now her fear for him became frenzy and she returned to her chambers and walked up and down them wringing her hands and muttering her own incoherent prayers, though she felt them superstition and useless. The women, forgetting their own whimperings and fear, watched her sullenly and glanced at each other with unspoken questions. Was the foreign woman sickening? They drew together, huddling, for protection.

She paused before them suddenly and stared down at them and hated them for no reason but that they were witnesses to her uncontrolled anguish.

A faint coolness, or a numbness, touched her heart and she became calmer. It was then that she heard a light tinkling against one of the bars of the window. She went to the window and looked without. Thalias stood there below, clad in sombre robes, his face shrunken and older, his eyes reddened. He tried to smile up at her, then bit his lip. There were but one or two men in the once-crowded courtyard and they were at a distance, talking together.

Aspasia hastily glanced behind her, but her women were rocking on their buttocks and chanting again. She leaned against the bars, her face full of pity and desire to communicate her sympathy to him. He understood. His once merry blue eyes became vivid with tears. He reached to his pouch and glanced about him, then withdrew a sealed letter and showed it to her. Aspasia's heart jumped. It could be only from Thargelia. Despairingly, she looked again at her women. They had as yet seen or heard nothing. Her thoughts flew through her head like distracted birds. Then her mind became clear. In the next chamber commodes had been prepared for her and the women so that they need not go down to the latrines in the courtyard. There was a small window there. She glanced down at her waist, which was clasped with a silver cord set with garnets and amethysts, a trifle she had fancied in a bazaar and which Al Taliph had bought for her. It was of several lengths so that it could be wound and twisted pliantly about her slender body and even about her breasts.

She looked down again at Thalias then pointed towards the window of the other chamber and turned back to the women. Sighing, she went into the adjoining chamber, which had no door. She closed the thick blue and gold curtains behind her then ran silently to the window. Thalias was standing below. Swiftly she unwound the gilded cord about her waist and, holding one end, she let the other through the bars of the small window very quickly, her breath tight in her throat, her eyes on the distant men.

Thalias deftly seized the end of the cord and speedily tied it about the letter. It flew up the dusty wall like a moth and Aspasia retrieved it. Then Thalias touched his forehead in farewell and wandered away, ostensibly to the latrines.

The thudding in Aspasia's breast was harder and more painful. She looked at the closed curtains, moved to a wall and swiftly opened the letter, which read:

'Greetings to Aspasia, one dearer than a daughter:

'How joyous was I to receive a message from you, my beautiful child, for never are you out of my memory. How I cried with pleasure, for the hope of seeing you again. I shall do as you wish at once and seek a house for you, as you desire, in Athens, but it appears to me a strange house. I will not question you, for the messenger awaits my answer. You must come first to your home in Miletus where I will embrace you and hold you once more in my arms and we shall speak of many things. I await you and will invoke Hermes to bring you on wings to me.'

Aspasia thrust the letter into her bosom. The disposal of it would be another problem. Nor did she think just then how she could leave Damascus and Al Taliph. That was for the future.

But still a lightness came to her, like a wind of freedom through the bars of a prison, and her resolution, so long in abeyance, began to open like a hidden rivulet within her, at first doubtful and muddy, then springing into crystal.

As the evenings were sharply cool after the heat of the day a brazier was lighted in the chamber where she slept with her women. Aspasia was able to drop the letter on the coals where it flared a moment and then was but ashes. However, like the Phoenix, there rose from them a renewed life. It was only later while her women slept that she thought, But even if he will let me go, how can I leave him? I will leave my heart and my love behind and all that I am, and henceforth I shall be but a shadow from Hades. But I must go before he tires of me and I wander like an apparition in the chambers of the rejected, unwanted and despairing of any summons, weeping and mournfully sighing in the endless nights.

CHAPTER XIV

One morning Aspasia received a summons to go to the chambers of Al Taliph. She hastily drew a comb through her dishevelled hair, for in these days she neglected her appearance. She rubbed her cheeks and lips with a red unguent; she had become pale and drawn in her sunless and imprisoned state. She dressed herself in a hyacinth-coloured tunic and clasped a silver and amethyst necklace about her throat and touched herself with attar of roses. Then she hastened to Al Taliph's chambers. It was very early and this summons was most unusual. The two armed eunuchs at his door opened it for her in a dull silence, and she entered.

To her horror she saw Al Taliph reclining on his cushioned bed in an attitude of total collapse, his grey profile staring at the ceiling. Three slave girls huddled at a distant wall, and two strange men stood at the bedside, rubbing their chins and conversing together in low voices. They were Egyptian, she saw by their garb and their dusky features, and medical pouches were beside them. There was a horrific stink in the hot closed room of vomit and faeces, and Aspasia stood and swayed and suddenly trembled. No one noticed her or marked her arrival. Almost creeping, she went to the bed and looked down at Al Taliph. She bent over him and he became aware of her scent and her presence, and he turned his face to her and tried to smile. His eyes were sunken far back into his skull and were dim. The bronze metallic shine had totally left his cheeks, which were sunken also. His mouth was dry as dust, and he panted. A heavy sweat covered him with glistening beads.

He lifted his hand feebly to her. She fell to her knees and took his hand and it was burningly hot as if she had touched fire. In spite of her anguish this manifestation startled her, for it indicated very high fever. Al Taliph was obviously very ill and close to death. There is little fever in cholera, she recalled through the haze of her terror. She put her hand under the coverlets. His belly was swollen, and he winced and moaned though her pressure was gentle. The Egyptians looked down at her in surprise, and exchanged glances with upraised brows. Forgetting everything but her beloved's extremity Aspasia continued her examinations and for an instant his old ironic amusement shone in his eyes. The area on his right side was especially prominent and had a thickened feeling under her fingers. Again she pressed gently on it and he exclaimed and pushed away her hand.

Aspasia flung back her loose hair and looked up at the physicians, and they attempted to smile disdainfully. Then they saw her large and wine-brown eyes, glowing with imperative authority. 'He does not have cholera,' she said, and her voice was strong and clear. 'How long has he been ill?'

They were silent a moment and then one of the physicians said, 'For several days, Lady. Why is it that you say it is not cholera?' But his voice was almost respectful and did not have the contempt in it for women which the Aryan peoples invariably displayed.

'I was taught considerable medicine by a famous physician in the house of Thargelia in Miletus, and it has been my abiding concern. Tell me, sirs. Has my lord had frequent bloody stools, and hard colic?'

The younger of the physicians moved closer to her with interest and now his expression was grave. 'It is true,' he said, almost as if she were a colleague. He forgot that she was but a favourite concubine, a mistress, hardly possessing a status above an adored slave woman. 'But this can occur in rare cases of cholera also.'

'There is little fever in cholera,' said Aspasia, addressing him while the older physician thoughtfully stroked his beard. 'Does he vomit profusely, as in cholera?'

'He vomits, but not very frequently.'

Aspasia, still holding Al Taliph's hand, sat back on her heels. 'But in cholera, as we were taught, there is no thickening and swelling of the right region of the belly, and there are clear faeces or brownish or murky, and no bloody ejaculations except in the most rare of instances. Tell me, is his urine deficient, or not present?'

Now the older physician drew closer to her also. 'His production of urine is almost normal, despite his vomiting and diarrhoea. Sometimes he retains water he has drunk.'

'He is in deep pain,' said Aspasia. 'He cannot endure a touch on his belly. This is not true of cholera, which affects the bowels but little.'

The older physician tried for indulgence. 'What is your diagnosis, Lady?'

'The flux,' said Aspasia. 'It is very serious and can be fatal, but it is not so serious as cholera.' She trembled again and held Al Taliph's hand tightly as if to imbue him with her own young strength.

'The flux?' said one physician, disbelieving. 'We see that very often, and this seems not the flux.'

'It could be, sirs, that it is because my lord has a virulent case of it. In Egypt, I have heard, it is endemic and so is more benign than in these regions where there is little defence against it, and it is therefore overwhelming.' She clasped her hands together and lifted her face to the physicians imploringly. 'I beg of you, lords, to let me treat Al Taliph, for the flux is not rare in the region where we live, among slaves and the poor. It is rare only among the rich and the comfortable. Let me treat him! He is almost in extremity. It can do no harm.'

Al Taliph's hot hand lifted feebly to her throat then her cheek, as if both touched and rebuking. Again she gripped his hand and held it tightly. 'What have you been giving him, lords, in treatment?'

'Purges,' said the younger physician. 'And herbal wine.'

'O gods!' Aspasia murmured, and shuddered. Then she said, 'I have your permission to order his treatment?'

They glanced at each other again, smiling, shrugging. 'Love,' said the younger, kindly, 'can often accomplish what the most skilled physicians cannot. His case is desperate. Your care can do no harm.'

'Aspasia,' said Al Taliph in a very weak voice. But she looked at him fiercely. 'You are in my hands!' she cried. 'You shall obey me, or die!'

Intense astonishment touched his sunken face, and he said nothing.

Aspasia beckoned to the huddled slaves near the wall. 'Open the windows, lest my lord stifle, and fan him gently. Fetch me cool water with Syrian whisky, a full goblet of it, in the water, and soft cloths. Bring at once a large goblet of goat's milk, with three spoons of honey in it and a half spoon of salt. Order, from the kitchen, the boiled juice of beef in quantity. This, heated, must be given him every half hour, the milk and honey and salt every two hours. Hasten!'

The slaves remembered that this alien woman was a sorceress, and hurried to follow her commands, making the sign against the evil eye. The physicians said, 'That is not the treatment for the flux, Lady. We give but boiled goat's milk and rice.'

'I have said that in your country the flux is not so vehement, easily cured by rest and care. O gods! From what house did my lord contract this?'

She looked at Al Taliph with the eyes of a mother reproaching a child. 'Lord, if you had but remained in this inn you should never have sickened!'

He tried to laugh but it was a feeble thing. She nestled her hand against his cheek and he kissed the palm. 'You must help me,' she said. 'You must not contradict my orders. You must struggle to retain what is fed to you. Thank the gods it is not cholera.'

He looked at his eminent physicians with the old satiric

glint on his face but to his amazement the physicians nodded. 'We leave you, lord, in the most competent of hands,' the older one said. 'We shall see you at evening.'

They hesitated. Then they each formally lifted Aspasia's free hand and kissed it deferentially. Al Taliph was more amazed. Aspasia acknowledged the accolade with a dignified inclination of her head, and an inner gratitude that she was not dealing with Aryan physicians who would have dismissed her like an impudent slave. They left her in a stately fashion; she smiled at Al Taliph with tears in her eyes, and his fingers suddenly entwined themselves in her hair.

The slaves brought the cool water and the strong whisky in it, and Aspasia bathed Al Taliph with the mixture. She made him drink of the honey and milk and salt, then stared at him threateningly when he made a gagging sound. 'You will only have to drink it again,' she said, and he made a wry face. Within an hour she forced him to drink the pungent beef broth. While waiting she sat beside him on the floor and watched his face constantly and pressed her fingers against his wrist and his throat. The feverish pulse began to subside. Long before evening he slept in exhaustion.

At evening the physicians returned and examined their patient. Then they said to Aspasia, 'Lady, you have brought your lord back from the gates of death, and we do not know if it is your solicitude or your treatment.'

She never left him for many days, except to bathe and to partake of food for herself. She would not let a slave approach him without first washing hands and face with lye soap and water and wine. She watched his excretions. She fed him with her own hands, sternly admonishing him when he complained. She bathed him several times a day with the whisky and water and his fever fell each time.

'Once,' she said to him, 'you remarked that I was a veritable child. But women become mature humans and leave their childhood behind them. However, this is not true of men, particularly when they are ill. They are the most petulant and intransigent of children.'

His strength was so returning that he could say almost with his former power of voice, 'That is a woman's illusion.'

'What we see in men is also an illusion, the most fatal of all,' she replied. 'If Hera and Artemis and Demeter and Athene Parthenos did not guard us women, and comfort and guide us, mankind would have long disappeared from this earth.'

'Would that have been so terrible?' he asked her, teasingly.

'Not at all,' she said and they laughed together. Never had they been so tender, so dearly as one, not even in passion. But the resolution was gaining in Aspasia's mind. Her lips were taking on a new firmness. I am young no longer, she would remind herself. I am now nineteen years of age, and I must take up my life lest it be too late. The infirmities of age come quickly to women. Then her heart would become weak and heavy and she would weep when she was alone.

She said to him lightly one evening, when he sat up in his bed to eat the food she had prepared for him, 'I will return you in good health to your wives and your women, and they should be grateful.'

He paused and looked at her intently. 'You do not speak of yourself, my dearest one.'

She looked at the windows where the sun lay redly in a lake of emerald, and she said, 'I hear far winds and they echo in my soul.'

He fondled her intimately, not understanding, and she smiled through her tears then fed him again. He could not have enough of her ministrations and when she slept on her cushions beside him he would rise on his elbow and look down on her pale face.

It came to him that she was no longer young but that she was more precious to him than life itself, and all other women were as naught. He could not speak of this to her. She would not comprehend, being a woman. She sighed in her sleep and he wondered why she sighed. 'Far winds?' That was ambiguous but women were full of fancies and they meant nothing. He touched her hair and slept also, content.

CHAPTER XV

There was a great garden in the city, filled with birds and monkeys and fountains and many strange animals. The cholera had subsided and the city teemed again with noise and bazaars and caravans and music and shops and laughter and bells, and the temples were crowded with those who gave thanksgiving that the plague had gone.

Al Taliph and Aspasia sat side by side on a marble bench in this vast garden, watching the changeful colours of the fountains as they threw up their transparent arms in the sun. The armed eunuchs stood about them, and Aspasia's attending women. Their litter waited, its carved golden roof shining in the light. Aspasia was at once sad, weary, and hopeful. Al Taliph held her hand in his under the shelter of her crimson cloak, and her eyes, above the veil, smiled upon him. He was still weak and sometimes he had fits of shivering in the night, but it was obvious that he would soon be well. His gauntness was decreasing.

'In four weeks I shall be able to travel with my caravan,' he said. 'We shall return home.'

She did not answer. She had averted her eyes. 'You will not be sorry to leave Damascus?' he asked.

She shook her head. A scarlet bird alighted near them, avid-eyed, then lifted its wings in the sun and was gone.

'I owe my life to you, beloved,' he said. 'Had it not been for you I should now have been gathered to my fathers. Tomorrow, I will take you to my jeweller and anything he possesses is yours. It is a poor sign of gratitude for my life, but it is the only recompense I can make.'

She bowed her head and said to herself, Alas, is that all?

Then she said, 'Lord, I want no more jewels, for I have much from your generosity.'

'How, then, can I repay you, Aspasia?'

A cool sweat broke out over her body. She must speak now or never have the courage to speak again. She lifted eyes clouded with tears to him and from behind her veil she whispered, 'Lord, let me go, in peace, with your blessing.'

He was astounded. He turned so that he could more fully look down into her eyes. 'Go, Aspasia? Where would you go, and why?' He could not believe it.

'I wish to return to my old home in Miletus for a space, and then go to Athens to open a school for young women who desire to be more than a mere bauble for men, and who wish to live as surely the gods intended a woman to live, for does not Athene labour endlessly, and Artemis, and does not Demeter attend the land, and is not Hera queen of Olympus and ever dutiful? The goddesses are potent in their sex. It was surely intended for earthly women to be important also, in their lives.'

Al Taliph was incredulous. 'You desire to leave me?' he asked.

'Lord, I must.' Now her tears ran over the edge of her veil.

There was a sick tightness in his chest, as if he had been wounded to the death. His hand left hers. He stared before him and she shut her eyes lest she weaken and implore him not to grant her wish.

He said, 'How have I offended you, Aspasia, that you wish to desert me and leave me forever?'

Ah, she thought, if you had but loved me, even a little, I should not flee from you, core of my heart. But men cannot love to the measure of our hope, and that is their nature. Even if they love, the love is evanescent, and a new woman is a consolation and a forgetting. I do not reproach you, my darling; I reproach my own folly in that I have hoped when hope was impossible. I had forgotten what I had learned in the house of Thargelia and that was my grievous error. I am a woman.'

Because she had not spoken he continued: 'Then you tended me not out of love but as a slave would attend a master, a dedicated slave thinking of duty?'

She said in a low voice, 'I have remembered our years together, and our affection and our joys, and you are a man of worth, lord, and must be preserved.'

'For what, for whom?' he asked with bitterness.

'You have wives and sons. Are they nothing to you, sire?'

He thought of three of his sons, now young men, of whom he was proud, and who had fortunate futures and who loved him. Though fathers did not cherish their daughters there were two whose beauty and gentleness were dear to him.

Aspasia said, 'Return to your family and their love for you. You are still their lord and their protection. Is that not enough?'

He did not speak. His eyes changed with his thoughts and with his rebellious passions. Then he said, 'Is not what I have given you of any value, Aspasia?'

'Lord, it is of inestimable value. I will never forget you. But I must go.'

He paused, and felt ill again and undone. 'Is there naught I can do to persuade you to remain with me?'

Yes, she answered in herself. You can tell me that you love me – which would be a lie – and swear to me that above all things I am eternally dear to you. She said, almost inaudibly, 'There is nothing which is in your power, lord, that can persuade me, for what I desire you cannot give me. It is true that you can take back your jewels and set me defenceless on the streets, as once you threatened. How I shall live then I do not know. So, I beg you to let me keep them and to set me free.'

'You believe I am cruel and ungrateful?'

O gods, she cried inwardly, is gratitude all you know, my beloved? A heavy faintness came to her. 'I ask for no gratitude, which is a poor and reluctant and resented thing. I did what I had to do. Let us not speak of it again. There is of a certainty one thing you can still give me: peace.'

'You have known no peace with me?'

She put her hand to her throat where the pain was enormous. 'No,' she said.

He was silent. The pallor increased on his face, but when she touched him in alarm he flung off her hand, and she shrank.

'Peace is for the dead,' he said. 'Are you foolish enough to believe it is attainable for the living? Surely Thargelia taught you better!'

'We are, as usual, conversing, but we do not mean the same thing,' she pleaded. 'The peace I desire is not the peace you would understand.'

He motioned to the litter-bearers. He said, 'I only understand that you wish to leave me. I owe you much, Aspasia. I owe you several years of pleasure and conversation and the contemplation of your beauty. You have been my companion in my empty hours and have filled them with contentment and delight. No other woman has been to me what you have been, and I, too, will never forget.'

'The world is full of complaisant women,' she said, out of her pain. 'I will not be hard to replace.'

This wounded him more than anything else and he made an abrupt gesture. 'I have a caravan leaving tomorrow. Do you wish to be part of it?'

Tomorrow! Then there would be no last parting, no last embraces. It was well, but it was also agonizing. 'Yes,' she said.

'I have servants who will take you to where you desire to go. I trust that pleases you, Aspasia.' He spoke dully and without emotion. 'As for the jewels, they, too, are in gratitude, and I will also send to you a purse of gold coins.' He paused and

146

smiled at her sombrely. 'Go in peace, Aspasia, if that is what you desire above all else.'

They returned to the inn in a silence too sorrowful for words. That night he sent to her a large purse rich with gold coins – but no final word, no entreaty, no avowal. Her women gathered her possessions together and put them in her chests, gloating and smirking when she could not see them. They whispered to each other, 'The foreign woman has been dismissed, and contentment will come to the lord's house again. She has the evil eye. We will all rejoice in the harem when she is absent.'

The caravan departed, with Aspasia's tent. There was no last farewell from Al Taliph, no sign of his solicitude. Aspasia thought, he has already forgotten me. She lay on her cushions in the tent and when the caravan began to move she rose and moved aside the flap on the tent and stood in the doorway. Al Taliph was not there. The gates of the inn closed after the caravan, and it started on its long journey. Had Al Taliph appeared she would have run to him and would have implored him not to let her go.

Unfortunate are we, she thought with crushing despair, when the gods grant our prayers! She was empty except for the dolorous woe that blew through the shell of herself and whispered of desolation, of the breaking of a heart, and the ending of life and immortal loneliness. She shed no tears. The dead do not weep for themselves. They can only remember.

CHAPTER XVI

Autumn came again to Persia and the great caravans began to move to their many destinations. But Al Taliph accompanied none. 'I am still recovering from a grave illness,' he would say to his friends and his fellow merchants. 'Too, I am no longer young.' They accepted this explanation, for they were gentlemen. But it was whispered everywhere that the beauteous Aspasia, the crown of his harem, his adored one and the adorable, had disappeared from his house. Had he banished her or had she died in Damascus?

Serah, one of Aspasia's attendants in Damascus licked her lips. What she had to say was too important to be whispered in the harem. It was also valuable. It would bring a good price. Who would pay it? Eventually she thought of Kurda, who had not gone to Damascus. He would pay the price. But he disdained to gossip too much with the women of the harem, and he was busy in attendance on Al Taliph, as he loved him and was full of consternation at his appearance.

Serah at last sought out Kurda, who listened with glistening eyes and a salivating mouth. He licked his lips. He gave Serah the gold coin she had demanded and even deigned to pat her shoulder approvingly, and with glee. Then he questioned the Raïs of the caravan, who questioned the men who had driven Aspasia's tent. After several weeks he found one of the men in the courtyard who had observed a peculiar matter, and still another.

Kurda pondered. How would his lord receive this information? With fury and denial and punishment? Or, with gratitude? Kurda would sit at night on his bed, rubbing his hairless chin and debating in himself the proper approach. At last he could wait no longer and sought out Al Taliph in his library. He entered silently and Al Taliph, gaunt and gloomy, looked at him with impatience. Kurda bowed. 'Lord,' he said, 'I have news for you, if you can endure it, concerning the foreign woman whom you banished nearly a year ago.'

Al Taliph started to his feet, and his bones became like hard metal under his skin, 'Speak!' he cried, and there was a leaping and fluttering in his breast. Had Aspasia been found? Where could he seek her?

Kurda glanced about him, and hesitated. 'It will anger you, lord, and I am fearful that your anger will fall upon me, who am guiltless, instead of the man with whom that woman betrayed you.'

Al Taliph stood motionless. He stared at Kurda and his parched mouth became quiet and still. Finally he said, 'There was no man, no lover. But tell me your idle tale – for I know you hated her – and I vow I will not punish you however absurd or vile the story.'

Kurda looked at him beseechingly. He said, 'The man is one of your companions, your friends, who has accompanied you on a caravan. He is Damos of Damascus, once a guest in your house.'

Still staring at Kurda, Al Taliph slowly seated himself. He recalled the night when Damos had dined with him and he had offered Damos the little girls and Aspasia had intervened. He recalled that prior to this she had become agitated on her arrival in the dining hall, and he had wondered if she had recognized one of the guests. 'Go on,' he said to Kurda, and his dark hands clenched on his brocaded robe.

Kurda, despite his fear, told the story well, and in sequence. He had found one of the men who had driven Aspasia's tent. The man had seen Damos ride up to the platform, on which Aspasia was standing; the man had seen her leave the tent and creep to the rear. Curious, he had also crept along the other side of the tent and had observed that the foreign woman had given Damos a letter. They had whispered together, or spoken in low voices, and so the man had not been able to hear the rapid conversation. Aspasia had seemed to be imploring Damos.

'The driver spoke to his companion about this strange event,' said Kurda, watching Al Taliph fearfully for any gesture of violence towards himself. 'But the companion had only replied that as Damos was your friend, lord, and a guest in the caravan, the foreign woman was only sending you a message, for it was known that you had not seen her for several nights. So the man shrugged, and forgot the incident, believing the explanation for it.'

Al Taliph did not speak. Kurda's throat became dry; he could see but those terrible eyes fixed upon him.

The woman, Serah, had seen a far more serious incident in Damascus. She had told him, Kurda, of Aspasia's obvious restlessness, imprisoned as she was during the cholera. She had continually paced up and down her chambers like a demon, her expression growing wilder every day. Then one afternoon Serah, who was engaged in her prayers against the plague, had seen Aspasia suddenly halt near one of the windows and gaze downwards as if something or someone had attracted her attention. After a moment or two she had gone into the chamber where the commodes had been placed, and had carefully closed the curtains behind her. Serah had run first to the window and saw below the lord's friend, Damos, who was gazing upwards at the window of the smaller chamber beyond. To Serah's astonishment she saw that Aspasia had untied her jewelled cord and was extending it through the bars to Damos, and Damos instantly caught it and wound a letter in it. Aspasia then had swiftly drawn it upwards, and Damos had wandered away.

Serah had then run to the curtains and had drawn the edge of one aside and she discovered Aspasia in the act of reading the letter, which she then had thrust into her bosom. Serah did not speak of these odd matters to her sister attendants, being prudent and not desiring to be an idle gossip. But she had watched Aspasia and later saw her furtively drop the missive on to the coals of the brazier.

He, Kurda, on being informed of these events, had made inquiries and had not only heard the tale of Aspasia's giving Damos a letter or message while the caravan was on the road to Damascus, but had found two other men of the caravan who had been in the courtyard alone while Damos was furtively conveying the missive to Aspasia. They had pretended to see nothing. It was of little interest to them at the time, for they had not seen Aspasia clearly at the window, but had known Damos well, for had he not ridden beside the lord during the journey on many occasions? If he was making an assignation with a woman of what matter was it to them?

'Either of these revelations alone, lord, would be serious though a possible explanation could be found for one,' said Kurda. 'But combined they have unspeakable import.'

Al Taliph was silent for a long time. He did not believe for an instant that Aspasia had been unfaithful to him. He recalled that Damos was a Greek and it was surely probable now that he had known Aspasia before, though he had denied ever living in Miletus, or of even visiting that city. Therefore, he had lied. Al Taliph remembered that Damos had invariably shown Aspasia deferential kindness, and that he had spoken of her to Al Taliph in the inn when Hephzibah had visited Aspasia. His voice had been gentle, as if he were speaking of a great lady, and not a courtesan, and had permitted his wife to converse alone with her, a peculiar thing for a virtuous Jew to permit.

Had he been a random patron of Aspasia's when she was in the house of Thargelia? No. Thargelia delivered only virgins to distinguished or illustrious or wealthy men, and Aspasia had been a virgin in his, Al Taliph's, bed, and of that he was convinced. There had also been a pristine quality about Aspasia, a freshness, an inexperience, which could not be assumed and certainly not to a man of Al Taliph's knowledge of women and their bodies.

Aspasia had been lured from her lord, or had induced Damos to assist her to flee, but for what reason Al Taliph did not know. Damos, deprived of a loved and loving wife, had remained in Damascus, nurturing and consoling his children and had wept when Al Taliph had bidden him farewell. Nothing could soothe his grief for the loss of Hephzibah, and his sorrow was genuine. He had not feigned his despair. Therefore, there had been no sensual communication between him and Aspasia.

Yet, but for him Aspasia would be in this house, and he, Al

Taliph, would not be on the verge of madness. From whom had come those letters, sent, received, on the road to Damascus and in Damascus, itself? There was but one answer: Thargelia. Yes, it could only be Thargelia. Al Taliph felt rage. He would go to the house of Thargelia as soon as possible and would drag Aspasia from the infamous purlieus. Or, his rage subsiding in a tide of hope, he would induce her to return to him, even if she had gone to another protector.

There was still the matter of Damos, who had betrayed his friendship.

Kurda stood before his master, waiting, watching the changeful expressions on Al Taliph's face, the arching and falling of his eyebrows as he thought, the red blood in his cheeks, the tightening of his mouth, then the loosening, then the paling of his colour.

'I have a task for you, Kurda,' Al Taliph said, and his voice was smooth and calm. 'But first let me present you with this purse, in token of my gratitude.'

Kurda was overwhelmed with elation and love and kissed Al Taliph's hand. 'Command me anything, lord!' he cried.

'You must go to Damascus, and you must contrive to have a man murdered quietly – Damos of Damascus. Do not do it yourself. Hire assassins. Do not return until the mission is accomplished.'

'To hear is to obey you, lord!' cried Kurda, joyfully, and ran to prepare himself for the journey and to plot Damos' death so dexterously that he, Kurda, would never be suspected of the conspiracy.

Then Al Taliph went to Miletus and sought out the aged Thargelia. She received him with every graciousness and every evidence of pleasure. She said to him at once, 'But why have you not brought my daughter, my loved Aspasia, to visit one who has such affection for her? Tell me, lord, how she fares in your house. Has she borne you children?'

Al Taliph regarded her with eyes like the points of daggers. He was sick with disappointment and the loss of his hope. He said, 'Has she not written to you, Thargelia, you who loved and cherished her so much?'

'I have had no word from her, Al Taliph, since she left for your house, nor have I written her myself. Why do you gaze at me so strangely? Is not Aspasia well?' Her simulation of alarm and dread was excellent and he was deceived.

'She is well,' he said to Thargelia and took his departure, refusing her offer to let him examine the young maidens in her house.

When he returned, after several months, he found Kurda at home. Kurda said nothing but only mutely nodded, with grinning satisfaction. Al Taliph gave him another purse.

Then he delivered himself up to despair for a long time.

PART TWO

Pericles

'Above all men, he was the most just.'

Zeno of Elea

CHAPTER I

After the learned man Zeno of Elea had seen Pericles, son of Xanthippus and Agariste, Xanthippus visited Zeno at his house. Concluding warm greetings, Xanthippus said, 'My son's mother, who is interested in appearance, which she insists is the first door to power, complains that Pericles' skull rises too high above his brow and features.'

'Does a great man mourn if he is not accepted by the acclamations of inferiors, the obscure, the unimportant? No. He rejoices, for what is commonly accepted is execrable and degrading and of little worth. A tumbler, an athlete, a jokester, a buffoon, a pugilist, a songster or an actor is applauded by the low multitude, whose appetites are the appetites of the barnyard. Who would wish to be applauded by such?'

'You are implying that my son is not of the mundane world?' said Xanthippus, with humour.

'Lord,' said Zeno with dignity, 'I was never mistaken in a pupil. Had I not looked into the calm, direct and radiant eyes of your son and had not seen what I have seen, I should not have consented to tutor him. He has a stately presence, even at his young age, and stateliness is to be much admired. I consider him the handsomest of youths, though he is but twelve years old. There is manhood in his demeanour, authority in his glance. I predict a future for him which will surmount the future of lower men, and which will ring through the ages.'

'I implore the gods that he will be a great soldier,' said the father.

'You speak as a soldier,' said the teacher, and smiled with indulgence. 'Your son, I believe, will be of military genius – I have observed him – but he will be the glory of his nation also. I have consulted the oracles at Delphi.'

'But that is superstitution,' said the father, who was extremely superstitious though in many ways sceptical and pragmatic.

'It is said,' the teacher remarked, 'that superstition is the child of experience. Who knows what controls the destiny and the affairs of men?'

The father thought, and stroked the fine white linen of his robe.

'You have mentioned "the glory of his nation." What is more glorious than a soldier?'

'It is said,' the teacher murmured, 'that history is the shadow of great men. Or, of monstrous men. Military genius is admirable, for it preserves a nation in its physical aspect. But there is another genius: the flame of intellect. Your son will possess both. As I have said, I have consulted the oracles of Delphi, and I swear that Apollo answered me.'

The father was incredulous. 'Apollo answered you, Zeno?'

The scholar averted his eyes, smiling, before the bright face of cynicism. 'I believe so, or a reasonable power. I am not a hysterical woman, nor a man given to idiot dreams. I weigh. I ponder. But something in my soul informs me that you son is not of common cast, nor is he concerned with common aspirations.'

Zeno of Elea, hailed by fellow philosophers as the creator of dialectic, was a young slight man with a thin, white and pointed face in which his black eyes were great orbs of scintillating light, dominating all his features. The perceptive listened to him with awe and rose when he entered a room or stopped to speak in a colonnade to students, and felt, when he had departed, that for a moment or two they had stood in the presence of an irresistible force, and that the very air had vibrated. His simplicity, they believed, was the simplicity of marble lighted by the sun, or, again, the simplicity of fire.

He had a considerable patrimony but lived without ostentation in the suburbs of Athens, content with a little square white house over which grew vine leaves on a lattice. He had no slaves, and attended to his own wants, even to making his own goat cheese and baking his bread and drinking the resinous wine of his own grapes.

He accepted but few private pupils, and then only one at a time and only when he was convinced that the pupil had unusual qualities of mind and spirit. Also, he was known as the master of paradoxes, and delighted in uttering them, so was in frequent danger of the pious and orthodox authorities and priests of Athens, for he often asserted that but One had existence and that belief in Many was in error. 'Yes, yes, Zeus, of the Unknowable can be given a name, but only Zeus,' he would say, though he acknowledged that sublime poetry lived in the concept of Many, and that monotheism could not be truly comprehended by the finite minds of men. 'If men cannot be simultaneously in ten thousand places, and have a universal awareness, then it is impossible for them to understand the omnipresence of Deity and omniscient consciousness, and instant and boundless cognizance.' So far the priests had not tormented or harassed him excessively for they thought him mad and of no importance.

Xanthippus had visited him one evening in his silver-decorated litter carried by six grandly-attired slaves. He had never met Zeno before, though he was aware of his fame, as he was a powerful politician as well as a notable soldier who had been a captain of a squadron which had annihilated part of Xerxes' fleet at Mycale. An astute man, he was also aware that ostentation would not impress Zeno, but he was a man who loved luxury and the trappings of riches, and, as he had said humorously to his wife, Agariste, he was no pretentious hypocrite who visited a wise man on foot in dusty sandals. Zeno was inspecting his new olive trees when Xanthippus arrived, and he turned his head and mildly studied his visitor. He had seen Xanthippus at a distance on many occasions, and recognized him, and came to greet him without apology for his stained hands and the withered leaves on his narrow shoulders. There was soil on one of his sunken white cheeks. But nothing could diminish the black splendour of his eyes nor the sudden lucidity of his smile. Xanthippus was unaccountably touched and when he looked into those eyes he was moved as many men were moved.

So he alighted from his litter instead of reclining on his cushions and addressing Zeno through parted curtains. He held out his strong soldier's hand, and Zeno took it with child-like guilelessness. Yet the shrewd politician and soldier understood that Zeno was no simpleton and possessed little vulnerability. He was armoured in his virtue.

In his turn Zeno studied his visitor, and was surprised, as always, by the face of Xanthippus, which denied his professions and his valour and genius as a military man. Xanthippus was tall for a Greek, and his body had the litheness of an athlete and the suppleness, and a peculiar swiftness of movement; he implied implicit power and masculinity. His face, long and narrow and pale and smooth, had the contemptuous delicacy of a Persian aristocrat. (In truth, he admired the Persians whom he had defeated.) This gave his expression a subtle arrogance, which had made him a great favourite with women. He wore the pointed short black beard of the Persians, and his nose was thin and aquiline and his mouth sensual and red and full. But his eyes were the colour of a Greek sky at noon, intensely and incredibly blue, if hard and clear. His eyebrows were black, as was his hair under the white hood of his robe, beginning too close at the inner corner of his eyes and then sweeping upwards the temples, giving him a cynical look that intimidated the less subtle.

'Greetings, Xanthippus, lord,' said Zeno.

'You know me, Zeno of Elea?' asked Xanthippus, with some surprise.

'I have seen you at a distance, Master,' replied the philosopher. He gestured towards his small white house, now smothered in the polished green of the spring grape vines.

'May I offer you my own wine and cheese and bread and a portion of fruit?'

'I thank you,' said Xanthippus. He gave Zeno a sharp and piercing glance of curiosity. Zeno's serenity and lack of tremulousness suggested that any explanation would inevitably come in good time from the other man and so needed but patience.

Xanthippus was accustomed to servility even from his equals, but Zeno was not servile. He stood aside to let Xanthippus precede him, but the soldier paused to look about him at the green land, the orchards, the groves, the high ground which permitted a view of the silver port of Piraeus, the acropolis with its crown of new low temples, and Athens, herself, white and rose-tinted in the first blush of sunset, and rising on her hills. Beyond lay the sea, flowing in aquamarine and streaks of running purple, and the ships at anchor, swaying in the breeze and the tide. Some were moving out to sea, and their white sails were full of blazing light. The soldier was not sentimental, though at secret heart he was a poet. As he gazed at the peace of the scene, and at Zeno's burst of gardens surrounding his little house, and at the goats grazing nearby, and inhaled the scent of the innocently lewd spring earth and grass and flowering tree, he felt the pride and humility and exultation of being a Greek. It was no wonder to him – though he did not believe in the gods – that the gods frequently preferred the noble earth of Greece to Olympus. And, most certainly, the daughters of the earth. The sea wind was as warm and pure as silk, as fresh as linen washed in the sun.

'This,' said Xanthippus, 'is a joyous place.'

'Yes, so it is, and so it will be in the future. Joy and beauty, passion and delight, and absolute resonance of mind and spirit.'

Zeno entered the house and placed upon the table a jug of goats' milk, a plate of ripe cheese, olives, some coarse but sweet-smelling bread, a ewer of wine, a bowl of herbs, honey, and asparagus and young berries all tart and exciting in their fragrance. There was also a little bowl of fresh garlic and a pitcher of vinegar and a yellow mound of pungent goats' butter. The plates and the goblets were of the red clay of Greece, and were the utensils of peasants. The spoons and the knives were of the basest of metals and the napkins of the roughest of linen.

'A feast,' said Xanthippus. His words had been but courtesy but he was surprised to feel a deep and contented consent in his heart. He sat down on a bench at the table and Zeno poured a libation to the gods and Xanthippus raised his eyebrows. Zeno smiled. 'If they exist, it will please them,' he said. Xanthippus laughed a little. He said to Zeno, 'I have a son, twelve years old. Pericles. I need a tutor for him, and I have heard much of you, Zeno of Elea.'

Zeno looked alarmed and anxious.

'Lord, I accept but few pupils, and only one at a time, and at my own desire.'

'What are your requirements for a pupil, Zeno?'

Zeno hesitated. He looked about his room as if in apology and dismay. 'Master, I take but unusual pupils, ones who intrigue my mind and excite my interest.' He raised his extraordinary eyes fully to the face of the soldier. 'Do you believe your son is such?'

Xanthippus pursed his mouth, then drank deeply of his goblet, which Zeno immediately refilled. The red sunlight struck on the face of Xanthippus and Zeno became interested, for he saw in full the half-disdainful, half-delicate formation of that subtle countenance.

'I believe my son has unusual qualities, even at his early age. He is grave. He is thoughtful. He has a certain reserve. He is interested in many strange things. He is disciplined, of himself. He needs no admonitions, no thrashings, no rebukes. He is of one piece, like the element of stone, like the configuration of marble.'

'Alas,' said Zeno.

Xanthippus was astonished and leaned back on his bench. 'Alas?'

'Such men are dangerous,' said Zeno. 'They know from the womb what it is they desire and none can turn them from it. They are imbued with destiny, and that is disastrous for other and lesser men.'

Xanthippus was inordinately flattered and pleased. 'It is possible,' he said, 'that I have exaggerated my son's qualities, as a father.'

'I hope so, and yet I hope not,' said Zeno, and he who was abstemious refilled his own goblet for the third time and drank hurriedly from it. He folded his large white hands, the hands of a sage, on the table and contemplated them. 'I will see your son,' he said.

'I will send a litter for you tomorrow,' said the soldier. He rose and Zeno rose with him and accompanied him to the gate where the slaves awaited. When Xanthippus had left him Zeno leaned on the gate and stared into the distance and brooded and once or twice he shook his head as if both excited and despondent.

CHAPTER II

Zeno looked between the embroidered curtains of the litter and at the hills of Athens already trembling with heat and radiance though it was still early morning, at the clustering white houses with their red tiled roofs and the lifting clouds of shining silver dust that wavered over everything and at the passionate blue of the Grecian sky.

The house of Xanthippus glittered white in the sun and the roof was like sparkling rubies. It was surrounded by a low white wall over which spilled a tide of red, purple, rose and white flowers and, beyond them, a barrier of pointed cypresses. But as the house was on a rise of land it was not entirely obscured. There was a slave at the gates attired as a soldier and he opened them and assumed a military posture. Now Zeno could see the grounds, all red gravelled paths and flower beds and exotic shrubbery in bloom and enormous Chinese vases filled with blossoms and polished green branches. The house was tall, of two storeys, with Ionian pillars which gleamed in the sunlight, and the atrium was cool with fountains and the scent of fern. It was among the more fastidious of the houses of little Athens, and all its appointments were elegant, and the artistic soul of Zeno approved.

He entered the coolness of the atrium and was greeted formally by Xanthippus who immediately suggested refreshments and the two men seated themselves in the shade of a wall of the outdoor portico and a slave brought a fine wine chilled in the waters of a spring, soft pale bread, fruit, excellent cheese, a plate of goose meat and one of cold pork in its own jelly, artichokes in olive oil and garlic and new berries still wet with dew. Zeno saw that the plates were both of silver and of the best ceramic design and the goblets were Egyptian glass wreathed with silver vine leaves and grapes.

A slave stood behind him with a long fan of palm leaves which, as it waved, not only brought a cool breeze but kept off flies. Xanthippus poured a libation to the gods, and smiled at Zeno, who followed his example. A babble of high female voices and laughter came from the rear of the house and the women's quarters. Xanthippus said, 'My wife, Agariste, is not stupid and ignorant as are most of the Athenian wives, for she was tutored in her father's house and has,' he paused and smiled, 'an elevated opinion of herself and her intellect. Nevertheless, I have found her counsel felicitous on a number of occasions, and she has flashes of wisdom which can be daunting to a man. She has desired to see you after you see our son. I trust this will not offend you.'

Zeno hesitated, then inclined his head. 'I have visited the School of the Courtesans and have met there women of extraordinary intellect as well as beauty, and have conversed with them to my edification. Thargelia, who conducts such a school in Miletus at this time, is a woman of magnificent gifts of the mind and spirit, and it is a delight to visit her.'

'Ah, yes,' said Xanthippus, who possessed a mistress who had been a protégée of the School, 'she is a paragon of what women should be but are not. Perhaps it is fortunate for our nation, for, it is written by the Sibyls, when women dominate a nation and their men and intrude their voices into politics and the arts of war and intellect that nation will decay and fall.'

The overseer of the hall came and Xanthippus commanded the presence of his son, Pericles.

The young Pericles entered the portico with his attendant slave, an elderly man with a beard. Zeno looked at the child who was twelve years old. Xanthippus looked at his son with smiling pride and said, 'His mother, as you may know, Zeno of Elea, is the grandchild of Ceisthenes, who drove out the sons of Pisistratas, and thus put an end to the Tyrants and attempted to return to the laws and principles of Solon. But that, as we know, was an impractical dream. My wife said to her slaves, being near her time of delivery of my son, that she was brought to bed of a lion.' Xanthippus put his dexterous tongue into his cheek and winked at Zeno.

The sun in the portico was blinding and vivid even at this hour. Pericles stood in the reflected brilliance quietly and with containment, almost as if indifferent to the scrutiny of a stranger, and as if his thoughts were fixed on some distance. He was tall for one so young and slender but muscular. He seemed much older than his years. He was clad in the short green tunic of preadolescence with the Greek key as its border on the bottom and about the sleeves, and his legs were slight but firm and his feet, in their sandals, long and narrow. His body had that elegance and grace much admired by the Athenians. His face showed the thinness but strength of his patrician bones, so subtly formed that they appeared to lie close to the flesh and to dominate it. His nose was slightly aquiline and his pink mouth was full and faintly sensual but finely carved and controlled. His eyes were of so pale a blue between pale lashes that it was almost as if they had no hue but were the eyes of a statue. His hair was the colour of bright flax and curled at his nape and about his cheeks, and his white neck was long and thin and upright and flexible.

All this made for a certain exquisite and masculine beauty except for his brow, which, though the colour and rigidity of marble, rose to an unusual height as did the crown of his head, and gave an elongation out of proportion to the face, thus diminishing and dwarfing it. Such a grotesque height would have attracted the attention of the priests and authorities as being abnormal and Pericles, had he been born of less illustrious parents, would have been allowed to die entombed in a large vase. For the authorities did not permit deviations in body or distortions of countenance or other grotesqueries to survive.

Zeno, in deference to the boy – for were not children susceptible to adult stares? – did not direct the full power of his eyes on Pericles, but fixed them at a point near the child's cheek.

'Greetings, Pericles, son of Xanthippus,' said Zeno in his high kind voice.

The boy responded, 'Greetings, Zeno of Elea.' Zeno was surprised at the depth of Pericles' voice, for it was not the piping of children.

'I have told my son of you, Zeno,' said Xanthippus, 'and that I am attempting to persuade you to be his tutor.'

For the first time Pericles looked fully at Zeno, and again Zeno was surprised, for it was not the wary and suspicious stare of a young boy but the calculation and weighing of a man, fearless yet cautious.

Zeno, gazing at the youth, knew with all his intuition that he had no need to question Pericles to discover his intelligence. Those pale eyes were implicit with cold inner fire and intellect, with judiciousness and latent power, and glowed with that radiance which can come but from an unusually intelligent mind. Pericles had brought his attention to Zeno from a far place where his thoughts were engaged, yet when he had done so it was with a certain piercing and cogent vigour which was totally aware and focused, and not diffused or vague.

Truly, thought Zeno, a most remarkable child – if one can call him a child – and one with potential terribleness.

Zeno had never said this to another prospective student, but he said it now: 'Do you accept me as your tutor, Pericles, son of Xanthippus?'

At this the youth smiled urbanely, and flashed a glance at his father. 'I do,' he said, and Zeno, laughing a little inwardly at himself, thought: I have been given an accolade!

'He reads and writes adequately,' said the subtle Xanthippus, who had understood the exchange and was gratified. He fingered his black and pointed beard and struck an attitude in his chair. 'Then, it is settled,' he said. 'You will not find my son stupid, Zeno of Elea, but possessed of a mind of curiosity and eagerness to be enlightened and guided.'

I doubt if he can ever be guided, except by a woman and then only on occasion, thought the wry Zeno.

'His mother has been educated by tutors in her father's house,' said Xanthippus, 'her father being deluded that women possess intellects.' He smiled. He held out his hand negligently to his son, and Pericles went to him and took that hand and leaned against his father's shoulder.

Zeno could not restrain himself and he said, 'Pericles, it is not in your nature to accept anyone immediately. Why have you accepted me?'

'I have read some of your writings,' said the youth.

Zeno raised his eyebrows. 'And what did you think of them, my child?'

'They are lucid,' said Pericles. He smiled at Zeno and it was as if he were a man, cognizant and a little amused.

Zeno became grave. 'That is a compliment,' he said. 'If the young can understand a sage then he has succeeded in being intelligible.'

He saw that Pericles was regarding him with that disturbing convergence of his which permitted no intruding thought at the moment.

Xanthippus dismissed his son with a kiss on his lips, and Pericles bowed formally to Zeno and took his departure with his slave. He did not run, flailing his limbs aimlessly, as did other children. He walked with the firmness and quiet of a man. Zeno said to Xanthippus, 'Your son is not a child. He is a man, and I am honoured to teach him.' His eyes ached from the light and from his thoughts.

'Perhaps it is true that my wife was brought to bed by a lion,' said Xanthippus, and laughed. 'A white lion with a golden mane. Does not my son resemble such?'

Zeno did not answer frivolously as Xanthippus expected. He considered, and then he said, 'Yes.' Xanthippus looked at him dubiously, then he shrugged. He struck his hands for the overseer and when the slave entered Xanthippus said, 'Summon the Lady Agariste from the gynaikeion [women's quarters] to attend her husband immediately.'

Agariste entered the portico attended by two female slaves with the customary short hair and simple long tunics and bare arms and feet. But Agariste wore a peplos of saffron linen with a golden girdle intricately wrought, and she was so tall that she had no need of the high-heeled shoes worn by other rich Athenian ladies. Her shoulder pins glittered with jewels and there were many jewelled rings on her long, white and very slender hands and bracelets on her narrow arms. She had a noble figure if one too thin for the taste of many men, and her bosom swelled under the folds of the peplos in a delightful fashion and it was evident that she had no necessary recourse to the strophion to elevate it. Her hair was naturally fair and of a fine gilt sheen, and so abundant and so full of tendrils and waves that she wore no false wigs or supplements to increase its bounty. It was bound with golden ribbons. Zeno saw that it was from his mother that Pericles had inherited the strong refinement of facial structure, the milky complexion, the carved mouth and aquiline nose and the almost colourless blue of the large eyes. But Agariste was haughty and cold whereas her young son was grave and stately.

'Zeno of Elea, the Lady Agariste, the mistress of my house,' said Xanthippus, who admired, respected but heartily disliked his wife. He loved her in his way for her gifts of character and her beauty and her family history; however, he frequently discovered her tedious for she had no humour at all but only arrogance.

She bowed slightly and coldly to Zeno. Xanthippus did not invite her to be seated and she could not sit without her husband's invitation. She glanced swiftly at an empty chair of ebony inlaid with pearl and when Xanthippus said nothing a slight flush ran over her face.

Studying her, Xanthippus finally said, 'You wished to speak with Zeno of Elea, Lady?' He leaned back in his chair, then negligently lifted a citron to his mouth and sucked at its juices.

Mortification heightened her colour. She did not look at Zeno but addressed her husband: 'Lord, you consider him an adequate tutor for our son?'

Zeno began to pity her. He said, 'Lady Agariste, I find Pericles most exemplary, and I feel destiny in him. Therefore, I have consented to teach him.'

Agariste, her humiliation growing, yet heard Zeno's voice and, more to her liking, his words. She turned her face to him though she kept her eyes averted. She had a voice as chill as snow and as colourful. She said, 'Zeno of Elea, you repeat what I have heard in my dreams and have seen in my visions. I do not feel that you are exaggerating or flattering, but speak only the truth.'

'It is true, Lady,' said Zeno.

'You are pleased, Agariste?' Xanthippus asked, as if addressing a superior favourite among his slave women. He shifted seductively in his chair.

Agariste inclined her head and Zeno had to admire her

composure and dignity for all she was a woman of no pleasant ways.

'Good. Then you may retire,' said her husband and waved his hand graciously.

He knew that she had intended to question Zeno sharply, and to impress on him the honour he had been offered, and that she had intended to cow him while she, too, studied his theories and words. She had hoped to engage his mind and make him admire her attributes. Throwing up her noble head she turned and, accompanied by her maidens, left the presence of the men, her peplos as quiet as yellow stone. Xanthippus watched her leave and affected to study her figure and her movements as men study the gifts of the hetairai and are about to choose among them. Zeno did not find this risible.

Xanthippus saw this and smiled. 'The Lady Agariste is a female of many talents and not only beauty,' he said. He paused. 'Her conversation is chiselled out of granite.'

Zeno could not help smiling. 'I will return at dawn to-morrow to begin the instruction of my student,' he said, and took his leave.

He believed the oracles at Delphi to be fraudulent and ridiculous and the imposture of priests hungry for lavish offerings from the superstitious and the gullible. Still, an oracle had predicted the defeat of Xerxes and his barbarians when the very thought had been preposterous and even priests had fled their temples. Another had predicted the future fame and glory of Greece, and Zeno, not often mystical, believed that implicity.

Five years ago they had announced the birth of a great hero who would bring down the imperial lightning from Olympus and from the hands of Zeus upon this small city of only forty thousand souls, the majority of whom were slaves, and would write the name of Athens in immortal marble for the blinkless stare of the centuries.

CHAPTER III

'It has been asked from the beginning,' said Zeno to his pupil, and with a courteous glance at Agariste who sat nearby, listening keenly and severely, ' "What is man?" The first brute in the skins of animals asked that when he suddenly contemplated himself in quiet pools in the primeval forests. "Who am I?" he asked. "I mate and live and breed and eat and defecate and die as do the animals which I hunt. Yet, I discern a difference. What is that difference which makes me a man?" He was less moral than the beasts of the jungles and the plains and the mountains. He discerned that the beasts had their own code of morality, discipline and behaviour, which could not be violated except at the cost of death or destruction.

'Was he less than the beasts after all? In all the capacities of their bestial nature they were superb, decisive, confident. He, himself, was not. We know that man possesses few instincts, and that he chooses by his own will, to a large extent, what he will think and what his future shall be. That is the crucial difference between man and the other beasts. The Choice. Does that ability make him an outlaw in the very natural world in which he was conceived, or does his disobedience to the law make him superior to them? He is not at peace with himself.

'We speak of the dominance of reason in men's affairs. Reason has been analysed. It is based, they say, on the observation of a common reality, an admission of what reality is. But what is reality to me is possibly not reality to you, Pericles, or to other men. If we are to know what man is, we have to know what reality is.'

'On what, then, can we base our lives and sculpture our features?' asked the young Pericles, who was now fifteen years old.

Zeno reflected. 'It is necessary for objective laws, for we are a lawless and passionate and wicked and vindictive species. We have agreed that it is necessary for the survival of our tribe to have objective laws, though we are vehemently at war with law, both subjective and objective. We do not accept, as the beasts accept. Of what mysterious fruit have we eaten in that we are rebels even against ourselves, and challenge even the gods?'

He looked into the pale and thoughtful eyes of his pupil, which told him nothing except that the young Pericles was thinking.

'No one has truly defined what is a man. The answer may be in the mind of God. It certainly is not in ours, no matter how emphatic the priest or the philosopher or the scientist.' Zeno smiled slightly, and ate a date.

'Young Anaxagoras has said that we are men because we have opposing thumbs. But so do various monkeys, and they have never raised a temple nor formulated a body of laws of their own. Others have said we are different because we think, that we are conscious of thinking, that we are conscious of ourselves. I have observed some dogs and notably the Egyptian cats. I am convinced they think, also.' He laughed.

'You are inconsistent, Zeno of Elea,' said Agariste, as she sat with her son and his tutor in the outside portico in the growing sunset. 'You set paradoxes and then smile at them as if with pleasure. You pose questions but never answer them. You hint of mysteries, propound them, then dismiss them as trivialities.'

Zeno glanced at her with pity. She sat like a princess in her lemonwood chair inlaid with ivory, with her female slave behind her waving a long palm-leaf fan; her hair was like wheat in the late sun. She advanced her intelligence, not with calmness and modesty or as even an equal, but with a kind of triumphant defiance and overweening pride. In this, thought Zeno, she does not confirm the theory that women are intelligent. He smiled at Agariste gently.

'Lady,' he said, and was somewhat vexed that the young Pericles was watching him with a spark of amusement in his eyes, 'it is my intention to have my pupil ponder on my questions and paradoxes and seeming contradictions and inconsistencies, and formulate answers and theories of his own, which we will discuss.'

'I believe it is the duty of a teacher to present facts and the reasons for the facts,' said Agariste, with severity.

'Lady,' said Zeno, 'there is a vast difference between philosophy and what we have universally agreed is the truth.'

'You do not agree that there is any absolute truth?'

Zeno hesitated. He studied the gardens about the house, the walls overflowing with colour, and beyond them the silver ribs of the hills of Greece, thrusting out between the firs and the cypresses and olive groves that covered them like a mantle which quivered in the evening breeze. But the zenith yet was like blue fire.

'Absolute truth, Lady,' he said at last, 'is not to be known by men, just as no man can reach any truth by himself alone. The absolute truth, like absolute reality, is the prerogative of God and none other.'

'You do not believe, then,' said Agariste, 'that men are like gods, though Homer has hinted of it?'

'I do not quarrel with Homer,' replied Zeno, 'for he was a poet and the majority of men are not poets. We are more akin to the beast of the field, and once we understand him we can begin the painful climb to our own mystery – from that mutual standing ground.'

Agariste tossed her head. Pericles said to his tutor, offering him a blue and white bowl, 'Refresh yourself with an apple, Zeno.' Zeno looked at him sharply and saw a subtle gleam on the boy's face, and he wanted to laugh but refrained out of respect for Agariste.

'You do not deny the reality and truth of Thermopylae?' said Agariste, with umbrage.

'I know we held the Persians there to some extent,' said

Zeno. 'But, as many in the east assert, perhaps all is illusion.' He bit into the apple Pericles had given him and sipped a little wine. He stood at the table, rather than sat, for though like many sages he preferred to sit Agariste irritated even his gentle and serene state of mind.

'Illusion!' cried Agariste, moving strongly in her chair so that her pale blue robe was agitated, and her breast rose up and down in disquiet. 'That is not only a foolishness, Zeno of Elea, but treason!'

Zeno closed his eyes briefly. He heard a faint chuckle near his elbow and knew that it came from Pericles, who was leaning back on his student's hard stool and enjoying himself at both his mother's expense and his tutor's.

'You do not even wear a dagger!' cried Agariste, exasperated by Zeno's silence, which she interpreted as a deprecation of her intellect as a woman. 'What is a man without the smallest weapon with which to defend himself?'

Zeno deplored this. Agariste was a woman of mind, but she could descend to trivialities and personal attacks on those who offered a thought which conflicted with hers.

He said, with mildness, 'From whom, and what, Lady, should I defend myself? I am a humble philosopher and teacher.'

Then Pericles spoke. 'Zeno, there are many who would attack you. You may believe yourself the least inoffensive of men, but a number of your ideas and words have aroused antagonism in the city.' He beckoned to a slave near the doors of the house, and when the man approached he said with a sudden authority which surprised Zeno, 'Bring the illustrious Zeno of Elea one of the lord Xanthippus' daggers at once.'

He then looked intently at Zeno and said with firmness, 'It is my decree.'

The slave brought an Egyptian dagger of considerable value, set with turquoises and amethysts and deep red stones, some of them intricately carved. 'This is very valuable as well as beautiful,' said Zeno. 'Will not the lord Xanthippus object to this gift when he returns?'

'He has the highest regard for you,' said Pericles. 'He would deny you nothing.'

Zeno fastened the dagger to his worn silver belt. It felt awkward against his thigh. Pericles observed him with a mocking smile. 'I trust you understand how to use a dagger, Zeno?'

Zeno became grave and his glowing face darkened. 'I know how to use a sword also,' he said.

Pericles raised his pale golden eyebrows. 'In war?'

'In defence,' said Zeno. He looked intently at Agariste, who was calculating the value of the dagger, and Pericles saw this. He turned with courtesy to his mother but also with imperiousness. 'My mother,' he said, 'may I request that Zeno and I be left alone for a discussion?'

Agariste rose at once and her slave with her, but her lovely face was crimson. She exclaimed, 'Am I of so inferior an intelligence that I cannot understand this – Zeno?'

'We will speak as men.' Pericles turned from his mother, overtly expecting her obedience, and gave his attention to Zeno, who was embarrassed again for the poor woman. She left immediately, her head high, and again Zeno pitied her.

When Agariste had departed Zeno sat down, placed his sharp elbows on the table, and contemplated the cheese and wine and bread and honeycomb and fruit and olives before him. Zeno nibbled; he was not aware he was nibbling. His thoughts were far away.

At last he said, as if meditating to himself, 'You have asked me if I am afraid of weapons. And I replied that once I carried a sword, but discarded it. I killed two men with my sword.'

Pericles was amazed. He said, 'But you refuse to be present when I take my fencing lessons!'

'True. It is my own remembrance. Many men deserve to be executed but it is a horror to the executioner. I cannot forget the men I killed – though they eminently deserved to die.'

'We have a conscience,' said Pericles, and made a mouth of derision which was also half-humorous.

'So do animals,' said Zeno.

He looked again at the domestic animals. He said, 'You have observed the mating instincts of these?'

Pericles said, 'Yes.'

'Then you know it is the way we human beings mate also.'

Pericles was faintly amused. 'Yes, that I know. Our bodies are as much animal as the bodies of the beasts.'

Zeno nodded. 'It is when we depart from the profound instincts of our nature that we become less than the beasts.'

Pericles frowned. 'Elucidate,' he said.

Zeno said, 'There is a philosophy which is recent in our history, though it is ancient in practice. But we Greeks like to give a white cloak of morality to our sins, though older civilizations are more cynical and pragmatic. We Greeks say that our wives and our concubines do not entirely satisfy us, and that men cannot feel true love for a woman, who is lesser and inferior and has no mind or soul of any consequence. Therefore, we must seek our ideal love and perfection of understanding among our own sex, for exultant exchange of ideas. Do not men live by ideas and poetry and communication?'

Zeno continued. 'If love between men, of the same sex, were confined to argument and ideas and conversation and the excitement of the exchange of theories, none would have objection.'

Pericles was silent.

Zeno said, after a pause, 'But when men substitute other men in the physical capacity of a woman, then they enter into a twilight world not only of perversion of nature, but in the perversion of their own minds and souls.'

Pericles' light blue eyes widened innocently, and he said, 'Is that possible?'

Zeno fixed his own eyes upon the youth and thought, 'Ah,

176

that feigned innocence!' He said to Pericles, 'Let us be men. Let me say this: The love between a man and a woman, if really love, is a great mystery and a great glory. It exalts, it edifies, it elevates, it makes them one flesh, almost immune to outward calamity, steadfast, the deepest intimacy any human being can know, beyond friendship, beyond the mere breeding of children.'

Pericles said, smilingly, 'You have not married.'

'I have loved,' said Zeno. 'I have loved many women, but have found none whom I wished to marry.' He paused. 'Some years ago I engaged a young scribe, for my friends wished what I wrote, and said, to be recorded. So, I found an erudite youth called Phelan, of much education and refinement and an intuitive and deductive mind. I took him into my house, where he could write down my musings and my sudden thoughts, as well as my dissertations and my theories.'

Zeno rubbed his chin thoughtfully. 'If I had been more discerning I should have noticed that Phelan was a youth of too much delicacy and sensitivity, and that he had a girlish appearance. He was also given to emotion and impulsiveness, and his responses were unseemly in a man. It is true that great poets and other artists can be moved to tears by the grandeur of a sunset or a statue or an epic – but Phelan could be deeply moved by the nuzzling of a lamb or a young goat, and would weep at the soft texture of linen or the sight of a young child bubbling saliva. These are womanish manifestations, but I hardly noticed them.'

Zeno watched Pericles with an inscrutable but observant eye as he spoke in his quiet and harmonious voice.

But Phelan's extreme and even hysterical sensibility did not decrease with time, nor did his high ecstasies for all that Zeno said, even the most inconsequential. This was sometimes embarrassing to the sage, but he was by nature indulgent and kind. He, himself, had become so engrossed with the exhilarating excursions of his mind, and excursions into the minds of others, that he failed to see the obvious:

Phelan was in love with him, as a woman loves a man.

'It is extraordinarily dangerous for a man to live by his mind alone,' said Zeno to the listening Pericles, 'for then he can stumble on the merest pebble in his path and break his neck, a pebble that even an infant would have avoided. It is true that Phelan often made me uneasy, with his obvious adoration and worship of me – which I unwisely attributed to his youth and to a gentle lack of sophistication. Then one day I said to him, "You must not constantly follow me about, Phelan, as if precious rubies were falling from my lips when all I wish is to scratch my anus in private." I had hoped to make him laugh, but he only blushed and looked at me with abject reverence and said, "Rubies, Master, fall from your lips even when you are silent." He turned his head suddenly and kissed my hand, then fell upon his knees, clasped his arms about my own knees, and confessed his love for me with such passion, such stammering candour, that repelled though I was I could not feel disgust but only pity and sadness.'

Zeno sighed and drew his hands across his eyes and looked at the last red rays of the sun over the purpling western hills. 'I should not have been so aghast, so startled. The evidence had been before me for a long time, and I could see it all at that moment, and despised myself for my blindness. I raised up Phelan as kindly as I could, speaking calmly, but he threw his arms about me and kissed me on the lips, as a wild girl would do. It was a wanton kiss, but still it had some innocence and a childlike recklessness.' Zeno looked at Pericles, and said, almost inaudibly, 'Do you understand, my pupil?'

'Yes,' said Pericles. 'I have heard of all this from my several companions, though not with the honesty you have shown, my teacher, nor the pity and understanding.'

'Ah,' said Zeno, and he was relieved. He said, 'And what do you think of it, Pericles?'

The boy shrugged. 'I find it neither repulsive nor attractive. But you have spoken of the attack on you by armed men.'

'I find it difficult to come to an absolute decision and to act

178

with authority,' Zeno confessed. 'So, though I sweated openly and cringed inwardly at the necessity, I discharged Phelan and sent him home to his father, writing the latter that I had come to the conclusion that my "immortal words" were not worth the recording, and remarking on Phelan's extraordinary intelligence and competence and loyalty.

'Phelan left me in tears with prayers to reconsider. Such men as Phelan have a woman's secret intuition. It took me hours to induce him to leave my house, whereas another man would have forced him to leave within moments. There are times,' Zeno reflected, 'when I believe that kindness is often cowardice rather than a noble virtue.'

When Zeno had been a youth his father had sent him to the best fencing school in Athens. Though Athenians did not make the finest soldiers, they having too much humour and satirical intelligence, they could fight almost as valiantly as the Spartan when forced to do so. 'It astonished my father even more than it astonished me,' said Zeno to Pericles, 'when I became an excellent swordsman, for both of us had believed that cold metal and I had no sympathy. When I was pronounced perfect by my fencing master my father gave me a fine sword of my own, keen as a razor, as viciously pointed as a woman's tongue. It had a gold hilt set with jewels. To please my father I wore it constantly.'

He paused, and his face became melancholy. 'I slept with it in my bed, even when with a woman companion. It saved my life, shortly after I had dismissed Phelan.

'For, one moonlit night my house was invaded by two armed men in cloaks and hoods. They burst open my door and advanced upon me with daggers glittering and bare in the sharp moonlight. Fortunately I was still awake or I should have been murdered in my bed. Hesitation would have cost me my life. I sprang to my feet and seized my ready sword, and rushed at the nearest man and impaled him. He fell at once, his hood falling from his head, and he died without a sound. I saw it was Phelan.

'My horror at this almost caused my own death, for I stood mute and frozen for an instant or two, seeing the dark hot blood welling from my poor secretary's heart. Then, through the corner of my eye I saw the other man lunging upon me. I moved aside and he inflicted a slight wound on my left shoulder. A second earlier and it would have pierced my heart. Then I struck at him with my sword and it entered his belly, and he fell, clutching at himself and groaning, and his dagger flew from his hand.

'I knelt beside him and raised his head by his hair, and saw that he was some coarse ruffian or a slave, and I hated him as I could not hate Phelan, who was still a youth and this was a man of middle age and brutal. I beat his head savagely on the floor and demanded an explanation. I did not recognize myself,' Zeno added, smiling sombrely, 'but I believe it was Phelan's death that enraged me, and broke my heart. The fact that Phelan had desired my extinction seemed less heinous to me than that this man, a stranger, had desired it also.

'The brute confessed that he was a slave in the house of Phelan's father, and was devoted to the youth on whom he had lavished a father's affection. Phelan had told him that I had insulted him "mortally," had abused him before companions in the colonnades, had ridiculed him and reviled him as a man of no intellect. And then, with invective, had dismissed him, urging him to lower his ambitions to carrying wood for the baths. He had incited this slave to rage, then had begged for advice, and the slave had assured him that only my blood would wash out my iniquities against the son of an illustrious house. Phelan had then suggested that his slave accompany him to my own house for that very purpose. So, they had come.'

Zeno was then silent for so long that Pericles finally said, 'How was this explained to the city guards and the judges?'

Zeno rubbed his chin and looked towards the west where a racing purple cloud had begun to cover the falling sun, thus darkening the landscape so that the white houses and buildings shone like bare bones in the quickening gloom.

'It was of Phelan's father that I thought,' said Zeno. 'So I dragged the bodies far down the slope of my hillside and let them fall below, and I threw their daggers after them.'

Pericles looked incredulously at the small stature and slightness of his teacher.

'It is remarkable what strength can be summoned in an emergency,' said Zeno. 'I was desperate not only to save the sensibilities of Phelan's father, a friend, but to conceal from him his son's aberration, for he is a proud man and an eminent soldier and would have died of grief to learn of his son's – peculiarity – and also to learn that that son, without pro-vocation, had hired a slave and had accompanied him to kill a sleeping man. I returned to my house and washed my floor with lye and water to drive away the bloodstains. At dawn I went to the temple of Ares, who was never my favourite god, to offer sacrifice for the souls of the men I had been forced to kill, and to display my gratitude for the strength Ares had chosen to give me in those most awful moments.

'After the authorities had conducted their investigations they declared that Phelan, and his slave, had been murdered by thieves when on their way to visit me.'

Zeno fell silent again and Pericles waited. Then Zeno said, 'Since that time I have never carried a sword, though it hangs on the wall of my house. I avoid circumstances and situations wherein I could be induced to display my swordsmanship in defence of my life.'

'Such circumstances and situations cannot always be avoided,' said Pericles. His fair hair shimmered like polished gold in the mingled light and darkness of the approaching storm. 'You often walk to your house and refuse my father's litter. Suppose you were truly set upon by thieves and had no means of defence. Would you die meekly? Is that not cowardice in itself?'

Zeno reluctantly laughed. 'I have taught you too much logic,' he said. He looked down at the dagger fastened to his girdle. 'I think I shall keep this weapon, after all, and wear it always, as do other Athenian men. Self-defence is no crime; to refuse to defend yourself is the instinct of a slave, not a man.' He sighed. 'Still, it is a monstrous comment on our times that sometimes we must kill in order not to be killed.'

He suddenly stood up as if seized by restlessness and walked to the parapet outside the portico and stared at the murky west. Pericles slowly joined him and they gazed down at the city and up at the sky. All at once lightning struck a scarlet crevice in the heavens and soon thereafter thunder bellicosely roared in answer. For an instant Pericles was illuminated in vivid eerie light and Zeno looked at him with new comprehension. It was as if a white and gold statue had been precipitated into being.

Thank the gods, thought Zeno. I had thought him too controlled, too much in command of himself, too removed. Thank the gods for men who can be moved to disquietude!

The storm increased and the palms lashed and the earth exhaled a hot odour as of both panic and desire, and dark and brilliant shadows raced over the city below. Zeno touched his pupil on the shoulder and said, 'Do not be too much disturbed. Life will crush your heart or turn it to stone. It is inevitable. But, you have your choice.'

Pericles lifted his eyes to the dusky height of the acropolis. 'I have a dream,' he said, as if he had not heard Zeno at all. Then he turned and smiled at his teacher. 'A dream of marble, but it will be alive.' From the women's quarters the slave girls had begun to sing, accompanied by the tinkling notes of lutes, and to Zeno it sounded very brave in the face of the rising storm. It is all the answer we can return, he thought. It is all we can say to the terrible gods. Courage.

It was inevitable that Xanthippus' unorthodox views on gods and governments come to the attention of both the priests and the government and that they should be extremely interested, for many envied him. Moreover, there were the letters from his discreet friends sadly denouncing him, and some were men of consequence, and had power and riches.

Xanthippus was politely invited to appear at noon next day before the priests and the Ecclesia for a 'consultation,' for he was too respected a man to be seized and dragged before them, and he was rich and powerful. It was the intention of some of the priests and the judges merely to rebuke him and restrain him, but others wished his death though they feared him. The hero was not a mere chattering philosopher or fervent teacher, whose fatal disposition would cause little comment, yet that fact made him even the more dangerous.

When Xanthippus received the summons he went to his concubine, Gaia, in her beautiful small house which he had given her. Lying in her bed he told her of his predicament. She sat beside him, naked and rosy as Aphrodite newly risen from the sea, her tawny hair thrown back so none of her delights were hidden. Her nipples were like tight rosebuds and her mouth was a warm flame. While she listened gravely her agile mind was busy. She knew a man of formidable influence in Athens, who greatly admired Xanthippus, and for an hour in her bed, unknown to Xanthippus, he would do her bidding and listen to her pleas.

'Tomorrow, at noon?' she murmured. 'Then, I must hasten and pray in the temple of Pallas Athene who is all wisdom and protects the wise, and surely you are wise, my Xanthippus.'

Xanthippus loved Gaia more dearly than he knew, and he was naturally indulgent towards women. So he shortly left her so that she could go to the temple. He restlessly went to his groves of olive trees. After he had departed Gaia summoned one of her slaves and sent him with a message to the man who ardently desired her. She bathed in scented water and slaves rubbed her body with perfumed oils and brushed her hair until it shone like an autumn leaf in the sun. She arrayed herself in a soft blue peplos with one arm exposed, on which she fastened a bracelet which her heretofore disappointed suitor had sent her nestled in a bower of lilies. She felt no pang of sacrifice or aversion. Men were men, and every man offered pleasure and took it with joy and gratitude, and she knew well how to please and all the arts of love. She pondered on which art he particularly liked, and which posture. She smiled. She loved Xanthippus, and this excursion would do him no harm but much good, and he would never know. She was a dexterous woman. She prepared to enjoy herself also, for a passive woman was no real lover. Slaves changed the silken sheets of her bed and sprayed perfume about her room and she studied her perfect body contemplatively. She would even endure the perversion of flogging for Xanthippus. She prayed that the man who would visit her would prefer more exotic and tender delights. However, a woman never knew a man until she had lain with him, for all a man's childlike simplicity. Or, she mused, was it really a brutish simplicity? No matter. She rubbed more scent on her loins and commanded a repast in the atrium when her visitor arrived. Her kitchen was famous.

'Ah, Athene,' she said aloud, 'you are the goddess of wisdom, sprung from the brow of Zeus in full apparel. But Aphrodite is the most potent of all the gods, and everything that lives bows before her.'

Xanthippus, who also admired Gaia's mind, for she had been well trained in that also, had given her a small alabaster statue of Athene Parthenos. She had it moved from her bedside and an indecent statue of Aphrodite and Adonis substituted. She smiled at the entwined lovers. She would ask no jewels; she would ask only for the life of Xanthippus. Later, if Teos desired a permanent arrangement, she would deal with that gracefully.

Xanthippus went to the Court of Justice on the Pnyx which was half-way up the acropolis. The Ecclesia and the priests were waiting for him in a semi-circle in a small circular room of brown and white marble. They sat severely and solemnly in their chairs. The priests contemplated their clasped hands which lay on their knees, and they appeared to pray for wisdom and enlightenment. The judges appeared more brisk and portentous. All wore white robes, like statues. Along one rounded wall was a row of marble benches for advocates and other interested men. Only two sat there today, and one was Zeno and one was Teos, one of the great dissolute citizens of Athens.

No one spoke when Xanthippus entered except for a robed man near the bronze double doors who announced in a voice like Nemesis: 'The noble lord, Xanthippus, enters to be judged.' Xanthippus paused for a moment for he recognized Zeno and Teos, and his black brows lifted. A philosopher and a lascivious man of Athens were all who cared enough for his fate to appear in his behalf, or at least to listen! His faint smile widened. None was so ineffective as a philosopher, and Teos, notorious for his fat living and his women and his gaiety and wealth and his lack of interest in politics, was certainly the strangest of advocates for an accused man!

Xanthippus was only casually acquainted with Teos, for they had nothing in common. They met occasionally in the houses of mutual friends, but Teos' crude jests, his flippant manner and his way of laughing boisterously offended Xanthippus who thought him light-minded and a fool and a rascal – for it was well known that Teos used bribery to manipulate government to grant his requests. He was no soldier, betrayed no concern for the fate of Athens, was good-natured to the point of ridiculousness, and appeared to prefer the company of low fellows, and even freedmen, to his peers, and could often be found drinking foul wine in dirty and crowded taverns among thieves and scoundrels from the waterfront and from filthy alleys of the city.

He bored Xanthippus, who usually avoided him. 'He is a perpetual youth,' Xanthippus would say, 'with desires like a satyr and the discriminations of the basest of slaves and the intelligence of a fish.' Sometimes he had found himself impatiently disliking this happiest of men who never engaged in weighty matters and found existence without a purpose and who rejected any responsibility except for his own enjoyment. 'There is a time for everything,' Xanthippus would say, 'and there is a time to be a fool, but not always.' Xanthippus, who was genial enough himself, and often found life ridiculous and without an object, and liked a jest as well as any other man, was frequently angered that Teos seemed to find him heavy and ponderous and without humour. In fact, the sort of man he, Xanthippus, despised himself.

Yet here Teos, the irresponsible, the flagrant, the reprobate, the fool, the man without imagination or subtlety, who knew nothing of poetry or the intricacies of the law, sat with a profound philosopher like Zeno as advocate of Xanthippus! There was something humorous in the situation, Xanthippus told himself, but he could not as yet discern it. Certainly Teos was no close friend of his and had never found his company entertaining or desirable. As for Zeno, he was suspected by the very priests and judges before whom he sat in silent dignity – and in his unimpressive appearance.

'Where is your advocate, lord?' asked one of the judges, a severe man of massive countenance and cold eyes.

Xanthippus stood before them, and all at once he wanted to laugh. He bowed to the lonely marble bench where sat Zeno and Teos. 'These are my advocates,' he said, and his neat black beard twitched. Three of the most important judges and priests studiously examined the parchments before them and their faces were sinister and momentous.

Someone cleared his throat noisily. A priest lifted a parchment.

'Lord, Xanthippus,' he said, 'you are accused of impiety and a disrespect for government and its just decisions. It is alleged that you do not believe in the gods and have no regard for their sanctity.' He looked at his fellow priests. 'For this, death is the only punishment. For, who has protected Athens and all of Greece but the gods, especially Athene Parthenos, our patroness? You are accused of jesting at her virginity and making lewd implications concerning it.'

Xanthippus could not repress himself. He raised a long thin hand. 'Surely that is a lie,' he said in his pleasant voice. 'Athene does not have a lovely countenance and is not alluring, for wisdom is forbidding and is not seductive in the least. What man desires wisdom above all things? I have yet to find such a man. Men prefer the thighs of women to any dissertation of philosophy or any theory – except if they are incapable. Wisdom, in short, is the refuge of impotence.'

Even the bribed judges and priests could not prevent themselves from gasping.

One said in a hoarse voice, 'You do not believe in the gods, lord?'

Xanthippus was beginning to enjoy himself, though it was a reckless and deadly game. He spread out his hands eloquently.

'Only a fool does not believe in something greater than man, for do not the stars obey inscrutable laws, and the sun and the moon? Who has laid down this law and this ineffable order? Men? But men are helpless insects, and have no knowledge of why they are here and what is their ultimate fate. Can they order, these insignificants, the wheeling of constellations and the Pleiades? What decree of man can forbid the rising of the sun and the illumination of the heavens? Who ordains the tides, and the seasons? Can any man demand of the mountains, "Remove yourselves"? Can a man say to the sea, "Retreat"? Who can order the fruitfulness of the olive trees and the fields and the palms? Who has given man awareness and harnessed the winds? Has any judge forbidden a volcano to explode, or a tempest not to disturb the waters? The moon changes by law, yet no body of men can regulate the phases of her. It is impudent of men to believe themselves all-powerful and in control of their merest existence.'

Xanthippus had spoken with an eloquence and sudden passion which amazed even himself, and Zeno stared at him incredulously and for once Teos looked grave.

A priest said in a severe voice, 'But it is alleged that you have jested at the very divinity which you now defend.'

Zeno rose in his small stature and lifted his hands and all looked at him, as if startled that he was present.

'A wise man jests at the impertinence of ignorant men who would tear down the gods to their own meagre level and make them equal to themselves or even less.'

'You do not believe that the gods have laid down a system of laws for the behaviour and the obedience of men, Zeno of Elea?' asked one of the priests.

Zeno smiled. 'I am not being judged,' he replied. 'But I will reply to your question, lord. We can find the will of God only through prayer and in solitude and in meditation. We can find His laws in the laws of nature, which He has ordained. What governs the humblest grain of sand or the merest sheaf of wheat also governs man. The law is of one piece. The suns obey Him and know His laws. Let us reflect on them. For law and order are of the nature of God, and are open to the innocent eyes of children and are confused and elaborated upon and made obscure only by the perverted sophistries of men.'

He smiled at the priests and the judges. 'My friend, Xanthippus, has been accused of impiety. But the true sacrilege is the making of God in the likeness and image of

188

man and attributing to Him all the passions and errors of mankind, and all the savagery, and believing that we can comprehend Him in the slightest. Of this crime Xanthippus is innocent. Who among you, sires, is competent to say that he knows anything about the Unknowable? Xanthippus has repeatedly asserted that this is beyond our competence, and who can deny it in truth? To differ with this truth is to be truly impious.'

'The gods have given us the capacity to comprehend them,' said one of the priests. 'Do you deny that, Zeno of Elea?'

'Who has said we can comprehend them?' asked Zeno. 'The gods, themselves? No. Only arrogant men have declared that, men without intelligence.'

He sat down, looked deeply at the silent priests and said in his sonorous voice, 'Who among you dares to declare that he knows the attributes of the Godhead and is acquainted with His nature? Who dares to commit that blasphemy before the face of this august assemblage?'

The oldest of the judges, and the one most heavily bribed by Teos, was becoming impatient, thinking of the noontide meal which he had missed and for which he yearned. He pushed aside his parchment and said, 'Zeno of Elea has put it cleverly and with precision. We are not presumptuous men; we would be presumptuous indeed to hold a dialogue concerning the gods with Xanthippus, who knows no more than we.'

Xanthippus bowed and bent his head mockingly. 'It is perhaps merciful that we are all ignorant men, for to know even a portion of the truth would be death to us.'

But one of the judges, who had not been bribed, said, 'There is the matter of insolence towards the law. I have here an accusation of an anonymous friend of the court to the effect that Xanthippus has declared his disrespect and ridicule of our democracy, and that he has not paid his just taxes.' He glared at Xanthippus, for he hated the other's aristocracy and fame and riches. 'Answer. lord,' he continued. 'What is your contention against the liberty you enjoy under your government, laid down by Solon?'

Xanthippus had a witty reply to this but for once he held his tongue. He assumed a thoughtful expression, but his thin and delicate face flushed with the anger he was repressing. He raised his eyebrows. 'Are you asking me to define liberty, sire?' he asked.

The judge said, 'That is my implication.'

Xanthippus looked at him and his blue eyes became like bright and polished stone. 'What is liberty? The right of a man to demand that his government let him be and refrain from meddling with his private affairs and his life, and regulating his conduct which offends no one nor interferes with the rights of his fellows. The right of a man to own property and to pay taxes upon it for the good of the commonweal and the protection of his property and his country from internal and external enemies. The right of a man to live in peace with himself and his neighbours and to enjoy the fruit of his hands and his intelligence. The right of a man to be a man, and to live unfettered by paternalism and the officiousness of petty bureaucrats. In short, the right not to be a slave. These are simple and honest rights. Anything more is oppression.'

'You believe your government does not rise to these expectations?' asked one of the judges.

Xanthippus did not answer for a moment. Then he said in the softest voice, 'Noble judge, do you believe our government rises to these expectations?'

The man shifted his eyes then thundered, 'That is not only my belief but my knowledge!'

'Sire,' said Xanthippus, 'who am I, a mere soldier who offered his life for his country and have served it with blood and honour, to dispute you, who were never a soldier but instead a member of a more honourable profession? As for your knowledge, sire, I plead ignorance of it.'

Teos chuckled aloud, and the priests and the judges glanced

at each other, some with rage and frustration and some with only half-hidden amusement.

Then Xanthippus, the intrepid and the sophisticated, lost his precarious temper.

'You speak of Solon!' he cried. 'But Solon envisioned a republic of just laws, under which all men would be free, and free, above all, from capricious and rapacious government. A nation where men could openly speak their dissent and plead for redress of wrongs – the wrongs of government against its people. We do not have such a republic, gentlemen. We do not have a republic at all. We have a degenerate democracy, the rule of the witless mob who have bellies but no minds. Under this condition we can be absolutely certain of but one thing: The world is ruled by fools, and this has always been and will be, for fools presume wisdom by their very overwhelming numbers, and what politician or judge will dispute numbers? You, gentlemen?'

Teos groaned inwardly. Now this Xanthippus had spoken his death sentence. Those whom Teos had bribed also groaned inwardly. One said sternly, 'You differentiate between a republic and a democracy, Xanthippus? Are they not one and the same?'

'No,' said Xanthippus with quiet emphasis. 'One is representative government. The other is government by chaos. Which, gentlemen, do we have in Athens today?'

The priests and the judges studied their parchments. They had no reverence for a brave man who was also a notable soldier, and they knew that such as Xanthippus was dangerous to their very existence. Still, many feared him, and the others feared that Teos would ask for the return of his rich bribes. After a long silence a judge cleared his throat portentously and gave Xanthippus an ominous look.

'It is alleged that you have cheated on your taxes, Xanthippus. What is your reply to this?'

Xanthippus laughed softly. 'Where is my accuser, sire? Bring him forth and let his records be examined with mine, and I will wager my life that drachma for drachma I have been more honest than he.'

When they did not answer he added, 'Or, is justice dead and not merely blind? Do we have government by vicious informers or government by impartial judgements?'

Again when they did not answer immediately, he said, 'But only you can reply to that. That, too, is beyond my competence as a mere soldier.'

The heaviest bribed judge said with eagerness, 'Then, Xanthippus, you plead incompetence both as to the nature of divinity and the nature of law?'

Xanthippus bowed. 'Sire,' he said, 'I am the most incompetent man present, and possibly the most ignorant, if that is possible.'

The judge said with haste, 'Your humility is worthy of you, Xanthippus, and is duly noted by the Ecclesia and this court, and therefore the severity of your fate will be mitigated.' He looked furtively at Teos who was slightly frowning. Teos had asked that at the most that Xanthippus be ostracized until he, Teos, had tired of the delightful hetaira, Gaia. In memory he tasted her lips again and smelled her perfume and remembered her embraces.

Seeing the frown of Teos the judge spoke with even more haste. 'Therefore, it is the judgement of this court, and the Ecclesia, that you be ostracized from Athens until we, in our mercy, are inclined to recall you. We are not insensible to your fame, Xanthippus, which was justly earned, nor is your city ungrateful. You are not guiltless, and this you know in your heart – though your guilt was caused by ignorance and incompetence. Be thankful that you live under a just and benign democracy, which takes no vengeance on its – incompetent – enemies, who speak not from malice but from benightedness.'

At this Xanthippus started to laugh aloud, but was seized quickly by both arms by Zeno and Teos, who led him towards the door. He threw off his friends on the marble steps and said to them with hilarity, 'I have been saved by a philosopher and –' He halted and stared at Teos with sudden amazement. 'And Teos. Why were you there, Teos, you who never interested yourself either in religion or justice?'

Teos smiled with the utmost cheerfulness. 'Am I not your beloved friend, Xanthippus? Have I not always admired you?'

'No,' said Xanthippus.

Teos took his arm again with a fond look. 'My litter awaits. Permit me the honour of taking you to your house.'

When Xanthippus arrived at his house he sent for his wife, gazed at her without emotion and with only indifference, and said, 'I have been ostracized for an indeterminate period, but have not been deprived of any of my substance nor will I be imprisoned, or killed.'

Agariste wept, but he did not stay to hear her protestations or her laments. He went to Gaia who received him with her customary joy and he was consoled in her warm round arms and with her kisses. He did not know why, but even as she smiled tears ran down her rosy cheeks.

From his villa on Cyprus he wrote to his son, Pericles:

'Above all things a man must love not only his own liberty but the liberty of others, or he is less than a man. True, liberty is an abstraction but is this not true of all perfect things? We must however, strive towards it though never can we fully attain it. It is our noblest duty to love all that is perfect, for perfection is the Shadow of God and we may, at our will and desire, rest in it, though never seeing That which casts it.'

Pericles was astonished at reading this from his urbane and mocking father, who had never revered the gods but had questioned their existence with laughter. He was deeply touched.

CHAPTER V

Pericles was widely admired among the youths of his acquaintance, yet there was a remoteness about him which rejected
intimacy while inspiring reverence in others and a desire to
approach him nearer, a desire invariably frustrated. There was a
Tantalus quality in his nature. When he left his fencing school,
which was conducted by the expert freedman, Chilio, he
never appeared anxious to have companions on his walk to his
father's house, yet he was always surrounded by eager and
fawning companions who often went out of their way to
accompany him.

There was, in the fencing school of Chilio, a youth of
sixteen who was scorned and ridiculed even by the master,
though the youth was of a distinguished house and his father
was a great soldier. His name was Ichthus, which meant fish,
and this alone would have aroused hilarity among cruel youth.
He was ashamed of the name, himself, but his mother, who
claimed to be dedicated to Poseidon, and hinted that she
had, as a maiden, been seduced by him, had insisted on the
name. Pericles, though he scorned the youth, never engaged
in baiting him or laughing at him, but would watch him at a
removed distance with an inexplicable expression, at once
wondering and dismissing.

Ichthus was as tall as Pericles, who was taller than his fellows,
and very slender and bony, and his skin had a peculiar pallid
transparency which seemed to cover a body containing no
blood. This gave him the appearance of chronic illness, for
even his lips had no warm tint. His nose was large and his
very light brown eyes were almost completely round, and
started hugely when he was confronted by a novel thought or
word, and were lashless. His wide flat mouth was tremulous

and betrayed too much sensibility. He stammered and would sometimes become speechless with shy fear of those about him. His thin retreating chin was not notable. His tutors and his mother loved him, and his father despised him as a weakling. Besides having tutors, he attended the same academe as Pericles. It was only his skill at fencing, which he detested, that brought him any measure of toleration from his mates. He had a high shaking voice like an adolescent girl's, which aroused mirth when he spoke quickly, and his light brown hair was straight and dull and blew in the wind, for it was very fine. He loped rather than walked and his garments never fitted him flatteringly.

There were times when Pericles felt a slight pity for Ichthus, and when the latter was beset too hard by his mates Pericles would interfere with a quiet word or a quelling glance. Sometimes the pity rose to the point of anger and protectiveness, which also annoyed Pericles. Ichthus was nothing to him, he would remind himself. He had no admiration for him except for his learning and his intelligence. When occasionally he found himself followed meekly at a distance by Ichthus, Pericles' vexation would heighten to the point of urging him to a cruel word, which he usually suppressed. Ichthus is a poor thing, the fifteen-year-old Pericles would think. Nevertheless, he has a right to an existence without harassment, as all men have, though he must be wary of voicing heretical thoughts.

One day Pericles stayed later at his academe to discuss a point of logic with his teacher, with which he hoped to confound Zeno that night. As he had delayed, his usual servile companions had left for their homes. Moreover it was a blustering day full of grey clouds so low they even obscured the top of the acropolis, and rain that resembled, in its stinging, the prickle of little shards of glass.

Pericles wrapped his warm woollen cloak about him tightly and pulled the cowl of it over his tall head. There were few abroad and those mostly in litters carried by shivering and running slaves or in covered chariots. Pericles began the descent down the hill from the school to begin the ascent to his father's house. Struggling with the gale he did not see that Ichthus, full of rapture and alight with love, was following him helplessly like a guarding slave. Pericles walked rapidly but Ichthus, with his long legs and light body, had no difficulty in keeping pace with him, though he lingered some distance behind, fearful of Pericles' displeasure at discovering him and not wishing to intrude on someone he regarded almost as a deity.

Athens lay below and the Agora also, crowded and beginning to shine with yellow lights as with stars. Pericles began the ascent to his father's house. He came upon a grove of dark cypresses, towering like spires and clustered together. He was almost past them when a large man, hooded and wrapped in his cloak, fell upon him with upraised dagger which glittered wanly in the dim light.

'Die, son of Xanthippus, traitor!' he shouted hoarsely. Pericles was athletic and agile, and he dodged the blow, springing to one side, the hood falling from his face and so exposing it to wind and rain. The man was much taller than he, and stronger, and his features were hidden, yet Pericles had the impression of ferocity and hate and swarthiness. In an instant he concluded that his best defence was flight and he was fast of foot. But the man was faster and powerful, and he seized Pericles by the hair and again raised his dagger.

I am lost, thought the youth, but though he was terror-stricken he began to fight for his life. He seized the upraised wrist with its weapon and clung to it with both hands. The man swung him off his feet like a monkey clinging to a branch and tried to dash him to the ground. Pericles curled up his legs, swinging helplessly but with determination. He tried to shout for help, but the wind bore away his voice. His feet scraped the ground and his knees were abraded by stones, yet all he knew was the screaming of his heart and the necessity to hold the murderous arm. In the meantime the assassin was belabouring him with the fist of his left hand over the head and the back, and blood spurted from Pericles' nose and from his forehead into his eyes.

Then suddenly he was dropped and fell heavily to the ground and he heard a cursing and a howling, muffled. Rising to his hands and knees he stared upwards, disbelieving. Ichthus danced near him. He had stripped off his big woollen cloak and had thrown it over the attacker's head and shoulders and body, and had drawn it tightly, holding it with one hand while with the other he was enthusiastically stabbing the stranger with his own drawn dagger though the folds of the garment. Ichthus' long tunic fluttered about him like the tunic of a dancer, and his long thin legs were active and swift. All this Pericles saw in an instant or two. He pushed himself to his feet, drew his dagger and rushed upon his assailant also, stabbing recklessly and with cold rage.

The man sought to save himself, but the two youths were more than equal even to him, and he was blinded and smothered by the cloak. Frantically he kicked at the two he could not see, and blood ran down his legs. He began to weaken from the many wounds, one near his heart, and he groaned even as he struggled. Finally he reared upwards like a dying horse, and fell heavily to the earth, where he writhed for a few moments then lay still on his back.

The two youths stood over him, panting, their bloody daggers in their hands. They stared at him. They wiped the sweat from their brows with the back of their left hands. Their breath whistled shrilly. Then Pericles bent and pushed aside Ichthus' cloak and lifted the cowl of the murderer. The man was a complete stranger, with a black beard.

'He is dead,' said the gentle Ichthus in a high and exultant voice, and he kicked the fallen man in the side.

'I do not know him,' said Pericles. He could hardly speak

from exhaustion and his breath was still fast. He watched Ichthus pull his stained cloak from under the man and wrap himself in it. Then Ichthus looked at Pericles and said, in a stammer, 'You – you – are not injured, Pericles?'

'You saved my life,' Pericles said. 'For that, I am always, into eternity, grateful, my dear Ichthus.'

'It was nothing,' said Ichthus, his heart bounding with joy.

'Then it follows that my life was nothing,' said Pericles with wryness. Seeing then that Ichthus was abashed and uncertain at his words, he embraced him.

A city guard appeared out of the swirling storm with drawn sword, shouting. He seized Ichthus by the shoulder roughly, and Pericles said in a weak voice, 'He rescued me from this unknown vagabond and thief and murderer, who attacked me, doubtless for my purse. He is my schoolmate, and I am Pericles, son of Xanthippus.'

The suddenly craven guard then insisted that he accompany Pericles home. Instinctively, though he did not know Ichthus, he ignored him as always did others. Ichthus stood aside shyly, accustomed to this treatment, and when Pericles looked over his shoulder and begged him to accompany him to his father's house Ichthus dumbly shook his head, and to save himself from further embarrassment he loped away as lightly as he had approached. Pericles watched him go, with wonder, affection and gratitude, and he said to the guard, 'That is the bravest man I ever knew, and I owe him what I am and whatever I shall be.'

CHAPTER VI

Agariste said to her son with that haughty sternness which she
had adopted towards him during the past years, for she feared
that he found her less than interesting since the death of
Xanthippus: 'You are of an age to marry and beget sons in your
father's memory.'

Pericles was invariably kind and courteous to his mother but
he no longer took her seriously. 'Alas,' he said, 'I might beget
only daughters.'

Agariste refused to recognize this lightness and said, 'I have
in mind my beloved niece, Dejanira.'

Pericles did not have to pretend disbelief and aversion.
'Dejanira! The widow of Hipponicus? She is older than I. She
is at least twenty-six, and has a son, Callias – '

'Surnamed "The Rich",' said Agariste. 'Riches are not to
be despised for all we are aristocrats.'

'You are jesting, my mother,' said Pericles who was clad
only in a short tunic because of the heat. He crossed his long
white legs and surveyed his mother with what he hoped was
indulgent affection. 'Not only is Dejanira older than I, a
widow with a son, but she is stupid and ugly, short and fat,
and has a face like a pouting sow. Her voice is like the string
of a lyre which is out of tune, shrill and twanging, and to hear
her speak is an assault on the ears. Certainly you are jesting.'

Agariste's face, still severely beautiful and august, flushed
with anger. 'You prefer your hetaira, that ignoble and shameless woman who is a physician?'

'She is at least intelligent and lovely to behold, my Helena,
and she is my own age and has a merry tongue, while Dejanira's
conversation, like Medusa's head, can turn anyone to stone out
of sheer fatigue. When she is not complaining she is whimpering, and when doing neither she is eating or sleeping. More-

over, she sweats and smells and not even the attar of roses which she so lavishly uses can obliterate it. Does she not ever bathe? Her garments, too, swell over her body as over a keg, as if she were perpetually pregnant, and her peploses and tunics, though costly, appear to be the clothing of a slave girl who works in the fields, and they are stained. She also waddles.'

He stood up as if to dismiss the conversation as absurd. But Agariste had the persistence of a bee lured by a dish of honey and the more she was resisted the more stubborn she became. 'Your remarks are obscene, my son,' she said, 'and revolting, and unworthy of an aristocratic man. Does appearance seem to you of the utmost importance?'

'You have always said, Mother, that appearance is most important, yet now you imply it is not.' He was becoming slightly irascible not only because he was afraid to annoy his mother too much, for had not his beloved Helena said that her heart was affected, as was evident to Helena by Agariste's new bluish pallor and the throbbing of vessels in her long white throat when she was in the least agitated? Pericles loved his mother still, though of late she was making him increasingly irritable with her pretensions and arrogance. Too, he was a notable soldier but he was becoming involved in politics in which he was not as yet notably successful.

Agariste said, ignoring her son's last remark, 'You forget that her father is an Archon [Magistrate] of Athens at this time and can be of invaluable assistance to you.'

Pericles regarded his mother in silence. He was somewhat surprised as he always was when she revealed a sharp shrewdness concerning the ambitions and the thoughts of others. He had not as yet informed her that politics attracted him immensely, yet in some way she knew, though he had not confided his intentions to anyone else, with the exception of Anaxagoras, whom his mother loathed.

'He must have bribed well to be elected,' he said.

'My brother would bribe no one!' cried Agariste, turning very pale and trembling. 'We are of an honourable house!'

'Even aristocrats love power, and their second love is money, however vulgar that appears, and they will use the second for the first without hesitation.' But he hardly believed that the Archon, who was a proud and repellently virtuous man, had bought votes. He would use influence, yes, to procure what he wished, but gross gold never, not truly because he despised money but because influence was more dainty and did not publicly smell. Moreover, influence could not be traced, a fact which the prudent Archon must have considered long and carefully. Pericles had never liked his uncle and Xanthippus had detested him and had often mimicked him for the entertainment of Pericles.

Agariste was protesting Pericles' observation about his uncle but Pericles did not listen. He was thinking; he made wry mouths. Was the abominable Dejanira his rapid path in the steaming fields of politics? He shuddered at the thought of her, but Pericles was inordinately ambitious. He reviled the Ecclesia for their oppressiveness, their stultifying of Athens, their crass and degenerate democracy. He believed that, in politics, he could affect the liberation of Athens and her new empire, make her great and free her for mighty things. At times he felt he could actually feel her throbbing but stifled heart under his feet; he yearned to give it room for expansion, for glory. The military man had little influence over the government. A man of resolution, determined that his beloved country would spread shining wings over the world, had one access to the needed power: politics. Even the profound Anaxagoras had so admitted, with sadness, while deploring the fact.

Can I endure Dejanira even for Athens? he thought, and he knew the answer. Athens was worth anything a man could offer her, his adored country; any sacrifice would be as nothing. His stomach turned, but he said to his mother, 'Let me consider it. Perhaps you could induce her to wash, my mother, and reduce her stink, at least for the wedding night.'

'Your remark is not only disgusting, it is unkind,' said Agariste. But she knew she had won, and she smiled her frigid but delicate smile. 'Dejanira is a healthy young woman and you are not accustomed to the fragrance of health. You prefer the odours of closed chambers where you and your companions drown yourselves in wines and garlic and romp with lewd women. Such as your Helena, who has no respect for her sex but must engage in the abattoirs of surgeons and dabble in filth and forget that she is a woman.'

Pericles laughed. 'I have not observed that she ever forgets she is a woman,' he said, and Agariste blushed at the implications of this and averted her head as if to avoid seeing something unspeakably lascivious. She lifted her hand to protect herself from any further mention of Helena, a gesture which Pericles found not only annoying but affected. Helena was like a rose that bloomed ebulliently and lustily and she was as candid as any unsophisticated youth for all her intellect and humour and sometimes bitter understanding of mankind. Robust, tall and somewhat plump, her laugh was loud and strong, and she loved a jest more than anything else, and did not pretend horror at a rude joke fresh from the military camps. Rather, she enjoyed it and would add an epigram to it besides.

I can forget Dejanira in Helena's arms, thought Pericles, smiling fondly, though Helena is owned by no man and is herself only and her bed is available to me seldom.

Zeno of Elea had retired to his small estate, and thankfully. His place in the life of Pericles was taken by Anaxagoras as a companion and a very dear friend, and from Anaxagoras Pericles learned much asceticism and the ability at all times to maintain a personal dignity even under intense provocation.

Anaxagoras was a tall and slender man with an elongated and serious face, a very sensitive mouth, and a thin long nose with a sharp tip. His brow was smooth and invariably calm, his cheekbones distinct and broad. Though middle-aged, he walked with the awkward grace of youth. His gestures were disciplined but eloquent. His dark hair seemed painted on his fragile skull and his ears, though unusually large, were translucent, so that they appeared rosy against the natural paleness of his complexion.

His fame as a mathematician and astronomer had reached Athens long before he arrived there from Asia Minor, and he was received with accolades and affection from his Athenian colleagues, even if the never-sleeping Ecclesia was able to restrain its enthusiasm without much difficulty. So he came under its stringent eye because of his scientific knowledge and teachings and writings. Contrary to the convictions of the Ecclesia, whose ideas of Deity were extremely limited, fixed and dogmatic, and therefore all the more vehement and passionate, Anaxagoras was guilty of posing questions, advancing dubious hypotheses and drawing unorthodox conclusions. When he was accused of impiety in insisting on 'mechanism' in the universe, he would reply that this was an exercise in semantics, and 'mechanism' was the law of the Divine Mind, and he was then accused of inconsistency, for did not 'mechanism' imply a machine ungoverned by the creative Mind? He would throw up his hands in despair. He had no tolerance for those who would oppose inquiry, no matter how 'impious' it seemed. 'The only impiety,' he would say, 'is a denial that the Divine Mind is larger than the mind of man.'

Pericles had heard of Pheidias the sculptor, who was the same age as Anaxagoras, but busy as he was he had not yet encountered him. Anaxagoras soon changed that. He took Pericles to the studio of the sculptor, who now had a considerable fame. He had already executed the incomparable chryselephantine Athene for Pellene and the Marathon memorial at Delphi. The mighty bronze statue of Athene, which towered on the acropolis and was a landsight for sailors, had been designed and cast by him. He had many students; some of the more gifted imitated him expertly.

He was an Athenian, and though still fairly young he was balding, and he had a shy sweet smile infinitely touching and self-deprecating. His body was slight and bending like a young sapling, but his face was plump and rosy and frank, which gave him an appealing aspect. His workshop was as modest as himself, and as dusty, and as stained with paint and the shavings of metal, but as noisy as he was quiet. He greeted Anaxagoras with affection, touching him gently on the shoulder and smiling bashfully into his eyes. He looked at Pericles with some timidity, for he was afraid of strangers.

'My friend, Pericles, who is a notable soldier and, alas, a blossoming politician, has been very anxious to know you, dear friend,' said Anaxagoras. Anaxagoras was dressed as humbly as the famous sculptor but nothing could reduce his aspect of self-containment and grandeur. Pheidias led his two visitors outside his workshop into the small but perfect garden of myrtles and oaks and sycamores surrounding gravelled walks and one single flowerbed with a fountain in which stood one of his own works: a little but exquisite bronze statuette of Psyche with a butterfly on her shoulder, her wings outspread, one delicate foot poised on her pedestal.

A student brought wine and cheese and olives and honey and bread to a rough plain table under the shade of an oak, and a dish of dates and figs. Pheidias made no hypocritical apology for the simplicity of this light meal and as the three sat and ate and drank Pericles gathered that food was of small importance to the sculptor and to Anaxagoras also. In the background, from the workshop, there came a constant hammering and the sound of youthful voices.

'It is my dream,' said Pheidias, 'to see Athens the supreme centre of beauty as well as philosophy and science.' He glanced up at the acropolis. 'I can see a temple there, to Athene Parthenos, and a statue of her before it of ivory and gold, a vast statue facing the dawn, heroic and terrible and commanding, gleaming against the blue sky.'

204

'It is not an impossible dream,' said Pericles, and Pheidias was pleased again by the sonorous quality of his voice. 'I, too, wish for the glory of Greece and though Anaxagoras here despises politicians it is necessary to be one to obtain the money to bring a dream into reality.'

When Pericles and Anaxagoras left Pheidias, Pericles carried with him a gift from the sculptor, an ivory figurine no longer than his index finger, and it was of a lovely woman with a clear and valiant face. He put the figurine on the chest at his bedside and would gaze at it for long periods, filled with yearning and desire. Once he dreamt that she grew and stepped down from the chest and was a tall woman and that she smiled at him and bent over him and whispered, 'I have hoped for a man like you. We will find each other.'

Pericles secretly hoped that something dire would happen to prevent his marriage to Dejanira. But the winter day in the month of Gamelion dawned crisp and especially bright and vigorous, which Agariste said was a good omen, but Pericles considered it disastrous. He had seen Dejanira at family festivals, when her husband was still alive, and he had had the heartiest, if derisive, sympathy for him. He remembered that Dejanira had never had the slightest prettiness even as a child and young girl and now, as a widow, she seemed particularly abhorrent to him. Before her marriage she had had, at least, a slender figure and kept herself reasonably hygienic with the help of slaves. Even these had departed.

Ah, well, he said to himself on this day Agariste proclaimed was auspicious, I suppose worse things can happen to a man than marriage, though at the moment I do not believe it. He decided to get drunk, though as a rule he was careful in his drinking. By noon he was sleeping in his chamber, snoring, and though Agariste, on hearing this, tightened her mouth, she had to admit to herself that perhaps he had reason, considering Dejanira, about whom she had no delusions. But Dejanira was rich and her father powerful, and a man could do worse than marry her, especially an ambitious man like Pericles.

As Pericles slept in an aura of sour wine he dreamed again that the beautiful little figurine Pheidias had presented to him enlarged to the height of a tall and slender woman, and that again she bent over him. But this time she kissed his lips and laid her hand tenderly against his neck and whispered, 'I am coming to you, O my beloved!' He felt the warmth of her mouth; it was as fragrant as a lily, and soft as a feather, and her hair, silver-gold, fell over his throat and his shoulders and hands. Her eyes, so close to his, were as brown as choice autumn wine, tinted and flecked with gilt and sparkles of changing light. She seemed radiant to him and vital and she smiled. He came abruptly awake, searching for her in the dimness of his chamber, his eyes strained and enlarged, so real had she appeared, so imminent. He was certain that he could smell the odour of lilies. He turned on his side, his heart beating fiercely with yearning for what was only, surely, a dream. The thought of Dejanira now was unbearably repugnant to him so that he had to restrain himself from rising and fleeing his house and the city of Athens, itself, to roam the world for the vision he had dreamed. At length, groaning, he put the figurine against his lips and kissed it, then placed it under his pillow and slept again until almost sunset. When he awoke he felt dulled and numb and without feeling, which, he thought, was fortunate.

CHAPTER VII

Among the wedding guests was the shy and emotional Ichthus, who was, from a calm and philosophic view, deplorable in his lack of self-restraint. His feelings were ever visible, in the constant slight trembling of his face and in his ardent and fervid eyes. He seemed always on the verge of flight; his sensitivity was that of a man who has been flayed. A felicitous word or a kind smile could provoke him to tears. He haunted the colonnades, following the philosophers and listening, and sometimes he would cry out as if unbearably moved. The philosophers found this gratifying, if amusing. Their students did not. They did not know that here was an undefiled soul who yearned for beauty and justice and truth and could not understand a world in which these were so terribly lacking. Worse, he could not express in eloquent speech the majesty he perceived, and so could only mumble though his spirit vibrated. His tongue was as if paralysed.

However, he could write. He wrote anonymously, and broadcast his writing throughout Athens, employing young lads to toss pieces of parchment in public places, and against the doors of houses. His polemics were potent and galvanic. They rang with passion and eloquence and fire. He questioned everything, but with humility, if it pertained to the Godhead. However, when he questioned government it was as if a volcano had broken its stony fastnesses and was pouring lava and flame over the city, full of wrath.

His particular hatred was for the hypocritical democracy of Athens, which pretended to serve the people but only served politicians. The Ecclesia did not ignore the writings of Ichthus. They set their spies searching for him. Only one person was convinced that he knew the author of these fiery writings which were disturbing the minds of the people and forcing them to think of their government even above their petty daily affairs. That man was Pericles. He was determined that he must speak to Ichthus for the latter's own sake. Prudence, prudence, he said to himself, as if addressing his shy friend. Then he would add with bitterness, 'Dear Ichthus, the truth is a deadly spice and can poison the administrator. I agree with you, but the time is not yet. Prudence, no. Patience, yes.' Then he would ridicule himself for his own discretion. More nations, he thought, were destroyed by indifferent patience on the part of the people than by perhaps any other destroyer. A people which had too much tolerance for evil deserved to die in its own leniency. There was a difference between indulgence for natural faultiness and indulgence for wickedness. The first was civilized, the second perfidious.

Then Pericles reflected that there was nothing more invincible than a just and uncorrupted man who set out to right wrongs. Gentle and timid though Ichthus was he had the soul of a Hercules bent on cleaning out the Augean Stables though he died for it. Rightful anger was a frightful weapon, stronger than Damascene steel, and he who used it must beware that it did not turn in his hand and slay him. Pericles decided that at some time during the wedding festivities he would speak quietly to Ichthus and urge – what? Self-preservation? Such was the cave in which shivering cowards died of their own inertia. If men had any reason for living at all it was for truth and honour and justice. For anything less, for compromise, a man was only a devouring beast intent on his miserable security and appetites.

Pericles thought of his father, Xanthippus, and his heart burned. What should he say to Ichthus which would not be a soothing lie?

Pericles, with his best man and his other friends, went to the house of Daedalus, Dejanira's father, to the wedding ceremonies. He was so preoccupied with his dream of the beautiful mythical woman and the problem of Ichthus that any thought of his own state was numbed. Seeing his abstraction his friends became silent.

The house of Daedalus was already seething with gay guests, and was wreathed in laurel and olive leaves and somewhat dejected flowers wilting in the cold air. The Ecclesia, many of them, wore the bland and smiling faces of politicians and greeted everyone as if they were the honoured.

Daedalus, though very rich, was frugal and so the cloths on the table were of the coarsest linen and the spoons and knives thinly plated with silver. Here were no rugs or precious murals but only small statues of the household gods on wall pedestals. The bare stone floor was icy. There were no silken curtains at the windows; heavy dull wool hung there instead. No braziers warmed the air except for a thrifty one in the centre of the hall. The Archon boasted of his austerity; Pericles decided he was less austere than mean.

Pericles saw his bride at a distance, clad in a demure tunic of blue linen with a toga over it of a darker blue. She was veiled and had a wreath on her large round head which appeared to set solidly on her shoulders with no neck intervening. Her friends sat about her, chattering happily, but she was stolidly silent as always except that occasionally her thin voice, laden with complaint on this, her wedding night, could be heard over the voices of the other women. Her mother, as stoutly shapeless as herself, sat sullenly at her side. Semele was very pleased by this marriage of her daughter to the handsome and distinguished Pericles. But if one were to judge by her wary and sulky expression one would have guessed that she was in ill-temper and morose. Her greying hair was lank by nature, though for these festivities it had been painfully curled and waved and bound in red ribbons. Her clothing was brown; she wore no jewellery. Like her daughter, she had a truly snout-like nose, with large gross nostrils, a low sallow forehead and sallower fat cheeks, a thick mouth sharply downturned, and very small sunken black eyes constantly darting with suspicion of all things. Her chin was greasy.

As for Pericles he sat among the men, at Daedalus' right hand, and he was filled with dark gloom. He looked at his veiled bride and shuddered inwardly. He usually drank with care and moderation but now he resolutely strove for drunkenness. The wine was execrable if strong. Fortunately Daedalus had thought to provide Syrian whisky and Pericles, wincing, drank it down, then hastily ate a piece of brown rough bread. He had become accustomed to army food during his campaigns, otherwise the dinner would have revolted him. The wedding feast would have been despised by slaves in the house of

Xanthippus. Pericles drank more whisky. Finally a warm haze enveloped him from the potions and a dreamlike apathy flowed over him. Voices seemed louder and incoherent. The forced laughter of the men became jovial to his ears. He thought to himself, Nothing lasts forever. He could forget this nightmare tomorrow, this visitation of harpies, this presence of Medusas.

A young male slave listlessly moved among the guests carrying a basket of sesame cakes and intoning, as was traditional, 'I have eschewed the worse; I have found the better.' Ho, thought Pericles, and felt a wild impulse to roar with laughter. He looked at the table where his bride sat. Dejanira still wore her veil, but she was avidly stuffing her mouth under it, greedily, as if starving. Her whining voice drifted to him occasionally and he thought, I hope I am not moved to strangle her tonight. Would that not be rude of me? Tut, tut, I am a gentleman. The whisky permeated his mind mercifully at last and he wanted to sleep. There was an acrid odour in the air which he disliked. He did not know that it came from the whisky in his goblet and on his clothes. Daedalus scowled. His son-in-law was certainly behaving strangely. The Archon did not delude himself – for he had eyes – that his daughter was desirable except for her money and position. However, he resented this open display of intoxication on the part of Pericles. If he continued to drink that abominable whisky he would become unconscious and that would be a scandal. The whisky was also costly and was being wasted. He motioned away a slave who would have filled Pericles' goblet again but Pericles seized the bottle himself and poured the contents into the receptacle and drank it down in one gulp as if it were army wine. He began to shake with laughter, and his friends were alarmed. Open public laughter was foreign to Pericles who had a stately decorum at all times.

Then came the presentation of gifts to the bride. She and her mother eagerly inspected all, cleverly guessing at their price. Then they were satisfied, looking at each other with satisfaction. The guests had not forgotten that the bride was the daughter of an Archon, who could be a malevolent and dangerous enemy. Pheidias had presented a figurine of Hera so charmingly cast in shining bronze, and with details that were so incredibly living, that the guests exclaimed in sincere admiration. Pish, thought the Archon. It is nothing. It is worth but a few drachmas. The sculptor had fame; he ought to have presented a figurine of ivory and gold at the very least. Daedalus was insulted. He looked at Pheidias surlily under his tight eyelids. Fame! For such cheap trivia? Bah. He, Daedalus, would remember this offence.

It was now the time for the procession to take the bride to her new home. The marriage wagon was prepared; two white horses were attached to it. Pericles never remembered how he, staggering and laughing, was got into the vehicle beside his still-veiled bride, but it vaguely seemed to him that something of sturdy bulk was his support and against which he helplessly sagged as the wagon proceeded over the cobblestones of the city, swaying and lurching. It was early night, and the stones glistened whitely with frost and a full moon was a cold and blazing ball skipping through thin black clouds. People rushed to their doors to see the procession, which was very large and noisy as it followed the wagon. The whole wedding party was on foot, carrying flaring red torches; flutes and lyres could hardly be heard over the roaring of the marriage hymn. Little boys began to follow the procession, capering like fauns, and the guests threw coins at them and sweetmeats.

Agariste had left the house of Daedalus to return to her own house, there to greet the bride and bridegroom. She looked about the perfection of the house, comparing it with the chill meagreness of her brother's, and gave orders to slaves who were splendidly dressed. She waited, pale and composed in her rosy robes, her shoulder and hair pins sparkling in the light of fragrant lamps, her golden hair seemingly carved on her head. She was satisfied with the decorations of the atrium. The house was embellished with laurel, olive and myrtle leaves and late flowers, and there were many handsome braziers warming every room. An odour of nard drifted through the house as if on a balmy breeze.

The procession was now at the doorstep, the wagon leading. Male slaves ran out to assist the bride and her groom. Dejanira heavily lumbered down, her veil flowing. The slaves had some difficulty with Pericles, to the laughter of the guests. They had to lift him down and then hold him upright. He had begun to sing a ribald ditty of the city streets and this increased the hilarity of the guests, who joined in – to Agariste's humiliation. She was not certain of the meaning of some of the coarser words but she guessed their import. Dejanira stolidly and silently walked at the groom's left hand, trudging like a milk-maid.

On entering the atrium, Dejanira was showered, as was traditional, with dried figs and nuts. Her little black eyes darted under her veil, surveying the festive scene but above all the luxury of the house which she considered too costly. Agariste was apparently prodigal with money. Dejanira, having been reared in a frugal household, was busily deciding in her mind that as she was now the mistress of her husband's house she would be firm in its management. There were too many slaves; there was too much lavishness. The beautiful rugs would be rolled up and carefully set aside except for occasions of festivity. The murals would be covered with cloths to preserve their lustre. She did not admire her aunt, whom she considered pretentious and unwomanly in her learning, and Agariste would soon learn who was mistress in this house. As she thought these things she munched on the bridal cake of sesame and honey, the crumbs littering her veil and falling on her bloated breast. The juice of the quince she had been given ran down her chin.

Pericles was glazed of eye and deeply red of face. The guests propped him upright. It was evident that he was not very conscious. He was led to the bridal chamber and dropped on the bed, where he sprawled. The bedside lamp was glowing with golden light, and it shone on the figurine which Pheidias had given him. The bride entered, still munching. The door was closed behind her and she was alone with her groom. In the atrium Daedalus formally bestowed Dejanira's dowry upon her husband's surrogate.

Dejanira lifted her veil and regarded Pericles and now her large face flushed and her black eyes gleamed. Having been married before she knew how to deal with a drunken husband. She slowly removed all Pericles' clothing, strongly moving him from side to side until he was a fallen white statue on the bed. She stood for some time, surveying him. She was smiling and her breast began to heave. Dear love, she said in her mind, I have adored you since first I saw you at a family festival, and you were but a child and I was little older. My dream of marriage to you has come true at last. Now I shall lie beside you and hold you in my arms as I have longed to do for many years.

She divested herself of her clothing until she stood only in her shift. She hesitated, then removed the shift and stood in the short massiveness of her nudity. The lamp glimmered on the bulges and ripples of her fat expanses. Her more than ample breasts swelled and tightened; her shapelessness quivered, and her obese thighs, thickly veined in purple, trembled. She gleamed with oil. She took the pins from her hair and the black and lightless mass fell over her shoulders and back and breasts. She blew out the lamp and climbed into the bed beside her sleeping and snoring husband.

She put her hand on his chest and pressed her head against his shoulder. She began to pant deeply. Her hands roved. Her breath was burning on Pericles' flesh.

He was dreaming again of the lovely figurine which was rapidly becoming the supple form of a woman. He could see her face as if illuminated by the moon. She was lying beside him and murmuring endearments in his ear; he could feel her breath on his mouth, his cheek, his belly. 'Love, love,' she whispered. 'My own beloved. I am beside you. Take me.' Her hand was hotter and hotter, and roamed deliciously, and he began to shake with delight.

'Heart of my heart!' he cried aloud and Dejanira closed her eyes on a spasm of joy. He rolled upon her, groaning with ecstasy, clasping her tightly in his arms. He saw his love's red lips and brown eyes, smiling up at him in ethereal moonlight which existed only in his intoxicated mind. A fragrance of lilies floated up to his nostrils. 'Sweetness of my soul,' he said.

And so the marriage was consummated but Dejanira did not know that it was a woman of a dream with whom it was consummated, in the blackness of the chamber.

CHAPTER VIII

Pericles knew that his leadership in Athens was precarious. He was dealing with a vagrant democracy and not the republic of Solon. He was dealing with judges and bureaucrats and the unpredictable Archons and all the other Myrmidons of a corrupt mob-controlled government. He might be assassinated. But he had long ago decided that too much prudence would result in inertia. He did not have the philosophers' fatalism or renunciation. He was driven by a vital dream, as he had been driven from childhood. He loved his country. He would rescue her from the rule of the base, the disorder of mindless rebels. Often he would gaze up at the acropolis and imagine there a crown of light, a diadem of brilliance, the rise of the free western world as opposed to the elaborate despotisms of the east.

He talked of this with Helena, his random mistress. She listened not only with sympathy, but with understanding. 'You need a hetaira of mind and greatness of heart,' she told him. He tried to embrace her, laughing, but she moved out of his arms and said, 'I belong to no man, and am not your hetaira, beloved. You must have a woman solely dedicated to you and not to a dead love.'

She pondered, and then her face became cheerful. 'I think I know the lady,' she said, looking at him with brightening mischief. 'A young woman, a protégée of Thargelia of Miletus, most beautiful, most accomplished. She has opened a school for girls of good family, wealth and position, here in Athens. Surely you must have heard of her.'

'Aspasia?' he said, and made a mouth of distaste. 'She is notorious. She has fashioned her school on the school of Sappho of Lesbos. What would I have to do with a Lesbian?'

'Sappho has been unjustly maligned,' said Helena with reproof. 'But why is it more reprehensible for a woman to love another woman, than a man to love a man?'

'You would not understand,' said Pericles, smiling. She slapped him lightly on his bare shoulder and said, 'That is the foolish reply of all men to an acute question from a woman. It tells us nothing except you will tell us nothing. Let us return to Aspasia. She was once the companion, the mistress, of a Persian satrap. She left him two years ago, heavy with jewellery and gold. The oppression of women in Persia is even worse than it is in Greece, and she is determined on the eventual emancipation of all women, as am I. If you laugh, my love, I shall drive you from my house. Your attention, please.

'I have heard from Aspasia, and from Old Thargelia of Miletus, too, that from early youth it has been the dream of Aspasia that women's minds must be respected as well as their bodies loved, or lusted for, and that they have a mission in this world as well as a duty to bear sons to their husbands. They have talents unique to them, and who knows how many female geniuses have died in childbed? We have souls as well as genitals.'

'I have never denied that,' said Pericles. 'I have an intelligent mother of many attributes, though she is growing waspish in her age. This is no wonder. Dejanira is the sole authority in the house and it is a case of older arrogance meeting younger arrogance, and Dejanira's vindictiveness is awesome – and dangerous – to encounter. So even my poor mother is silenced by her and I console her frequently, reminding her that it was she, not I, who desired this disastrous marriage.'

'Do not distract me from the subject of Aspasia, Pericles. Aspasia is no Lesbian. It is reputed that she is very discriminating in the choice of lovers. It is said that she has had many, but this I do not believe, for she is fastidious and is concerned only with her school. Many of your more enlightened friends have placed their daughters under her tutelage. She not only teaches them the arts of song and dance and music but gives them an excellent education besides, equal to that of men. Zeno of Elea teaches them at intervals; philosophy and dialectics.'

'For what end?' asked Pericles, with a gravity that pleased Helena. 'What can an educated and intelligent woman do in this world?'

'I am a physician,' said Helena, running her fingers through her auburn hair, which streamed over her bare breasts and shoulders. 'It is true that I am considered infamous, but that is not of great moment to me. Many of my patients are men of distinction – and money, for I have a reputation, and a school of medicine and a large infirmia. I am very rich. I am not alone among my sisters, and many of the hetairai have married noble and famous men, men of family, who have regard for a woman's intellect and gifts. Have you not promised me that you will help women to attain their status in life, and so be regarded as human and with respect?'

'I have sworn it,' said Pericles. 'If I had daughters instead of two sons I could not be more determined.'

'Good.' She gave him a rewarding kiss. 'I will give a dinner for Aspasia, and you will be one of my guests.'

Pericles became wary. It was one of his convictions that, with the exception of Helena and a few more of the hetairai, women of intellect cared nothing for personal beauty and did not cultivate it in themselves and regarded it as trivial. He had been careful not to let Helena guess this opinion, which he held in common with other men. His mother, too, had been an exception. He said, 'What is her appearance?'

She regarded him closely with her large blue eyes. 'Is that of importance?'

'I dislike harpies,' he said. 'No one, man or woman, should neglect a pleasing aspect.'

Helena sighed. 'Aspasia is considered the most beauteous woman in Athens, for all she is no longer young, being twenty years old. Have you not heard of her loveliness? For a powerful man who hears and sees everything you have been very ignorant. I will give that dinner in my house and you must come. Aspasia's voice is as lovely as her appearance, though it is no soft or gentle one, and not fluting. She is also very amusing.'

'A paragon,' said Pericles. 'Still, you have not told me of her appearance, except that she is beautiful. I have discovered that when a woman says a woman of her acquaintance is charming she is invariably no rival and is repulsive to men.'

'You are speaking of mean and trivial women who have minds like pigs,' said Helena. 'When I say a woman is beautiful she is truly beautiful. Aspasia is as tall as I, but slender while I am robust, and her body would make Aphrodite envious. She has hair of so pale a colour that it appears spun from both moonlight and sunlight.'

'I must meet this famous Aspasia,' he said.

She smiled in relief.

'I will tell Aspasia that she is to meet the most powerful man in Athens,' she said, laughing gleefully.

'Except for the damnable Archons and the rest of this government,' he said.

'Dear love, you have forgotten that Pericles is also of the government.'

That conversation with Helena had occurred last night, and he

217

had almost forgotten it, for his mind was too disturbed today as he sat in his hot offices in the Agora and considered Athens and her government. He could hear the roar of the heavy traffic on the streets which surrounded the Agora, and the clamour of thousands of impatient voices. Common Athenians were noisy and insistent, unlike the aristocrats among them. This was not surprising; the market rabble in every country were alike. In other countries, however, the market rabble did not vote, except for the rising city-state of Rome, in Italy. Pericles promised himself to visit Rome, which was reputed to have been founded on a fratricide, but which was also reputed to be sternly moral and virtuous and full of industry. It was said that Rome also had a representative government and this savoured of a republic, in embryo at least. He had already received a request from the Roman Senate to permit it to send him a commission which desired to study the laws of Solon and his legislation.

I am afraid that they will be disappointed in the government we have! he thought, moving his buttocks restlessly on his chair. But it will do no harm to inspire a young nation with the dream of Solon, though we have not achieved it ourselves.

A guard in plumed helmet and leather armour knocked on the bronze door then opened it tentatively. Seeing Pericles' glare he almost retreated; then his courage rose. 'Lord, the noble thesmothetai Archon, Daedalus, is here to consult you on a grave matter.'

Pericles muttered something particularly obscene and pithy concerning his father-in-law, then rose and nodded at the guard. He put his thumbs in each side of his silver girdle and cautioned himself to discipline his vexed thoughts. When Daedalus entered, Pericles greeted him amiably enough and led him to a chair. Daedalus was drier and more wizened than ever, and leaner of body and more skull-like of facial appearance, and his brown long robes were dusty.

Daedalus regarded his son-in-law's stateliness of form and his dignity of countenance. He both secretly respected and resented Pericles, who always appeared incomprehensible to him. But he incessantly complained of him to Dejanira who agreed with him that Pericles was a difficult man, if a kind husband and indulgent father, and that he lacked the proper respect for an Archon.

'How may I serve you, Daedalus?' Pericles asked. 'Cool wine, bread and cheese and fruit? I have some fresh plums and grapes in that closet yonder.'

Daedalus waved away these suggestions. 'I have no time for dallying, Pericles. I come to you on a matter of great importance.'

Pericles doubted this but he inclined his helmeted head gravely and seated himself on a corner of his desk, and waited. Daedalus wished he would sit down in a chair, for Pericles' presence was overpowering when too close.

'You have heard of one Ichthus?' said the older man in his grating voice.

'You know I have not only heard of Ichthus, Daedalus,' said Pericles in a gently perilous voice. 'But you know he is one of my dearest friends and that he saved my life when we were young.' He paused because he was suddenly alarmed; he hid the alarm from his detestable father-in-law, but he grasped his elbows tightly. 'Ichthus is of a most distinguished family, as you know, Daedalus, almost as distinguished as mine,' and certainly more honourable than yours, he added to himself.

Daedalus, always careful of himself, heard the warning in Pericles' voice. But he was a malicious man, and sharp malice made him less afraid of Pericles today than he customarily was. Pericles, he reminded himself, was not entirely invulnerable. There were still things he could not do in spite of his position.

'I know all about Ichthus' family,' said Daedalus. 'His father was ostracized for heretical opinions and died in exile. Despite your gracious opinion of Ichthus, Pericles, the family is not notable. Nor is it rich.'

Pericles waited.

'Ichthus wasted his patrimony by buying and freeing worthless slaves, and on his activities, which are both impious and subversive of government.'

Daedalus watched Pericles closely but Pericles' face remained impervious. 'I know of Ichthus' dedication to the freeing of slaves,' he said. 'I find it admirable, for did not Solon demand this also? It is not unlawful, this bestowing of liberty on the unfortunate who are suffering under the whips and tortures of cruel masters. Mercy is not to be despised. You have mentioned my friend's "activities". What are they?'

Daedalus lifted a hand which appeared fleshless. 'He is your friend, is he not, Pericles? Surely you must know that he is the author of seditious writings denouncing the government and accusing us of all vileness and oppression, of corruption and the defilement of the laws of Solon, of faithlessness towards the people of Athens, and crying for our overthrow.'

He still watched Pericles, but Pericles remained as if uninterested.

'Your friend,' said Daedalus, in a weighty tone. 'Do his activities not offend you?'

'I do not believe he does these things,' said Pericles. His remark was apparently idle and amused. 'If he did what you have accused him of, then surely I would know. He was a guest at my wedding. We were schoolboys together. I count him closer than a brother. No, I do not believe the foolish charges against him. The world is full of malevolent men. Ichthus probably offended one of them without intention, for he is timid and retiring and gives the impression of weakness. Therefore he is open to enmity; in particular the enmity of the brutal.'

Daedalus lost his temper. 'If he is truly your friend, then you are in danger, yourself, Pericles! I have only this advice to give you, for you are the husband of my daughter, and you are ambitious: Deny that you know much of him. Declare, if asked, that he is but a slight acquaintance, from childhood. If pressed and reminded that he is often seen in your company, denounce him, and feign horror when told of his writings.'

Pericles' heart was thumping in his chest. But he maintained his attitude of serenity. He knew that Daedalus hated him, for all his pride in him. He also knew that Daedalus' position as an Archon would come under scrutiny, for was he not the father of Pericles' wife? So Daedalus was impelled to protect both his own station and the station of Pericles, however he might resent the latter.

Pericles said in the most detached voice, 'Have public charges been made against Ichthus?'

'Seven thousand ostraka have been received,' said Daedalus, again watching Pericles closely.

But Pericles laughed aloud and slapped one of his knees. 'I doubt if Ichthus knows *seven* men in Athens! What absurdity is this?' Then he made his face serious. 'Those who signed those potsherds are liars and libellers, and should be prosecuted for defaming the gentle character of a harmless and merciful man.'

He stood up and began to pace the room indignantly, breathing loudly so that the outraged sound would reach Daedalus' ears. 'Illiterate peasants from the country, who must have friends sign the ostraka for them! It is not unknown that many men have been ostracized or even executed by the Assembly, upon receiving forged potsherds produced in the thousands at the command of a venomous man who desired some revenge on another man, or had malignance in his soul. It is not unknown that citizens have been suborned and bribed to send in the ostraka, if a criminal desires the fortune of the accused man, or his position, or envies him for one reason or another.'

Daedalus cried, 'Are you accusing the Assembly of corruption, of being the creature of designing and evil men?'

I can accuse them of much worse, thought Pericles, his teeth clenching together. He stopped his pacing, his back to Daedalus, and pondered. The situation was terrible. At all costs Ichthus must be saved.

Daedalus said, seeing that Pericles would not reply to his question, 'You did not know that we have discovered, through confidential and unimpeachable sources, that Ichthus is really being condemned for his writings, and that the Ecclesia has hundreds of such writings in its possession. Ichthus has not denied the writings, when confronted.'

Pericles held himself very still. What a fool was Ichthus for not denying the authorship of the inflammatory writings! But what a man of fearless integrity lived under that inoffensive exterior, that retiring demeanour! Athens would be free and saved if only two thousand of his kind lived in the city.

'This is in addition to the ostraka,' Daedalus added, exasperated by Pericles' silence and his turned back. 'Have you nothing to say, husband of my daughter?'

Pericles slowly faced his father-in-law and for an instant Daedalus was frightened, though Pericles' features were still serene and the light eyes still indifferently blank.

'I have this to say, Daedalus,' he said in a slow and steadfast voice. 'I will defend him before the ostrakophoria and the Ecclesia.'

Daedalus started to his feet, holding his arms above his head, and his countenance was distorted. But before he could speak Pericles abruptly left the room.

CHAPTER IX

Pericles loved his sons, Xanthippus, eight years old, and Paralus, two years younger. Miraculously, neither resembled their mother. Xanthippus resembled his grandfather of the same name and Paralus, though he had Dejanira's black eyes, had Pericles' colouring and stature. Xanthippus had his grandfather's high sense of humour and mischief and quick intellect and slight and elegant body and was already famous for his vivacious wit. Paralus was more serious, somewhat inflexible of character, took life, even at six, as a sober affair and rarely laughed or played pranks, was stronger than his older brother and taller, and moved ponderously.

There were no other children, for Pericles had not called his wife to his bed since the birth of Paralus. He was afraid that the gods might not be so benign with other children and that they might be born looking like their mother and with her immovable obtuseness. Moreover, Dejanira became more and more repugnant to him, more unbearable to his nostrils. Worse still, she adored him and would look at him with imploring eyes when she saw him, and he pitied her the more inexecrable she became to him. Therefore he avoided her, though admitting that she was most able in household affairs and was increasing his fortune through frugality and expert managing.

Dejanira's son by Hipponicus, Callias, was now sixteen years of age, and was a male replica of his mother, being short and massive and fat and disagreeable of temperament. He sullenly resented his brothers for their appearance and their accomplishments, and would console himself that he was surnamed 'The Rich', for he had been his father's heir. He was as miserly as his mother and dressed as meanly as a slave and his tutors despaired of him. He was no athlete. He preferred cockfights, the bloodier the better. He also liked to gamble, but as he was not averse to cheating he was rarely invited to participate with the companions at his academe. He hated Pericles and ridiculed him to his mother when she would permit it.

During the past few months Pericles had conferred with his bankers concerning Dejanira's dowry and the increase in it, for he had come to the conclusion that he must divorce his wife. Though seeing her seldom and rarely close by, he found her presence in his house more and more intolerable. He saw the misery of his mother, who had no escape from Dejanira as he did, with his hetaira and other women of even less repute.

He saw the mutinous expressions of his slaves who resented Dejanira and who complained to the overseer of their bad food and crowded quarters, and the overseer complained to Pericles in their interest. For Pericles was a kind master and treated them as paid servants rather than slaves, and often rewarded them lavishly and if petitioned enough he would free them, warning them, however, of the perils of freedom. When, at Dejanira's secret orders, distinguished guests had been served a poor wine in richly ornamented bottles, he had decided that he could endure Dejanira no longer. That wine was symbolic of the climate of his house. He had upbraided Dejanira for his mortification and she had burst into tears, had tried to embrace him, and had wept, 'I only sought to save you money, lord.' He had spurned her then as one spurns an importunate and untrained dog.

Not even the fact that his sons had considerable affection for their mother could deter him any longer from divorcing her. They could see her in the house of Daedalus at regular intervals. He was afraid that some of her coarseness might be conveyed to them and he loathed Callias as much as Callias hated him. Pericles, always pragmatic, feared that Callias might infect his sons in some fashion. As for Dejanira's own feelings, he did not consider them, for he doubted she possessed any capacity for devotion though she had been repellently passionate towards him when he had called her to his bed out of a sense of duty and compassion. He no longer pitied her. He must rid himself of her and as quickly as possible. As yet the unfortunate woman had no premonition that her husband's lawyers were already preparing for the suit.

On this evening after Daedalus' visit to Pericles' office Pericles wished to be alone while he considered the deadly danger to his friend and how he must protect and save him, for, on inquiry among his friends in the Agora, he had learned that not mere ostracism was contemplated for Ichthus, but death. The King Archon had been consulted but two hours before, and even Daedalus had not known, though he had been informed of it an hour after he had left Pericles.

Pericles did not know that at the very time that he was attempting to eat his dinner Daedalus was in terrified and raging consultation with Dejanira.

'Pericles will destroy us all if he defends that Chilon!' he cried to his daughter. 'He is already in bad favour among men of influence, who not only mention his resemblance to the Tyrant, Pisistratus, but assert that he is aiming at arbitrary power. He has been accused of cynicism in that he, an aristocrat, has set himself aside from his fellow aristocrats, and espouses the humble merely to make his position secure. It is noted that though he pretends to be the friend of the common people he keeps far from their presence and lets them see him rarely. He is too ambitious, sinister, ambiguous, to have many influential friends. It is no secret that he was the instigator of the banishment of Cimon, who was truly beloved, for he coveted Cimon's power. Yet, my daughter, he connived with Cimon later to have Cimon appointed commander of the fleet while he ruthlessly plotted with him to gain power in Athens for himself, with Cimon's consent. It is even rumoured that he had procured the murder of Ephialtes, the great and popular statesman!'

Dejanira whimpered and wrung her fat hands together and squinted through her tears. 'I know of none of this, my father, and it is possible they are lies inspired by envy.'

'Hah!' exclaimed Daedalus fiercely. 'I believe it all, though he is the husband of my daughter! He desires to be a monarch! The aristocratical party justly fears and hates him, for they consider him a traitor to his nation and his family, and his ancestors. They rightly fear his power, which he unlawfully took upon himself – '

Dejanira said with a spirit unusual with her, 'Father, that is not true! The citizens of Athens raised him by his merits.'

'Silence, woman!' cried infuriated Daedalus, lifting his

hand as if to strike her. She subsided and renewed her whimperings, shrinking from her father.

'The aristocratical party has induced Thucydides the Alopece, kinsman of Cimon, to oppose him, a good and intrepid man. He will succeed! Thucydides is no hypocrite, to woo the people to advance his own power. You have not read the writings on the walls of Athens, infamous accusations against Pericles scrawled by the very people he defends against the aristocrats. I tell you he lusts to be king and that Athens will not endure!'

Dejanira could only sniffle forlornly. Her father regarded her with exasperation. 'He is your husband,' he said. 'He is the father of your sons. You must prevail upon him to listen to you, that if he continues his plan to defend Ichthus not only he may be destroyed, but you and your children also.'

Dejanira broke into fresh tears, and her face turned very red. She averted her face and said, 'I have no influence on Pericles, my father. Rarely do I encounter him. He avoids me. I fear he despises me. I enter his chamber no more, not since the birth of Paralus. He has abandoned me for dissolute women. You have said that when you spoke to him today he turned on his heel and left you, after daunting words. You are an Archon, a man of position. If he will not listen to his father-in-law, why should he listen to me?'

Daedalus stood up, shaking with rage. He looked down at his stricken daughter and he, who rarely felt pity, felt it now. He laid his hand on her head and said in a trembling voice, 'My daughter, I did not know of this indignity laid upon you, and your mother did not know for she would have told me. There is but one solution: You must leave him and petition for a divorce, and return to your father's house with your children. Only then will the people realize that you are blameless, that you renounced your husband for his treason, and removed your children from his house lest they be dishonoured and punished in their father's name.'

'Leave Pericles?' wailed Dejanira, her small black eyes bulging with grief. 'He is my husband! I love him, no matter the humiliations he has heaped upon me, and in the presence of the very slaves.'

Daedalus seized her fat shoulder and shook it. 'Have you thought of your parents, my daughter? I am an Archon. Do you not realize that not only you and your children will be destroyed by the impetuous actions of this man but your parents also? Five innocent people! You will let us all die, or be exiled and our fortunes confiscated? You will serenely permit yourself, and your family, to live in dire poverty far from Athens, on some barbarous island? Have I begotten a human daughter, or a female Cyclops who sees with but one eye but who is blind to those she should dutifully love?'

Dejanira could not speak for her own terror and anguish. She wrung her hands and sobbed deep in her breast.

'Speak to him!' her father commanded. 'Speak to him this night. If he is adamant, send me a message and I will dispatch litters for you and your children and you will return to your father's house and will procure a divorce. Tell him this.'

Dejanira pressed her hands to her breast and her stolid face was contorted with fear and suffering and hopeless love. She whispered, 'I will try. I swear by Hera that I will try. That is all I can promise. If I fail,' she paused and wept louder, 'I will return to your house, my father, and that tomorrow.'

'And he will be forced to return your dowry and what has accrued to it,' said Daedalus, sighing with relief. It seemed to him, as a covetous man, that the loss of Dejanira's dowry would be a worse blow to Pericles than the loss of his family.

Dejanira said almost inaudibly. 'He loves his sons. He may not permit their removal.'

'Then, once you have left his house, and he is ruined, we will petition for the return of your children from the nefarious influence of their father. Do not be distressed, my daughter. Attempt, as your duty, to prevail upon him to reconsider. If not, then you must flee at any cost.' He rubbed his bony hand over his face and sighed. 'I am a man not without influence. Your children will be given to me as their guardian. I would that I had never consented to this marriage, but my sister besought me to consent.'

Dejanira was not without shrewdness. She knew it was her father who had proposed the marriage and not Agariste. She thought of Agariste with a sudden venom, Agariste who did not conceal from her her contempt for her daughter-in-law.

'It was through me that he was assisted to power,' said the Archon. 'One must never forget it. Would that the Furies had paralysed my tongue before I did that!'

He embraced his daughter and departed, and after long and shivering thought Dejanira sent a slave to Pericles, beseeching him to permit his wife to visit him immediately. She consoled herself with the thought that Pericles might listen to wise counsel for the sake of his sons if not for her sake. There was also his mother, who would be in deadly peril.

Dejanira paused and stared into space. Agariste. Much as she disliked the older woman and much as she had tried to relegate her to an inferior position, Agariste, at the last, might be a formidable ally. Waddling fast and ponderously, she went to Agariste's quarters.

Agariste had not surrendered her own exquisite and tasteful rooms to the new mistress of the house. After dining at night she would retire to her chamber and go to bed, for she was increasingly infirm and physicians spoke of her heart. She very seldom slept deeply but only drowsed, to awaken to gaspings for breath and a piercing pain in her heart. She had fallen into a sick doze when a slave entered her chamber softly and said, 'Lady, the Lady Dejanira would speak to you for a moment on a matter of the most extreme importance.'

Agariste, blinking in the soft light of the lamps, forced herself to sit upright. Her breath was loud and struggling in the fine chamber. A warm night wind scented with roses blew into

228

the room through the open window. She stared at the slave. What would Dejanira have with her, she who had never entered these rooms and had never been invited? The two women avoided each other as much as possible. Dejanira had never asked her advice except on a few occasions. Whenever they did speak together Dejanira would gaze at Agariste with sullen resentment and, as always, would try to impose her authority as mistress of the household on Agariste. She was invariably and coldly rejected by the older woman, but still she persisted in her stubborn way. Only yesterday they had had a quarrel, Agariste disdainful and aloof, Dejanira stammering with surly anger and insistence. At last Agariste had said, 'You may be the daughter of my brother, the Archon, but to me you have the manners of a kitchen wench, and an insolent one. Your father is my brother, and so is descended from a noble house, but your mother is as vulgar as you and had only money to distinguish herself. She has taught you well and you are as insufferable as she.' Dejanira had heavily stamped away, muttering and helpless.

Agariste said to the slave woman, 'The Lady Dejanira wishes to speak to me? Is one of my grandsons ill?' She pushed herself even higher on the bed and was frightened, for her son's children were very dear to her.

'I do not know, Lady,' said the slave woman. 'But the Lady Dejanira implores you to receive and listen to her.'

Agariste sipped at the cup of medicine at her bedside, and trembled inwardly as she awaited the coming of her daughter-in-law. She pulled her shift more easily over her still beautiful breasts, but her face was haggard and lined with pain and very white, and her golden hair had long lost its lustre and was dull and streaked with grey.

Dejanira entered the chamber, sobbing. Then she sank, unasked, on to a fragile chair – which creaked ominously with her weight – and began to wail loudly.

'In the name of the gods, tell me!' cried Agariste and turned even paler. Dejanira was stolid and without much emotion, so Agariste assumed that the news she brought was appalling. She wanted to strike that shapeless woman in her anxiety.

Dejanira said, 'We are ruined, we are destroyed, and all with us!' Her voice was hoarse and harsh and she rocked on her massive buttocks and her tears streamed. 'Pericles has brought the Furies down upon us, and we are lost!'

Agariste regarded her incredulously. Her impassive son, so remote and self-disciplined and laconic in speech except when addressing the Assembly, could hardly have been so impetuous and reckless as Dejanira indicated. She sank back on her cushions and said in a cold and peremptory voice, 'Tell me.'

It was almost impossible for Dejanira to tell a coherent story for her thoughts invariably flittered on to irrelevances. So Agariste was forced to strain her attention upon the flood of stammering words which poured from that thick wet mouth. Loud sobs interrupted the flow; Dejanira spoke of the honour of her parents, the delinquencies of the slaves in her husband's house, the depredations of the cooks on the larder and the money, the fate of her sons, her threatened self, her father's fear and offer, his importunities that she talk with Pericles, her general dissatisfaction with the ordering of the household, her fright, impending bankruptcy, her premonitions of disaster which had haunted her for many months, Pericles' indiscretion and his mistress, her unfortunate fate which marriage had brought upon her, the failure of Pericles' last investment in ships to Egypt, her meekness and virtue under insufferable trials in his house, the lack of appreciation she received for all her scrupulousness and thrift, and sundry other things.

Agariste wanted to scream. She reached out her thin hand and clutched Dejanira's enormous wrist. 'Tell me!' she almost shouted. 'You fool! Can you not bring your feeble wits to order and enlighten me? What has all this to do with the disaster you spoke of?'

The flood of meaningless complaints came to an abrupt halt, and Dejanira was outraged by her aunt's voice and the fierce seizing of her wrist. She strove for dignity. 'Have I not been telling you, Agariste?' she said. 'But you will never listen to me! We are undone.'

But Agariste's eyes were quelling and enlarged, so Dejanira dropped her head and her moist face became sullen. She could hardly remember her father's specific denunciations of Pericles, for she was always confused by rapid speech, which she could not follow. But Agariste, sitting stiffly upright on her bed, was finally able to grasp a little of what Daedalus had imparted to his daughter. Agariste thought rapidly. Surely Pericles was not insensible to the peril and jeopardy into which he was hurling his family. He was not volatile or heedless. His emotions, however stirred, did not rush him into fatalities. His friendships were temperate if strong. Anaxagoras had taught him that; but he was innately prudent. Agariste was again incredulous, though she knew that Dejanira had so little imagination that it was impossible for her to be inventive, and exaggerate.

She broke into Dejanira's sobbing and said, 'I can hardly believe this of my son. I will go with you to his chambers, for your slave woman has announced that he will see you.' She glanced at Dejanira contemptuously and rose with difficulty and threw a white toga over her nightdress. Her heart was painfully thumping but her countenance was composed. 'Come,' she said, and led the way from her chamber, and Dejanira followed her like a servant, moaning over and over. Agariste walked like a goddess, proudly suppressing her pain, and thinking, and Dejanira trailed after her like an obese shadow, sniffling.

Pericles was sitting in his library, but he was not reading. His face was closed and intent. He looked up at the two women and frowned, but he directed his attention at once on his mother. He saw her translucent pallor and requested her to seat herself, but he did not invite his wife to do likewise.

'I was informed that only Dejanira wished to see me,' he said, but his tone was gentle towards his mother. 'You are ill; why have you risen to visit me this night?'

Agariste waved her hand in the direction of Dejanira but did not look at her. In a few concise words she repeated what Dejanira had told her, and the threats of Daedalus. She had an orderly mind and could speak shortly and clearly. As she did so she watched Pericles' face. It had become impassive again, a marble mask which concealed his thoughts. When Agariste had stopped speaking he leaned back in his chair and was silent. His mother waited. Dejanira's sobs and random exclamations filled the library. Her black hair was dishevelled, for she had been running her fingers through it constantly in her distraught state. Her cheeks were blotched, her eyes and nose red. She mumbled over and over about bankruptcy, her father's position as Archon, ruin, exile, confiscations of estates. But neither Pericles nor Agariste heeded her.

Then Pericles said to his mother, 'It is all true, that I must defend Ichthus, for he is a simple, just and good man, and he speaks the truth. He also, unfortunately, writes it, and broadcasts it.'

'You understand the consequences if you fail, my son?'

'I have weighed them. I shall not fail. I must only induce Ichthus to recant and plead for mercy, for he values my opinion and guidance. He is a man of fervour, but tractable. I have been thinking of all this for hours, and I have come to the conclusion that a brief ostracism will be his only punishment.'

Pericles was not so confident as he appeared, but he wished to allay his mother's fears and to soothe her.

Agariste sighed with relief. Her son was the most powerful man in Athens.

Then Pericles turned to his wife for the first time and his face was even more impassive and hard. 'I must inform you, Dejanira, that I am about to divorce you. You have made my house untenable and caused disorder and dissension in it. You must leave my house tomorrow and return to your father, taking your son, Callias, with you, but my own sons must remain.'

Dejanira's lumbering thoughts were stirred into disjointed confusion. She was also filled with despair. She broke into loud and hysterical weeping. She attempted to go to her husband but Agariste restrained her. The mother said to her son in a dispassionate voice, 'This is for the best. We have been an unhappy household since your marriage, Pericles. Unhappiness is not to be suffered if it can be removed.'

She stood up and took Dejanira firmly by the arm and forced the younger woman to look at her. 'You will have observed that none of us is in danger, and it is all your father's fevered imagination. Go to your quarters at once, there to prepare to leave this house in the morning.'

Dejanira struggled with her briefly, while Pericles watched, then subsided. She burst out into a storm of denunciations, complaints, pleas, importunities, incongruous arguments. Pericles closed his eyes wearily. Sweating, Dejanira exuded an offensive smell and the fastidious Pericles drew in his nostrils, as did his mother hers.

'Come,' said Agariste. But she pitied Dejanira who had been so brutally dismissed and rejected. 'There is no use in crying this way. Tomorrow is time for reflection and decision.' Dejanira stared at her with bulging eyes, and licked away the moisture on her upper lip. She thought that Agariste was assuring her that she would not have to leave this house. Her breast heaved and she permitted Agariste to lead her away.

She said to the silent woman as they walked through the halls, 'I love Pericles. He is my life, my love. On our wedding night he called me his sweetness. I have never forgot it. He embraced me not only with passion but with joy.'

Agariste raised her eyebrows, disbelieving. She was also surprised that Dejanira could love in this manner, and with such vehemence. Again, she pitied the younger woman and her touch on Dejanira's arm was kind and comforting. Yet she knew that Pericles' decisions were inexorable.

CHAPTER X

Though Anaxagoras had told Pericles that a man who could not command his body and his emotions to his will was not a full man at all, Pericles found that he could not sleep that night. He had disciplined himself to make firm decisions and then act upon them with no regret and no wistful glances back over his shoulders. A strong decision, which later proved catastrophic, was far better than vacillation, which weakened a man. One was action, the other inaction; one was life, the other a dim death. Pericles had long before decided to divorce his wife. Still, he had not been insensible to her wild grief and protestations of love, and her lamentations. These had not shaken his decision; compassion was often cowardice, which one later regretted. Or, one became hostile and angered, knowing that he had succumbed to artful manipulation, and had been betrayed by maudlin deceit on the part of others.

To him, the situation of Ichthus was far more grave. Unable to sleep, unable to reach a decision – he was innately a prudent man for all his resolution and character – he rose long before dawn and sent a message to the barracks that he would be leaving immediately. A sleepy slave brought him a cool melon, a delicately broiled fish, light bread and wine for his breakfast. He ate, brooding, and tapped the table with his fingers. At moments he was furious with his endangered friend for his indiscretion; Ichthus had also placed his few friends in jeopardy, and his widowed mother and his relatives. But in the next moment Pericles would say to himself: He is a brave man, and courage is more to be desired than any other virtue. He did what he must. That is all a man can do.

Pericles' guard of six mounted soldiers, helmeted and

armoured in leather, arrived and he rose and went to join them. His chariot waited outside, with two fine white horses. He always drove it himself. It was not the splendid car of the aristocrats, all gilt and enamel, but Pericles was no man for personal ostentation, for all he had one of the most lovely houses in Athens. He jumped into the chariot and took the reins from a slave, to whom he spoke kindly, thanking him. He was unaware that his mother had died peacefully in her bed in the night. Even the household did not know it as yet.

As the cavalcade swept down the hill, the soldiers carrying torches, Pericles glanced at Piraeus, the port of Athens. Some red torches still burned there, and there was some sluggish movement of lanterns. Athens still slept.

When the company reached the level of the Agora Pericles began to wonder why he had arrived so long before his usual time, forgetting his sleepless hours and his sense of pressure and unease and anxiety. Ichthus, he thought wryly, would not die before noon, if he died at all. There was the matter of his trial. He brought his horses up short with a sharp command as a young man suddenly appeared on the road before him. The young man dodged and danced lightly up on the pavement, and he turned an antic smiling face on Pericles and half-mockingly saluted. He had a Pan-like appearance, and there was an air of goatish agility about him. He had a very ugly little face with a nose that resembled a persimmon and was most undistinguished, a thatch of roughly cut hair, and an incongruous little beard trimmed to a casual point. His big ears stood out from his head like the handles of jugs.

Pericles recognized him though he had never exchanged a word with this young man who was already noted for his arguments and his philosophies and his teachings in the colonnades of the Agora and near the temples. Anaxagoras spoke approvingly of him, and with some little amusement, as an elder. But Athens teemed with philosophers, all hungry and vehement and self-assured even if humbly dressed and often barefoot.

The morning light lay in his eyes as he contemplated the halted company and Pericles, who rarely smiled, found himself smiling. 'Were you coveting death, Socrates?' he asked, flicking his whip idly.

'Do we not all, even the happiest of us?' returned Socrates with an impudent grin. He was not awed by this most powerful man in Athens, whom he had often seen in the Agora. 'And why should death be feared? If it is an endless sleep, do we not woo sleep? If there is life beyond it, then that too is good. Death is not to be abhorred.'

'It is too early in the day for philosophy,' said Pericles, and Socrates grinned again, inclining his head. The company went on. Pericles reached his offices and went to his separate room through a mass of petty officials and scribes who were just beginning to arrive. He sat down at his desk and began to frown and to ponder. A huge restlessness seized him, nameless and unformed. He faced the problem of Ichthus fully. His mind was fresher than it had been during the dark hours of night. But he was conscious of a physical weariness. He went silently over the arguments he had prepared for his friend, and clarified some of them.

A young scribe brought a bowl of fruit and a goblet and a small jug of wine and set it down before him. Pericles nodded without speaking. He glumly drank a little wine and ate an apple. The door opened and Anaxagoras entered, a man of grandeur for all his simple long tunic. He sat down opposite Pericles and said, 'Our friend, Ichthus, is to be tried tomorrow before the Ecclesia.' He poured a little wine for himself in a goblet Pericles silently offered. 'He will,' said Anaxagoras, 'surely be condemned to death. On that the Ecclesia is determined.'

When Pericles said nothing, Anaxagoras continued: 'The time is at hand when no man will be permitted to criticize government, however mildly, nor speculate on the gods.'

'I intend to go to the prison this morning. I will attempt to persuade him to be cautious, and not to blurt out damning facts about himself, nor orate in defence of freedom.'

Anaxagoras waited, looking at Pericles with his noble eyes. Pericles stood up and began to pace the room, cursing half under his breath. 'I will try to persuade him, for his own sake, and the sake of his family, to be discreet. Discretion is not to be despised, when a man's life and the lives of his family are endangered. If I fail – '

He stopped. Anaxagoras still waited. 'If I fail,' said Pericles, 'I have but one recourse: to defend him before the Ecclesia, even if I have to say that he is mad and so is not responsible for his writings.'

'But the Ecclesia desires his death above all other things. If you persuade them he is mad, they will incarcerate him for life.'

Pericles, who had begun to sweat in his extremity, removed his helmet and wiped his damp hair. 'You pose no solutions,' he said.

'In life, there are no solutions. A man can only do the best he can with the guidance of his reason. I grant you that Ichthus is not notable for reason. He is no philosopher. He is only a man who loves his nation and would die for it.'

'I love it also. But I must deal with bureaucrats, and may the Furies scize them!'

Pericles called for his chariot and his guards. He drove up the acropolis to the prison of 'the Eleven', or the Criminal Commissioners, where Ichthus was confined. It was a for-midable and grim place, and only heinous prisoners, suspected of being enemies of the State, were incarcerated there.

The guards were awed when they saw Pericles and his company. He was readily admitted, and with incredulous wonder, by the guards, to the cell of Ichthus. What had this powerful man to do with a criminal?

As Ichthus was not only a citizen of Athens but was of a notable family his cell was commodious and light and clean. A member of his family had brought a soft carpet to cover the stone floor, and some light furniture and a comfortable bed. Pericles motioned to the guard to open the door, and said with stern authority, 'I will call you when I wish to depart.' The guard saluted, Pericles entered the cell, and waited impatiently for the sound of the guard's retreating footsteps.

Ichthus exclaimed, 'Pericles! Oh, never should you have come to this place!' His high voice was still almost feminine in its intonations.

Pericles hesitated, then held out his hand and Ichthus took it. Tears shimmered in his eyes, and Pericles looked away. 'Why should I not have come?' he asked. 'Am I not your friend?'

Ichthus glanced at the barred door with a sort of terror and he raised his voice and said with loud emphasis, 'No, never were you my friend, Pericles, son of Xanthippus! We knew each other slightly, but that only.' He drew a trembling breath. 'If you have kindness, lord, please leave me at once and forget' – he could not speak for a second or two – 'forget you ever saw me.'

Pericles understood at once. His enemies were always accusing him of possessing a heart of marble, for he was almost invariably cold and distant in his manner, unlike the majority of his clamorous fellow Athenians. But now his strongly disciplined face softened and he felt a plunge of pain. He put his hand on Ichthus' shivering shoulder, pressed it firmly, and Ichthus sat down on the bed again in a posture of anguish. Pericles drew up another chair and sat near him and once again studied him, and now with gentleness.

'Ichthus, my friend,' he said, in that sonorous voice which could always move the emotions of others, 'you have come to a sad pass, against which I warned you years ago.'

'Yes,' said Ichthus, who could not move his eyes from the face he loved so much and adored almost slavishly, 'you have warned me.'

'You did not listen,' said Pericles.

Ichthus made a desperate motion with his long and sensitive hands. 'I obeyed One I loved much dearer.'

'The Unknown God,' said Pericles.

Ichthus nodded. 'What is my life?' he said. 'It is nothing besides that obedience.'

Pericles made a wry mouth. 'Have the gods communicated to you their desires, Ichthus? Have they spoken to you in the night, and especially Pallas Athene? Is that not presumptuous? How do you know their commands, their wishes?'

Ichthus put his hand on his slight breast. 'I hear the voice of God in my heart. God is the enemy of tyranny, of all that oppresses man, and to obey God is better than to obey an unconscionable government.'

Pericles frowned. It might be possible to save this pathetic and innocent man, this fervent and honest man, but he would always be in danger of retribution. At the end, he would be murdered. Pericles rubbed his chin, and the rings on his fingers twinkled in the rising and falling light of the lamp. He moved nearer to Ichthus and lowered his voice.

'You have a mother,' he said. 'You have sisters, and cousins, all who love you. Do you know their fate if you are found guilty by the Ecclesia of heresy and treason?'

Ichthus briefly closed his eyes on a spasm and the lids wrinkled. Then he opened his eyes and regarded Pericles straightly, and Pericles saw the valour in them, the steadfast light shining like a star.

'They know what I must do,' he said. 'They know I can but obey, and fight for my country, that she might be free once again, and a sun to the world of men.'

'Do you understand that it is very probable that all your goods and lands and money will be seized, your family dispersed or ostracized, if you pursue your course?'

'I know,' said Ichthus, and Pericles could hardly hear him.

Pericles said, and with some painful exasperation, 'It is very heroic, and very honourable, Ichthus, but it is a sacrifice no man should ask of his family!'

He stood up and began to pace the cell with rapid and clanging footsteps, and Ichthus watched him mournfully. Ichthus said, 'I have talked of all this to my family, and they know I must do as I must do.' When Pericles did not reply but only increased the rapidity of his pacing, Ichthus said, 'What would you do, my dearest of friends?'

'I would not have you die,' said Pericles. 'You are one of the few men of probity I know, one of the few I can trust. You saved my life. For that alone I shall always be grateful. But more than that you taught me a tremendous lesson. You are my friend, and I can say that of only a small number.'

The fervent light slowly began to return to Ichthus' face and he turned eagerly towards Pericles. 'Then, you would despise me if I betrayed all that for which I have lived! And all that is mighty to you, yourself, Pericles!'

Pericles was silent. He felt old and heavy and very tired and sick. He thought of Anaxagoras and what the latter would have felt at this conversation. Pericles could see those piercing and noble eyes. They seemed to have fixed themselves on him, in this cell, glowing and unwavering.

Once more he stood up and began to pace the cell, his head bent, and Ichthus watched him, following his course back and forth with his enormous eyes. The lamplight fluttered in a hot breeze which came through the windows. The scrolls on the table stirred restlessly.

Ichthus spoke again and again imploringly. 'What would my life be worth to me if I lied to myself, if I ignobly recanted and if I were permitted to slink away like a beaten dog? How could I live with myself? How could you live with yourself, Pericles, if you followed your own advice?'

Pericles sighed. He did not stop his pacing. He fingered the sharp Damascene steel dagger at his girdle, and felt the faceted gems in the hilt.

He stopped before Ichthus. 'I fear I could not live with myself,' he said. Ichthus clasped his hands together and his eyes were radiant and full of reverence.

'So,' said Pericles, 'I have but one recourse. I will defend you before the Ecclesia.'

The radiance died instantly from Ichthus' eyes. Terror and alarm suffused his face, which had become deathly yellow. His mouth opened on a great cry.

'No! That you must not do, Pericles! You have formidable enemies. They would use your defence of me to your destruction, your ruin, and even your life!' Horror gripped him, and confused agony.

'All through the night,' said Pericles in so stern a voice that even the distraught Ichthus caught his breath, 'I have pondered this and have come to the conclusion that I must defend you, if you refused to be discreet. Let us speak no more of this. I, too, Ichthus, must do as I must do.'

Ichthus fell on his knees before his friend and raised his clasped hands to him. He almost grovelled.

'No! I will not accept this monstrous sacrifice! I will not permit it! Who am I, compared with you, Pericles, son of Xanthippus, the glory of our country?'

'You are my friend,' said Pericles. 'You are even more: You are a brave man.'

He reached down to lift Ichthus to his feet. Ichthus' eyes stared wildly in his extremity of dread and suffering, then roamed about the cell, then returned to Pericles. He swallowed visibly. Tears began to flood from his eyes. He flung aside Pericles' hands and moaned over and over, 'No, no, no. This you must not do! Athens needs you. You must not die for me, an insignificant man!'

Then, before Pericles could move, Ichthus' hand darted out and seized the hilt of Pericles' dagger. He leapt to his feet and sprang back from the other man, and he smiled deeply, a heartbreaking smile, the dagger high in his uplifted hand.

'Farewell, dearest of friends! Live for Athens!'

Before the startled Pericles could move one foot Ichthus had plunged the dagger into his breast. The blood spurted forth, and Ichthus staggered. Pericles caught him in his arms and swayed with the weight that had become heavy and flaccid.

Pericles lowered him on his bed, and his hoarse panting filled the cell. 'Gods,' he muttered. He leaned over Ichthus who lay on his bed with a beatific smile on his face, a smile of love and triumph. Pericles looked at the dagger which stood upright from Ichthus' chest. Blood flowed all about it. Pericles began to tremble. The jewels on the hilt glittered in the lamplight.

Ichthus tried to speak, but he died, still smiling that ecstatic smile of loving triumph. At the very last he had touched Pericles' hand consolingly.

Pericles, never looking away from that piteous countenance, so gently victorious, so dauntless, forced himself to stand upright, though all his flesh was shaken.

Again, Ichthus had saved his life. He covered his eyes with his hand and began to weep.

CHAPTER XI

The King Archon looked at Daedalus with an inscrutable expression. He said, 'You have brought grave charges against the Head of State, Pericles, son of Xanthippus. It is true that the Head of State must be beyond reproach, even if he is just a man as are the rest of us. In his official position he must not be guilty of malfeasance, however he may be only a human being in his private life. You are enraged, my friend, that when your daughter refused to divorce him he brought suit for annulment.' The King Archon raised his hand. 'Let us not be emotional. Your cries have been hysterical. Bear with me. The affairs of your daughter, Dejanira, have no bearing on the conduct of Pericles. Many men divorce their wives or seek annulment. The government is not concerned with the domestic problems of their members.

242

'You wish to have your grandsons, Xanthippus and Paralus, returned to the custody of their mother, under your guardianship. Pericles is their father. Men have full disposal of their children, and this must not be denied Pericles. The children are content with their father, and adore him. Let us not be concerned with children, who are insignificant. It is womanish to consider children; they are nothing until they are men. Before that they are unripe, and disorderly. There is no room in our national life for such. Their future belongs to their fathers and not their raging mothers, who think with their wombs and not with their minds – if they have any.

'What are your other impetuous charges? Ichthus died in his cell by his own hand, with the dagger of Pericles. You deny this. You have said that Pericles, the notable Head of State, deliberately murdered Ichthus to prevent that unhappy man from "betraying" his connections with Pericles! Had Pericles wished the death of Ichthus he could have had him quietly poisoned with the hemlock cup. Or, he could have repudiated him with contempt. Why, then, murder? It is ridiculous to believe for an instant that Pericles, the Head of State, reduced himself to the status of a common alley murderer!'

'I hate him!' cried Daedalus.

The King Archon frowned. 'Government has no room for personal sentiments. Government is orderly – or should be – and detached from the aberrations of female instability. As Solon said, women should not be permitted to interfere with affairs of State. Go to. If you would not be prosecuted for libel, my Daedalus, you will control your tongue and your twitters. It was you who arranged the marriage between your daughter and the noble Pericles. Now, for some reason known only to you, you wish to destroy him. I do not admire Pericles, but I know what is ridiculous. Let us be done with this nonsense.'

Daedalus rose in all his skeleton height, his teeth clenched.

'I will have vengeance!' he said.

The King Archon shrugged. 'If Pericles is mysteriously

243

assassinated I will remember your words.' He added, 'I am not in agreement with the design of Pericles to waste the public money on the raising of monuments and temples to the glory of Athens. I am not in agreement with his policies. I do not admire his defence of what he calls "the middle" between the aristocrats and the rabble. The rabble is only the offal of a society. It needs to be controlled at all times. I do not distinguish between the market rabble and Pericles' advancement of merchants and shopkeepers and artisans and skilled labour, and the mean professions of physicians and lawyers. What are the people? Dogs. Nevertheless, he has been a prudent and determined administrator. His opinions are his own. Only time will tell whether he has been right. The sober people of Athens love him, and the sober are not to be despised. Let us wait. In the meantime, my friend, control yourself.'

'May Hecate and the Furies devour him!'

Again the King Archon shrugged. 'The gods have their ways, and they are not known to us. If Pericles flourish or die, that is their judgement. Please leave me. I am wearied with your outbursts and denunciations, none of which are relevant.'

Pericles did not know for whom he mourned most deeply – his mother or Ichthus. He was filled with hatred of the faceless man who had betrayed Ichthus. Ichthus had written his broadcasts anonymously. Therefore, only one he had loved and trusted could have delivered him to his enemies. But, was that not always so? Who was it who had said that a malicious enemy was less to be feared than an avowed friend, full of protestations of loyalty? He, Pericles, had few friends, not only because he was a politician but because he repudiated all fawnings, all declarations of dedication to him, all vows of eternal faithfulness. He was especially suspicious of the latter. Yes, friends were to be feared.

He was determined to discover the dear friend, the trusted

and loyal friend, who had been the cause of Ichthus' arrest and death. No doubt, if apprehended, he would virtuously protest that what he had done was in the interest of his country, which came above friendship. Of such stuff were liars made. Malice was the one dread and terrible trait which all human beings possessed, though they differed in other traits. It was inspired by envy, private cruel ridicule of the victim, greed, or some petty imagined offence the victim had inflicted on his destroyer. Often it was only the result of the heroic character of the victim; men can endure anything but profound virtue in another. For some reason virtue inflamed hate among mankind, just as vice receives its secret admiration. We are an evil species, thought Pericles, and why the gods do not eliminate us must be due either to their indifference to our fate, or their benignity.

Now he sought the beloved and trusted friend of Ichthus. He could not be denounced publicly, for the government would praise his loyalty to it. He must be murdered and before his murder he must be told why he was being done to death.

So, night and day he pondered on the identity of the avowed friend of Ichthus. Then he would exert fear on one he would employ to kill that friend. He went to the mother of Ichthus, who was ill with grief. 'Who was my son's best friend, lord? You were, though you saw him seldom. He would have died for you. His closest associate? An old schoolmate, Turnus, whom my son pathetically loved. He has been with me often, consoling me, offering me his selfless services – '

'Ah,' said Pericles. 'Did Ichthus leave, in his will, any treasure to Turnus, son of Patroclus, who is one of the Archons?'

'Yes,' said the bereaved mother. Despite her composure her face twitched. 'He left him one-third of his patrimony.'

Money is always an inducement to betrayal, thought Pericles with intense hate and bitterness. He left the unhappy mother, saddened by her distress; he was burning with 'renewed anger and determination. He made some inquiries concerning Turnus and discovered something secret which enraged him further.

He then explored the backgrounds of his friends. Who was the one who feared him most? Pericles thought, ruthlessly.

He sent for Jason, son of an illustrious father, who was not only a bureaucrat of formidable power but was tied to Pericles' service by the most potent respect. He was a tall quiet man of middle age and of a gentle manner and scrupulous in his duties, not, in this case by fear, but because of his character. He was famous for his natural magnanimity, which was not a pretence, and his sympathetic attitude, again not pretence. He had never been known to do a cruel or unjust act; his probity was beyond any doubt. He and Pericles had been schoolmates together, and both the youths had protected Ichthus. He was also a patriot and loved Athens little less than did Pericles. Pericles had considerable fondness for him and often consulted him on difficult matters. However, without any hesitation Pericles chose him as the destroyer of Turnus, whom Jason despised.

Jason not only respected Pericles, but returned his affection. Pericles counted him as one of his few friends. He greeted Jason with his usual restraint, but smiled at him and gave him his hand in the privacy of his house. Pericles ordered wine and pastries for his friend, and while they drank and ate together they discussed affairs of state. Jason was somewhat puzzled. They had discussed these affairs only yesterday. Jason fixed his grey eyes on Pericles with curiosity, but being a courteous man he did not ask why he had been summoned almost at sunset from his office.

Pericles' manner abruptly changed and his eyes took on that blind look which was so daunting to others. He said in a low voice, 'I have thought, today, of your murder of your wife, Calypso, two years ago.'

Jason turned very pale and stared, without speaking, at Pericles.

'It is true that she deserved to be murdered,' said Pericles, in a soothing tone, and nodded. 'She was notable for her evil temper and viciousness. Did she not abuse you and your children by your dead first wife? Did she not lie to you so that they would not inherit your estate? Did she not attempt to degrade your daughter in your esteem? Did she not, at the last, betray you, for she was a woman of considerable beauty? But, you loved her, and trusted her despite her enormous defects of character.'

Jason's mouth and throat became so dry that he made a retching sound. After an attempt or two he found his voice. 'Why do you recall this to me, Pericles?'

Again those blind eyes turned themselves on Jason, who had begun to tremble. 'Yes,' said Pericles, 'your wife deserved to die. Yet, you could not kill her, yourself. You hired an assassin, and paid him well. Then he began to torment you, demanding more than his fee on the threat of betrayal. He would write a confession, he said to you, and then would flee back to his native Arabia to escape punishment himself.

'You came to me, your friend, in despair, for you knew I was discreet and remember friendship. You laid your case before me. You thought of hiring another assassin to dispose of the Arabian. However, you feared that he would also betray you. Murder is an endless chain. The assassin did not know that I was your friend. I had him investigated. He was a thief, though he had concealed the fact well, and he had murdered others. Yet, there was no valid evidence against him, for he was clever and adroit. Now, I had the evidence. He was duly executed.'

'Yes,' whispered Jason. For the first time he saw a baleful glow in the depths of those unreadable eyes.

Pericles sighed and leaned back in his chair as if wearied. 'There is one dread thing I have learned in this world of men, which I did not make. I keep full dossiers on friend or foe, sworn to most solemnly by myself. It is known that I am not malicious – but I trust few if any men, even yourself, Jason.

'Do not be offended. I consider that friendship is a very frail thing, and friends unpredictable. The brother today can become your most mortal enemy, with or without provocation, tomorrow. It is human nature.'

Again Jason whispered; he felt that he was dying. 'Are you my enemy, Pericles?'

Pericles smiled slightly, though his conscience was troubling him. 'Not yet, Jason,' he said frankly. 'But I have a dossier on you which I hoped I would never need to use. I must protect myself. I trust I will never need to use it and deliver you to executioners. But, as the Egyptians say, who knows what tomorrow will bring?'

'You are going to use that dossier against me, Pericles?'

'Not unless you force me to do so, either by becoming my enemy or by any violation of your duties. You can trust me a little better than you can trust others. Tell me. You have the name and know the whereabouts of the second professional assassin whom you considered employing against the first?'

Jason swallowed. 'I do,' he said.

Pericles nodded. Jason said, 'You wish someone murdered, Pericles?'

'Yes. Turnus, the son of Patroclus. I have discovered that it was he who betrayed our poor friend, Ichthus, to the authorities. Love and trust! What enormities follow such! Perhaps they are justified. No matter. I want Turnus dead, as quickly and as secretly as possible. It might be that your assassin can contrive an accident for him, as the first contrived it for your wife.'

'Turnus, the son of Patroclus, the Archon!' Jason's face almost disintegrated with his shock. 'He betrayed Ichthus? That is indeed a crime of calamitous proportions. His father is very powerful. He will not lightly accept an accident to his son. He will investigate. Woe is me!'

'Do not be distressed. He will be disposed of swiftly, the assassin. I have another thought. He will be caught in the act of murder, and will be dispatched at once before he can speak.

I promise you that. I will order this. The details will be arranged most meticulously.'

Trembling more than ever, Jason bent his head and pondered. After a while he looked at Pericles straightly. 'Why can I not give you his name and you arrange the – murder – yourself, my friend?'

Again Pericles smiled. 'I am the Head of State.'

Jason clasped his hands together convulsively. 'I detest murder.'

'So do I. But sometimes it is – effective – and necessary. Was it not so in the case of your deplorable wife?'

Jason winced. 'I was driven almost to madness. But murder leads to murder – '

'I disagree – my friend.' He withdrew a large purse of gold coins from his girdle and laid it on the table between himself and Jason. 'I would not have you bribe the murderer yourself, Jason. This is my money. There is another matter. Before the assassin kills, in whatever manner he devises, he must say to Turnus, "This is vengeance for Ichthus." Let Turnus think of that before he dies. Otherwise the murder will be pointless.'

When Jason did not speak Pericles said, 'The first assassin was truly inventive. Calypso was inadvertently hanged by her rich necklace of pearls, which she accidentally caught on a hook in her bedroom. I trust the second assassin is as inventive. Only you can know. But you must not tell me.'

Still Jason did not speak. Pericles sighed. 'If Turnus is not executed – we must call it a just execution – then I will be forced, in honour, to make public my dossier on you, my poor friend.'

Jason spoke weakly. 'Then you will be asked why you had not shown the dossier heretofore.'

Now Pericles' eyes became young and candid. 'My dear Jason, I was only thorough in my investigations and did not wish to prematurely accuse you! The dossier was completed only yesterday!'

'I never thought you would injure me, Pericles, or ruin me.'

'Have I done so? Never will I do it unless you become my enemy, or fail in your authority.'

'That I will never do, and so you know it, Pericles.'

Pericles shrugged. 'Make no rash promises, Jason, for you are only a man and also possess malice, the one evil which all men, regardless of virtue or station, possess. I trust you as much as I am capable of trusting – which I confess is very little. Sometimes men are driven to malice, against their very scruples. Tell me, Jason. Is not Turnus deserving of – execution?'

'Yes, that is true,' said Jason with reluctant honesty.

Jason stood up, slowly, his hands visibly shaking. He looked down at the purse of gold for a long time and Pericles watched him. Then Jason took the purse. Suddenly he was resolute. 'It will be done,' he said.

Pericles embraced him. 'Do you think this is an idle petty judgement on my part, and that I rejoice in it? No. I am not only Head of State. I do not know any assassins.'

'You will destroy your dossier on me when this is done, Pericles?'

Pericles was silent for a moment and then he shook his head with true regret. 'No, Jason. That I cannot promise you. One day you may become my enemy. I pray this will not happen, for I love you.'

When the distraught Jason had departed Pericles was filled with gloom. He had been ruthless, even more ruthless than customary with him. He disliked himself for the misery he had imposed on Jason. But Jason was only a weapon in behalf of justice.

Five days later Turnus suddenly arose from a dice game with his friends and called for his chariot in a condition of great agitation. He then raced off in the direction of his father's house. The horses mysteriously bolted, or he had whipped them in too great a frenzy, and he was thrown from the chariot and killed, smashing his head against a marble column. His friends spoke of his sudden pallor at the gaming table, his staring eyes, then his flight. Among them was Jason.

Pericles sent for Jason, who came into the offices silently, his face grey and still. Pericles closed the door and said, 'Nemesis rode with him.'

'Yes,' said Jason. He briefly closed his eyes. Pericles said, 'Your assassin is very clever. Unfortunately, my agents had no time to eliminate him, for I had had no word from you.'

Jason was silent. He bent his head and gazed at the floor. Pericles continued: 'We must know his name and where he lives.'

Jason shook his head. 'He will never speak – that assassin.' Now he looked up at Pericles and his tired eyes were still and intent. He repeated, 'He will never speak.' He laid the purse of gold Pericles had given him, on the table.

Pericles stared at the purse for a long time. He was filled with pity. At last he said, 'You must tell me nothing.' He went to his closet, unlocked a brass chest and withdrew a sheaf of papers rolled and sealed. He put them into Jason's hand. 'I, too, will never speak. Here is your dossier, my friend. Destroy it as soon as possible.' I hope I do not regret this, Pericles thought to himself somewhat ruefully.

Jason said in a faint voice, 'He was a most iniquitous man.'

The next day Anaxagoras said to Pericles. 'God took His own way in avenging Ichthus.'

Pericles smiled at him blandly. 'Was it not fortunate? I did not have to intervene.'

Anaxagoras answered the smile with his own, though reluctantly. 'Who shall limit the instruments of God? He often employs men to carry out His will.' He drank from a goblet of wine and said, 'However, do not presume too often, Pericles, in deciding that what you do is His will. He may have other plans.'

CHAPTER XII

Pericles arrived at the house of his beloved Helena, who greeted him with her usual robust and rosy smile, and embraced him. 'I fear I shall lose you tonight, O Apollo.'

'Never, my Hebe,' he said, kissing her soundly and stroking her auburn hair in which were diamond pins he had given her. They were no brighter than her eyes. He smacked her rump and she led him from the atrium into the dining hall, laughing. She whispered a short lascivious joke to him, and he smiled in appreciation though he did not admire lewdness in women except in the bedchamber. But physicians were famous for their improper jests.

The dining hall was already filled with guests, though they had not yet seated themselves. Slaves went among them with wine, beer and whisky and various savoury titbits. The silken curtains at doors and windows moved in a brisk breeze and there was a sullen stalking of thunder in the hills and an occasional flash of blue lightning. Beautiful Egyptian and Damascan lamps of glass and gold and silver stood on the long waiting dining table, and hung from the frescoed ceiling where nymphs and satyrs and fauns frolicked in intense colours. The table was strewn with late roses and lilies and ferns in delicate patterns and the air of the dining hall was suffused with their fragrance. The chairs and the divans, both at the table and against the yellow marble walls, were rich with silk and velvet of many hues, which were all harmonious. Even the Chinese vases, overflowing with blossoms in the corners and against the walls, had been chosen with meticulous taste for their form and their decorations. Helena was a physician; she was also a woman of great artistry and discrimination.

Helena rarely if ever entertained dull and stolid matrons so Pericles knew that the beauteous women present were rich and courted and beguiling courtesans, all selected for their appearance, wit and intelligence and gifts of entertainment. With pleasure he observed that his friends, Zeno of Elea and Anaxagoras, were among those present. But with surprise he saw the roughly clad young man, Socrates, with his goatlike beard and vivacity and ugly face. Even more to his surprise, Pericles saw that Zeno and Anaxagoras were listening to him intently and with evident pleasure. Also present was the shy sculptor, Pheidias.

Pericles had halted in the archway with Helena and so he surveyed the guests, particularly the women, before entering the hall. Beautiful women were no novelty to him; he knew most of them present and had enjoyed their loveliness and their conversation. Then he saw the stranger, and his heart rose like a fountain in him and he was lost.

She was the woman of his figurine and of his dreams, with whom, in a drunken fantasy, he had consummated his marriage with Dejanira. She was not young; she was in her early twenties and so had lost the first freshness of youth. But she had the maturity of a ripe pear, of opalescent grapes ready for the trading. She was speaking gravely to Pheidias, a goblet in her hand, and the sculptor appeared entranced. She was much taller than Pheidias, and, unlike the other women's her hair, a cobweb of silvery gold, flowed simply down her back and almost to her knees. She wore a garland of pink rosebuds. She had the easy grace and slenderness of a trained courtesan, and the courtesan's elegance of movement and gesture. Her robe was of green silk, Pericles' favourite colour, and seemed to flow about her body like tinted water rather than fabric, and so outlined her body. Her breasts were high and full, her waist delicate and fragile, her hips swelling daintily. Her waist was entwined with a girdle of gold, blazing with gems, and there were armlets clasped about her round white arms and bracelets about her small wrists and a multitude of flashing rings on her hands. She wore golden shoes, also ablaze with jewels, and when she moved a little Pericles saw her ankles, as beautifully wrought as a statue's. There was, to Pericles, a strange air about her, a lack of personal consciousness, a lack of artifice, in spite of the splendour of her garments and her jewels, in particular a necklace of incomparable opals set in rubies and diamonds. Her intimate attention was not on herself, unlike other women, but upon Pheidias to whom she listened with intensity and respect. The sculptor seemed almost animated in her presence, forgetful of his shyness, his eyes glowing eagerly. He had lost his stammer; his gestures were vehement; he shone with excitement, and Pericles marvelled.

Pericles looked at her face, disbelieving that any countenance could reveal so faultless a contour, whether she was in profile or facing him.

'Aspasia,' whispered Helena, smiling broadly. 'The harpy, the Medusa.'

Aspasia, though listening with all her attention to Pheidias, had noticed Pericles immediately and knew who he was. An instant glance had revealed his tall stature to her, his strength of compact body, his tawny mane of hair like a lion's, his air of power and assurance, not flaunting but immediate. She had seen his face, calm and impassive and rigorously controlled, his strong straight nose, his carved severe lips. He is puissant, she thought, a man of men, and Helena had not exaggerated in her buoyant enthusiasm. He had eyes so very pale that they seemed to have no focus at all. She doubted that they ever overlooked anything, even of the smallest importance. Above all, he had Olympian grandeur.

She was stirred for the first time since she had left Al Taliph, and she was annoyed with herself. She had vowed never to look again on a man with interest or provocation. How different they were, the man of the unknowable and intricate east, and this western man who had the appearance of immovable marble. She saw that his eyes were fixed on her, those inexplicable eyes which revealed nothing. No doubt to him she was just another beautiful woman, ripe for exploitation. She would enlighten him. Helena had assured her that Pericles was not as other men, but the sceptical Aspasia had not believed this.

Helena embraced Aspasia and exclaimed, 'You grow more entrancing every moment, my dear friend! Behold! Pericles, son of Xanthippus, Head of State, has deigned to grace our dinner tonight. I have told you much of him.' She glanced humorously at Pericles, who took Aspasia's hand, bowing, and kissed it.

'Rumour has not lied of you, Lady,' he said, and she was pleased by his eloquent voice.

'Of what has it said concerning me?' she asked, and he saw the bright watery lights in her eyes dancing.

'Only that which was laudatory,' he replied. He still held her hand and smiled down at her.

'You are gracious, lord,' she said. 'But I do not believe you.' He saw that she had a mischievous look, almost saucy, and that she suddenly appeared as a young girl. He held her hand tighter, when she tried to withdraw it. She frowned slightly and her smile disappeared. She felt a tremor through her body; where his lips had touched her hand there was a burning, a smarting, which ran up her arm. She had not felt this for five years and she was frightened. She was confused; she saw the pallor of his eyes and knew him to be inexorable, and all at once she was excited and the tremor was stronger in her flesh.

The guests repaired to the dining table, laughing and vehemently arguing, and Pericles, forgetting even his Helena, led Aspasia to the chair which stood beside the ornate divan reserved for him as the most distinguished guest. He could smell her perfume, that of lilies, and he wondered if that had pleased the Persian satrap, and that she wore it in memory of him. He felt a pang of jealousy. Nard became her more, or heliotrope. She was the most beautiful woman he had ever seen, though he saw that she was not deliberately voluptuous, and used no conscious arts or seductions. There was a certain pure clarity about her, almost virginal, for all she had been a courtesan. He no longer believed in the vile rumours about her. She had put from her, like a garment, the lessons she had been taught by Thargelia, the artifices and smirks and graces destined to lure and hold a man. If she had any passion now it was for her school. He had heard that she had had lovers in order to obtain money for her young ladies' tutoring. He knew it was not true. The satrap had left her a fortune. He must have loved her dearly, Pericles thought, with a stronger pang than before, and now with resentment. He decided he hated the satrap who had brought her to his bed from Thargelia's house.

Slowly, during dinner, Aspasia began to be more acutely aware of Pericles, in spite of her despondent thoughts of Al Taliph. She began to glance at him sideways, and saw the clear hardness of his features, which had no hints of softness or sentimentality. Almost imperceptibly his expression would change, while he conversed. She became frightened by her own fascination with him, and turned to listen to others.

Helena said with her robust smile and laugh, 'Pindar has said that the best of healers is good cheer, so let us drink to this night and this gathering, for this moment is all we have.'

Aspasia gave her a look of fondness and for the first time she truly smiled and said. 'Aeschylus has remarked that the pleasantest of all ties is the tie between host and guest. And so, let us drink to our dearest Helena, who condescends to teach one of my classes twice a week, in the art of medicine.'

After the toast had been drunk and the singers and harps had struck a lighter note, Pericles said to Aspasia, 'Tell me of Persia, for I admire the Persians.'

Again she hesitated, and the pale veil of sadness drew down over her features. Then she began to speak to him alone in a quiet voice, as the guests had begun to jest among themselves and Helena was telling some of her more indelicate stories. Aspasia spoke of Al Taliph with difficulty yet with candour. As she became more eloquent, and saw that Pericles was regarding her with disconcertingly intent eyes, she was less constrained. A warmth pervaded her. She discovered she could now speak of Al Taliph without the overwhelming pain she had endured for five years. In fact she laughed gently now and then as she related some tale of his unpredictabilities and his acrid conversation. Yet she was not able to conceal from Pericles the sombreness of the aristocratic Mede, the bitterness under his sallies.

'I should have liked to have known him,' said Pericles, when she fell silent, smiling to herself at some memory. She looked up, started, and said as if with amazement. 'He should have liked to have known you also, Pericles!' She knew this was true, and was even more astonished.

'In his terrible way, he was a great man,' she added, and now without any sorrow at all but only with admiration. 'He never said a crafty or deceptive word, yet he was most elusive and inexplicable. He could be frightful, and then the kindest of men. We did not understand each other, yet – '

'You loved each other,' said Pericles. His jealousy seized his throat. 'How fortunate was he to have had your love, Aspasia!'

'He was spared a deep suffering: He never knew I loved him,' she replied, and all at once her face was no longer young but grave with years.

She could feel the warmth of his body, now so close to hers, and the scent of fern which rose from his garments. It was all like a threat – or an embracing – and she feared both. She half-started to her feet, involuntarily, in instinctive flight, then sank down again and a bright haze seemed to cover her eyes and she felt weak and undone. She looked timidly into his face and saw there only kindness and approval, and she thought again that there was something Olympian about him, something splendid, and a soft melting came to her and for some reason she wished to weep. She saw his strong white hand near hers. She longed for him to touch her, yet she shrank. Never had she experienced such an inner trembling, such a tumult of feeling, and she did not understand it. This was entirely different from her passion for Al Taliph, and she endured no pang of betrayal.

When Pericles and Helena were alone Helena said with an arch smile, 'So, you have fallen in love with my beauteous Aspasia? Ah, do not suddenly look so stiff and annoyed. I have watched your face for hours. She loves lilies and the scent of them. Send her a sheaf tomorrow. You have touched her heart.'

'She is like a nymph who has never been awakened,' said Pericles.

The cynical Helena said with demureness, 'Then, awaken her. For the last time, my Hercules, you may enter my bed tonight, in a farewell. I am not unhappy. My heart rejoices in your future happiness. But Aspasia will be hard to woo. I must pray especially to Aphrodite tonight.'

Pericles, lying with Helena in her bed, found that he could embrace her, not as a lover, but only as a tender brother or passionless friend. With alarm, he thought of impotence. However, Helena understood and kissed him with cool tenderness. For the first time, she thought, he had truly loved a woman and therefore – for a time at least – he would be indifferent to other women. Yes, I understand, she reflected, for when I had my beloved I saw no charms in other men, but alas, as I am a faithful woman, I still find few charms in them, remembering my love.

Aspasia lay sleepless in her chaste bed in her small and delightful house adjoining her austere school. The moon stood in her window, as white and pure as Artemis, and as cold. She turned from it, restlessly. She could think of nothing but Pericles, not as yet with joy, but with yearning and fearful agony. Al Taliph had been like a sleek and sinuous leopard, revealing eyes which reflected secret emotions but which would not answer an inquisitive glance. Pericles was like a lion, stately and regnant, deliberate and lonely, resembling a mountain. The man of the east and the man of the west were singular in that both possessed enormous strength, yet one had the strength of the unknowable and the other the strength of steel, flashing yet icy. One moved with subtle grace, the other with overt power.

She thought of a fragment which Sappho of Lesbos had written: 'Now Love masters my limbs and shakes me, fatal creature, bitter-sweet.'

Again, she was frightened and was full of the instinct for flight. Then a deep sweetness came to her, a surrendering sweetness, and she wept and smiled, then slept, and dreamt that she was a girl again in a moonlit grove of myrtles.

PART THREE

Pericles and Aspasia

'Not houses finely roofed or the stones of walls well-
builded, nay, nor canals and dockyards, make the City.
But men able to use their opportunity.'

Alcacus (611–580 B.C.)

CHAPTER I

Daedalus, father of Dejanira, stood before the King Archon, shaking with hysterical rage, and cried, 'It is infamous! A man in his position, who takes a notorious harlot, an open courtesan, to his bed and often to his house, should be impeached by virtuous citizens! At the very least, the ostraka should be used against him. He is a public outrage; he is a spendthrift; he is devious and unapproachable. He is robbing the treasury of the labour of the people, for his fantasies in architecture and his patronage of low artists and sculptors and barefoot philosophers!' Daedalus almost choked with his rage; he had become incoherent. When he could find his breath he burst out again: 'A harlot, a notorious and infamous woman, who flaunts the modest feminine decencies and flaunts herself in public and debauches young girls! There is not a woman of immaculate morals who does not avert her eyes at the mention of her impious name! The people despise Pericles and demand redress and his removal from public office.'

The King Archon stroked his beard and said in a conspicuously moderate voice, to express his disapproval of Daedalus' excesses, 'Go to. There is not a man of any distinction, or wealth, who does not have a hetaira. This is accepted. Do we not all marry stupid or illiterate women of family and money to breed us sons and enhance our wealth and govern our households? And do we not all, in flight from what we have married, acquire a beautiful and loving and intelligent woman to soothe our exacerbated senses?

'Pericles is like all of us. He has fled from stolid women and their meek whinings, and their shrill little rages. Why, then, should he be singled out for blame? It is hypocrisy to do so. To denounce him is to betray our own iniquities.' He smiled at

Daedalus slyly, and the other's skeleton features flushed with harsh scarlet.

The King Archon continued: 'You may deplore Aspasia. At the very least she is educating young ladies who will not merely stink of the kitchen, the barnyard and the breeding pens. They will be a joy to their husbands. They even may make their husbands so fascinated by them that they will eschew the hetairai and even harlots. As Pericles has said, women belong to the human race also, a saying that some may doubt, considering their wives. At the best, intelligent women may give us sons fit to be called members of humanity, and daughters who will not only possess beauty but be entertaining. Let me ask you this, Daedalus: Do you consider your wife to be enthralling?'

Daedalus suddenly looked sick. Yet he became even more infuriated, and his mouth kept opening and shutting soundlessly, which the King Archon thought a blessing.

'You have called Aspasia impious, Daedalus. In what manner? She is teaching the girls in her school to question and not merely to accept. If that is impiety, let us have more of it, especially among our sons.

'You have said that the people despise and hate Pericles, our Head of State, that they demand his impeachment or ostracism. Who are the people you speak of, Daedalus? The market rabble, who want no monuments to glory and history and the gods, but only the satisfactions of their bellies? Shall we descend to the pigpens which infest our society, or shall we raise our eyes to the dreams of Pericles? Is a fat and well-fed beggar, who lives on the industry of others, preferable to a man of vision, a man who works in honour and sobriety, and loves his country not for what his country can do for him but what he can do for his country? Those who regard their country only as a smelly trough in which they can wallow and devour are a terrible danger to all of us.

'Those who love Pericles and would defend him to the death are not only intellectual aristocrats but men who earn their own living with pride and work and dedication, whether it be at the loom or in the field, in the manufactories or in the shops or the vineyards. These we dare not offend, for they are the life of our nation, our city-state. They are the hope of our survival through the ages. But the market rabble are our death.'

Daedalus swallowed with difficulty and found his voice. 'There is always the ostraka to be used against officials or persons like Pericles.'

The King Archon sighed both with exasperation and disgust. 'If it were possible, and left solely to my judgement, I would not permit the ostraka to be employed by men who cannot read or write, and so have no clarity as to the significance of their votes. I would permit a citizen to vote only if he has been measured for his intelligence, his awareness of why and for whom he votes, and is literate. Voting is an awesome duty and a momentous privilege. It should be confined to the responsible who see less their own advantage and more the advantage of their country. I fear, alas, that this is an impossible dream.'

He saw that Daedalus was still having difficulty in speaking, and he waited with obvious patience. He saw that Daedalus had not listened to him in the least, and that he was concerned only with his furies and his emotions.

So the King Archon, who was a benevolent man for all his stern principles, said, 'Let me refill your goblet with this good wine from my own vineyards. Wine is the blood of old age.'

'I am no drunkard!' cried Daedalus, with an offensive gesture.

The King Archon refilled his own goblet. 'Nor am I,' he said in an equable tone which did not entirely cover his anger. 'Moderation in all things. Is that not the saying of us Greeks? I am never immoderate,' and he looked meaningly at Daedalus. But the latter had never considered himself immoderate so the rebuke did not touch him.

Daedalus said, clenching his fists on the table before him, 'Pericles, it is said, would marry that woman – that woman for whom he had his marriage to my daughter annulled! If that is not a public scandal then nothing is!'

The King Archon smiled. 'Have no fear of a marriage between them. Had not Pericles, himself, a few years ago, ordained, with the approval of the Assembly, that no Athenian citizen may marry a foreign woman? Aspasia is an Ionian. Therefore, he cannot marry her. He is a prudent statesman; for him to repudiate his own law would indeed cause an outcry, and justly so, for many are the Athenians who cannot marry the women they love, for they are foreigners. They have obeyed the law. Therefore, Pericles must obey the law. When rulers flout the laws they have personally fostered they are criminals. Pericles is no criminal.'

Then his kind face became stern and hard. 'There is the matter of your grandson, Callias. He has been proscribed from the meanest and lowest of gaming tables, and taverns, and from nearly every establishment in the Agora. That is because of his furious conduct, his arrogance, his reliance on his riches – '

'He is but a youth!' shouted Daedalus, forgetting the superior position of the King Archon. 'It is but his high spirits, his young exuberance!'

'Youth is the time for discipline, for the exercise of self-control,' said the King Archon, and his eyes darkened. 'If a man does not learn these in his youth, he will never learn them. You speak of high spirits and young exuberance. Was it those which caused him almost to murder a man in a tavern? Had he not been rich, as you have mentioned, and had you not interceded, he would have gone to prison. For the honour of his own sons, the half brothers of Callias, Pericles also interceded, though, I believe, with reluctance.' He shook his head. 'That is the one thing which vexed me concerning Pericles.'

'You have always, lord, had a high regard for him!' said Daedalus, forgetting his own prudence for a moment.

'Of a certainty. He is a man of public justice, of civic virtue, in larger matters. I would have done as he has done.' He became weary of Daedalus.

Daedalus stood up. 'I will have vengeance,' he blurted, and without permission he almost ran from the room, despite his rage, his robes flowing back from his emaciated figure. The King Archon laughed a little, and called for his scribes and for the lawyers, who had more important matters to discuss with him.

'Was that the Archon, Daedalus, who blew from here like Boreas, lord?' asked a young lawyer.

'It was. He is an old man. Yet he sprang from this room as if pursued by Nemesis,' said another.

'I fear he was,' said the King Archon, smiling. Then he thought of Callias, whose petty crimes and insane assumptions and malignities, his cunning and coarsenesses, his joy in cruelties, his swaggerings and roughness, had earned him a dissolute fame of his own in Athens. Only his riches, and his family, protected him from the wrath of many. They often saw him drunken on the streets, or belabouring the slaves who carried his elaborate litter, or stabbing innocent street dogs, or reeling after young maidens accompanied only by women attendants. He was infamous and avoided, and this inflamed him.

It was only with his mother and his grandparents in the house of Daedalus that he was accorded any tolerance. His rude appearance, his bulky body, his stolid countenance were exceptionally like his mother's, but he did not have her docility, her capacity to love and to endure. He heard her wails over her lost sons, Xanthippus and Paralus, and he hated his brothers, for he wanted all attention and affection on himself, though he had none to give himself. He knew that Dejanira preferred her other children above him, those youths who were the sons of Pericles. Often he had fantasies in the night of murdering them. He listened to the stammering diatribes of his grandfather against Pericles, and the weeping denunciations of his grandmother, and he pondered. He had enormous vanity; he was convinced that his aspect was that of a prince, and that his intellect surpassed that of anyone in Athens. Though tutors had despaired of him, and though students had driven him from the colonnades of the Agora where they were listening to philosophers, he considered them lamentable fools, and had cursed them for their shouts of derision. His tongue was full of blasphemies, and threats. He had already killed two inoffensive slaves, one an old man, the other a child. Though Athenians did not regard slaves as human, but only as things, they were appalled. Callias believed that all envied him, which pleased him, and he was the bitterest enemy of all who dared to belittle or laugh at him.

His deepest hatred was concentrated on the lofty Head of State. He became certain that not only was Pericles his enemy but that Pericles was hated by the whole of Athens. So, for many midnights, he pondered on Pericles, after listening in the dining hall to the imprecations of Daedalus on his former son-in-law. What would cause Pericles the agony he deserved? To lift one's hand against the Head of State or even an official of government meant execution. Even an open threat was punishable. Callias believed himself as invincible as Hercules, so great was his egotism. But something warned him not even to speak of Pericles with so much as an oath, in public or in private, among his debauched companions. Pericles was famous for his ruthlessness.

So Callias concentrated on Pericles, and listened to the outcries of Daedalus against him, and the whore, Aspasia, who had displaced his mother, as he had been taught to believe. The shame of Dejanira became his. How dared such a woman sit on the chairs his mother had sat upon, and lie in the bed of Pericles? Dejanira's degradation became his. Was not Aspasia the infamy of Athens, as well as a notorious courtesan, of whom the lewdest stories were told? She was also impious, it was openly declared, and the mortification of all pure women. Pericles loved her. It was enough.

Callias began to plot. Should he cause the death of Aspasia it would not only mortally wound Pericles but it would bring accolades from Athenians on her assassin. At one stroke he would avenge himself on Pericles and become the hero of Athens. Pericles would not dare to seek revenge on him, no matter the loftiness of his position. So Callias believed.

But how contrive the opportunity of murdering her? She had guards about her house and her abominable school, which had inspired the indignation of good citizens. She never went abroad unattended. Virtuous Athenians might find her contemptible, and comic poets might lash at her with witty verses on the stage and in the taverns – even before Pericles, himself – yet she was feared as the mistress of the most potent Head of State. She was also courted and admired by the patrons of her dinners. No one, not even her most intense enemies, could deprecate her beauty, which was renowned in Athens.

Her beauty. To destroy that was to destroy the woman, herself, make her repulsive to Pericles, visit him with mourning and despair, cause even the most devoted to turn from her with pity and revulsion. Slow though the wits of Callias were, they were also cunning and dogged. He went, hooded and alone, to the dark abode of an old woman notable for her brews and her potions. Many called her Hecate, and she had even preened herself on the name, and had cackled. Her house was avoided, not only at night but by day also, for it was rumoured that she could cast evil spells. Nevertheless, she had her customers who went to her for love philtres and amulets and curses upon their enemies. Barren women visited her, and became fertile. She told fortunes, and multitudes whispered that she was a seeress. Officials considered her mad and so did not apprehend her, for they had heard that she was lavish with gifts to the temples. She was rich, if not honoured. There were those who said she was one of the Sibyls in disguise. Her house was set in a grove of heavy sycamores and guarded by fierce dogs on chains, which she could loose in an instant – it was said – by uttering a single guttural word. The house, though small, was luxurious and filled with treasures given to her by grateful patrons. Daedalus, who proclaimed himself above superstition, had execrated her, calling her the scandal of Athens.

Callias trusted no one, so he did not send a slave to acquaint Hecate that she was about to be visited by a noble lord. Slaves babbled. If his grandfather heard that his grandson had visited such an ominous woman he would be wrathful, even with him, and declare him a disgrace. Besides, Daedalus was an Archon, who had public responsibilities, and was a cautious man. Callias knew that Daedalus had tried to injure Pericles through Aspasia, but only by way of legal channels, and that furtively. It must be done by the utmost stealth, so that none would suspect the son of an aristocratic house.

Callias, though rich, was frugal. He thought of intimidating Hecate with threats, when he found himself, still hooded, in her house, his features hidden, and so to force her to accept only a gold coin or two. But she insisted on fifty gold crowns, and when he complained that he was a poor man, she laughed at him and offered to set one of her snarling wolflike dogs on him and drive him off. He had worn humble clothing, but she saw that his large hands had never laboured, but were soft and fat, and she heard his voice, which, though coarse, was not the voice of a peasant or small shopkeeper.

She threw back her haggard and dishevelled locks, which resembled grey snakes, and said, 'It is not only the acid which you buy, but my silence. That has never been broken, though I have been threatened with torture more than once.' She grinned at him like an evil mask in the theatre, and cracked her gaunt knuckles. Her house smelled of incense, and the walls were covered with ghastly murals of harpies and furies and Gorgons and serpents and dragons, all lit by the light of brass lamps, and all surging with frightening colours. Callias had a thought of murdering her with his dagger after he had received the acid, thus retrieving his purse and leaving no witness behind him, but as if she heard his thought – though she could not see his malevolent face – she loosed two dogs who sat before her and made the most sinister sounds, their red eyes fixed upon him. He shrank, and she cackled, and she knew she had guessed his intentions.

Her carved brass chest of large proportions stood by her side, as she crouched on her silken chair. Callias, with an oath, flung his purse on to her bony knees, and she opened it and counted the coins. She nodded her head with satisfaction, opened the chest and withdrew from it a glass vial filled with a murky crimson liquid. 'Throw this upon your enemy's face, and never will he see again, and none will dare look upon his countenance for very horror. It will be more dreadful than the face of Medusa. The acid will burn like a fire that never was, and will consume all it touches. Flee from it immediately after it has been flung.'

Callias, without speaking again, left her with exultation, the vial carefully wrapped in parchment, and then in leather. He now had only to arrange an encounter with Aspasia, to come close enough to her to throw the acid fully into her face. She would not die, but she would pray for death then and later. It was a most fitting revenge on Pericles, who adored her, it was said, as if she were a goddess who had condescended to love and lie with him.

For a number of days he skulked about her house and her school, wary of guards, clad humbly as if he were a workman or a man from the fields, his face hooded, his gait slouching, his head bent meekly. He saw slaves coming and going, and guests whose famous faces he recognized, and none noticed him, not even the guards. Once he saw Aspasia's litter, but it was guarded also, and the curtains were closed against the hot sun which could injure her celebrated complexion. It was reported that in the city she showed her bold face at night, without shame, and her eyes stared fearlessly before her and were not averted. But Callias knew that she was always surrounded by admirers who could seize him in a moment, and doubtless slaughter him.

It was impossible to get into her house, guarded as it was. As Callias was forced to wait his frustration made him frenzied and even inclined him to recklessness. He thought of becoming the hero of Athens, even if he died for it. But always he recoiled from that end, and always he knew he must be anonymous. That infuriated him against Aspasia. He desired glory, but the price was too high, though his act no doubt would be applauded. He lost interest in being a hero, if he would not be here to be acclaimed. He had also learned that Aspasia had many powerful friends who would avenge her, no matter how much the citizens of Athens might approve of his act.

He told himself that he must be fearless, for the honour of his family. But he was afraid. He forced himself to the first real and concentrated thinking of his life, and he sweated with the monstrous labour of it.

Eventually, after long days he came on a plan which was all folly, but from its boldness it might succeed. What had he heard Daedalus say sourly one night? 'Money is all things, and with it one can even seduce the gods – who created it.' Callias had found this eminently true, and for a unique hour he wildly pledged to himself that he would not be frugal, as was his nature, but throw with golden dice.

He went to the lowest quarter of the city where lived and prowled the most audacious and venturesome rascals, criminals hiding from the law, willing to face all things for money, and as heedless of mercy as the vultures they resembled – bloody men armed in their spirits with congenital evil. Not only would money lure them, but wickedness itself, for that was their climate.

Callias knew their taverns and frequented them, but never did they know his name, for he feared his grandfather as he feared no other. He called himself, to them, Hector. He roistered with them, drank with them, and they recognized him as one with their own natures, and so did not rob him or murder him. They guessed that he was not of their birth, and this flattered them, as he sought their company. Moreover, he bought wine for them, out of gratitude that they accepted him. Some considered that in an extremity he might come to their aid through influential friends. He often implied this, boasting. He and they knew that should they be arrested they would be immediately executed, for some of them were escaped murderers as well as thieves.

He entered the sinister tavern they preferred, and flung a purse of spilling gold on the table before the wine merchant, who was as evil as his customers. 'Spare no wine tonight!' he shouted. 'I have plans of greatness, of fortune, for a number of you!'

They shouted with joy and delight, and scrambled for the coins and Callias watched, satisfied. Then he asked for Io, a harlot who catered to these men, a very young girl not more than thirteen who had the face of a dryad, as innocent as a lily, and with pure blue eyes. She was a favourite of Callias, who often slept with her on her squalid bed, and she liked him for he gave her a gold coin instead of a copper one. They sent for her at once, dragging her from her bed where she lay with a malefactor. She was in her short shift, which revealed her gleaming white thighs and her child's arms and part of her budding breast. Her hair was black as a sable wing, her mouth soft and rosy, her countenance virginal. She was also very dull and of little wit, and as obedient as a puppy. No one had ever heard her speak, though she heard, and the only sounds she could make were squeals and gasps and small shrieks. She was most beguiling in appearance. She might have been the daughter of an aristocrat, for she had strangely delicate gestures, for all the grime of her flesh and garments and feet.

Callias studied her, and knew his judgement and memory had not failed him. She was perfect for his purpose. She would ask no questions, for she possessed neither curiosity nor understanding. She had only a stainless beauty untouched by her propensities, which were as vile as her face was untainted. She exhaled sweetness despite the rankness of her surround-

273

ings. She had been found as an infant, wandering the noisome streets, and had been taken as a slave by the wine merchant's wife.

'Io, my love,' said Callias, fondling her immature breast, 'you are about to attain fine garments, and soap, and fragrances.'

CHAPTER II

In the two years Aspasia had been his mistress – or, as the surlier Athenians called her, 'his harlot' – Pericles had never wearied her for an instant, but was constantly in a state of joyous wonder that she always seemed to possess a new countenance, a new variety of character, a new and startling revelation, for him. He would leave her in a state of gravity, and when he saw her next she was scintillating with mischief and humour, or, if gay, she would show him a temperament of such seriousness the next time that he was reminded, again, that she was not a light woman but a woman of profundity. There were moments, especially when she was wearied, that she presented to him a face almost plain, and pale and thoughtful, even old, and tomorrow she would be a blaze of loveliness, shining with colour, and as young as an untouched maiden. She would on one night spend hours discussing the plans of Pheidias with him, and the next time she would throw her round white arms about him and say, 'Kiss me. It is a night for love.' It was, Pericles would think, as if he possessed a harem of entirely different women, all of whom worshipped him and were adorably complaisant though in different manners.

Once he said to her, 'I will repeal the law I have made, that no Athenian citizen can marry a foreign woman.' Above all things, he desired her for his wife, fearing the inconstancy of human beings. But she said, 'That would give a mortal lance to your enemies, and especially to those men who love but cannot marry an alien woman.' To herself she said, 'Many men are more faithful to their mistresses than to their wives, for whom they invent faults in excuse for their betrayals. But a free woman can leave them at any hour, and this they know, and so must be faithful lest beloved women leave them first for men more tender and considerate and bountiful.' To hold Pericles, who was, after all, only a man, she must withhold also.

They entertained their friends in Aspasia's house, rather than in his, though Aspasia's house was smaller even if more beautiful in a very austere and elegant way. The house adjoined the school, a square building surrounded by colonnades where girls could study and read and converse and walk and look upon the composed beauty of the gardens. The girls lived in the school's dormitories, under the guidance of their teachers, and guards. At sunset the gardens echoed with their laughter as they played ball or practised archery or threw the discus or splashed in the pools.

Callias had meticulously surveyed walls and gates. His desire to destroy Aspasia, and thus destroy Pericles, grew daily. His first plan had been to throw the acid into Aspasia's face, himself. But like all physically powerful, bullying and loud-voiced men, he was a coward. He studied all possibilities and had finally concluded his plans down to the smallest detail, for he had the cunning mind of the stupid and malicious. He had been told that Pericles spent at least three nights a week in Aspasia's house. When his cut-throat friends informed him that Pericles would not sleep that night with Aspasia, that he had spent the night before with her, and that he was due to address the Assembly this morning, he completed his plans. He did not know that Aspasia and Pericles had entertained guests the last night, that Pericles had been somewhat overcome with wine and conversation, and had remained in her house, from which he would go to the acropolis.

This morning, as usual, they walked together through the gardens just after dawn.

'I have received a letter, some days ago, from a very rich young man who lived in Corinth,' said Aspasia, holding Pericles' hand in her soft fingers, like a trusting child. 'His parents died of the flux just recently, and he has been left with a little sister, thirteen years old. As he is often absent from his house he fears for her safety. Her name is Io. He has slaves to attend her, but is sedulous regarding her welfare. He has heard of my school, and wishes her to be with me, and so he is bringing her to see me. He spoke of her shyness and vulnerability, for she has been unusually protected, even more than is usual among the Greeks. He will arrive with his sister either today or tomorrow, for my inspection. He mentioned that she has had tutors and is considered very intelligent, in spite of her youth and inability to converse with strangers.'

The sun was rising higher. It was time for Pericles to leave. Aspasia never asked him when he would return, for this made men impatient and gave them an uncomfortable feeling of restraint, deadly to love. Pericles, on visiting Aspasia, brought with him but two guards, mounted like himself. He went to join them, after a last embrace with Aspasia, and disappeared behind the school. She stood there, enjoying the morning, and gazing about her with pleasure and comfort. Even when she was old, she thought, she would love all this and remember. She looked idly at the distant gates and the walls. Two guards stood inside the gates, well armed. She smiled. Pericles protected her thus, not that he truly considered she was in any danger, but because it gave him confidence.

A company stopped outside the gates, a handsome chariot with an awning, in which sat a young man and a young girl. It was accompanied by four horsemen, helmeted and armed. They sat on their horses like soldiers and the early morning light glanced off silver harness and helmet and made the hides of the animals glimmer sleekly. So the girl, Io, had arrived with her brother, with considerable ceremony. Aspasia walked slowly down the red gravel path, then paused. The guards were talking with the company. Then one came towards her and said, 'Lady, the lord from Corinth, one Nereus, and his sister, Io, have arrived. They crave an interview with you.'

'Let them enter,' said Aspasia, and stood, waiting. The guard returned to the gates and opened them. The occupants of the chariot climbed down, and the chariot with its white horses, and the accompanying soldiers, remained outside the gates. The young man and the girl entered the gardens alone, which Aspasia idly thought was a little curious. She looked kindly on the approaching young people. The brother, Nereus, was fair and tall and dressed richly if quietly in a robe of crimson silk with a girdle of gold and a mantle the colour of his robe. His smooth head was gilt; he did not affect the hyacinthine curls of the Athenians. Aspasia's attention was directed at the girl, and she saw before her a child of an absolutely pure countenance, smooth as a lily, and as sweetly pale, with thick black hair, unbound, under a veil of blue the colour of her wide and staring eyes. Her dress was white linen, bound with silver, and her mantle was of blue traced with a silver design. Her feet were shod in sandals of silver, twinkling with gems. In her hand she bore a small object wrapped in a red and blue silk cloth.

Callias, on his horse outside the gates, gloatingly observed that Aspasia was alone in the gardens, with not even a distant slave in evidence, or a gardener. His men outnumbered the guards; still, he was afraid, as a coward, of entering the purlieus of the house and the school. If the guards, after the fearful act, attempted to seize him and his companions, they would be unhesitatingly slaughtered. As for the two within the gardens, they were of no moment to him. They might be able to flee and rejoin the company. If not, then let them perish. This he had not told the spurious Nereus, who had been reassured that the company would wait and bear the two off in safety.

Nereus, who was a thief and a murderer, though young and

fair, greeted Aspasia with a proper bow and said in his culti-
vated voice, 'Lady, it is gracious of you to receive us, and we
are humbly grateful. Here is my sister, Io, of whom I have
written to you. I pray you will receive and nurture her,
though she is shy and seldom speaks. She will observe her
childish silence.'

Aspasia bent her head and smiled tenderly at the young girl,
for always she was moved by youth. She saw the fixed eyes, and
then she hesitated, for there was no intelligence in them, but
just an empty staring which their beauteous colour and form
could not conceal. She said, 'You say she has been tutored
well, Nereus?'

'Well indeed,' he said. 'But she has not been exposed to
public gaze, and so does not speak readily to strangers.'

His left hand pinched Io's upper arm, and this was her
signal, which she had rehearsed many times under the brutal
guidance of Callias. She began to unwind the silk which concealed the deadly vial of fuming acid. She did not look away
from Aspasia, who said, 'Let us withdraw to the outdoor
portico, where we can converse. Then I will show you,
Nereus, my school.' It was her thought to question Io, about
whom she had become uncertain. The girl had an infant's
eyes, blank and uninhabited. Moment by moment Aspasia was
becoming convinced, regretfully, that Io was not a candidate
for her school. Still, she had been mistaken before. She would
not dismiss the two until she was completely convinced of
Io's unsuitability.

She turned to lead the way to the outdoor portico of her
house, but Nereus said, 'My little sister has brought a gift for
you, Lady, and wishes to present it to you now.'

Aspasia faced them again, smiling. The last fold of the silk
fell from the vial and Io gripped the vessel in her hand, staring
at Aspasia's face. She had lifted the top from it with a swift
movement. At that instant a buzzing wasp flew before Aspasia's
face and she quickly stepped aside and waved her hand at the
menacing insect. It was this that saved her, for even as she

moved and made her gesture the girl flung the contents of the vial in the direction where she had been standing.

Hissing, and flaring redly, the acid arched in the early sun, and fell on the grass near Aspasia, where it burst into flames and exuded a stench which was intolerable. Aspasia recoiled with a cry of terror.

Nereus had received his orders. If, by some unseen misadventure, the acid failed he was to stab Aspasia in the heart as rapidly as possible. He saw the blazing acid on the grass; it was creeping in a thin serpent of fire through it, away from Aspasia. He drew his dagger and furiously advanced upon the shivering and horrified woman, while Io merely stood there, blankly staring and expressionless. At that moment Pericles and his men rounded the side of the building. Nereus saw them. He was a brave murderer, however, and would have completed his task had not Aspasia, herself, seized his wrist and flung his arm upright and had brought her knee swiftly to his groin. She screamed wildly; Nereus dropped his dagger and doubled over with a yell of pain. Pericles struck his horse with his whip and rushed towards the three, seeing the crawling flame, and the struggles of Aspasia, for though agonized Nereus had gripped one of her ankles and was twisting it, intending to bring her down where he could the more easily kill her.

Callias saw all this from his safety beyond the gates. He made a signal and the empty chariot and his horsemen began to roar away. However, Pericles' men raced after them, though they were outnumbered. They had one advantage which they did not know as yet: Callias' men were not soldiers and though they carried swords they hardly knew how to use them with any dexterity. So, they all fled. Pericles' horsemen pursued, and the guards at the gate ran in their way with drawn swords.

Pericles shouted for more guards, and he seized Nereus by the hair and pulled him from Aspasia. Io simply sat down on the grass and began to fold and unfold the discarded silken kerchief, and gaze about her unwonderingly. It was not Pericles' intention to kill Nereus, who was much slighter and smaller than himself, and so he had to control his murderous rage, for he wanted information about the assassins. He caught Nereus about the throat and choked him into submission, then threw him on the ground and held him there with his booted foot. He looked over his shoulder at Aspasia, who was hugging herself with her arms and shuddering and weeping. He said, in a very calm voice, 'It is over. Do not fear, beloved. Return to your house and await me.'

'They wished to destroy me,' she said.

'That I know. I will soon discover why, and they shall be punished.'

She repeated over and over, 'They wished to destroy me. Why?'

'Go into your house,' he said with terrible sternness, and then she obeyed, her head bent, her face in her hands, her hair lifted about her in the wind. Pericles' face had drawn itself into formidable lines. Nereus feebly tried to stir, and creep from under that inexorable foot, and Pericles deftly kicked him in the temple. Nereus sprawled laxly, unconscious.

In the meantime the house guards appeared, running over the grass, swords drawn. The acid had stopped its crawling, and now was just a small smoking trench in the grass, without fire, and only with smouldering sparks here and there. Pericles said, 'Take this murderer and lock him in some room and guard him constantly. Do not injure him. He must be questioned.'

Alone, and waiting, Pericles looked down at the black trench in the grass and for the first time he, too, began to tremble both with rage and horror. He felt undone. He looked at the sitting girl, Io, who had begun to hum softly to herself, winding the multi-coloured scarf about her wrist and raising it now and then to see the glimmer of it. Pericles' first impulse was to kill her, and then he saw the vacancy of her young face, the untenanted aspect of her eyes. She was no more guilty of this atrocity than the birds in the trees, he thought. He said to her, tempering the roughness of his voice, 'Who sent you here, wench?'

She heard him, with her slow wits, then she lifted her face and gazed at him. She only knew that he was a man; she had been taught seductiveness. She inclined her head and regarded him with blue eyes as shallow as a puddle deposited briefly by rain. She said in an infant's voice, 'Hector. Do you – bed, lord?' Her voice was uncertain, like the voice of a very young child. She began to gurgle incoherently, and Pericles frowned. To Pericles the imbecility of the girl impressed him with a kind of frightfulness, as if she were an elemental and not a human being. He saw that she had no conception of the enormity she had tried to complete. She was beyond good or evil, for she had no soul. Pericles felt himself in the presence of something innocently appalling yet supranatural, from which the human spirit must recoil.

A female slave came into the outdoor portico and Pericles called to her and she came running. 'Take this child to your quarters,' he said, indicating Io. The slave led Io away by the hand, and Io went with docility and unasking, and without resistance. Pericles shuddered. The garden was bright and lonely about him, smiling in the risen sun, but there was only tumult and fury in his heart. He dared not think of what Aspasia had escaped, as yet. His whole mind was set upon vengeance.

The soldiers and the guards, panting and dusty, returned with but one man, who was slightly bloody and dishevelled. That man was Callias, surnamed 'The Rich'. The others had been slain after a hard battle. The only reason the guards had not killed him was because he had cried, 'I am the grandson of the Archon, Daedalus, and if you murder me you will pay to the last drop of blood! Take me to Pericles, for my mother was married to him.' To the last he was a coward, thinking only of his own life, and never of his grandfather or his mother, who could be crushed under this scandal and attempt at murder or worse. He thought himself above the law, as all the stupid did, and therefore had privileges. He also believed that Pericles would spare him.

Pericles wondered at his own lack of surprise when Callias was dragged before him into the atrium, bleeding from several superficial wounds, and as grimy as a peasant. His face was bestial and defiant, though his eyes flickered when he saw Pericles.

Pericles contemplated him as one contemplates something unspeakably obscene. He said to the guards, 'Take him away, and put the brand of slavery on his forehead.' Callias shrieked and struggled futilely, but the guards overpowered him and bore him away. Sudden nausea took Pericles. He bent his head to his knees for a moment or two, then accepted the iced wine a male slave mutely offered him. He thought of Daedalus and Dejanira and considered the pleasure he would feel when his soldiers flung Callias at their feet with the shameful brand of slavery on his brow. Forever he would be marked as a thing, and not a man. This was more desirable than any other punishment.

Aspasia, as pale as death still, came into the atrium and stood mutely before him, seeing his silent and mingled rage and hate and emotion. He was leaning back in his chair now, his eyes closed. After a little he became aware of her presence and looked up at her. She watched him as she said, 'I have taken the liberty, lord, of countermanding your order to have Callias branded as a slave.'

He sat there and gazed at her and she had never seen the face he now presented to her, the blind and menacing face, and she stepped back, affrighted. But he said quietly enough, 'You dared to do this thing, Aspasia? You dared to disobey me?'

'Yes, lord.' She clasped her hands tightly to her breast and felt her first terror of him. Never had he seemed so imperial in his short white tunic, his helmeted head, his fixed expression, and never so dangerous. She had often been afraid of Al

Taliph; in comparison that fear was nothing to what she felt now. She trembled visibly, but kept her features as still as possible.

'You doubtless have an explanation for this mortal affront, woman?'

Never had he addressed her in such a voice and with such chill insult. She bowed her head and said, hardly audible, 'I do, lord. You have two sons, and they are brothers of this Callias. Would you have Xanthippus and Paralus kinsmen of a slave?'

He had not thought of this. He considered what she had said with profound shock. She continued, 'Would you also have it laughed through Athens, by your enemies, that you had been married to the mother of a slave?'

He stood up and slowly paced up and down the atrium, his hands clasped behind his back, his head bent. She watched him and said in a shaking voice, 'The disgrace would be bad enough. But the punishment you decreed for him is beneath you, lord.'

He stopped with his back to her and said in a tone hard with scorn, 'What would you suggest, O Sibyl?'

She went to him and touched his bare arm imploringly. 'I suggest that he be beaten soundly by my overseer of the hall, before my slaves, then taken in chains before the King Archon, who is your friend. Let Callias be exiled for life. Are you not Head of State, even above the King Archon? He will not deny your demand.'

'Callias is pestilential,' said Pericles. But he was thinking; he rubbed his jaw with his hand and stared before him. 'He deserves death. Would it not be better to have him killed and then buried in some unknown spot?'

'It is beneath you, lord,' she repeated.

He thought of Turnus and smiled grimly. He knew that Aspasia was appealing to his pride and not to his justice. She was a woman and thought as a woman. Wise as she was, she did not fully understand a man. He said, 'Had that wasp not saved you, Aspasia, you would be deformed for life, hideous to the eye, or you would have been murdered. Yet you appeal to

283

me for mercy for the assassin who would have done these things to you!'

'I am not insensible to what I escaped, lord,' she said. 'I, too, have imagination. I am not as weakly compassionate as you may think. I was less his intended victim than you. He wished to strike at you, through my destruction. For, have I offended him in any way? No. For what he tried to do to you death is too feeble. My suggestion is far more ghastly. When he is thrown before the King Archon, command that Daedalus be present. Daedalus is your enemy, and mine. He will never outlive the shame, that his grandson attempted murder, that Callias is a miserable demon, worthy of the utter contempt of honourable men, that he stood before an assemblage in chains, like a common criminal.'

He looked at her now and she saw the tight ruthlessness of his smile. 'You are very artful, beloved. Still, there is much merit in what you have said. Let it be done.' He clapped his hands loudly and the overseer of the hall entered the atrium, and bowed. Pericles said, 'Bring to me one Nereus, who is under your guard.'

Nereus was dragged into the atrium, manacled, and flung on the floor before Pericles, who spurned him with his foot. Then Nereus rose, and he had the quiet manner of the born aristocrat, for all his face was bruised and bloody.

'What have you to say for yourself?' asked Pericles.

But Nereus said nothing. He wiped blood from his mouth with one of his chained hands. Pericles contemplated him, his eyes narrowing. 'I know your father,' he said, 'one of my friends, and he is of a noble house and a man of probity and honour. I recognize him in your face, and I saw you as a child. Your father drove you from his house, with grief and despair and just anger. I know your crimes.'

Aspasia listened to this with astonishment.

'You are more nefarious than Callias, who is a pig, a fool, and a gross creature,' Pericles continued. 'For you chose your evil life. You darkened your father's house. He is still suffering from the infamy. How shall I punish you, so that men will know and avoid you for the rest of your life?'

He glanced at Aspasia, and she said, 'Let him be branded, and not even his father will have one pang of pain. Then deliver him into the hands of a slavemaster, who will send him far from Greece. He has kept his silence, for he is a man of birth. He will not defame his father further.'

Nereus' mouth shook, and yet he did not speak. When the overseer led him away by his chains he walked proudly. 'No,' said Pericles, 'he will never give his name, and never will his father know. There is some advantage in being an aristocrat. At the last they suffer punishment without whimpering or an outcry.'

He went to Aspasia and took her gently in his arms and kissed her brow and her lips. She rested against his breast, but she was still afraid, remembering his aspect when he had up-braided her. As if to console her he said, 'Your advice was excellent, and I am grateful, my beloved one.' Her fear left her as she thought that Al Taliph would never have spoken so to a woman; he would have felt no gratitude for this offence to his pride, however judicious. She clung to Pericles, and for the first time in this day of horrors she wept. He held her tenderly.

CHAPTER III

'Alas,' said Aspasia to her friend, Helena, as they sat in the outdoor portico of Helena's house, 'perhaps it had been better that I perished than Pericles suffer the present calumny and vituperative attacks. Would I not give my life for him? He is in danger because of his associations with me and with philosophers and scientists – accused of impiety – such as Anaxagoras and Zeno and Pheidias and Socrates, to name but a few. The Archons, the Ecclesia, the Assembly, and all the dreary scum of government hate him for using the public treasury to enhance and glorify Athens. They would prefer to pocket the gold, themselves, or to advance what they call the public welfare, which means, in the raw reality, the buying of votes for themselves.'

Helena was as rosy and robust as ever, and realized that they saw in Pericles a threat to their hope of an easier and more abundant life, at the expense of taxpayers. They hated him in that he had told them that a man should earn his bread with his industry, and not with mendicancy. They knew he despised them openly, and regarded them as a peril to their country.

They seized on Aspasia – they the filthiest of fornicators and adulterers at every opportunity – as an example both of impiety and of lasciviousness. They cried that she influenced Pericles in his office. She was a degraded woman, a courtesan, and never a matron. She was scandalous, in that she corrupted young women with learning. She entertained suspect philosophers – who sneered at the gods, and scientists who debated the existence of the gods – in her own house. Therefore, Pericles and Aspasia have insulted Zeus. If Pericles was not deposed the gods would avenge themselves on Athens. Woe!

Daedalus said to the King Archon, with hysterical fury, 'He would have branded my grandson, of a noble house, as a slave! Had it not been for some merciful slaves, who smuggled him out of that detestable woman's house, he would have been disfigured for life! Now my beloved grandson, Callias, has been exiled; such was the decree of Aspasia, the whore of Athens, who rules us in the name of Pericles. Is that not monstrous, that a harlot is more important than the government, itself?'

When the King Archon did not answer, Daedalus screamed, 'Who is Aspasia, that she dominates our lives? My grandson was only attempting to redeem his mother, his house, his pride of family, his position. For his manly intentions, for all he holds dear, he is a vagabond on Cyprus, and can no longer return to his loved family, and his weeping mother.' The King Archon considered him thoughtfully as he stroked his beard. He said, 'Yes. Daedalus, you and I are old men, and often our memories fail us but our prejudices, on the contrary, become more fiery. If I am wrong, correct me: If I remember, your grandson was not smuggled out of Aspasia's house by righteous and merciful slaves. He was brought in chains, after a flogging, to the court of the Assembly by Pericles' soldiers. The Assembly does not love Aspasia, just as they do not love Pericles, but they are men frequently just. They were appalled at the attack on a woman who had done your grandson no wrong, and who, though despite her faults and her convictions, is not only a beautiful woman but a learned one. I do not admire her, you will understand, for women are contentious enough without an education, and learning could make them even more disagreeable.' He stroked his beard again and fixed Daedalus with bright intent eyes like a bird. 'I am informed that it was Aspasia who prevented Callias from being branded with the brand of a slave.

'Daedalus, your grandson had no reason for malice towards Aspasia, except that I have heard he is naturally malicious. He was striking at Pericles. It was Pericles' own plea that this not be brought too strongly to the attention of the Assembly, and the Archons and the Ecclesia. You know, most certainly, what the punishment is for an attempted injury against the Head of State?'

This was a somewhat specious remark, and the King Archon knew it. He also knew that Daedalus' fury would prevent him from detecting the adroit fallacy. Daedalus could now only stand and shiver with rage and clench his hands at his sides and glare at the King Archon with mingled fear and blinding temper.

Finding his voice at last he almost yelled, 'Lord, it is common talk in Athens, and in all of Greece, even in Sparta, that Aspasia is impious, that she teaches the deluded girls in her school that the gods do not exist, or if they do they are not cognizant of man and therefore honour given to them is a delusion!'

The King Archon became grave. 'Who has told you this, Daedalus?'

'It is common knowledge, lord!'

'What is "common knowledge", Daedalus, is a common lie, in my experience. Are we men or old women who idle away the hours in slander? When you have some authentic evidence against Aspasia, bring it to me and I will give it all my attention. Now you must leave me. I have matters of *consequence* to consider.' So he dismissed Daedalus. Privately, he thought it would have been wiser of Pericles merely to have had Callias murdered and buried far out at sea or in some isolated spot. Then there would have been no public scandal – something no politician can afford. But, he had chosen the honourable way. The King Archon sighed. Sometimes honour could well be confused with folly, and was often less excusable. It was also very dangerous.

Pheidias sat in the cool atrium of Pericles' house, where the centre fountain made a plangent sound against the night silence, which was broken only occasionally by the rippling and poignant music of nightingales. Even the trees were still and the moonlight seemed to come from an unmoving orb of alabaster. The dried brown grass of summer exhaled an odour of aromatic dust, pervasive as smoke. The hour was late; even the vociferous Athenians were now in bed and, to Pericles, blessedly quiet.

The two men sat at a table over which hung a lamp, and they were leaning forward to study the scrolls Pheidias had spread before them.

Pericles marvelled, as always, at the genuine humility of genius. He became for a time engrossed more with Pheidias' shining face, his joyous descriptions, his passionate ardour, than with his plans, and Pericles' cold and judicious heart was deeply moved as rarely it was moved.

Pheidias sighed with exhausted delight. 'It will be perfect, a most glorious example of the Doric order.' He hesitated. 'I remember, lord, that you said you preferred Corinthian columns.'

'I do not – now,' said Pericles. 'It could be nothing but Doric.' Then he, too, hesitated. 'The cella – There is the base in these plans for the gigantic statue of Athene Parthenos. You still believe that the statue should be of ivory and gold?'

Some of the light went from the face of Pheidias. 'I am not successful, at least to myself, when I work in marble. It has a rigidity which demands a certain ruthlessness and power. A man must have rule over his materials; he must command them. Marble intimidates me. It has a monumental challenge which only the strongest can answer with a greater challenge. But the gentler materials, the more fluid and compliant, the kinder, are to my hands living, and our souls are in sympathy. However, lord, I have students who are greatly gifted, and will work in marble under my direction, including the statue of Athene Parthenos.'

He could not understand Pericles' slight smile. 'No,' said Pericles, 'it will be as you desire, a gold and ivory statue.'

Pheidias was joyous again. Then he was suddenly dejected. 'It will cost far more than a marble statue, for it will be a towering work, and gold is very precious. The treasury may refuse it.'

'They will not refuse me,' said Pericles, with some of that haughty and overbearing manner which his enemies detested.

They went on to discuss each metope in detail, and the chariot of the goddess and the painted friezes. Sometimes Pericles winced, thinking of the cost, and the miserable little men of the treasury who would bay like wolves to the moon of the public's avarice. But as the light of the false dawn made the east dim as a pearl he was overpowered by the massive dream of Pheidias. He could see the terraces and fountains and gardens which would adorn the grounds of the rising acropolis to the huge temple of Athene Parthenos, and the lesser temples scattered about and below it. It would resemble a fortressed mountainous city of marble and colour and flowers and dark cypresses, soaring and gleaming and blazing, not only over Athens but over all the world. The climbing white stairways, broad and polished, would know the feet of great men who would come to see and remain to adore, and to walk dazed among all those golden sun-struck colonnades and stand refreshed at the profusion of fountains, and look down upon the silver city on the violet sea. They, and all others after them, the multitudes who would come here through the centuries, would know the glory that was Greece. The vision overcame Pericles, for it was as though he had heard a solemn prophecy.

'It will be almost worthy of God,' he said. 'He will know it is the most glorious offering that a race can humbly present to Him, in His honour. He will not despise it.'

CHAPTER IV

The youths, Xanthippus and Paralus, sons of Pericles, were infatuated with Aspasia, and loved her. Pericles was pleased by this, for never, therefore, would his sons marry inferior or stupid women but would demand of a woman not only a pleasing form and countenance but a superior mind also.

As Xanthippus was approaching marriageable age, for he was seventeen, Aspasia would introduce him to some of her maiden students in the gardens of her house. Athens professed to be outraged at this impropriety. A young man of family did not choose his bride. That was the prerogative of his parents, and the parents of the girl. However, the parents of Aspasia's students did not object, for was not Xanthippus the son of Pericles? Moreover, were they, the parents, not themselves enlightened? Too, Aspasia never permitted Xanthippus to be alone with any of her students. This was not because of seemliness but because she knew human nature, and remembered Thalias. Youth was hot enough without providing it with encouraging opportunities, and the maidens had been entrusted to her care.

Daedalus, hearing through the gossip of slaves that his grandsons were being taught impiety and corruption by Aspasia, brought himself to confront Pericles in Pericles' own house. It had been the first impulse of Pericles to refuse him an audience, then he relented and received Daedalus with iced courtesy and offered him refreshments. But Daedalus, more vitriolic with age, furiously declined. 'I will not dine in this infamous house!' he shrieked. 'I have degraded myself in behalf of my grandsons, and it is a vomit in my mouth.'

'Visit the latrines, then. I will wait,' replied Pericles. 'I am Head of State. You are but an Archon, and I have politely granted you permission to speak to me.'

They both stood in the atrium, for Daedalus would not sit. His usual high colour had paled to a deathliness. Pericles felt some pity for this old man, and so stood in a waiting attitude, his arms folded over his chest.

'My grandson, Xanthippus, visits the young courtesans in the house of that unspeakable woman, Aspasia! It is rumoured that he will even marry one of them!'

Pericles' mouth became fixed as marble. 'The young ladies in Aspasia's school are of aristocratic names and of impeccable houses. Shall I inform the parents of those maidens that you have slandered them, have called them concubines and harlots? Their fathers are powerful, as you are not powerful, and they would destroy you.'

Daedalus trembled with fear. He flung out his arms. 'I do not mean the students,' he stammered. 'It is said that Xanthippus is induced to consort with the female slaves in that house.'

'Of a certainty, that is a lie, and that you know, Daedalus.'

'I would believe anything of that woman!'

Pericles controlled himself. 'The Lady Aspasia has enabled

Xanthippus to know the daughters of great families and to choose a bride for himself. He has taste and discrimination. Of a surety, if he chooses a maiden who is a student of Aspasia's, he will not commit the appalling folly of marrying a stupid and ugly woman. His son will be no Callias, whose name is infamous in Athens, so much so that no gentleman will consider him as a husband for his daughter, in spite of his inherited riches.'

'His name is not infamous! He has been the victim of pestilential people! If he has done foolish things it is because he was distraught over the dishonour done to his family! Has he not vitals, not emotions, that he cannot be overcome with shame and sorrow? His riches have been held against him. No matter. He is living in loneliness and sadness on Cyprus, and that is the only reason he cannot marry an Athenian maiden, for what parents would permit their daughter to share exile?'

Pericles laughed lightly. 'I know he is living in luxury in Cyprus. He is flattered there and fawned upon. He is no wandering vagabond. His house is magnificent, and full of slaves. He entertains lavishly. Many an Athenian maiden of a great house would be permitted to marry him and with alacrity. He does not desire marriage. He has concubines. I have sent emissaries to Cyprus to hint that if he desires he may be recalled to Athens. He has repudiated them. He can commit licence in Cyprus which he could not commit here. What! You did not know this?'

'I do not believe it!' cried Daedalus. 'We receive mournful letters from him, stained with his tears, for he longs for his family.'

'You believe I am lying?' asked Pericles in a dangerous voice. Daedalus flinched, and retreated a step before that face.

'Perhaps he is exaggerating,' he said. 'But what man does not want to return to his loving family?'

'Callias,' said Pericles.

Daedalus trembled. Then he looked up to see the mingled derision and sympathy in Pericles' eyes.

Pericles said, 'I have told you. He could marry – if he wished.' He paused. 'He could return soon – if he wished. He does not wish.'

Daedalus was distracted. He flung out his arms, despairingly. 'You have called my daughter, Dejanira, stupid and ugly. She is virtuous and faithful. Are these not gracious attributes?'

Pericles closed his eyes for a moment, wearied. 'I grant you that Dejanira has virtues. They do not appeal to me. I am grateful to her for my sons. I respect her name. We had no quarrels. But all that is past. I have given you time, and it is precious to me. I must ask you to leave.'

Daedalus started away, then swung around, his garments flurried. 'I will not forget!' he exclaimed, raising his hand in an oath. 'I will not forget! I implore the vengeance of the gods – in whom you and that woman do not believe! They will not be mocked.'

He trotted from the atrium and into the outdoor portico, where his litter awaited him. Once behind the curtains he burst into tears, and his mouth moved with imprecations. He was not without power, and Pericles had many enemies. He began to plot. His old face twisted and contorted with hatred.

Aspasia took Pericles by the hand at sunset and led him into the cool tranquillity of her gardens.

'Why do you smile, my golden one?' asked Pericles.

'I am thinking of our son,' she replied.

He was astonished, and seized her arm. 'Our son?' he exclaimed.

She bent her head.

'I have waited to tell you, lord. I am with child. I am certain it will be a son – your son and mine.'

When he did not speak but only gazed at her with enlarged pale eyes, she said, 'We will call him Pericles, after his illustrious father.'

He frowned, released her arm, and removed himself a pace. 'He will not be legitimate.'

Aspasia touched his arm. 'You can adopt him, sire. Then he will be truly yours.' She felt some anxiety. Was he not pleased? Was he angered that she had been careless during one heated night?

Then he turned to her, his face lighted, and he took her in his arms. 'I am thinking of your danger, my sweetest. After all, you are in your thirties now. Have you consulted Helena?'

'Yes.' Aspasia was moved. 'Despite my age, she has said I am in the most supreme health. She will tend me, herself. She has had many instructions from the young Hippocrates, who has visited her school and her infirmia.'

'I must see this Hippocrates,' said Pericles, but he was frowning again, alarmed for Aspasia.

'Do not disturb yourself, lord. It will be well. But, tell me. Are you pleased that I am to bear your son?'

'It may be a daughter,' and Pericles laughed. 'If she resembles her mother I will adore her.'

'And – if it is a son?'

'I will discipline him. He will be a worthy son of Athens.'

They held each other, breast against breast. Pericles put his warm arms about her and kissed the top of her head. But her thoughts were troubled. Pericles was now being called the man on horseback, the dictator, and the comic poets were becoming more ribald and bold in their attacks on him on the stage. She cared nothing for calumny directed against her, but she deeply feared for Pericles. As she had fled for her own sake from Al Taliph so she often considered fleeing from Pericles for his sake.

She was hated, derided, accused of unspeakable things, and she knew this was because of Pericles' association with her, and his passion for her.

'Why do you sigh, my love?' asked Pericles, lifting aside a lock of her hair and peering down, in the growing darkness, to see her face.

'Did I sigh?' she said. 'It is the nature of women to sigh, for do we not love men even though you do not deserve it?' They laughed together, for Aspasia had never forgotten that Thargelia had said that a melancholy woman was disliked by men and left to her miserable sorrows, and that a woman must always pretend that her sighs were pleasure or teasing or trivial and meant nothing. Even though she knew that Pericles loved her and would defend her with his life and often comforted her, Aspasia also knew that she must not be melancholy too long. Men might be moved by a woman's tears, but not if they were chronic, and Pericles was a man after all.

They went into the house together, hand in hand, to dine and then to go to Aspasia's chamber to love and sleep under the moon. When Pericles slept beside her, surfeited, Aspasia pondered again on the fate of women, and felt, again, the old rebelliousness. Her new fears returned and she stared, sleepless, into the dark. Whether a woman's destiny was due to custom or innate nature was impossible to know.

CHAPTER V

What Daedalus lacked in personal power he made up in vituperations against Pericles, whom he now hated with a frenzied hatred. His fellow Archons began to be wearied by him, though they agreed with him and hated Pericles hardly less than he did. But while he merely frothed they consulted how best to depose Pericles and obtain his exile as an overweening and dictatorial Head of State. He was not invulnerable, so far. They dared not, as yet, pass resolutions against him and consult openly with the others of the government how to bring about his fall. They could only insidiously discuss with the many others the situation of his extravagance and his outrageous contempt for the weighty and heavy pendulum of government and its confusions and vacillations. 'It is true that he is Head of State,' they would say, 'but that does not make him a god, not in our form of democratic government! Nor does it give him the power of a despot. He is answerable to us,' and they added as an afterthought, 'and to the people who elected us.' He sought to be king, with absolute powers and had not Solon, himself, warned of ambitious men?

Daedalus urged his daughter, Dejanira, to marry again, for she had many mercenary suitors who were also of noble if impoverished families. But she shuddered away from him, weeping, and declared that she loved only Pericles and still considered herself his wife, and that if he would permit her she would creep like a dog to his feet. Daedalus loved his daughter; therefore he was scandalized at this abjectness, and ashamed. So, he upbraided her, only to be answered by loud sobbing and a wringing of her hands. Once she even said to him, 'Callias deserved his fate; I do not pity him, though I love him as my son. He received only a measure of justice. Another man would have been executed for that act.' Daedalus did not see the certain nobility of Dejanira's words – for she had lost a measure of her obtuseness. He was only aghast and accused her of being an unnatural mother.

She believed herself blameless for the dissolution of her marriage, for had not Pericles on their wedding night declared his passion for her and had he not embraced her with desire? What had she done to deserve banishment from his house? But still she said to her father, 'I despise such as Aspasia, but he had forced me from his bed long before he saw her. She is only a hetaira, and Pericles is of an illustrious house. I do not believe he loves her, for how could such an abandoned woman be respected by such as my husband? No, she is a passing fancy; there will be others.'

Daedalus, beside himself, shouted at her, 'Do you not hear the gossip that she is with his child?'

Dejanira closed her eyes suddenly with grief and anguish. Daedalus went on: 'He is not only not ashamed that he has lacerated the sensibilities of decent men. He flaunts her condition to all who will listen. Yes, I know that the hetairai often bear children to their lovers, though it is loathsome in the eyes of the virtuous. But at least their lovers do not boast of the vileness as does Pericles.'

Dejanira opened her tearful eyes. 'It is not in Pericles' nature to boast, my father.'

'Hah! And how do you know this thing? Pericles was perhaps speaking the truth when he said to me that you were stupid.'

Seeing her suffering, and seeing her shrinking, he felt some compunction. But the next moment he was again incensed that Pericles had made his daughter suffer such despair. When Xanthippus and Paralus next visited his house he said to them, 'Are you not ashamed that your father has begotten an illegitimate child by his hetaira, his whore? Have you considered what this will do to your name, his lawful offspring?'

'What will it do?' asked Xanthippus, a bland expression on his lively face. Paralus nudged him in his side, for he saw the brilliant mischief in his brother's eyes and he was innately more compassionate than the irrepressible Xanthippus. But Xanthippus said, 'We honour Aspasia, for she is not only the most beautiful woman in Athens, but is kind and loves us. She adores our father, and gives him laughter and consolations. Her situation is quite common and there are few outcries against it.'

'You do not care for the humiliations of your mother?'

Paralus said with his father's own gravity, 'My mother is no longer the wife of my father. What he does does not injure her in the esteem of others, for she has no part in any of his affairs.'

Daedalus seized on this with hope. 'You do not, then, approve of your father?'

Paralus had more respect for his grandfather than did the youthful satyr, Xanthippus. So he replied, 'I did not say that. Forgive me. I meant that what my father does, or my mother, is not the concern of either. They are not one.'

Xanthippus struck an orator's attitude and quoted from

Homer: ' " There is nothing stronger and nobler than when man and wife are of one heart and mind in a house. A grief to their foes, and to their friends great joy. But their own hearts know it best." ' He grinned at Daedalus. 'That best describes my father and our beloved Aspasia.'

Paralus did not like this baiting of the aged Daedalus who stood blinking, now, trying to comprehend with his senile wits. So he said, while frowning formidably at Xanthippus, and resembling his father acutely, 'Do not mind Xanthippus, Grandfather. He loves to tease. He means nothing by it.'

'I never say a word which is not pertinent,' said Xanthippus, who affectionately made fists at his brother and stood in the attitude of a pugilist.

After Callias, Daedalus loved Paralus best. He was afraid of Xanthippus and his acid wit, and so disliked him while still loving him.

He said, 'Pindar has asserted, "Strive not to become a god. Mortal aims befit mortal men." ' (He had heard this in the Assembly only yesterday.) He added, 'Your father strives to become a god before the people, for their worship. Men are but mortal; they are as dust before the gods, something your father does not realize.'

Xanthippus shook his naughty head and imitating Paralus' gravity he proclaimed, 'Sophocles has said, "Wonders are many, but none is more wonderful than man." My father is a wonder. Therefore, he is as wonderful as the gods.'

'Your syllogism lacks something,' said the temperate Paralus. 'My father is not mad; he is above the folly of considering himself divine and his decrees are not infallible.' He smiled. 'One should not quote philosophers as the ultimate authority, for they dispute with each other and are frequently contentious. They are also not quite sane, in our own dull interpretation of sanity.'

'It is true,' said Xanthippus, 'that you are frequently dull, my brother,' and they laughed in each other's eyes and pushed each other. 'You should encounter Pan!'

Daedalus was not following this quick exchange. He said with bitterness, 'Your father is trying to lead us into war again. Who profits by war, except tyrants such as he?'

'Hah!' cried Xanthippus. 'Has not Homer said, "All dreadful glared the iron face of war, but touched with joy the bosoms of the brave"?'

Paralus said quickly, 'Poets, too, often disagree with each other – as do the gods. I doubt, Grandfather, that our father is warlike, though he is a soldier. He is trying to unify Greece, and if he appears devious at times we must trust him.'

Daedalus was incredulous and his eyes bulged. 'Trust your father? I should prefer to trust the harpies!'

'It is a matter of taste,' said Xanthippus, and was thrust from the room by the more forceful Paralus, to join their mother. While they travelled down a corridor Paralus said to his brother, 'Why do you torment that poor old man, who has nothing but his hatred to feed him in his age?'

'Hatred is the bread of Hades to which he is destined,' said Xanthippus, who knew little mercy and found life ridiculous. He did not have the cold control of either his father or brother. He had only wit and intellect, and a huge sense of humour which others found infuriating. Above all things he loathed stupidity, and could not forgive it, though Paralus often told him, 'Blame stupidity not on the intransigent nature of him who possesses it, but on his fathers who bequeathed it to him and on the gods who decreed it. Does a swine ordain his snout, and the monkey his lice, and the vulture his stink? We are what we are, not by our own desire, but from the loins of our fathers and the wombs of our mothers, and nothing can change that, not government, not alms, not learning, not prayer. We are fixed in our natures from our conception, and we cannot escape our fate.'

'We can try,' said Xanthippus. 'At least it is in our power to order the filthiest aspects of ourselves. Do we defecate in the streets? No, we go to latrines. Let the stupid go to theirs and learn discretion, so that they do not offend others.'

'We can perhaps teach the stupid,' said Paralus, sighing, 'even though they destroy those who would teach them,' to which Xanthippus disagreed and said, 'You have refuted your own argument.'

They loved each other dearly, they so dissimilar, and they entered their mother's quarters in amiability, and arm in arm. Dejanira was overjoyed to see them. They visited her at least once weekly but she greeted them as if she had not seen them for years, with embraces and smiling tears. She did not immediately inquire about their health but asked about their father with an eagerness they both found moving. Their grandmother lurked in the background sullenly with an air of chronic disapproval. She listened to the conversation, grunting, and as she, like other Greek women, did not believe in idleness, she was sewing industriously. But her eyes, black and small, darted about like cockroaches. She had affection for the sons of Pericles, though her love was for her grandson, Callias. So she felt some sullenness towards Xanthippus and Paralus, who did not resemble her or her daughter in the least. Her animosity towards Pericles extended to his sons, if not with the hatred she had for the father. This conflict of emotions made her irascible and her grunts always became very loud in the presence of the youths. Though they showed her the courtesy she deserved as their grandmother they ignored her after the greetings.

The youths conversed with their mother in an atmosphere of ease and love. She stroked their arms and fixed her eyes on their countenances, seeking for signs of Pericles. She asked about their academe. She had heard that Xanthippus was almost espoused to the daughter of a great house. Xanthippus shrugged. 'I have met the maiden in the school of Aspasia, and she is sweet and kind. Why is it necessary for a man to marry? Is marriage all?'

To which his teased mother replied earnestly, 'Yes, it is all.'

Xanthippus was about to enter on his military service and he affected to find it onerous, but he was the son of Pericles and the grandson of Xanthippus, and he always thought of this with a pride he was careful to conceal. He talked with his mother, but he was easily bored with those whose minds were lesser than his, and he was soon yawning despite the stern glances Paralus gave him. At last, in spite of Dejanira's entreaties, both youths protested that they must return to their father's house, as the hour was late and they had a military guard waiting in the courtyard. The poor woman clung to them, kissing them and leaving her tears on their cheeks, and imploring them to visit her as soon as possible.

They mounted their horses. An abnormally large orange moon stood in the dark sky and gave the earth a curious illumination, so that every pillar and wall shone with a saffron light and every shadow was sharp and black. The hills were bathed in a wash of lemon yellow and the crowded and rising columns of the acropolis temples appeared to be made of gold. Athens, below, glittered with red torches and lanterns and lamps, restless and unsleeping. The autumn air was pungent and the wind cool. Fallen leaves rattled on the road and scurried before the horses like brittle small animals. Xanthippus began to sing the newest ribald ditty of the streets, to the amusement of the guard, and he added a few more stanzas of his own which were even more lewd. The horses pranced a little; hoofs clattered on stone. Xanthippus was in high spirits, as usual, while his brother merely smiled and made reproving sounds which were not entirely sincere.

The military guard carried torches and rode close to the brothers, watching every door and alley. They glanced at rooftops, for the light of the moon was very vivid. But they did not see the archer who was awaiting them, crouched on a roof and hidden by shadows. He did not rise until the company was directly below him, and he stood for an instant or two like a black faceless demon from Hades against the orange moon. A guard uttered a loud cry. But the archer was swift and skilled and he had chosen his target.

There was a whirring sound in the air, as deadly as that of a hawk, and the arrow found its lethal way into the right eye of Paralus, and he fell into the path of the horseman behind him.

Instantly, all was uproar and shoutings and the screaming of horses, and the hissing of fallen torches, which spewed off showers of red sparks on the stone. Horses wheeled frantically and reared. Xanthippus, careless of danger, swung down from his horse and threw himself on the body of his brother, and felt the blow of a horse's hoof on his left arm. Everything became confusion and oaths; men and horses crashed into each other. One horseman veered about and raced towards the house, dark and closed, on which the archer had stood. But he had disappeared, vanished like a phantom.

CHAPTER VI

Helena would not permit visitors to her patients in the infirmia, in order to limit meddling and noise. 'The patient's welfare is more important than your curiosity, or even your love,' she would tell anxious relatives. 'He must rest if he is to recover. Who knows what diseases you may bring to him unwittingly? I have studied with Hippocrates, who says that the well may carry with them infections which will overcome the sick or the feeble.'

She had a pleasant room for relatives and friends outside the infirmia itself, scented with flowers and a fragrant fountain, and with comfortable chairs. There she would converse with the visitors and tell them evil news or good. Her physicians would sometimes accompany her, with an air of deference when she spoke. In this room her voice was firm and strong. When visitors lamented the fate of the sick she would say, 'Sophocles has said that it is better never to have been born at all in this world. Why do we grieve if one dies? Socrates says that a good man has nothing to fear in this world or the next –

if it exists, and that death is only sleep, and who does not desire sleep? Death is our portion; it comes to us late or soon and none can escape it. We must accept it, as we accept life. The wise law-giver of Athens, Solon, has advised us never to call a man's life happy until it is over. Think on these things, and you may envy the dying.'

For these remarks, delivered to the relatives of an expiring patient, she was considered heartless and without sympathy. She told her friends, sighing, that if a physician became one with his patients he would not be able to practise his art and would spend his days in fruitless tears. At all times, he must be as remote as Olympus, if his mind and intellect were not to be clouded by emotion, and yet must understand human suffering and grief. But they must be objective, not subjective, lest the patient himself suffer.

She would not permit alleged sorcerers or miracle-workers into her infirmia, nor would she allow a patient's neck to be garlanded with amulets. 'It is true', she would say, 'that the mind rules the body more than the body rules the mind, and sometimes superstition is as strong as a draught of medicine. But let me and my other physicians decide whether a man or woman is ill of the soul or of the flesh. If of the soul, you may bring amulets – for the soul is easily persuaded and is subjective. But if he has an illness of the body an amulet will not cure cancer or cut for the stone or deliver a child in difficulties. The body is objective, and does not believe in amulets.'

Still she was beginning, more and more, to believe that a man's will to survive was most potent. She said to Pericles, 'Your son will live, but he has lost the sight of his eye and nothing can restore it, not even the gods. It is miraculous that he is not dead or paralysed, for the point of the arrow pierced his brain. He is a valorous youth. He is determined to live and does not spend his painful hours bewailing that his sight will now be only partial. He is glad that he is not blind. As for Xanthippus, you may take him to your house, for he had but a broken arm and shoulder. He will not be comfortable for some time. However, he is more disturbed about his brother than is Paralus, himself, and vows vengeance.' Helena's high colour faded and her face, usually robustly cheerful, darkened.

'It is being sought,' said Pericles, and his voice, though quiet, had a terribleness in it. 'This was not a private vengeance or a sudden impulse, the attack on my son. The attack was directed at me. I have no foes but political ones. Even if the King Archon himself is responsible for this, he will suffer.'

Paralus was the first person of high family to be a patient in the infirmia, for all households had their own physicians. But Pericles believed Helena to be the most learned of them all. Paralus had been brought here at Pericles' request, almost in a state of extremis, and he was in one of Helena's handsome private quarters, guarded at all times, both within the chamber and outside the infirmia, and in every corridor by armed men with drawn swords. Not a morsel of food or a goblet of wine or water was permitted to enter his mouth without its first being tested for poison. His favourite dog slept at his side, as alert as the guards at any sound it did not recognize. In the next chamber Xanthippus had been housed. The brothers had been here a week.

Pericles said to Helena, 'Aspasia pleads to be allowed to visit Paralus.'

'Of a certainty my dear friend may visit one she loves so dearly, who is like a son to her.'

'I am fearful her grief may affect her in her pregnancy.'

Helena laughed shortly. 'A pregnant woman is doubly protected, and she is as strong as a span of horses. Nature protects burgeoning life more than she protects those already born. Let Aspasia come, to relieve her anxiety. Her very countenance will soothe and delight Paralus.' She hesitated. 'Aspasia is well guarded, also?'

'I have doubled the guard – in my house. I have taken her

from her own. She does not breathe without being heard. I lie beside her with my drawn sword in my hand.'

Helena said, 'The attack upon Aspasia was a private malice, though directed at you. The attack on your son was doubtless political, as you have said. Therefore, it is more dangerous, and more formidable. I doubt that your political enemies will attempt to injure you through Aspasia, for they regard women as trivial and insignificant, no matter who loves them. Guard your son, Xanthippus, as closely as Paralus is guarded. Guard yourself above all.'

'Base dogs!' Pericles exclaimed. 'They dared not attack me, myself! They knew it would arouse the rage of those who trust me. They therefore struck at me through my son, in order to frighten and intimidate me, and cause me distraction, and give me a warning. They wish me to withdraw in fear for my family, because though they whisper of impeachment and my ouster from office they know the people are with me. I will not withdraw! But I will find the perpetrators of this mischief and will ruin them.'

'They may be too many,' said Helena, thinking that a civil war could well be precipitated. She said, 'Let me advise you, my dearest Pericles. Do not cry out publicly that this is a political matter, lest you open the gates of hell, to the injury of Athens. Say always it was some dastardly criminal, who wished to rob or who had a private spite against you. Demand openly that Athens employ more street guards in order that blameless citizens might be safe from murder and theft.'

'What pusillanimous advice!' said Pericles.

She smiled. 'Perhaps. But think on it for a moment or two. My advice is wise. You will lull your enemies into complacence, while you search them out. An open attack on them will invite an open attack on you, whatever the consequences to themselves, for they are desperate.'

Pericles considered. As he was rarely if ever moved by emotion he began to see the wisdom of Helena's advice, though it galled him and angered him.

'I suggest,' said Helena, watching his white face closely, 'that you proclaim a high reward for the discovery of the "single criminal". Make the reward so high that the hired assassin will be more than tempted to betray those who employed him. Offer him sanctuary, if he comes to you, which he possibly will. Money, with death, is no temptation. In the meantime, breathe no word of your true suspicions. Accept the condolences and the sympathy which the government is offering you, and do not search each face fiercely with your eyes. They must suspect nothing, though it is most possible that the greater the vehemence of indignation expressed the greater the probability of guilt.'

Frowning, and running his fingers through his hair, Pericles said, 'Some of my horsemen have sworn that they saw not a single archer, but others on other rooftops, waiting to see if the first succeeded. I do know that arrows were found in the shoulder of Xanthippus' horse. Had he not flung himself instantly on the body of Paralus he would have been murdered. Only the second arrows convinced me that my men were not hysterical.'

'Then, above all, say publicly that it was but a single criminal who had attacked your company, and your enemies will be deceived. But I will wager that after you offer your reward there will be an unusual number of dead criminals found in alleys. Your enemies dare not let them live.'

'What it is to be a politician!' said Pericles, with bitterness. 'If a man seeks to help and glorify his country and make her strong before her enemies his own people will leap at his throat and call him malefactor, a thief, a mountebank, a liar! Better it is to smile and smile and smile upon the people and show a shining countenance than to raise them above the ruck.'

'But, is that not an ancient story of heroes?' said Helena, and refilled his goblet. They sat in the blue twilight in the outdoor portico for though it was autumn, it had been a warm and golden day. 'My dear Pericles, you will remember the ancient proverb concerning powerful men: "Walk softly among your enemies – with a sleeping sword." Do you desire the fate of noble men? Exile or death or maledictions or contempt or hatred? Heroism is splendid, and candour, but there is also judiciousness in all things – if a man would serve his country as well as possible.'

Helena, despite her convictions, had permitted the weeping Dejanira to visit her stricken sons. Dejanira volubly and tearfully questioned Helena about the identity of the assassin. Who would wish to injure her children? What was the power of Pericles if such could attack her sons amidst their guards? Athens had become a den of thieves who flaunted the law, and murderers who could kill at will. Where had been the city guards, that none were present? Helena, restraining her impatience, replied, 'These are evil days, as always the world has evil days. We must acknowledge this. Mankind is a race of barbarians, of primeval animals.'

'My father,' Dejanira replied, her face red and swollen with weeping, 'declares that it is Pericles who has been too tender towards criminals and the judges too merciful, and that we need a stronger man as Head of State. He is distraught. He has taken to his bed, my poor father.'

Helena was too kind to explain to this unfortunate and stupid woman that her father's incessant ravings and denunciations had assisted and encouraged the attack on Paralus. She could only shrug and repeat that these were evil days. 'No one is ever safe in this world,' she said. 'Those who seek safety and security are deluded, just as those who fight for peace inevitably must face war.'

Friends and enemies in the government all extended words of wrath and condolence to Pericles, and he watched their faces, friend and foe alike, seeking for those who had plotted his son's death. 'It is outrageous,' said the Archons, and Pericles smiled cynically but accepted their remarks with grace and apparent gratitude. They congratulated him on offering the huge reward for the apprehension of the assassin. Many offered a purse of their own also. It was a paradox which only Zeno appreciated, that Pericles' worst enemies were the most lavish in their offerings, and the loudest in their expressions of ire. But he knew that among themselves they were pleased, and sniggered, and that they whispered against him.

He said to Aspasia, 'My dear one, I am going to remove you, before the birth of our child, to one of my most secluded farms near Athens, with guards.'

Aspasia said, 'No. I must remain with you, lest fear destroy me. I am guarded here.' She gazed at him desperately. 'I have my part in your present persecution. Would it not be well if you did not see me again?'

He was both touched and irritated and said, 'Shall the lions flee before the jackals? Shall they whimper at shadows? You must obey me, for my peace of mind. You will leave for my farm tomorrow, at dawn, and none must know where you are save Helena and myself.'

He dared not accompany her to the remote and peaceful farm lest it be noted, so she left in the morning before the sun came up and few were on the roads. She was accompanied by strong and trusted slaves and soldiers, who were to remain with her. 'If the Lady Aspasia comes to harm,' he said to them, 'I will exact the utmost penalty not on one of you, but all. Therefore, you must watch each other sleeplessly, and report the smallest dereliction to me.'

Helena promised him that when the hour of the child's birth was imminent she would go to Aspasia, though ostensibly she was going to Epidaurus to pray in the temple of Asclepius, son of Apollo, who had been educated by Chiron, the centaur. There she would also attend a meeting of the new followers of Hippocrates, and study his methods and his teachings.

Pericles, on Aspasia's departure, was bereft. He visited Helena for comfort and encouragement, and inevitably, to soothe him, she took him to her bed. She was a sensible woman; she knew she was not violating his love for Aspasia, and that men needed the consolations and the soft words and hands of a woman in their extremity. Moreover, she was not afraid for him, as Aspasia was afraid. 'Love makes cowards of the most valiant,' she told him. 'Aspasia is a woman of valour and never knew true fear before, but now she is as weak as the daisy of the field for dread for you. I write her constantly that you are flourishing, though,' she added with a smile, 'I do not inform her that you find surcease in my arms. You and I are old friends, Pericles, but Aspasia, being a woman abjectly in love with you, would not understand for all her intelligence. We could not explain to her that we do not love each other, except as friends, and that our festivals in bed have no true meaning.'

One day Pericles received a sealed missive delivered by a cloaked and hooded man who put the letter into the hand of one of Pericles' scribes then fled swiftly into the crowds of the Agora. The scribe said with indulgence, 'Lord, the vagabond was very elusive and had a voice of import. Doubtless he wishes alms, or this missive contains a denunciation against you.'

Pericles smiled and opened the letter. It was written in a peculiar hand, hardly legible, but the wording was that of a cultured man. 'If the noble Pericles would like news of those who instigated the attack upon his son, Paralus, he will come at midnight tonight to a certain tavern which will be closed and locked but which, upon five knocks, repeated three times with a short interval between, will be opened to him. He may bring guards, if he so desires, but he must not permit them to cross the threshold of the tavern. He must enter alone. He will find it silent and deserted with but one candle burning on a central table. As he is an honourable man, and after per-ceiving a letter addressed to him on that table, he will leave a purse of gold, as promised, in the place of the letter.' The tavern was named; it was situated near the sea in a desolate and notorious section where few dared to venture except criminals.

Pericles, trembling inwardly, read and reread the missive. Was it a plot to lead him to his own death? Was it a snare to rob him of money? Was it fraudulent? A criminal could give a few names. Would they be, in truth, names of those who had paid for the attack on his son, in order to strike at his most vulnerable spot? He studied the letter over and over, gnawing his lip, rubbing his brow. He had an impulse to destroy the letter. The next moment he again read it. He had nothing to lose but a sum of money. On the other hand he had much to gain. He would tell his soldiers to surround the tavern so that if he were injured they could capture the criminals at once. There would be no escape for the traitor or the thief. Too, if Daedalus was named he would know that the message was mere trickery. Malice had done worse than to name an innocent man.

Then he had another thought. He sent for his most trusted officer, a brave young man whose courage and honour he had tested many times. His name was Iphis, and he was a distinguished soldier, short and massive, with glittering brown eyes and a square face under his helmet. Because of his small but powerful legs he waddled and planted his feet heavily, yet he could move like the darting of a sword.

He saluted Pericles and stood before him, waiting. Pericles gazed at him thoughtfully. Then he said, 'My dear Iphis, you know of the reward I have offered for the name of the assassin who attacked my son, Paralus.'

'Yes, noble Pericles.'

Pericles held out the letter to Iphis who took it and read it. The young man's face became as still and carved and hard as stone. He stood in silence for several moments then carefully placed the letter on the table before Pericles and stared down at it.

'Well?' said Pericles at last.

'Lord, it may be an ambush. You cannot go.' He looked directly into Pericles' eyes. 'I will go. I am not of your height, but I will wear a cloak with a hood and be seated on your horse, surrounded by my men, also on horseback. I will obey the instructions in that letter.'

Pericles placed a finger against his lips and looked down at the letter. Iphis said sternly. 'You are too important to Athens, lord, and you are Head of State, and the people trust you. To go as directed, yourself, would jeopardize not only your person but Athens as well. It may be that this letter is sincere and the rascal seeking money. We dare not miss the opportunity, however suspicious.'

Pericles was always frank with his soldiers and so they trusted him without question. He could be most severe and then most kind. He said, 'I hoped you would suggest this, Iphis, but I would not have suggested it myself. You may be in grave danger of death by going in my place. Do you understand this?'

'Yes, noble Pericles. But I will be armed, and will surround the tavern with my men, and I am a notable swordsman.' His complexion was browned with the sun and had the texture and folds of leather for all his youth, and his eyes were clear and penetrating as he gazed at Pericles. He had an aura of resolution. He added, 'I have no wife, no children, no kin. I have nothing to lose, but you have our country and your family. Who am I compared with you?'

Pericles stood then and embraced him, much moved. He withdrew a flashing ring from his finger and said, 'This ring is famous in Athens and I never am seen without it. When you ride at midnight, let it be conspicuous, so that it will deceive any watcher. Go to my house at once; you will be seen emerging on horseback at midnight, through my gates. I, myself, will go to my house within the hour, but will leave for the house of Helena, the physician, so that even my most trusted slaves will believe I am with her.'

He added, 'Do not return to my house when you have procured the promised letter. Seek me in the house of Helena, where I will be waiting.'

Iphis saluted. 'What shall I tell the overseer of your hall, sir?'

'Tell him you have a message which you must deliver to me, and to me alone. Then, at midnight, with your soldiers, leave in yawning impatience and say that you will return at dawn.'

When Iphis had left him Pericles pursed his lips and walked up and down his office, shaking his head. Iphis was indeed a notable swordsman, while he, Pericles, had not attended a fencing match for nearly two years. Iphis was also young while he was middle-aged. If danger there was, then it would be acute. Iphis was wary, and he had been warned. He would not give up his life easily, and his men would be there to guard him.

Before I had known Aspasia I would not have considered letting another man take my place in peril, he thought. But love makes us weak, even if we are powerful, and cowardly even if we are brave. What are even my sons compared with Aspasia? Iphis was right. I must also think of Athens. Those who trust me would be inconsolable, and my enemies would caper with delight if I were murdered. I stand between them and my country. Too, generals do not expose themselves carelessly to danger, for then their armies would be in disarray.

But he was still troubled.

Helena said to him in her house, 'You acted with wisdom. Iphis is intrepid. Athens is greater than you, and she is in your charge. Do not look so uncertain. Come. I have a most delectable dinner for you tonight and I will amuse you until Iphis returns.'

'You are too sensible,' he said, and began to smile.

She regarded him gravely without an answering smile. 'When you have the names – and they may be illustrious ones in government – what will you do with them? Have you considered this? You cannot punish those men openly, for then, in return, your enemies will become more united and more vengeful.'

'I have considered,' he replied. 'But I will find a way to eliminate them, without open accusations. However, I must be convinced. It is not my way to act with haste, and that you know.'

CHAPTER VII

Shortly after midnight, at the height of Pericles' apprehensions, Iphis rode up to the house of Helena where every lamp was burning. He bowed deeply to Pericles and bowed slightly to Helena as the friend of Pericles only and not to be considered seriously, though she was a physician of renown.

'Lord,' he said, 'it was as written in the letter. I knocked three times, as declared. There was no answer. I pressed against the door and it opened silently. None was there. On a single table, lighted with a candle, was a letter, which I have in my possession. A search of the tavern was futile. There was no sign of life or recent occupancy, though we searched.' He smiled grimly. 'It is apparent no one trusted us. I left the purse of gold on the table.'

He gave the letter to Pericles; it was sealed. He opened it and read it with astonishment. There were four names. One was the Eponymous Archon, Philemon, and the second was the Polemarchos Archon, Leander, the third a member of the Supreme Court (called Heliaia), Tithonous, and the fourth, also a member of the Supreme Court and the Boule, Polites.

These four men had appeared to be his kindest and most devoted friends, serious, bearded and thoughtful. Philemon, Leander, Tithonous and Polites! It was incredible; it was impossible. But nothing, he reminded himself, was impossible in this worst of all possible worlds. A man's enemies were frequently discovered as his friends, his friends, his enemies. He had even expected to see the name of the King Archon, who always greeted him formally and coldly, though with respect. The fact that his name had been omitted, and that of

Daedalus, gave credence to the letter. He had anticipated the names of those whom he believed were his overt foes. They were not here.

He had more than expected to see the name of Thucydides, his arch foe. He was not named.

He showed the missive to Helena, who read it carefully. She said, 'I believe every word. These men have been in my house. They always expressed their devotion and loyalty to you. This made me suspicious from the beginning. The more a man protests the more he is to be mistrusted.' She added, 'The man who wrote this missive was no tyro, no mere vagabond. He knew the truth.'

'I have dossiers on them all,' said Pericles, but his heart was weighted. 'I will study them tomorrow. It was only yesterday that Polites came to my house to speak with Paralus and bring him gifts of sympathy. As for the others, they surrounded me, weeping, and vowed that the dastardly assassin must be brought to justice. They pleaded with me to allow them their assistance.'

'The more reason for you to suspect them, Pericles,' said Helena.

'But what if the writer had a grudge against them and wished revenge?'

'You must study their dossiers,' said Helena. 'You may find truth there. If I remember, they are easy and elegant men, with sincere faces, and airs of integrity. Such should be doubted and watched.'

Pericles was very perturbed. He stared at the letter and said, 'I trust your judgement, but not always. I have known these men in my youth, in my childhood and early manhood.'

'So,' said Helena, 'they are envious of you. They saw your rise and your popularity. They ask themselves, "Why is he Head of State and not I? Was he more distinguished than I at our academe? Was he praised more by our teacher than I? Was he more industrious at learning, and did he receive prizes, as I received them? Is his house more notable? Is he richer? No! Therefore, why is he Head of State? Has he bribed voters and politicians? Has he poured out treasure to be elected, when I am more justified? Doubtless. Therefore, he bought office which I, as an honest man, would not have deigned to do. I am virtuous. He is heinous. He deserves punishment." '

'They were my comrades in arms,' said Pericles, and knew fresh grief.

'Hah!' said Helena, with a cynical face. 'So, they believe themselves to be at least your equal. Did you not defecate and urinate with them and exchange lewd camp jests and sleep among them? Who are you, then, to be loftier? That is their reasoning. I have discovered that when a man is accessible and amiable to his companions he is denigrated in their estimation. He is not only on a level with them but possibly inferior. He is not to rise above them; that is unpardonable. If they guess inherent superiority they are sleepless in their hatred.'

Pericles was silent. He looked at Helena, who was gazing at him with her large blue eyes and a tender smile, as a woman gazes at a child. He touched her shoulder and said, 'I will consider what you have told me. I fear you are correct.' He thought of his beloved Aspasia, who read his speeches before they were delivered, and who censored them, adding emphasis here, reducing emphasis there.

He said to Helena now, 'I hate no man but an evil and stupid one. How, then, could these men be my enemies? Your explanation wounds my heart, my wise one.'

'Think on your wounds,' she replied. 'They are not only valid; they bleed.'

The next day he summoned the King Archon to meet him in his offices. The King Archon came with his retinue, elderly, composed and as alert as the old bird he resembled. Pericles received him with ceremony and seated him and ordered refreshments. The King Archon knew this was a grave occasion, and waited patiently, looking at Pericles thoughtfully and with an expression that told nothing. In his turn Pericles studied the old man, for whom he had small respect as he had small respect for all other members of his government. But now he saw that the King Archon had a kingly aspect, and that it was possible he was a man of verity. How unique it is, thought Pericles, to discover a man of probity in any government!

He lifted a sheaf of papers on the table between them.

'My son, Paralus, was wounded almost to the death by an assassin, or assassins,' he said to the King Archon. 'But this you know. I have four names here, which are alleged to be those of the men who bribed criminals to kill my son. I also have their dossiers.'

The King Archon inclined his head. 'Yes,' he said. 'I have heard of your dossiers, Pericles, son of Xanthippus.' He paused. 'You would not have called me here if you did not trust me.'

'I trust no man absolutely, not even myself. But I trust you as much as I can, which, I assure you,' and he smiled faintly, 'is not in extraordinary measure.'

The King Archon smiled a little and again inclined his head. He drank some wine and ate a ripe fig or two.

Pericles gave him the missive Iphis had brought to him. The King Archon read it. He began to frown, and his bearded cheeks turned sallow with shock. At last he lifted his eyes and looked in aghast but quiet silence at Pericles.

'You do not expostulate,' said Pericles.

The King Archon shook his head. 'I can believe anything of mankind,' he said. 'Tell me. What do your dossiers show?'

'The Archon, Philemon: He is your cousin's husband. A few years ago he was accused of bribing the charioteers of Athens in the Olympic Games. He had much invested. Our charioteers lost to Sparta. Though accused, he was never brought to trial, because of your high position, and the name of his house. The news was quietly suppressed. You will observe that the charioteers confessed, under holy oath. You will see that I have corroboration.'

He waited for a comment but the King Archon made none. 'Ah,' said Pericles, 'then you did not know.' The King Archon tried to speak but could not and Pericles looked at him in sympathy. 'After all, it is considered a terrible crime to bribe anyone in the Great Games.'

The King Archon said nothing. Pericles sighed and continued.

'The Polemarchos Archon, Leander. He is in charge of metics, foreigners. For a large fee he had documents forged to show that many Ionians, not to speak of Persians, had their names inscribed in our public records as Athenians born in Athens. He did this because he had to return his wife's dowry, and he had spent her money in unwise investments, which had all melted away like butter under the sun. It is curious,' said Pericles, 'but he has been most stringent in his attacks on foreigners who were poor and desired only to come to Athens to work and practise their arts and live virtuously. Many of them, poor good men, were forced to leave our city, and lost all they had, which was very little in the very beginning. That was to assure his fellow Athenians that he held our city to be inviolate and not to be polluted by aliens.'

The King Archon retained his composure but his eyes flickered with pain. Pericles looked at the papers in his hands and said, 'Tithonous, a respected member of the Heliaia, the Supreme Court, from which there is no appeal. He has persuaded many of his innocent fellow judges – by his vote and oratory – that various dangerous criminals were innocent, if they came of rich families or had political influence. He would weep over their "wrongs", or say that they were young and heedless and meant no overt transgressions. He castigated fathers for the plight of their sons. The criminals went free. He received large sums from grateful parents for this.'

The King Archon closed his eyes as if he could not endure listening, but must.

Pericles said, still quietly, 'Another member of the Supreme Court, Polites. His wife, of whom he had tired, died under mysterious circumstances. He is rich and powerful. You will observe the names of the men who swore that he was with them far away when she was stabbed to death in her chamber. They did that, not out of venality, but because it was unthinkable to them that a man of such a blameless character and sober mien could have arranged the murder of his wife. But, you will observe, I have received letters from the murderers, themselves, from their sanctuary in Syria. Even murderers, it would seem, have consciences, occasionally. Or, perhaps, they had received less money than they expected. Their letters are beyond doubt. They described the actual murder as only participants could do, for many of the vile facts were unknown except to officers of our police.'

There was a long silence in the office. The King Archon spread his hands, palm down, on the table in a gesture of misery. Then he said, 'Pericles, you are not without guilt. These men should have been brought to justice. You did not speak.'

Pericles leaned back in his chair. 'I am a politician. Moreover, these men did not commit further crimes. To expose them would have destroyed the trust, more or less, our citizens have for politicians – and I am a politician.'

'They did not commit further crimes because they feared that someone knew the truth about them.'

Pericles lifted his eyebrows. 'True. But they did not know that I was the one. You asked me why I did not speak. Again, I must repeat I am a politician, and I have kept these dossiers for the day when I might need them. The day has come.'

The King Archon lifted his spotted hands and covered his face with them, leaning his elbows on the table, and Pericles felt compassion for him, for the old man was honourable. The King Archon said, 'I, too, am a politician, but I would have spoken.'

'I do not doubt it,' said Pericles. 'Perhaps you love Athens less than I do. It is also true that politicians keep their fellows in order, under threat of exposure. We scratch each other's backs.'

The King Archon dropped his hands and his bright and youthful eyes were lucent. He said, 'You scratch no one's back, Pericles, and no one scratches yours. I have watched you for many years. I knew your father well. He was a hero.'

Pericles looked aside. 'I am no hero, and have no pretensions to be one. My public life has been as clean as possible. I am guilty of no crimes against my country. Still, I am a politician.'

The King Archon rose and walked slowly and heavily up and down the room. Then he came to a halt before Pericles and said in a sick voice, 'What would you have me do?'

'Summon these men, tell them that you are aware of their capital crimes, and that they must go into exile at once, for life.'

'You wish me to tell them of your dossiers?'

Pericles bent his head. 'Yes, if you will. Tell them that if they depart without incident, without speaking, the dossiers will not be made public. Tell them I showed you the dossiers out of a spirit of public service, only.'

'They will know it is revenge.'

'They have no way of knowing how I came by this information, nor that I suspect them of bribing murderers to attack my son. How could they know? Let them suspect, in their exile. They have no proof.'

'Why do you not confront them yourself, Pericles?'

Pericles' smile was bitter and arrogant. 'I am Head of State. I would not demean myself to accuse my fellow politicians, of inferior station. That is your function, not mine. Again, I was moved to inform you only because my conscience began to annoy me – though I came on this information only recently.'

'That is not the truth, Pericles.'

'No, it is not. But you will not be lying to them. You do not know how long I have had this information.' He paused. 'I implore you to space the sentences of voluntary exile. I say, voluntary. Thirty days, at least, must expire between each rascal's invitation to leave Athens for ever.'

He pushed the papers towards the King Archon. 'These are copies. I will retain the others.'

The King Archon looked at the papers as a man looks at vipers. 'Would it not be better if I did not reveal the source of them?'

Pericles shrugged. 'Perhaps. But I am only human. I should like them to ponder the rest of their lives and wonder if the information was given to you because I knew of their bribery to murderers, or,' and he smiled coldly, 'that I was moved by civic virtue. It will make their years of exile interesting.'

'Knowing you, Pericles, I fear they will think it is civic virtue.'

'Perhaps. After all, they were my companions in arms. Let them believe that Nemesis overtook them. I will not know their thoughts, and that, to me, is regrettable.'

The King Archon took up the papers. 'I am an old man,' he said. 'I love my country. I have done no wrong to her, or her laws. This is very grievous to me. Had I had this information the malefactors would have been driven into exile long ago.'

'You are no politician, then.'

The King Archon bent his head and shook it slowly and heavily. 'I have heard that before, from my beloved hetaira. She has assured me that no honest man enters politics.'

'Let us encourage the honest men, then. Let us make it possible for honourable men, though poor, to enter politics. But that is only a dream of the perfect state, and no state is perfect.'

The King Archon sighed deeply. 'I often think of Solon,' he said.

'So do I,' Pericles replied. 'As much as the people allow me I attempt to enforce his laws. But, we must deal with the people and they are capricious!'

'And we fear them. Pericles, I will move as swiftly and as discreetly as possible. These men will be exiled – for their crime against your son – though they will believe it is for another reason.' He paused. 'Why is it not possible to

320

accuse them openly of the attempt on the life of Paralus?'

'On the unsigned word of an informer? Sire, who would believe it of such notable and ostensibly good public servants?'

'And you desire not to increase the mistrust of the citizenry for their government.'

'True. Not all politicians are venal. Incredibly, some of them are honourable men, and it is very hard for a man to remain honourable before a treacherous citizenry, who are, themselves, as fraudulent as their leaders.'

He added, when the King Archon was silent, 'I could have had these men murdered, and they deserve death. You will observe that I am merciful.'

The King Archon smiled strangely. 'No. I observe only that you love your country and would not have her plunged into chaos because of evil men.' He looked long at Pericles. 'I, too, look at the acropolis in the moonlight. For the sake of Athens and her glory and beauty you would do anything, except the dishonourable.'

He took his departure, walking as weightily as a very old sick man and Pericles watched him go and his face was sombre. He thought: The King Archon is wrong. I would do anything for my country, honourable or dishonourable.

CHAPTER VIII

Pericles had believed the King Archon to be neither friend nor foe, but only a just man. His coldness and formality were even more notable than his, though he was never pompous. Therefore, he had few acquaintances and fewer friends. What he thought in private was never revealed, not even to his hetaira.

When alone in his office with the damning papers before him the King Archon thought long and intensely. Pericles would have been amazed had he known of the respect and admiration the King Archon had for him, and how often he had rebuked his fellow Archons who had expressed rage or hate for or envy of the Head of State. The King Archon did not consider it wise to make personal friends of fellow politicians. That way led to subornation and the mutual 'scratching of backs', and was a betrayal of justice and of the people who trusted them. Justice and friendship, he would often think, are what Socrates would call a contradiction in terms. They who would serve justice publicly should keep aloof from human entanglements. So, he was a lonely old man, distant and cool even to his sons and daughters. If one of his sons had committed a crime he would have punished him as severely as any other criminal, with no outward aspect of distress.

He thought, as he sat alone in his private chambers: Pericles, after all, is only human. He would like these men, who are to be exiled, to know he was the avenger and the instigator, or, rather, suspect it for the rest of their lives. But that is most perilous for Athens, Pericles, and his family. These men have many powerful friends, and many male relatives of valour, and they would avenge the four, and they would eventually find means of destroying Athens through the destruction of Pericles. No, this must not happen.

He summoned Polites, Polites who had had his gentle young wife murdered – he, a member of the Supreme Court. The King Archon did not believe in lengthy explanations and accusations. Moreover, he must be sure that what had been revealed in the letter was true. So when Polites arrived, a man of fifty with a fine and aristocratic face, perfect manners and a candid expression, the King Archon, in silence, laid his dossier before him, and acutely watched his face. It turned a mortal white; his eyelids quivered; he seemed to grow old rapidly. So, it is true, thought the King Archon in despair. Polites finally looked up at him and said, 'Lord, do you believe this libel?'

'Yes,' said the King Archon, at once. 'But, I am merciful.

Rather than give this information to the proper authorities I will keep my silence, provided you leave Athens for ever, within two weeks.'

Polites cried out in anguish. The King Archon lifted his hand. 'Your trial could be prolonged, in the way of the law, but the people would believe it, as they are inclined to believe anything of public officials. Truth will out, though many do not believe this. Long investigation would bring your case to the light of day. I have said: I am merciful. If you challenge this dossier you will be ruined. You are accused of a capital crime. You would be put to death, and your estates confiscated. Be silent, then. Tell your friends that you are leaving our city for a considerable period – for the sake of your health. You may then keep your estates and your family can abide with you.'

Polites said, 'Who made this dossier?'

'It is not pertinent. In mercy, I do not advise you to challenge it. If you do, other accusations will be brought against you – I promise – and this time you would not escape justice as you escaped it before.'

Almost beside himself, Polites quickly named several men who were his enemies, execrating them, but the name of Pericles was not among them, a fact which made the old face of the King Archon ironic. He merely kept shaking his head, and repeating, 'I shall not tell you.' He dismissed Polites, who left him with an almost staggering gait, and he then summoned each of the other three in turn.

In every case guilt appeared on their countenances though they protested their innocence, even vowing the most sacred of oaths, that of Castor and Pollux. The King Archon closed his eyes in weariness and lifted his hand. 'Let that oath not condemn you before the gods,' he said. 'If you wish to withdraw it, do so now.'

After some hesitation the oath was withdrawn and the King Archon, who had prayed that at least one of the men had been falsely accused, was sickened. They had always declared their deep love for Pericles; they were his comrades in arms. They had voted with him almost invariably. Men of family, and proud of their city, they had approved of the Parthenon and other costly temples on the acropolis. They had frequently dined, and with pleasure and accord, with Pericles, and he had visited their own houses often. Two were of his own tribe. Why, then, had they attempted to kill his son and cast him into sorrow and misery? Malice and envy, the ancient human crimes, the old Archon thought. A man, even the best of friends, will forgive anything but that a friend rise above him and attain fame. Pericles had understood that, and the King Archon reflected on Pericles' own sorrow that his friends had betrayed him, had tried to plunge his heart into grief, and by no justification except that he had proved himself their natural superior. We are a wicked and incorrigible race, thought the old Archon, and why the gods endure us is a great mystery.

The King Archon, even more discreet than Pericles himself, did not send word of the results of his accusations to the Head of State. The news would reach Pericles soon enough. One man had said he would leave Athens soon to manage his estates in Cyprus; another claimed the air of Athens had injured his lungs – he must flee for his health's sake; another had said he was weary of public office, and would retire to the country; still another said his beloved wife wished to be with her family in Cos. Not one hinted that his absence was exile, forced upon him under threat. The King Archon, hearing all this, was deeply depressed, knowing now, beyond all doubt, that they were guilty.

Each of the four men went, weeping, to Pericles, to announce his imminent departure from Athens. They confided to him that they had been forced into exile because of false accusations, 'which would endanger the State, if I challenged them.' Pericles, who had trained himself, as a politician, to be somewhat of an actor, against all his principles, said in apparent wonder and concern, 'But, if you are

324

innocent, why not seek to prove it?' Their silence, their dolorous sighs, filled him with hate and he could scarce restrain himself. 'Let me help you,' he said, and none heard the iron under his words. They replied, 'It would imperil you, yourself, dearest of friends.' He heard sincerity in their voices, and marvelled. They truly meant it.

He almost pitied them, and he especially pitied Polites who had been a valiant lieutenant under Pericles' command, and who had proved his loyalty and love under dire circumstances. But Pericles had only to look at the sunken right eye of his handsome son, Paralus, to feel the return of his furious hatred. Paralus said to him, 'I live. I can see, if only in a flattened state. I am fortunate to be alive, and to have some sight. For a time my other eye was threatened, but Helena saved both my life and my vision. Alas, though, I shall never be a soldier as you were, my father.'

'Nor will you have comrades in arms,' said Pericles, and Paralus, who thought he knew his father better than did even Aspasia, was puzzled at the profound bitterness in his father's voice, and the look of terrible anger.

Xanthippus, now healed, proclaimed his discontent that he would have to serve his two years in the army. He did this to spare Paralus, who longed to be a soldier, and Paralus said, soothingly, 'The time will pass soon, and I will think of you as taking my place, for you must have the strength of two men.' His brother was now espoused to the young girl whom he had met in Aspasia's house, and the marriage would take place soon. Xanthippus was very happy. He sighed, and said, 'I would prefer not to marry, but it is my duty. I am like a virgin heifer led to sacrifice.' His dark face beamed.

Helena informed Pericles that the time for the birth of his child had arrived. He insisted, against her advice, on being in that remote farmhouse with Aspasia, and so she left one morning alone, except for two young physicians who would aid her, and he, Pericles, left the next day. He took with him only Iphis and a subaltern who was devoted to Iphis, for it was not his wish that he attract attention. The farm, though secluded, was but a four-hour journey on horseback. The roads were very poor, the Athenians declaring that good roads were not necessary outside the city. 'We do not travel,' they said, grandly, 'for where is there a spot more beautiful and important or renowned than Athens? If we wish to see the world and engage in commerce with other nations, the sea is our road.'

The olive trees were burnished with a fresh silver, and corn was thrusting moist green tips out of the earth and into the sun. Children played outside their houses, and the grapevines which grew up the sides of the houses were exploding with new tendrils, the garlands of Dionysius. The red mud ran with mercurial brooks, reflecting the sky. The ponds teemed with fish, and so did the rivers.

It is a goodly season in which to be born, thought Pericles, whose fair skin had begun to smart with the heat and the sun. It is a promise. He hoped for another son, but even a daughter would be welcome, a daughter who resembled Aspasia. Peace came to him. He saw his white farmhouse in the distance, surrounded by cypresses and sycamores; he saw his olive groves and his sheep and lambs and goats and cattle and horses, and he felt more pride than when he addressed the Assembly, which rose in a rustle of garments at his entry, and bowed before him. He could even forget hatred here and the hot sickness that often assailed him. Above all, politicians needed a retreat where they could observe their unimportance, and feel, however vaguely, the Presence of God, not the dutiful gesture to the Godhead which was expected of them in public, but the immanent Presence which touched the heart and the spirit with verity, and only in solitude.

Aspasia, with Helena at her side, greeted Pericles joyfully. He embraced her with delight, careful of her swollen body. Her face shone like the moon; never had he seen her so beautiful, so young, so radiant. She took his hand and kissed it, and pressed it to her breast. She gazed at him adoringly. She was in transports. She threw back her pale golden hair and laughed, and there were tears in her brown eyes. She even babbled incoherently, and never had he heard this before, and he held her again as one more precious to him than his own life. Helena watched them with indulgent affection and humour. One was a trained and experienced courtesan; the other was the most powerful man in Greece. Yet they were as bride and groom, awaiting their first child, parents as simple as peasants, and as innocent and unknown.

The food of the farm was theirs, as the three dined together: new cheese, dark rich bread, little carrots and lettuce drenched with oil and vinegar, young roasted lamb, broiled fresh fish from the river nearby, fowl fried in olive oil and tender as butter, soup of green peas with pork – and, always, the wine from his autumn hillsides.

Later, they retired to their rough chamber, where the walls were of unpolished wood, and pale gold. The floor was of stone; it was covered by no carpets, and was cool to the foot. The blankets were coarse, the linen prickling, and it was not bleached. Pericles held Aspasia in his arms; he would put his hand on her belly, to feel the kicking of his child. It was as if he had no other wife, no other children. The uncurtained windows were bare and open and they could smell the carnal passion of the warming earth and could hear nothing but the nightingales, the shrilling of insect voices and the night wind. Pericles had blown out the lamp. Stars gazed through the windows.

Aspasia slept, her head on his shoulder, her hands entwined with his, her round limbs seeking him, her breasts full and warm and preparing milk. Her hair was fragrant with the aroma of grass and sun. Her shift was of linen, and simple. She wore no scent. He felt her soft silken hair against his chin, and he kissed it. She sighed happily in her sleep, and murmured like a maiden awakened to love. Athens became unreal to him; his problems and his distresses were of no significance.

He held the whole world in his arms, the world of life and labour and veritable joy. A dog barked sleepily; a cow lowed in the barns. A horse stamped. The only discordant note was the voice of a guard speaking to another guard. The wedge of the rising moon peered in the window. Pericles slept.

The next morning, clad as a countryman, Pericles rode with his men and slaves over his land. This farm was not his most profitable; it was, in truth, a peasant's farm, including the farmhouse. His other farms were almost opulent in comparison, with villas for the visits of the owner. But he preferred this, a return to simplicity.

Aspasia was in the kitchen peeling onions for a soup when Helena joined her, and Helena smiled a little mockingly at her friend's humble occupation. Aspasia said with an almost child-like joy, 'Oh, if but Pericles and I could live here always, in such peace and such unaffected plainness! How happy we would be.'

'Nonsense,' said Helena, critically selecting a citron from a reed basket on the table and beginning to remove the peel. 'This is a novelty for you, dear. Go to. What, no Agora, no banks, no shops, no booksellers, no music, no dinners with philosophers and artists, no dancing, no pleasant luxury, no jewellery or fine robes, no solicitous services of slaves in the baths, no gossip, no excitement, no stimulation of the mind, no sophisticated conversation, no politics, no discussions of the arts, no meeting of thoughts? Pah. I agree that every man should have a little quiet land of his own to which he can escape and renew his peace of mind and be freed from the burden of thinking.' She laughed, her blue eyes sparkling. 'Oh, I can see you and Pericles here for all time, until you gnaw your knuckles for very ennui and dullness and too much quiet!'

Aspasia was at first offended, then she laughed and wiped her eyes with the back of one of her hands. 'How we pretend to ourselves!' she said. 'I have known nothing but opulence all my life and daintiness and excellent food and wine, and I admit I do not despise them. But, for a space, this is good. Let Pericles and I have this pretence for a little while.' She then asked of her friends in Athens.

'Anaxagoras is coming under attack, and I fear for him,' said Helena. 'All of Pericles' friends are being scrutinized, including me.'

Aspasia stopped smiling. 'You, Helena, who have given your life to the saving of others and the mitigation of their diseases?' She was incredulous.

'Ah, but I am a dissolute woman! My lack of virtue is beyond dispute. I am a black example to modest wives and daughters. I am unchaste, and impious. I go publicly into the market place with no attendants; I am the companion of many men. I wear no veils of discretion. I do not titter and cast down my eyes and say childish things, as do other women. Therefore, I am a disgrace, the shame of Athens.' She paused. 'As for Anaxagoras, and the others of Pericles' friends, they, too, are impious. They question not only government, but religion and superstition. They are leading the youth of Athens to disaster and rebellion against authority; they ask youth to think as well as merely to obey. These are capital crimes, of a certainty.' She sucked at the citron and her eyes were darkly serious. 'On one hand we hear talk of the splendour and glory burgeoning in Greece, and worship it. On the other hand we would destroy those who have brought this splendour and glory to our country. It is not a new tale; it is the history of every nation. But we never learn. After we kill heroes we elevate them among the stars. But the gods do that also, so what can we expect from men?'

Aspasia looked through the window at the warm and pellucid sky, at the far wide peace of the fields, at the stands of dark cypresses, at the orchards and the cattle and the lambs and the goats and horses, all exuberant in the spring air. Birds swooped and darted like coloured arrows in the lucent light. She was about to say something when she caught Helena's mocking eye, and so was silent.

'Of a certainty,' said Helena, 'a man who thinks will be forever unhappy, for who can come to terms with this world except the stupid? Still, it is better to think and conjecture and be unhappy than it is to be happy in ignorance. The divine discontent – it creates glory. Contentment? That is for the tomb.'

Aspasia said, her thoughts still with her dear friend, 'You are not afraid for yourself, Helena?'

The physician shrugged. 'Of what avail is fear? If one ponders on it long enough one becomes cautious, and caution has blinded and deafened and made impotent too many who should have been bold. I despise prudence – to some extent. I do not court death or any other punishment. But I must live as I must, according to my nature, or expire, one way or another. What is it?' she asked quickly.

For Aspasia had suddenly put her hand to her belly and had gasped. Her face had paled and sweat had broken out on her brow. 'A pain, a great pain,' she stammered, and all at once she was afraid. But Helena was calm. 'The child is due. Let us repair to your chamber, where I have placed the birthing stool and my instruments. Let the slave woman continue with this preparation of food.'

'Pericles,' Aspasia murmured, as another pain seized her, causing her to bend deeply.

'Nonsense,' Helena said with briskness. 'How can he assist? Men are only a trouble when women give birth. They become hysterical, and they dither. Let him look at his growing turnips and cabbages and talk of manure to his slaves; let him examine the new corn. Let us pray he does not return soon.'

She conducted Aspasia to her austere chamber and told the slave women to prepare towels and linens and oils and heat water and wine. She put Aspasia on the birthing stool and sat down placidly near her. If she was concerned about Aspasia's age – she was thirty-four – and this a first child, she did not reveal it. She talked genially of Athens and their friends and politics, but ever watchful, counting the contractions. They were still not very fast. Occasionally she rose and wiped the sweat from Aspasia's face with a cool cloth dipped in water of nard. She made no comment on this. She still conversed as she felt the other woman's pulse. Her conversation was matter of fact; she did not discuss the coming birth. When she saw Aspasia was in pain, she told her a lewd joke, and Aspasia laughed. The sunlight came through the window, and the fresh scent of the jubilant earth. A bird, whose feathers were blue and gold, lighted on the window-sill and sang. 'It is a good omen,' said Helena.

Aspasia began to writhe on the stool. Helena said, 'It is not a good thing for a woman in labour to lie in bed. Now you must stand and walk.' She took Aspasia's arm and led her up and down the chamber. Two slave women, crouching in a corner, wide-eyed, stared at the two. The garden slaves were singing; a fragrance of grass and lilacs blew into the room. A bee flew through the window and buzzed against a wall. A slave woman would have killed it but Helena said, 'Let there be no death here. It is an industrious thing, the bee, and we should honour it.'

Helena permitted Aspasia to lie on her bed for a few moments while she examined her. She said, with satisfaction, 'The head is already presenting itself. There are some physicians who hasten labour. I do not. Nature knows more than we. In your case, my dear, there will be little difficulty.'

Aspasia gasped. 'What women must endure!' she said.

Helena forced a yawn. 'It is no high tragedy,' she replied. 'Do we not all endure travail in our lives? Besides, in the case of giving birth it is not only women who suffer. We suffer with other female animals, who assign no importance to it.' However, she was somewhat concerned. The enclosed child's head was indeed presenting itself at the cervix, but the birth bag had not yet broken.

She made Aspasia walk again. Then she let her lie on her bed, and forced her legs apart. She hid a small instrument in her hand and then inserted her hand into the birth canal. She punctured the bag. Aspasia cried out as a gush of fluid mingled with blood ran from her. Helena was satisfied. Now the birth could proceed. She put Aspasia on the birthing stool again and knelt before her, her instruments at her side, and the high forceps which Hippocrates had invented. At her command a slave woman brought a pail of hot water and soap and Helena, as Hippocrates had taught her, washed the instruments and her hands over and over and then dried them on clean towels. The air was becoming warmer, more fervid. Helena, might have been a hearty and very plump countrywoman herself, as she knelt before her patient, her brow wet and streaming, her auburn hair darkening with water. When a strong contraction came she pressed gently on Aspasia's belly, pushing down. Aspasia's gasps and groans became louder. 'Do not draw deep breaths,' said Helena. 'It delays birth. Press down as I press, even if it increases the pain.'

Aspasia was very pale and drawn. Helena studied her. Then she rose and mixed a murky liquid in wine. 'Drink this,' she said. 'It will ease you.'

Aspasia, beyond speech now, drank obediently. Her mouth contorted. 'Opium,' said Helena. 'I give it seldom for it inclines to delay the birth and the child is also affected. So says Hippocrates. However, you are near delivery, so it will not injure you or your child.'

The opium rapidly affected Aspasia, and she entered a dreaming state. Now she could see Helena in a haze. Helena's voice came to her in a strong and peremptory fashion. 'Do not sleep. Press down your belly.'

But what have I to do with my flesh? Aspasia asked herself with superb amusement. It surprised her that Helena could be so obtuse. A sudden unbearable pain tore her, but it was still apart from her. She felt hands take her roughly, lift her, put her on her bed. There was one appalling convulsion, which slowly died away into night. She slept.

It was sunset, red and burning, when she awoke, flaccid and

exhausted. She was in her bed and Pericles was bending over her, smiling. He was holding her hand. She looked up at him and said, 'I have seen all things.' She heard Helena laugh.

'We have a son,' said Pericles, 'a beautiful son, with hair of gold and with blue eyes, and he is very fat. He is perfect.'

She clung to his hand. She said, 'Pericles,' and she spoke of both her lover and her child. She slept again, her cheek in the palm of Pericles' hand, and she sighed with joy that the pain was over and that her bed was soft and that her beloved would never leave her.

To Aspasia, her child was a miracle. No other woman had ever given birth to such excellence, such beauty. She was amazed at him; she examined him with awe. It was morning and Pericles sat beside her in his rude countryman's tunic, his knees already burned by the sun, his stern face youthful. 'Never was there such a wonder,' she said to him, and he smiled. Helena, standing near him, said, 'Life is always a wonder, and marvellous and full of mystery.' Aspasia knew compassion for her friend, Helena, who had never given birth. She felt the strong sucking of her son at her breast, and she was overcome with happiness. She said to Helena, 'Oh, beloved, if only you had given birth to a child!'

'The gods have been kind to me,' said Helena in a satirical voice, and she pushed Pericles' shoulder.

She and Pericles went outside into the lyrical morning light. 'What is it?' she asked of Pericles. 'I heard a messenger ride up to this house just before dawn, and I see that you are greatly disturbed.'

Pericles said, 'I have just received a message that Anaxagoras has been arrested, on the accusation that he has been teaching impiety and heresy, and that death has been recommended for him.'

Helena made a sound of angry protest. 'What will you do?' she asked.

'I must return to Athens at once, and save him.'

333

'Yes, you must go,' she said. 'Do not fear for Aspasia. Fear for Greece.'

'Do I not always? The gods have struck her with lightning and glory, but there are always men! We must invariably fight our brothers that even they may survive and not be the victims of their own crimes and stupidity.'

She put her hand on his arm and said with gentle affection, 'Go at once. Do not see Aspasia again, lest she be troubled. I will tell her later.'

CHAPTER IX

Pericles found Anaxagoras in the same prison where Ichthus had been incarcerated and had died. But Anaxagoras was not in a pleasant cell, for he was poor and only a philosopher. A dim lantern hung on the sweating walls of the corridor and shone fitfully into the cell, where Anaxagoras was lying on a bed of straw. Pericles had come directly from the road to this noisome place and was covered with silvery dust and was weary. Before he even spoke to his friend he said in cold rage to the guards, 'Remove my friend immediately to a large cell with a window, and bring him wine and fruit and cheese and bread.' He had seen a brown plate on the floor with a repulsive mixture on it, which Anaxagoras had not eaten.

Anaxagoras opened his great blue eyes and he started and gazed at Pericles with pleasure and raised himself on his elbow. His magnificent face was gaunt and drawn, but he had retained his air of utter serenity. He rose slowly to his feet while the guards unlocked the door of the cell. Pericles took him by the arm and, led by the guards, they proceeded to a larger, warmer and airier cell. A guard went for the ordered food and returned, placing it on a bare wooden table. During this interval Anaxagoras and Pericles did not speak, but only exchanged smiling glances.

When the astonished but respectful guards had left, saluting, Anaxagoras embraced Pericles and said, 'I am overjoyed to see you, beloved friend, but you should not have come here. You endanger yourself.'

'The time has come,' said Pericles, 'when one should not consider such danger, but how to preserve what small freedom we yet retain. Now, you must tell me the charges.' He sat down at the table and poured wine for Anaxagoras and broke bread and cheese for him. They began to eat and drink together. Anaxagoras sank into thought and looked dreamily at the wall. Then he said, 'I do not know. I was teaching in my small academe when the government guards arrested me. They told me I had committed an offence against the State, by impiety, heresy and corruption of youth, and so was an enemy of the people. On query they said the charges had been placed against me by Daedalus, the Archon.'

'So,' said Pericles. He had removed his dust-covered mantle and helmet. The light of the lantern flittered over his hard face and lofty forehead.

'I will, tomorrow, appear before the Assembly to defend you.'

'I beg of you, no,' said Anaxagoras, and his eyes filled with sharp anxiety. 'Your former father-in-law will halt at nothing. He has powerful friends in the government.'

'In short, they are striking at me through you,' said Pericles. His weary face flushed with rage, but his voice remained quiet. 'I will, then, be defending myself and my office against these scoundrels.' He thought of his son, Paralus, and Aspasia, who had been wantonly attacked in order to injure him. 'Do not protest. Had you not known me you should not now be in this predicament.'

Anaxagoras shook his head. 'You are wrong, dear friend. It would have happened to me eventually, even if you had not known me, as it has happened before to others.'

335

But Pericles was frowning in thought. 'Have they witnesses against you?'

Anaxagoras spread out his hands. 'Who knows? My students? My friends, with whom I have conversed often? It is impossible to know.'

'Be sure they have witnesses who will eagerly aid them to exile or imprison you or kill you. Doubtless, they are avowed friends.'

Anaxagoras regarded him with compassion.

'Tell me,' said Pericles, 'have you been expounding some new theories which conflict with the accepted religious dogmas?'

Anaxagoras sank into thought. Finally he said, 'They were extensions of what I have already been teaching. Only recently I repeated that there were no magical or supernatural or godlike interventions in eclipses, meteors, rainbows or comets. They were only manifestations of the eternal order, founded by God, and could be predicted. You will remember I predicted an eclipse of the moon three weeks before it occurred, and related that it is but the shadow of the earth between the moon and the sun. This enraged the authorities, who, on the eclipse, called upon the people to pray that the moon would not be obliterated. They sent criers through the streets, shouting, armed with torches and carrying statues of the gods. My students laughed. This was unpardonable, of a certainty. The priests were particularly enraged. Had they been a little more stupid they would have declared that I, Anaxagoras, through sorcery, had caused the eclipse, but then the whole populace would have laughed.'

He, himself, laughed gently, but Pericles remained sombre.

'I wrote a thesis,' said Anaxagoras, and Pericles winced. The written word was far more dangerous than the spoken. 'I said it was my belief that all things that exist now had existed from eternity, and would continue to exist, whether it was the material of the stars and their planets or the life of living organisms. Not their immediate manifestations, but in other forms. While all is flux and change, the innate patterns remain,

336

though giving rise to either more intricate manifestations or simpler on the base of their original matrix. This was because, I wrote, all matter, whether of stars or a blade of grass, are only an illusion of form, for all things are composed of infinite particles which are not matter at all, but only energy. In short, all things, suns, planets, galaxies, dust, trees, the earth itself, constellations, flowers, men, birds, insects, wheat, water, wine, houses and temples, mountains and marble, furniture and statues and murals, oceans and continents, are but one dynamic force and are indications of one endless pattern of energy which can change itself – perhaps by accident or by the will of God. There is only a Oneness in all that we see, hear, feel, touch, taste and smell, despite the apparent differentiations, and so variety of apparent objectivities is only an illusion. I even ventured,' said Anaxagoras, 'that nothing really exists but the Mind of God, which contains all manifestations and apparencies, and therefore is subjective.'

When Pericles did not comment, Anaxagoras said, 'To put it more simply, everything that exists is only in the Mind of God, and in His dreams, and there is nothing but His Mind.'

Pericles put his head in his hands and groaned. 'That neatly disposes of the gods, who, our priests say, are overt and material.' He laughed grimly. 'In short, as you surmise, the gods themselves are subjective.'

Anaxagoras looked depressed. 'That was possibly the conclusion of the priests.' He added, 'But, was my thesis blasphemous? God contains everything and all things. Surely that reveals His majesty. For He is all, and there is nothing else. He is Energy, itself, and weaves, like a weaver, patterns without end, and evokes changes which are yet the same. He cannot disobey His own divine Laws, which He established from eternity. If He once disobeyed His own Laws, then all would be chaos and darkness. He is the Law. If the Law disintegrates, nothing would exist any longer.'

'I see,' said Pericles. 'Our gods constantly disobey the laws of decency, morals and justice and mercy. Therefore, they do not exist – except in particles of mindless energy,' and he laughed without mirth.

'That is the interpretation of the priests of what I have taught. It is not mine.'

'Did you truly expect that the average man would understand your thesis?'

'One can only try,' replied Anaxagoras. 'It is the duty of those who teach to speak the truth, though all teachers know only a small portion of what they teach. There is such a thing as integrity.'

'Which is very rare,' said Pericles.

Anaxagoras looked down at his veined and elegant hands. 'I also wrote in that thesis, that there is but one God, and not a variety of male and female antagonists.'

'How thoroughly you disposed of all the goddesses,' said Pericles, 'and most of our gods.'

'Who were created in our own image – by men,' said Anaxagoras. He looked again into space. 'There is but one God, in Whom all things exist. I wrote, in my thesis, that the endless colours and forms of nature, in both land and sea, exist because He moved over the world in music, and in the diversities of His music rose the varieties which we discern, the multitude of varieties.' His blue eyes sparkled with fervour. 'Who shall limit God to the dimensions of men? Only blasphemers.'

'True,' said Pericles, 'therefore you must recant the truth.'

'If I do, then am I myself destroyed and there is no meaning to my existence.' His eyes glowed. 'I believe in one God, eternal and unchanging, even if manifestations appear to change, as a lute and a lyre and a drum change tempo though remaining themselves as entities, unchanging.'

He looked at Pericles earnestly. 'Do you understand what I am saying?'

'I am no philosopher, Anaxagoras. I am only a politician. I discern, dimly, what you mean, but only dimly. Zeno would understand you more.'

Anaxagoras sighed. 'Philosophers are also egotists. They deny all philosophies but their own, which they believe is divine revelation.'

'Including yours?'

Anaxagoras chuckled. 'Including mine.' Then his face became grave. 'I do believe, however, that future ages will understand what I have been saying. Perhaps to their glory. Perhaps to their death. When men grasp the fact that all apparent things are only energy, and that energy can be manipulated – it may be the end.' He was graver than before. 'I do not dispute with God. But would it be wise to give man the secret of the universe?'

'Perhaps,' said Pericles, 'God is weary of man and his stupidities and his evils. Therefore, He will give the secret so that man can choose between life and death.'

Pericles stood up and began to pace the cell. 'That is a terrible and momentous choice, considering the limitations of men's capacities. It is as though we gave the secret of guiding a fleet into the hands of children.' He looked at his friend. 'Our minds approach the universal but our tongues are the gross tongues of apes. We communicate with each other in the meagre language of the jungle, even while our thoughts are afire. That is the tragedy of mankind.'

'We must find a different mode of communication, then, Pericles. Mind to mind, and not tongue to tongue. For, despite what Socrates has said, there is no defining of terms which are relevant to every man. Our emotions intrude.' He smiled faintly. 'In the midst of discussions, sometimes flaming and exalted, my students have to repair to the latrines. When they have taken care of their animal needs the divine flame has left them.'

'Perhaps that is the curse which God has inflicted on man.' Pericles laughed. 'It is possible that God, Himself, does not wish us to complete our knowledge, so our intestines demand our attention.'

Anaxagoras said, 'In the middle of an elevated conversation

I spilled a plate of beans on my lap, and that ended the discussion, as my students hovered about me – picking up the beans and commiserating and wiping the debris from my garments.'

'It was possibly a relief for them. You terminated their thinking.'

He refilled Anaxagoras' goblet and leaned back in his chair. The friends were much refreshed not only by the wine and food but by their conversation. Pericles said, 'If I let this pass, and they exile or kill you, then I am guilty of betraying my country. So, I will not let this pass.' He looked at his friend, who was about to protest. 'I assume, for the sake of peace and your freedom and your life, that you will not recant, and beg the pardon of the government?'

'Of a certainty, no!' exclaimed Anaxagoras, astonished. 'I cannot deny the truth I know.'

'Hum. Do you recall what Sophocles has told us: "Truly, to tell lies is not honourable, but, when the truth entails tremendous ruin, to speak dishonourably is pardonable"? I agree. Again, it is not you who is on trial, Anaxagoras. It is the freedom of Athens.'

'You believe that Athens, and freedom, can be saved by lies?'

Pericles shrugged. 'When I was younger I would have denied that. Now I am a middle-aged man and no longer young and I know that in the cause of truth lies are sometimes necessary, paradoxical though that seems.'

'Did you tell that to Ichthus?'

'I did. But he was too emotional to listen and to understand.'

'And so he died for truth.'

Pericles shrugged again. 'It would have been better if he had lived, by a lie, so that he could later utter the truth and perhaps with impunity.'

Anaxagoras pondered. He was no passionate young man like Ichthus. Pericles said, 'Would you at least hold your tongue while I defend you?'

The older man began to smile. 'It may be a good comedy.'

Pericles picked up his mantle and shook it. 'I have not told you. I have a son, as young as the morning, and as beautiful.'

Anaxagoras rose and embraced him. 'He will be a glory to you and to Aspasia.'

'Who knows? You will see I am again melancholy. The dark Sisters, the Fates, have the thread of his life in their hands, for good or evil, and who can know what pattern they are weaving for my son?' He added, 'Or for me, or for you?'

Pericles left with a lighter heart than he had come. Anaxagoras was a sensible man. He had immediately discerned that he need not deny the truth. He had only to be quiet. Truth should not be shouted from the rooftops; it should move with the wise subtlety of the serpent, and often in silence. Then it was potent.

When Pericles had left, Anaxagoras sat thinking. Years ago he had rebuked Pericles for his proposed plan to save Ichthus. But age brought more hesitation, more weighing of facts, more thought for the future and its consequences. Too, Ichthus would have condemned himself openly before the Assembly and the Ecclesia, and that would have endangered Pericles beyond hope. Pericles, at that time, had not been above gestures, himself! Anaxagoras smiled wryly.

Before going to the place of judgement, before the King Archon, Pericles first went to his offices and studied some of his dossiers. He wrote some short notes on a tablet and put them in his pouch. He had dressed himself soberly, in a blue tunic and a grey toga and he wore black shoes. His helmet had been polished diligently. He had gargled with honey and water so that the full power of his sonorous and eloquent voice would not be impaired. Composing himself, for at intervals his cold and bitter internal rage became unusually intense, he went to the place of judgement. He knew that the King Archon, a noble and just man, would listen with gravity and detachment to the accusation and defence of Anaxagoras, but if he was convinced that Anaxagoras was indeed an enemy of the people and State, and a corrupter of youth, he would not refrain from ordering even the extreme punishment. Pericles had rarely seen him smile, for he took all things seriously.

The huge jury was already assembled, and Pericles, somewhat to his dismay, found that many members of the Assembly and the Eleven, and the Ecclesia were there also, all avid, like men in the theatre awaiting a bloody drama. The spring day was hot. The judgement hall was crowded and very warm, and the high small windows let in shafts of smarting sun and the effluvium of the Agora. When the stately Pericles entered, all eyes turned upon him, and he knew, as he had guessed before, that Anaxagoras was not the chief accused, but himself. Some of his friends were there, also standing against the ochre walls, a number of them with foreboding that one day, sooner or later, they would be the accused and suffer ostraka or death. They watched Pericles approach before the high seat and bench of the King Archon, and their quiet eyes were anxious.

Also before the bench was the Archon, Daedalus. Pericles turned very slowly and studied him as a gentleman studies some obnoxious sight – that is, with an expression of faint incredulity, faint astonishment, and cool aversion. The aged Archon, bent and even more skeleton-like than he had been at the marriage of Pericles and Dejanira, returned Pericles' gaze with venom, his face writhing and wrinkling so that he resembled an ancient ape with jaundice. His sunken eyes were fiery, vindictive and almost insanely fierce, and his mouth twisted as if he wished to spit but his throat was too dry. He trembled visibly with his hatred; his hands appeared palsied. All looked at both the men, some gloating and anticipatory, some with alarm. Anaxagoras became insignificant before these two mortal antagonists, who loathed each other.

At a silent gesture from the King Archon, Anaxagoras was brought into the hall, walking as tall and regnant as a king, for all chains dripped from his wrists. He moved with serenity and that dignity which only men who do not fear death can bring to cover them like an invincible armour. He was thrust before the bench, between Pericles and Daedalus. He bowed courteously to the King Archon. He smiled gently on Pericles and did not give Daedalus, his accuser, a single glance. Now the hall became very still, and all leaned forward so as not to miss a word or a gesture.

The King Archon spoke: 'Daedalus, you have brought charges against the teacher and philosopher, Anaxagoras, who stands before us. Repeat the charges you have made to me.' The King Archon's folded hands were clasped together on the bench before him.

Now Daedalus shook as if a wind had struck him. Some thought he would fall. Others believed he had been seized by a fit and would hurl himself to the floor, foaming and twisting in all his limbs. His dull garments of brown actually blew over his emaciated body. The King Archon observed this with silent detachment, waiting. Pericles pretended that he saw nothing. He was studying his notes. Quickly he glanced at some of the members of the government whom he knew hated him and had come here as to a slaughter. His face had taken on that deadly and daunting expression, and they saw it and a few moved uneasily. They were all powerful men.

Daedalus found his voice, as cawing as a crow. He pointed his finger at Anaxagoras and said, 'I accuse this man of impiety and heresy and the corruption of our youth! I have heard him speak, myself, to the innocent boys and other students, and my heart and soul were shaken with wrath and outrage, and, yes, fear of the gods whom he had so insulted!'

'You must be specific,' said the King Archon in a steadfast voice. 'Tell me. What has the prisoner said in your hearing?'

'That the gods do not exist, that they are fantasies of mist, that they have no being!' The caw rose to a loud croak, and a stammering. 'He denied the verity of the gods. With these ears I heard it, and that I swear by the sacred names of Castor and Pollux.'

Pericles' enemies affected to be horrified, and a loud

343

groaning filled the hall and men looked, as if astounded and aghast, into each other's eyes. Pericles smiled faintly and with obvious contempt at them.

The King Archon motioned to Pericles, who gave Anaxagoras, who seemed about to speak, a quelling glance. Then Pericles smiled broadly and shook his head as though he found the charge absurd and fit only for laughter.

His voice, clear and strong and vivid, rose when he turned fully to Daedalus. His brows lifted in pretended amazement and his smile was the indulgent one that one gives to a child or a senile old man. All listened acutely.

'My dear Daedalus, most honoured Daedalus, surely you do not believe that the gods are of our gross flesh and material, and are only enlarged men? You do not believe they are mortal and will suffer death?'

'No!' screamed Daedalus, in a frenzy.

'No?' repeated Pericles, in surprise. 'But that is what you imply. Homer has written that the gods ride on the wind, are often invisible and impalpable, can pass through matter and substance as if matter and substance did not exist, can change form and shape. They are protean. Do you deny this?'

'No!' howled Daedalus with fury.

'No?' said Pericles. 'Then you agree with Anaxagoras that the Godhead is immaterial Mind and that all apparent things dwell in It. For that is what he maintains, and I, too, have heard him often.'

Daedalus could not speak. Pericles said with kindness, 'You do agree with Anaxagoras in this?'

Daedalus still did not speak. He was shaking again. The King Archon said sternly, 'Answer, Daedalus.'

Daedalus wrung his hands. His eyes darted frantically. Pericles said, 'Perhaps it is you, dear friend, who defames the gods and would bring them down to the earthly gutter in which we all wallow?'

Daedalus spoke hoarsely, 'If that is what Anaxagoras maintains, I must agree with him.'

344

'You thought that when Anaxagoras compared them with radiant mist, with the deepest and most subjective adoration a man can feel, and that when he implied that they are not in our context of existence, you believed he was denying their being?'

When Daedalus was speechless again Pericles smiled at him tenderly. 'It is all a matter of semantics. You are not to blame, dear friend. We all misunderstand each other, for words are clumsy stones and they lie heavily in our mouths.'

'Do you wish to withdraw the charge of impiety, Daedalus?' asked the King Archon and his beard about his mouth stirred a little, as if with a smile.

'In that one instance,' Daedalus muttered. His bony cheeks had become dusky.

Pericles let the silence of the hall expand while he appeared to muse kindly on Daedalus, who looked at him with a helpless if ferocious malignity.

The King Archon said to the jury, 'The charge of impiety – that the gods do not exist – is removed from Anaxagoras.' He said to Daedalus, with some sternness, 'Do you wish to continue with your other charges?'

Daedalus gathered himself together as a vulture gathers himself, preparing to pounce. He pointed to Anaxagoras, who seemed to have withdrawn to a great distance and was meditating.

'This creature,' Daedalus said, 'has declared that eclipses are not supernatural manifestations of the gods, but are natural phenomena, and therefore are not omens, as our religious teachers have taught us! He has even declared that they can be predicted!'

Pericles' pale eyes enlarged in amazement. He stared at Daedalus as one stares disbelievingly when hearing incredible things. He said, 'But Anaxagoras did predict an eclipse of the moon very recently.'

Daedalus shrilled at him, 'Who can explain that? Was it chance? Was it some dire magic? Did some malevolent demon whisper it to him? Only he can tell!'

345

Pericles shook his head, incredulously, and turned to the King Archon. 'Lord,' he said, 'we Greeks boast, and with some reason, that we have a grand new age not only of the arts and philosophy, but also of science. I only pray to God, and with due reverence for Athens, that the Egyptians and the Chaldeans do not hear of this trial, and the words of Daedalus! How they would laugh at what they would call our pretensions to glory and reason!'

A deep growling roved through the hall and angry eyes focused now on Pericles, and men exchanged outraged glances. The King Archon remained calm. He stroked his beard thoughtfully. He said, 'Noble Pericles, we should like to hear you elucidate more on this matter.'

Silence fell again. Hundreds of eyes glared at Pericles.

He said, 'Lord, the Egyptians and Chaldeans through their wise men, their scientists, have been predicting eclipses almost to the exact moment for hundreds of years. Before Anaxagoras came to Athens he studied among those scientists.' Anaxagoras made a quick movement, as if to protest, but Pericles ignored the gesture and raised his voice. Now it was grave, earnest, almost confidential, even pleading.

'Let us pray that they do not hear of this folly. They are already envious of what we are accomplishing here. Let us give them no reason to jeer at us and call us barbarians, as they have done in the past. Their scientists would be appalled at the ignorance of – Daedalus. But one must excuse him. He is a very old man and has not had the advantages of an extended education in science.'

The King Archon almost imperceptibly smiled. The hall was hushed.

'Sorcery!' shieked Daedalus. 'It is only sorcery!'

Pericles shook his head sadly. 'So unlearned men through the ages have proclaimed, when confronted with something which refutes their prejudices, their unreason. But, we are Greeks. We have reached the Age of true Enlightenment, and what our elders believed was the truth we now see as superstition or obtuseness.'

'Heresy,' said Daedalus and flung out his arms.

Pericles now became stern. 'What is heresy?' he demanded. 'Is it not the impotent cry of those who do not know what true heresy is? True heresy is that which refuses to accept truth, which limits the capacity of man to think, which belittles our nature, which denies that we are more than animals, which would blind us to knowledge and prevent us from increasing our stature, which stands at the portals of learning with a savage sword, which will not let us enter the temples to look upon the manifestations of the Godhead, which fears the light and declares that it is darkness and an illusion. In truth, heresy is a denial of God, Himself! All that inhibits the increase of human knowledge, human wisdom, human reverence, human achievement, human awareness of God, human glory, is heresy. Heresy is that which cramps the soul and the spirit of man, those which emerged from God's breath. Heresy is that which would force us to walk in the dust and not lift our eyes to the heavens. Heresy is that which would fill up the footsteps of gods with mud, and declares that all things are dead and nothing is sentient, especially not the human mind. Heresy is that which worships stone and not that which the stone represents – the Being of God, His visage.'

His eloquent voice held everyone as still as the stone of which he had spoken. He turned to Daedalus with a gesture of repudiation, as if he were trying to control his indignation.

'It is you, Daedalus, who, by your own words, are a heretic! You would enclose the soul of Greece in clay and obliterate her features! If that is not heresy against God and man – ' He stopped, evidently overcome, and his loud breath was heard in the silent hall.

Daedalus shrank. He had not understood much of what Pericles had said, but now he was aware that he was in some danger, himself, and he could feel vexed and umbrageous eyes upon him from every quarter. The King Archon gently pulled his own beard and looked at the old man.

'Speak, Daedalus,' he said.

347

Pericles raised a respectful hand. 'Lord, he is an old man and his wits are confused and he does not recognize heresy when he hears it. Let us not be without mercy, without understanding. He has not had the advantages of this age of Athens. His youth was constricted, narrow. He accepted the word of ignorant men as the truth, of stupid teachers, as learning. Must we condemn him for what he did not know, for what he was not taught? If he has offended God, surely He has compassion, understanding the limits of Daedalus' mind.'

Daedalus clenched his withered fists and cried, leaning towards Pericles, 'I spit on you, wily liar and deceiver, who with words can addle the thoughts of just men.'

Pericles was never so dignified and aloof as when he wiped the spittle from his cheek. He looked imploringly at the King Archon, who rubbed his lips to quiet the involuntary smile which had begun to move them. But he said to Daedalus, with severity, 'This is unpardonable. We are reasonable men in this chamber. We are here to listen to arguments, and not to spit like unweaned children. If this occurs again, Daedalus, I will order the police to seize and confine you.'

As all honoured the King Archon they were moved to reluctant vexation against Daedalus, and even Pericles' enemies felt admiration for his dexterity and eloquence. Daedalus shrank; purple pulses beat visibly in his temples. He almost whimpered, 'Lord, King Archon, I forgot myself in my sincere anger against this Anaxagoras and against him who dares occupy the highest position in Athens while profaning her name and her gods.'

A faint murmur of amusement trembled in the hot air of the chamber, and smiles were exchanged among the jury.

The King Archon said, 'Let us continue. Your next charge, Daedalus?'

The frail breast of Daedalus heaved. He looked about to expire, but his glance at Anaxagoras was strangely violent.

'I have heard him say, with these ears, that in Greece wise men spoke but fools decided! He defamed our government – '.

348

Pericles gave such an exaggerated start, and looked so aghast that Daedalus stopped speaking. Then Pericles turned to Anaxagoras with a countenance full of pale reproach. All were then immediately attentive.

'My dear friend,' said Pericles to Anaxagoras, 'I cannot believe this of you, that you did not give the credit for those salient words to their author, Anacharsis, the Scythian philosopher, to his beloved friend, Solon, the sacred father of our incomparable laws! With Anacharsis did Solon agree, and in sadness. How is it possible that you did not attribute the words you spoke to Anacharsis?'

'I did,' said Anaxagoras, and his great blue eyes glinted with mirth. 'But it is probable that Daedalus had never heard of Anacharsis.'

Pericles covered his eyes with his hand and sorrowfully shook his head. When he dropped his hand there were actual tears in his eyes. Now he looked fully at the jury and then at the whole assemblage, which was showing signs of acute embarrassment.

'Alas,' said Pericles, 'this august company has been presented another evidence of piteous ignorance. Again, let us be compassionate.'

Daedalus almost went mad with rage. He even struck the sides of his cheeks with his clenched fists, and some of the jury involuntarily laughed until halted by the imposing frown of the King Archon. 'Let us have no levity here,' he said. 'This is the court of justice,' and he glanced at Pericles, ' "founded by the sacred father of our imcomparable laws ".'

The friends of Pericles stifled their happy chuckles and the jury and the members of the government assumed an air of gravity, though inwardly they seethed against Pericles and Anaxagoras.

The King Archon let his weariness become plainly seen. He said to Daedalus, 'Your next charge.'

'Pederasty,' Daedalus squeaked. 'The foulest crime against nature!'

No one moved. But Pericles turned and with slow glances like shards of ice he fixed one man after another with his eyes, and each man who encountered his glances shrank and huddled himself in his robes. But Pericles held them with those cold and rigorous looks and they could not turn away. Many were almost overcome with terror.

'Pederasty,' said Pericles, with loathing. 'No doubt every man in this chamber is horrified at the very word, and recalls his own virtue to mind. No doubt but that every man here is guiltless of such an act, and shudders even as it is mentioned.'

He, himself, shuddered elaborately. Then he took his notes from his pouch and studied them carefully, letting his brows lift to the rim of his helmet, and letting murmurs of shocked disgust rise from his lips. And each man, watching him, felt his terror increase, and each wondered what names were listed on those notes in Pericles' hand, praying that his own was not among them. The King Archon watched their faces and tight lines appeared about his eyes.

Pericles raised his eyes and said to Daedalus, 'And who was Anaxagoras' eromenos [male adolescent lover]?'

Daedalus' frantic eyes went at once to one of the Archons, who had two adolescent lovers, and what he saw on the face of his friend made him quiver, for the other Archon was a man of remorseless vengeance when offended.

Pericles patiently repeated his question, then added, 'You have accused Anaxagoras of corrupting our youth, and have said that he is the erastes [older male lover of an adolescent male] of at least one boy. It is true that our laws forbid pederasty, which openly flourishes in Sparta. But we are Athenians, and do not practise perversions. I have heard rumours, however – Let us continue with Anaxagoras. You have said that he is the erastes of a youth, or youths. You have not named names, Daedalus, though we have been patient. Is it possible, too, that you know those among us who do practise pederasty? If so, it is your duty to name them immediately.'

He looked at the King Archon with deep seriousness. 'Is it

not his duty to accuse others, also, of the crime of which he accuses Anaxagoras?'

'It is his duty,' affirmed the King Archon.

Fear nearly caused Daedalus' collapse on the spot, for he felt at least a dozen pairs of threatening eyes upon him. He tried to moisten his grey lips, but he could not speak.

'If a man accuses another man of a crime, and speaks his name, and knows of the same crime among others of his acquaintance, then in justice he should name them all,' said Pericles. 'Is that not so, lord?' he asked the King Archon.

'It is also the law,' said the King Archon. He looked at Daedalus. 'If you have the name of any eromenos of Anaxagoras', speak now, and also speak the names of those who are also guilty.'

Daedalus dropped his head on his breast. 'It is possibly only a rumour –'

'A court of law is not the place for rumour,' said the King Archon. 'You have uttered a vile slander against Anaxagoras, which is punishable. Therefore, you are fined five talents, Daedalus.'

When Daedalus was struck dumb the King Archon said, 'I have observed your countenance. You know of men here who are truly guilty, for I have followed your eyes. Speak, then, their names.'

It was then that the relentless Archon rose with a rustle of his robes and bowed to the King Archon. 'Lord,' he said, 'my fellow Archons and I have come to the conclusion that all that Daedalus has said is a slander, the foolish wet mouthings of a senile and pathetic old man.'

The King Archon gazed at him for a long time, then looked at several others, who tried to avoid his eyes.

He said, 'I agree with you, Hyperbolus. We have wasted precious hours of our time in this chamber. But when one of the position of Daedalus makes reckless charges against another we are compelled to listen, for is he not an Archon?' He paused and said with quiet meaning, 'And are we not all honourable men?'

He let his glance rove slowly over the jury. 'To what conclusion have you gentlemen come?'

Several members of the jury rose and said with reluctance, 'We agree that Anaxagoras is not guilty of any of the charges brought against him by Daedalus. We do not approve of Anaxagoras, but he has done no obvious wrong.'

The King Archon next turned to Pericles. 'Is there aught you wish to say, Pericles, son of Xanthippus?'

Pericles sighed, and wiped away non-existent sweat from his forehead. It was as if he were very tired. Then he addressed the whole assemblage, and only the King Archon and Anaxagoras heard the irony in his resonant voice.

'I have always been proud, as Head of State, of the nobility and balanced judgement of the men of Athens. We are all but human, yet sometimes we rise to grandeur, as the acropolis is now rising. What stands there, what is being built there, is a poor if beautiful reflection of the Athenian soul, the glory of that soul. Let no man now or in the future denigrate Athens, her integrity, her holy passion and reverence for beauty, her arts, her scientists, her philosophers. But above all, let all admire, in every corner of this world, the spectacle of our matchless impartiality, our craving for the orderly processes of law which were given to us by Solon. Where else in the world do such processes exist? Who can be compared with us? Despotisms abound, tyrannies which will not let a man speak the truth or lift his head as a man and not a slave, and who exact the last coin of tribute from their helpless people.

'But in Athens a man is free. His opinions may not be honoured or regarded highly, but he may speak them – as you have permitted Anaxagoras to speak. You have refuted slanders with that mighty sense of justice which only Athenians possess. There are some among us, I admit, who possess the tarnish of a despot's evil urges, but only a few. Only a few. But from those few may the gods deliver us!'

Even his enemies felt their hearts swell with emotion at this subtle flattery of themselves, and they experienced a thrill of gratitude for Pericles who had so elevated them in their own estimations. For a brief moment or two they actually loved him and forgot their enmity. As for the men who had known terror, they sweated with relief and were grateful to Pericles for delivering them from open accusations. Some of them said to themselves: 'That fool of a Daedalus nearly destroyed us. We must warn him to hold his tongue hereafter.'

The King Archon ordered the chains to be struck from the wrists and ankles of Anaxagoras, who stood there eyeing Pericles with a most peculiar smile. The King Archon then rose and all bowed to him, even the Head of State, Pericles himself. The King Archon retired from the chamber and a loud buzzing of voices rose as a storm of bees in the hall. No one noticed that Daedalus, staggering, was leaving like a gaunt shadow.

Pericles himself led Anaxagoras from the chamber. 'Come with me to my offices, for a little refreshment,' said Pericles. 'My throat is dry.'

'I do not doubt it,' said Anaxagoras. 'My dear friend, you are worthy of the most prominent role on the stage.'

'Tut,' said Pericles. 'Do I not always speak the truth?'

'No,' said Anaxagoras, smiling. Then his face changed. 'But I am afraid I have not heard the last of this.'

That night the unfortunate Daedalus, consumed by his own rage and defeat, had a seizure and died before dawn. To the last he cursed Pericles.

Dejanira, his daughter, wrote to her son in Cyprus: 'My dearest Callias, what calamity has fallen on this house! My beloved father, and your grandfather, has died in his bed, in our arms, weeping. Alas, it was his own fury against Pericles which killed him.' She then related what Daedalus had incoherently gasped before he succumbed.

On receiving her letter Callias lifted his hand in an oath and said, 'We will be avenged! Of a certainty, we will be avenged!'

CHAPTER X

Socrates said to Pericles, 'This, of course, is not the end.'

'In the meantime,' replied Pericles, 'let us not anticipate trouble before it arrives. Each day we live is a day gained.'

'We, your friends, are alarmed for you, Pericles.'

'So am I,' said Pericles, laughing.

'You are an orator,' said Zeno of Elea.

'Have I not had an excellent teacher – you?'

'Alas, what a world this is,' said Pheidias.

'When was it not? It was and ever will be a dangerous and precarious planet, full of evil and contention, of malice and envy, of death and fury, of murder and pillage, of lies and hatred. Human nature is, was, and always will be detestable and unchangeable. We are a monstrous species.'

He looked at his friends and added, 'With rare exceptions. But you are in this world but not of it. There is a difference. Future ages will proclaim your names, forgetting that you were outlaws among your contemporaries, just as they will persecute their own contemporaries who are superior, leaving them for future generations to extol.'

Zeno of Elea said, somewhat sadly, 'You grow more caustic and embittered with time, my dear Pericles. But then, you are not a philosopher.'

'Thank the gods! I, therefore, will not perish.'

His enemies in the government, however, declined to sanction the name of his illegitimate son, the infant Pericles, and refused that name on its records.

Aspasia was too wise a woman to attempt to soothe Pericles with the metaphorical substitute of a honeyed tit, as one soothes a fractious or frightened infant. She said, 'Our son is Pericles, in our minds and our hearts, and so he will be called among us and in our houses. The malice of governments is always present, and its attempts to punish its adversaries or those who criticize it. It should not be pertinent to our own lives. We should remember who and what it is, and disdain it.'

'Unfortunately, it has the power to defame, exile, depose and even kill,' said Pericles, who was both humiliated and angered at the insult. He knew now why some men like himself desire to be dictators, when inflamed, mortified or impatient with lesser functionaries of government. He knew that his own government, and many of the rabble, were accusing him of plotting to become a monarch or at least a dictator. He told this to Aspasia. She touched his cheek gently with her soft hand. She smiled and dimpled.

'That, too, has its worth, for it is only when the lesser functionaries of government, and the rabble, fawn unanimously on a man that he can attain despotism.'

Aspasia now lived almost always in his house, for he feared for her since the birth of his son. They resumed their dinners for their friends and the long and exciting conversations which ensued during them.

Xanthippus, the enthusiastic soldier, and Paralus, an avid student, loved their infant brother and played with him at all opportunities, remarking how much he resembled their adored father. The child had a merry temperament, like Aspasia, and his father's stateliness also. He was strong and vigorous. 'What an athlete for the Olympian Games he will be,' said Xanthippus. 'And what a soldier.'

The young men were now permitted to join the dinners and discussions in the house of their father. They saw that not only were gifted and beautiful hetairai present but the advanced wives of many of Pericles' friends. The dinners, because of Aspasia who presided, were becoming more and more famous throughout Athens, and hundreds of wives became rebellious against their husbands who kept them in subservience, and hundreds of daughters demanded the education given their brothers.

Pericles, however much he despised his fellow aristocrats

and the market rabble (who appeared to have too many things in common), had no desire to be a tyrant, not even over his mockers and foes. He might, in his secret anger, wish to bang their heads together and to order them to refrain from their iniquities, and command them, but his emotions were never translated into action. He only watched them assiduously. If others found it strange that the aristocratic nobles of Athens, fastidious and discriminatory, and the odoriferous rabble had a deep accord, Pericles did not. The aristocrats (though they figuratively and sometimes literally held their noses) consorted in private with the rabble. They pretended to deplore the 'tyranny' of Pericles, who opposed all laws giving the rabble free bread and meat and cheese and housing and demanded that they work for a living. 'He has no compassion on the unfortunate,' the aristocrats would say to leaders of the rabble. 'He has no mercy on the deprived and the humble. He despises those in want, and would have them starve. What is the treasury and gold of a people compared with a single human life? Should not taxes be used to alleviate distress and illness and starvation among our people? Are we not equal in our humanity? What pains Pericles in his flesh and belly pains the people of Athens also. He has physicians and medicine and fine food and shelter. You, our poor friends, have none of these. He builds grandiloquent temples and wastes your substance. While a gold and ivory statue is being raised in the Parthenon your children cry for bread, and you desire the barest amenities of living and have them not. Who can compare the house of Pericles with your huts? Our hearts bleed for you.'

None of the rabble appeared to notice that their friends, the aristocrats, parted not with a single drachma to relieve their alleged miserable state. When Hippocrates' influence persuaded physicians that infirmias for the destitute should be built, the very 'friends of the humble' opposed them, for such infirmias would cost them money in increased taxes. When Pericles insisted that the noisome hovels of the poor should be destroyed and more agreeable housing be built, his fellow aristocrats raised an outcry over his 'extravagance, and his hypocritical desire to be known, unrighteously, as a humanitarian.'

Pericles, bitterly, understood the motives of the wealthy aristocrats. They were using the rabble against him, to impeach him. If, he would say, these gilded traitors attained their object and became omnipotent, they would at once enslave and subjugate the poor whom they pretended to respect and pity. They, the lovers of the poor, the champions of the afflicted, lusted for power above all things. They, in their souls, hated the populace, and despised them.

Daily the rage of the rabble increased and became more vociferous and audible against Pericles. The aristocrats smiled happily under their noses. The middle class was alarmed at the growing hostility against the man they so deeply admired and trusted. They knew that he stood between them and exploitation by the lazy and worthless, and between them and their natural enemies – the rich patricians. They sent him delegates to extend their love to him, their trust, their faith. Though these were not scholars their deep instincts warned them that their destruction was being plotted by the aristocrats through their minions, the rabble. If they did not know that the aristocrats called them 'upstarts, who are inimical to the glory of Greece and would subdue her to the rule of dull merchants and shopkeepers,' they dimly suspected the truth. But they sensed, in their strong spirits, that if they disappeared and the aristocrats were solely in authority and the rabble were slaves, Greece would become a despotism.

Sometimes Pericles pondered: 'Who had said that a despotism meant wolves on the top and jackals on the bottom?' Aspasia said, 'I think you did, beloved,' to which he responded with gloom, 'It does sound like me.'

In the midst of all his worries the young city-state of Italy, Rome, sent a commission to him, through her Senate, of three earnest Romans, 'in order that you, lord, can instruct them in the creation of a perfect and just Republic, as established by your great law-giver, Solon, and which has made Greece the wonder of the world.' Pericles, on receiving the message announcing the imminent arrival of the Romans, laughed with mirthless and cynical hilarity. But Aspasia said, 'Why disillusion these honest men with the truth? Let them establish their republic, according to Solon, and perhaps they will realize the dream which Athens never attained, a dream which other nations may make into a glorious reality.'

'But these barbarian Romans are also men, and inevitably, despite their labours, they will become corrupt and establish a democracy and hence a despotism.' Yet secretly he felt a deep pity for the Romans and a sadness for their hopes. He prepared to receive them with solemn respect, and ceremony. This made the aristocrats restive and contemptuous. 'He will honour barbarians,' they said, 'barbarians without an aristocratic tradition, and entertain them lavishly at governmental expense, which will come out of the pockets of the working poor.'

He personally met and greeted the Romans at the port, clad in ceremonial attire, with an honour guard headed by his trusted lieutenant, Iphis. When the three Romans left the ship drums were sounded, trumpets flared and colours were dipped. Pericles advanced, bowing, then extended his hand solemnly to each Roman in turn. His perceptive eye swept them, and he felt a warm impulse of approval. They were short but bulky men, not fat though muscular, and about forty years old. They had strong and serious faces with large noses, dark eyes and firm full lips, and their hands were calloused and familiar with work. Their hair was severely cropped, their dress sober, and they wore no jewellery. They looked like farmers, for their faces were browned by sun, and their shoulders were massive. They wore plain leather shoes, crudely but sturdily made. Pericles saw clear intelligence in their eyes, though he detected from their sincere expressions that they lacked the urbane humour of Athenians. Each carried one small chest, and none had attendants. They walked weightily as men walk who have trudged the earth and have sweated, and have guided ploughs and have builded houses. They were men with a purpose, and Pericles trusted them immediately. It was obvious they were peasants.

He took them to his house in his large awninged car, which was drawn by four magnificent white Arabian horses bright with silver harness. They watched everything with grave and alert eyes, and did not pretend that they were not impressed as the car passed grand houses and elaborate government buildings. When they glimpsed the acropolis and the now completed Parthenon – shining like silver gilt in the morning sun – they audibly drew deep breaths of awe and admiration. Their knowledge of Greek was poor, and their voices were hoarse and loud, as are the voices who call to cattle and swine. They had the genuine dignity of simple men who esteem themselves without vanity, and who honour themselves and their country. Pericles loved them more and more. He pointed out spots of historic interest. They had, at first, been somewhat taciturn with him, as a superior man, but his manners, his kindness, his obvious respect for them as the men they were, reassured them and they spoke to him in the spirit of equality as members of government. They were not ignorant. In slow sentences they mentioned the history of Athens; they were conversant with the civilizations of Egypt also, and other eastern nations.

They knew much of Sparta, and questioned Pericles. He smiled. 'This is a most auspicious and pleasant occasion for me,' he said. 'I pray that you will not darken it.' They laughed loudly, an honest and knowing laughter. 'We Romans, too, have trouble with little city-states in Italy,' they said. 'We wish to live and flourish in peace and in trade, but others challenge us.'

'We are a tribal people,' one said with pride.

'So once were we,' replied Pericles. 'Now we are complicated and urban. Every man is his own philosopher in Athens.'

They detected cynicism in his voice and were concerned.

They inquired with true interest of Pericles' family, and he told them of his sons. 'My youngest is named for me, and he is an infant still,' he said. Now he became thoughtful. He could not speak of Aspasia as his mistress, and his son as illegitimate, for they would have been shocked to the very heart. He cursed himself for not earlier thinking of this emergency, for he already knew that though Romans respected and loved their wives they kept them secluded, and mistresses secret. How would he explain Aspasia to them, for it was not possible to keep them in ignorance long; they would meet others in government besides himself. So he said, 'I have a lovely wife of much intelligence, but Athenians do not regard her as my wife for she is a foreigner born in Miletus.'

He was both pleased and surprised when they laughed in comradeship, and spoke of the Sabine women whom their fathers had abducted and brought to Rome and made wives of them. 'To this day,' they said, 'many Romans do not acknowledge that those of Sabine ancestry are their equals. Are not men foolish?'

'Of a certainty,' said Pericles.

He was relieved. But what would these Romans think of Aspasia when she joined them at his dinners? Like Athenian wives, Roman wives could dine with their husbands only when they were alone. How could he explain the hetairai to them, for surely they would hear of the ornamental and learned courtesans. They would also learn that Aspasia had been one of that adorable company. He said, 'My beloved wife has been gifted with intelligence, and so she was educated highly. In consequence, she has come under suspicion as a woman of immoral character.'

One Roman hesitated, then said with candour, 'I have four sons, in whom my heart rejoices, but I have a daughter who is the sweet core of my heart. My sons are valorous and are soldiers, but their minds are not of great consequence. My daughter has the wit of a man, and I have a tutor for her, though my wife disapproves, being an "old" Roman. My daughter,

Calabria, swears she will not marry a man except of her choosing, and though this is reprehensible in a mere chit,' and he bridled with pride, 'I agree with her, for I saw her mother in the market and loved her at once and asked her consent after her parents had given me their heartiest approval. Had my wife refused me I would have withdrawn, in spite of my love for her, for she had a beauteous face. But Venus was kind and her son, Cupid, had pierced my wife's soul with his arrow.'

Pericles knew that the Romans had changed the names of the Greek gods, and he understood that his guest meant Aphrodite and Eros. So he said, as the host, 'Your wife was fortunate, and your daughter must be a veritable Minerva.' The brown countryman's face flushed with gratification, but he said somewhat sheepishly, 'She is a mere chit.'

But what would they think when Aspasia greeted them in the atrium? Would they consider her an outrageous and forward woman whom no man could respect? As they neared the acropolis they exclaimed at the sight of Pheidias' Athene Parthenos, glittering with gilt fire and august majesty in the sun. They were overcome with wonder and reverence. 'Minerva,' said Pericles. 'The patroness of our city.' They nodded solemnly.

The guard of honour on their horses trotted briskly beside the car, and crowds stopped to stare at the company, and many hailed Pericles in joyful voices while some merely remained sullen and silent. This surprised the Romans, for they were accustomed to respect given to the head of the government. Perceiving this Pericles said, 'We Athenians are very lively, and often are abusive to the Head of State, at least in language, and we are not disturbed. We accept it as evidence of freedom.'

When they arrived at his house, which the Romans considered a magnificent palace of possibly too opulent a taste – judging from their expressions – Pericles was happy to see that Aspasia was not in the atrium but only the overseer of the hall and the most handsome of the male slaves, all dressed exquisitely. Ah, I have not given her credit for her reticence and discretion and wisdom, he thought with tenderness. The house had been garlanded with laurel and wreaths of flowers, in honour of the guests, and it resounded with soft music and gently singing voices of unseen female slaves. Once more it was evident that the Romans thought this somewhat effete, and Pericles smiled inwardly. The overseer conducted the Romans to their assigned chambers and Pericles wondered what they would think of silken coverlets and delicate alabaster statues and Egyptian glass lamps and marvellous mosaics and Persian rugs, not to mention exotic scents and painted walls delineating nymphs and satyrs in somewhat liberated postures. One chamber wall depicted Aphrodite and Adonis coupled together in voluptuous enjoyment, both rosily naked, and Pericles went to his own chamber, laughing, and wished that he could overhear any scandalized comments.

When they emerged to join him he could scarcely refrain from mirth, for their faces were openly embarrassed. But they were men with manners, however recently learned, and they thanked him for his hospitality, even if at first their voices were constrained, and even if they avoided each other's eyes for a while. In his heart he did not deride them as ingenuous farmers, for so his own ancestors had been in a time less corrupt than this. He told himself that he must not, even in wine, tell them any lewd jests of the city, but must impress them as a man of gravity and open sincerity, for they expected this of him.

He conducted them to the dining hall, and they stared at its lavishness, which was yet tasteful. But they averted their eyes from the bawdy paintings on the walls and pretended that they did not exist. One furtively fingered, with hardly suppressed disapproval, the rich texture of the tablecloth, and one examined the knives and spoons, of beautifully wrought design, and another gazed at the silver plates. But as they were innately courteous, as were most men of the earth, they did not exchange meaning glances. He could almost hear their thoughts: This is truly inexcusable luxury, which we Romans dislike. However, one must remember that Greeks are not Romans, and Romans are not rich. The gods forbid that ever our children's children will become so decadent! Ah, thought Pericles, but they will, they will, when they reach affluence through your labours! In the meantime, may God bless your austerity, for it is like the clean air of mountains above a murky city.

One said, unaware he was voicing Pericles' thoughts, 'I have been in Egypt and it is very depraved, and very extravagant and – sensual.' When he coloured at what he considered unpardonable and covert criticism, Pericles said quickly, 'That is the history of nations when they become wealthy and debauched. We, in Greece, have not as yet become so, but I fear we will.' He shook his head sadly. 'Of a certainty, we will.'

He added, 'When a nation is agricultural, and cities are small, they are virtuous and ascetic. We have a philosopher in Athens, Socrates, who avers that cities breed infamous men, but the land breeds heroes.'

'We have heard of your Socrates,' said one of the guests, relieved that Pericles had not taken offence. 'We should like to see and to listen to him, for surely he is a great and honoured man in Athens.'

Pericles' mouth twisted a little. He said, 'Socrates is an immured man, by his own will, and it is difficult to approach him.' He could hear the shrill laughter of Socrates in his own mind at these words. 'Yes, he is honoured, though few understand him, among his students. He has said that the unexamined life is not worth living.'

The Romans nodded in assent. 'We examine our lives each morning, during our prayers, and search our consciences, for is that not our duty to God and our fellow men?'

'Indeed,' said Pericles with a most solemn face.

He was pleased when he saw the simplicity of the meal which the astute Aspasia had ordered. Yet the goblets were ornate and jewelled, and the Romans were openly taken aback and touched them dubiously. Cool beer was poured in the goblets and once again Pericles thought of Aspasia with gratitude. The following wine was one of which Dejanira, in her meagreness, would have approved. Pericles wondered where Aspasia had found it, and he drank it very sparingly.

There were no dishes with sauces, cunningly flavoured. The fish had been broiled simply, the tough meat was stewed, the vegetables were heavily burdened with garlic, and there was a dish of beans with robust pork. Pericles thought it all execrable and was again reminded of the frugal Dejanira. Aspasia, unlike himself, had known exactly what Pericles' guests would appreciate, and he marvelled, and saw that the Romans heartily enjoyed what was set before them. The meal was of their taste and their lives. He could hear their thoughts: Our host is not ostentatious or depraved. His table is commendable, if not his house. Moreover, his appetite is not voracious. He eats but little.

The Romans expanded. They gazed at Pericles with fondness. For all his house, he was one of their own, a man of asceticism and prudence. No doubt his wife has been indulged too much, and she had chosen what we have seen. Or possibly she had brought him an enormous dowry and licentious articles from her father's house. Perhaps he loves her too much, this handsome and elevated Head of State, and lets her have her female way. It is probable that she is very young and wilful in addition, and extremely beautiful. Such are hard to resist and oppose.

They smiled wisely at Pericles, as at a brother. They began to ask him questions.

CHAPTER XI

Pericles, on advice from Aspasia, had written a message to the King Archon; he was beginning to believe, however tentatively, that the old Archon was not unfriendly to him. He had written:

'Our friends from Rome are desirous of meeting our government. They reverence the laws of Solon – which, regrettably, we do not obey. The Romans are under the misapprehension that we have a perfect government, based on the laws of Solon. Therefore, their aspirations for their own government are very high, and they dream of an excellent republic. It would be most cruel to disillusion them while they are in Athens. If we deceive them well enough they will return to Rome and found a republic worthy of the honour of honourable men. The eldest is one Diodorus who is a member of the Roman Senate. They are all men of principle and conviction and the sternest probity. Senator Diodorus has expressed a desire to address our government in solemn session. I pray that the Assembly will not be too rowdy and will control any spasm of risibility before these simple but stately men, and will answer their questions in all due sobriety, remembering always that they are our guests.'

The King Archon, and the lesser Archons and the Assembly and Ecclesia, met Pericles and the Romans with all ceremony and composure. Elaborate compliments were exchanged. Once Pericles caught the eye of the King Archon, who rarely smiled. But now there was a grandfatherly twinkle in his eyes which Pericles enjoyed but hoped the Romans had not discerned.

Pericles wished that Aspasia had had the ordering of the feast which was set before the Romans. The latter were astonished and somewhat appalled at the rich dishes, the profusion of different wines, the Syrian whisky, the wreathed goblets of Egyptian glass glittering with jewels. They gazed at everything; they studied the fine tunics and togas of the other men, their gemmed armlets and rings and necklaces. Several wore a single gold ear-ring set with bright stones, in the Egyptian manner. Many were perfumed. The Romans, frankly, did not know what to do with the silver bowls, floating with petals, which were set before them for the dipping of their fingers. They watched and followed suit, and looked dumbly at each other. Singing girls, indecorously dressed, played lutes and lyres and flutes, and smiled openly at any man who glanced at them. Pericles saw the Romans wince. The King Archon said to Pericles, 'This is none of my doing, but our friends wish to impress the Romans, whom they consider country bumpkins.'

'I believe, alas,' Pericles replied, 'that the Romans fear we are decadent.'

'And, in a measure, are we not?' asked the King Archon, to which Pericles had no answer. The King Archon said, 'It might have been well had they visited Sparta instead of Athens.'

Pericles was relieved when the moment had come for Senator Diodorus to address the assemblage. He rose in his subdued garments and looked about him in a sedate fashion. The Athenians had become somewhat vehement with wine, but when they saw the temperate, if weighty, countenance of the Senator they fell into reasonable attention.

He spoke without grandiloquence. 'We Romans', he said, 'have founded a republic according to what we have heard of your holy Solon. Our knowledge was small until we came to your glorious city,' and he glanced kindly at Pericles, who bowed in his chair. 'Now our knowledge is vastly increased, and we are full of admiration and respect.

'Our Constitution is not yet complete. But we are establishing a system of checks and balances. We intend to diffuse power so that no one body of Romans can assume tyranny over others. I will say it more plainly: We intend to protect all

366

Romans against their government by establishing agents in government who will assiduously watch each other, so no one group will become too potent.'

The Athenians exchanged amused if careful glances, as do adults when an immature child speaks, but they saw that the King Archon was looking at them sternly.

'Under that Constitution we are in the process of completing, there will be strong emphasis on the unity and sanctity of family life, of patriotism, of the inculcating of our children with reverence for their parents, the inviolate status of a man's solemn word, self-control at all times, and, above all, the profound relationship between man and God.

'We Romans believe that the man who labours is the foundation of every just society, and by labour we mean every endeavour in which a man uses his mind and his hands, and respects the earth from which we have sprung. At no time will any man be permitted to oppress his neighbour, to exploit him, to defame him, to demean him. We will, at all times, strive for greatness and justice in our public and private lives, not the greatness of riches but the greatness of the familiar virtues. For he who is a good man, however humble, is more to be honoured than a king.

'We know that all men are born free and that it is the sacred duty of government to protect that freedom before the Face of God. That is the foremost duty of government. When that duty is depised or obliterated all else will be lost, for nothing can flourish in the absence of liberty. Our courts will be courts to which any citizen can appeal if any of his rights are threatened. We will teach our people that self-rule and self-sacrifice are the marks of a dignified man who reveres his God, his country and his humanity, and that the man who does not possess these is not a man at all.

'We prize industry and honest commerce. We will strive to live at peace with our neighbours and not war against them unless we are attacked. We will have no foreign alliances which can lead to wars and dissensions and bankruptcy. We will treat other states with deference but avoid entanglements with them. We will not permit any politician or other unscrupulous man to rob one section of our citizens for the benefit of another section, through the seizing of their property which they have earned and giving it to others less prudent and industrious. If a man will not work, then he must starve, and no politician will be allowed to alleviate his state at the expense of others. For we hold that what a man earns by his own labour belongs solely to him, and he shall not be plundered of it. It does not belong to the government; it does not belong to his neighbour. The rights of property will be protected at all times. If it becomes necessary for government to use a man's land, for the building of aqueducts or other public services, then that government must pay that man in full. If he does not assent even then, he will be allowed to take his case to the courts.

'Remembering that ancient nations were destroyed by crushing taxes, we shall tax our people for only what is necessary for our military services, for the guarding of our city through a system of police, for clean water and streets, for the support of the courts, for sanitaria, for sound buildings, for fighters against fire. The stipends for those in public service will always be modest; the honour is almost enough.'

He looked earnestly at his audience; many were carefully studying their jewelled hands.

'Riches,' he said, 'are not to be despised if they are acquired by superior work and intelligence. But the man who becomes rich by thievery and malfeasance in office or crafty dealings will be treated with contempt. He is a disgrace to his nation.

'In conclusion, then, we will build a state on the laws of your Solon, and the Constitution he desired will be ours. Frugality and thrift and open respect for neighbours will be taught our sons, and they will also be taught that law and order must rule lest we all perish in a welter of crime, and venal politicians become our masters.'

He sat down, after bowing to his audience. They looked to the King Archon for a signal. All near him saw tears in his aged eyes. He lifted his hands and clapped them in applause and the audience, however reluctant, and highly amused, joined him.

He turned to the Romans and said, 'May your city flourish, under God, and may your children's children remember you with piety and gratitude and honour, and may they never forget what you will write on your Twelve Tables of Law. Your republic, I prophesy, will become the wonder of the world. So long as your people adhere to those Tables they will never decline nor will dust choke up your temples nor foul men rise to power, nor any just man become the slave of his avaricious neighbour.'

He turned to Pericles, and Pericles rose and bowed to the Romans and said in a voice no one had ever heard before, so moved was it:

'Go with God.'

CHAPTER XII

Pericles had told the Romans, 'You have asked me of Sparta. Spartans devote their lives to war, Athenians to politics.'

'But they are an industrious people,' Senator Diodorus had remarked.

'They are also lightless, grim, unrelenting, suspicious and their lives are unimaginative. Their government is all-powerful, an oligarchy, and so their people are virtual slaves, always in terror of those who rule them with so much gloom and ponderousness. I admit they are valorous and patriotic; but their existence is one of monotony, endless labour without the reward of laughter or any ease. Their surliness is famous. Their women do the work of men, the children are never permitted to be children. They are afflicted by a conviction that the rest of Greece is conspiring against them, whereas they, themselves, are conspiring to dominate our country. There is a kind of madness in their souls, a darkness of spirit. They believe they are superior to all other Greeks, and their tread is the tread of iron. They have no humour and I confess I am terrified of humourless men. They are dangerous. You have spoken of freedom as the breath of life. The Spartans do not regard freedom as desirable for their citizens, nor, in fact, for any other state. If they have any cherished belief it is that they are ordained to force their manner of living on the whole world.'

Now the Spartans were directing all their determination against Pericles, who had far more power than when he had first come to the attention of Sparta, and had made Athens the supreme maritime queen of the seas. They jeered at his desire to make Athens also the empire of the mind through the help of his artists, his sculptors, his architects, his philosophers. 'Has it not been said,' they asked, 'that he whom the gods would destroy they first make mad? Pericles is a madman, an overweening dictator and tyrant.' So now they were fixed with the resolution of stubborn and narrow men that they must seize the maritime power of Athens. Labour, once held the province only of helots, became the duty of all men – except, of course, the oligarchy and the few aristocrats.

This, then, was the present anxiety of Pericles, who was weary of the constant small but costly and enervating wars and distractions. He knew that among his own Athenians there were rich and potent men who were sending emissaries or spies to Sparta, out of hatred for him. He knew that they were also secretly inciting the rabble against him, so that through his destruction they could assume authority. The word 'impeachment' was constantly on their lips in private. Only the accursed middle class of shopkeepers and little merchants and industrious men stood in their way, and these loved Pericles. Pericles called his foes traitors, openly, and they laughed at him.

Aspasia said to him in concern, 'Is there no way to reach an accord with Sparta and assure her that there is enough trade and commerce in the world for all cities?'

'No. Sparta has never relinquished her ambition and purpose to be all-powerful. Dreams take various shapes and war is but one of them. It is now trade – the rule of the world through commerce. It is the same goal: conquest.'

On a few occasions he sent his own trusted emissaries to Sparta, to conciliate her and to assure her that Athens had no imperial designs upon her, and that surely reasonable men could reach an amicable understanding in the name of peace. Sparta received those emissaries with what they could only report as brutal courtesy and a lightly controlled rudeness. Her demands for an agreement were absurd, and so Pericles was forced to refuse. 'These foolish little wars will continue,' he said, with mingled wrath and despair. 'Sparta is determined to subjugate Athens as she has subjugated her allies. Our treasury is ominously depleted and we may soon have to debase our currency. The debasement of currency invariably means the decline of a nation, and so Sparta is compelling us to do that.'

Aspasia said, 'A final confrontation with Sparta, then, is inevitable?'

'I fear so,' he replied. 'In the meantime we will try to avoid that confrontation as long as possible. I only pray that it will not come in my lifetime.' But he suspected that it would and often he would pace his chamber at night futilely searching for a way either to conciliate the irreconcilable or to threaten Sparta in one open and exasperated challenge.

His enemies were now accusing him of 'goading' Sparta to attack, or of inciting her through unjust suspicions of her motives, motives which Sparta candidly and consistently proclaimed. 'He is, first of all, a soldier,' his enemies told the rabble, 'and soldiers are not famous for hating war; they love war even for its own sake. His imperial ambitions grow hourly and Sparta knows that and fears us. If we war strongly against her she will retaliate as strongly and peace in our world will be a lost vision.' They appealed to the pusillanimity of the market rabble, its fearful self-love. The rabble scribbled lies and threats and libels on the walls of Athens. When they saw Pericles in

371

the Agora they either were sullenly silent or shouted at him before fleeing.

Pericles' enemies struck at him again and again through Aspasia. They said that she was the real power behind Pericles, that she was insisting that Sparta be attacked or made subservient, that her school was only a disguise for the procurement of free women for unspeakable purposes, that she induced young girls to engage in perversions with the ageing Pericles, and that, worst of all, she was impious. The comic poet, Hermippus, publicly accused her of these things. 'If I were a tyrant, as my enemies and Sparta say I am,' Pericles told Aspasia, 'I would have him quietly murdered or thrown into prison.'

'I do not fear lies,' Aspasia answered him.

He raised his eyebrows humorously at her. 'Then, my sweet, you are still an innocent, and I am amazed. Lies are far more potent than the truth, and far more dangerous. They have caused the death of more good men than any deadly truth has done. For human nature is inherently evil and it prefers lies, and delights in the suffering of the just which it has inflicted.'

'Then,' said Aspasia, 'we must remain serene and indifferent to evil, as Anaxagoras does, in spite of the pain imposed on him by the mobs.' She added, disturbed by Pericles' suddenly darkened face, 'Future ages will give him honour, as they will give you honour, beloved.'

'Unfortunately,' said Pericles, 'neither Anaxagoras nor I will be aware of that.'

Anaxagoras was growing old and tired. Enemies repeatedly stoned his little house and the disruptions of his academe were finally exhausting him. His voice no longer had the power to rise above derisive shouts and taunts, and the serenity and indifference which his friends so admired in him were giving place to deep inner sadness and a desire for even a precarious peace of mind and spirit.

One day he went to see Pericles in the latter's offices. The natural high dignity which had always distinguished him had not disappeared, nor his calm glance and composure. But his hair and his beard were white and his fine hands were tremulous. Pericles had not seen him for three weeks, and Anaxagoras' aspect today alarmed him, for it seemed to him that the philosopher-scientist had aged greatly even in that short time.

He poured wine for Anaxagoras, who gently refused other refreshments. He was long in speaking; he swirled the wine about in his goblet and absently studied it. Pericles was more alarmed.

'Do you bring me bad news, my friend?'

Anaxagoras hesitated, and seeing this Pericles said, 'Do not refrain from telling me. There is not a morning that comes to me with hope, but only with aversion, these days. I must armour myself afresh each day by deliberate will.'

'But you are much younger than I, Pericles.'

'You must remember I am a politician.' Pericles tried to laugh. 'Well, you must tell me. I assure you that my enemies have not as yet castrated me, try though they do.'

Anaxagoras still hesitated. Then he sighed. 'I must leave Athens.'

Pericles looked at him with astonishment. 'You would flee from your own enemies?'

Again Anaxagoras sighed. 'There comes a time in a man's life when he is weary of fighting, of struggle – when, in truth, he finds it too hard to endure and becomes tired of living. That time has come to me.'

'You are tired of living?'

Anaxagoras raised his eyes and looked at Pericles fully. 'Yes. If I am not to come to the desperate conclusion that no life is worth living then I must leave Athens, however dearly I love her.' Seeing Pericles' misery he added, 'It is my age, dear friend. I would have a little peace in my last years.'

'You were never a coward,' said Pericles, hoping to perturb that calmness and restore spirit to Anaxagoras. But Anaxagoras merely smiled.

'Is a longing for tranquillity in an old man cowardice? Even an old soldier eventually retires from the battlefield and the sound of drums does not quicken his blood.'

'I cannot endure that I will never see you again,' said Pericles. 'Now will all your friends be devastated.'

'You must explain to them,' said Anaxagoras. 'I have my limits of endurance, too. I have spoken of this only to you, for if I see the others and listen to their pleas I may weaken in my resolve and remain. At the end that would be a little death for me. It would be the end of all my hope.'

'Where will you go?' asked Pericles, and now he was most anxious.

Anaxagoras shook his head slightly. 'That I will not tell you for you may seek me out, and seeing you will cause me suffering and a longing to return.'

Pericles rubbed his suddenly tired eyes and his mouth and chin. 'You have little money, that I know. Will you at least permit me to give you a purse of talents as a gift? I should like to have that small pleasure.'

'I need very little,' said Anaxagoras, looking at him with compassion. 'But, yes, if it will truly please you.'

Pericles went to an iron locked chest in his cabinet and took out a heavy purse. He laid it before his friend. They both stared at it. A deep silence fell between them. It had been many years, too long to count, since Pericles had felt a desire to weep, but he felt it now, and with that impulse his growing bitterness was increased and his growing despair. He was always striving against hatred in himself even for his enemies. Now it was rising beyond his control.

Anaxagoras was pushing himself heavily to his feet and Pericles stood up also. Anaxagoras put his hands on Pericles' shoulders. 'Give me peace,' he pleaded. 'For I say to you, may the peace of God be with you, dear friend.'

'Go in peace, then,' said Pericles, but his expression was harsh.

'Do not grieve for me, Pericles. My hour for silence has

arrived, as it will, unfortunately, arrive for you. We cannot escape our mortality.'

When Anaxagoras had departed Pericles felt a great wound in his soul, a tremendous emptiness and loss. His reason told him that the loss of beloved friends, and the emptiness which follows, cannot be avoided, but his heart rebelled. Why could not Anaxagoras have lived out his few remaining years in tranquillity among his pupils and those who loved him? He had been driven away by evil, for all his explanation that he was only weary and old.

Aspasia wept when Pericles told her of Anaxagoras' departure.

'Who will replace him?' she asked.

'No one. A good man can never be replaced.'

'We have that to console us, Pericles. Bad men die and no one sorrows for them.'

Now Pericles spoke to her impatiently, he who was rarely impatient with her. 'But their evil endures after them. Have you forgotten history? The good descend into their graves, lamented only by their friends, or, if history does record them, it is only briefly. But the memory of evil men is too often glorified. How many statues are erected to good men? But forests of statues are erected to ruthless conquerors.'

'That is a sad commentary on human nature.'

Pericles shrugged. 'But a true one.' He paused. 'That one such as Anaxagoras was finally forced to flee is enough of a commentary.'

The friends of Anaxagoras were broken-hearted. Only Socrates kept his composure. 'At least they did not murder him,' he said. He smiled. 'He has escaped that honour.' He laughed, his high whinnying laughter. 'But I feel that I shall receive that honour one day, for which I am already grateful.'

They all tried to console themselves that Anaxagoras had probably found the peace he so deeply desired. But his absence tortured them. A vital element had departed from their lives, and it would never return. They were poorer. A golden coin

375

had been forever lost from their purses; the light of their existence had darkened in a profound measure. The sun would never shine for them as once it had shined, and their hope had lessened.

They never saw Anaxagoras again nor did they receive any message which might have consoled them, nor did they know where he was nor when he died. But one day Socrates said to Pericles, 'Our dearest old friend, Anaxagoras, left this world yesterday or the day before.'

'How do you know?'

Socrates' satyr eyes were sorrowful. 'How do I know? I do not know. Did I dream it and have I forgotten the dream? Or did his spirit pause beside me one night to bid me farewell? I do not know. I only know that I know.'

Pericles did not doubt him. Acrid tears came to his eyes and Socrates looked at him in commiseration. 'But does not death come to all of us? I say to you now, as I have said it before, a good man need not fear death, for if it be eternal sleep is not sleep pleasant? If he lives beyond his grave, then God will surely receive him with love, and embrace him.'

When Pericles' despairing face did not lighten, Socrates said, 'Let us compare death with a ship full of passengers. The ship leaves its harbour and we weep and say, "She departs, and never shall we see our friends again." But perhaps in another harbour a glad shout is raised, and the waiting ones say, "Here she arrives, and our friends with her!"'

It was then that Pericles could not restrain himself and he broke down and wept, weeping as he had not wept since his father had died.

Socrates thought, When a great man is moved to tears the world should so be moved also. Alas, it never is. We save our tears for mountebanks and liars and oppressors, when they die, and we hail them as saviours and heroes.

CHAPTER XIII

Thucydides, son of Melesias, was called the Old Oligarch because of his insistent and querulous dogmatism and pursuit of those he hated. Had not Pericles had him once or twice prosecuted for usurious practices he still would have hated the Head of State. Pericles was all he despised. The character of Pericles infuriated him. Among his friends he mocked Pericles' stateliness, his composure, his aversion for the mean and petty, his intense patriotism, his patronage of artists and philosophers, his Aspasia, and the illegitimacy of his son. Avaricious though Thucydides was, he spent his money almost lavishly to inspire outbreaks among the rabble against Pericles, cunningly aware that there was almost nothing the populace loved more than the ridicule of the prominent and the powerful, and especially the noble. Well knowing that mobs were naturally hysterical and believed any vicious rumours, he accused Pericles of not only prolonging the hostility between Sparta and Athens but of using that hostility to 'hide his derelictions and the depletion of our treasury'. The ignorant masses, Thucydides knew, were womanishly excitable and always solicitous for themselves, and that no matter what ill came to Athens they were eager to believe the fault was in their leader. Thucydides bribed comic poets and orators to blame Athenian troubles on Pericles' alleged indifference to the gods, 'which remains unpunished'. Was he not known to neglect them? Had he not been heard to say that 'there is only God', when it was obvious there were many gods and goddesses? His patronage of Pheidias and his approval of the enormous gold and ivory statue of Athene Parthenos on the acropolis was not the result of piety, for though it was complete it had not yet been dedicated. Moreover, it was shamefully expensive.

'Look at all those other statues and extravagant temples and gardens and terraces on the acropolis!' Thucydides would complain. 'No, it is not piety. It is self-aggrandizement on the part of Pericles. He also wished to enrich his sculptor friends, particularly Pheidias. Pericles' association with such pestilential ragamuffins like Socrates is a disgrace to Athens. Where is our former sobriety in financial matters, and our prudence and responsibility? Pericles has corrupted them all with his vanity and his desire to be known as the leader of culture and philosophy in Athens. Let us return to his sacrilege: He permitted Pheidias to represent him, and Pheidias, on the shield of Athene Parthenos, bold enough for any eye to discern! If Athene does not destroy Athens with an earthquake such as afflicted Sparta years ago it is only because she is merciful, or she is waiting for Athenians to avenge the insult to her.'

The envious rabble, who were already persuaded that Pericles should have spent the gold in the treasury 'on your abject needs and laudable aspirations for a better life,' were daily becoming more mutinous. Pericles lived in luxury. Why should they not, too, be more adequately sheltered and given other sustenance? To them Pericles embodied all the wealthy and the aristocratic. He, and he alone, was accused of delighting in 'the suffering of the poor', and in instigating it. He was selfish; he was too ambitious; he detested the lowly; he was a dictator; he was endlessly greedy; doubtless he had misappropriated funds from the treasury – to which they had never contributed through taxes – for his own enrichment. The jewels of Aspasia were famous. From what lowly pockets had the money come for these? He had plundered Athens for the adornment of a harlot, whose habits were shameful, and who was known for her own impiety. He was attempting to divert the attention of the outraged citizenry from his crimes against it by goading Sparta to outright war. 'It is well known', said Thucydides, 'that this has often been, in the history of nations, a tactic used by tyrants.' As an investor in various enterprises engaged in the manufacture of war material, and from which he, Thucydides, had enriched himself, Thucydides was careful never to attack those enterprises or his wealthy friends who were also invested in them.

As the masses do not think, they were easily persuaded that Pericles had a personal treasury of his own, gained by war and investments in war. They lusted for this imaginary treasure. That there were many men in Athens far richer than Pericles they did not consider, for did not several of them agree sadly with Thucydides and also accuse Pericles of the same crimes and were they not always loudly proclaiming their love 'for the meek and exploited?' Where was the hero who would rescue them from this cruel and merciless man?

On the death of his uncle, Daedalus, Pericles had permitted his sons, Xanthippus and Paralus, to attend the funeral of their grandfather. Moreover, he had encouraged them. He had sent the kindest of regards and condolences to Dejanira, which had caused her to weep more copiously than she had over her father's death. She had then written to Pericles imploring him to have her son, Callias, recalled from exile, unaware that on several occasions he had been so invited through the agents of Pericles on the latter's orders. Callias, for many years, had revelled in his exile, for he had escaped his reputation in Athens and there were no disapproving faces to annoy him. But he pretended, to his mother, in tearful letters, that he was languishing in exile. In some manner he had come across the information that Pericles, out of pity for Dejanira, had kept her ignorant of her son's refusal to return to Athens. This had made him gleeful.

But now he had learned of the more virulent attacks on the hated Pericles, his mistress and his friends, and Callias' vengefulness increased. He allowed himself to be persuaded to return to Athens. His mother, very fat and grey, and cumbersome in all her movements, greeted him with incoherent joy and embraces. 'I have been so lonely, so sorrowful!' she cried, covering his rough face with kisses. 'Yes,' he replied, 'that I know. I will not tell you of my own sufferings, dearest of mothers, and how I longed to return to this house, and my midnight tears. But behold: I am here, and I will never leave you – unless I am again forced into exile.'

Within a few days of his return to Athens he went to the house of Thucydides, which was almost as frugal as the house of Daedalus, and he offered his own money, and his talents, in the plot to ruin Pericles or at least drive him into exile 'with his harlot'. He was elated that the hatred of Thucydides and the latter's friends almost surpassed his own. The rich aristocrats in the plot thought him personally loathsome and obnoxious and disreputable, but they pretended to be overjoyed and grateful to him for joining them. He preened over their protestations of admiration for him, and their enthusiastic friendship, and became more conceited than ever, for when he had been young these patricians had avoided him, had publicly shown their contempt for him, and had openly held their noses when they had encountered him. Never had he been admitted to their houses or sat at any table with them. Even his riches had not been enough for any of them to offer him their daughters in marriage.

'He caused the death of my beloved grandfather,' he said to them, with meretricious tears in his eyes, and they nodded solemnly while they laughed inwardly. 'He exiled me, kept me from the affection of my dearest of mothers,' he would continue, and again they would nod with commiseration and sympathy. 'I will be avenged for the crimes against my house, and the crimes against my city,' he said, and they were intensely interested. What suggestions had he to offer? One must remember that Pericles had saved Anaxagoras.

'Who is now dead,' said Callias, 'after he was forced to flee Athens.'

'Pericles is more powerful than ever among his detestable middle class,' said his new friends.

Callias had a suggestion which at first revolted his friends with its crudity. Then when Callias was absent one observed,

'Its very bold uncouthness might make it possible of success. The old King Archon is dead, and the new King Archon hates Pericles as much as we do. Pericles is absent at this time at one of his villas with his concubine, for is it not high summer? Let us give the matter thought and move with circumspection so that he will not suspect us. Callias is stupid as well as cunning. If anything goes wrong we will arrange for him to bear the whole guilt.'

They chose the most influential of their members to bring charges of peculation against Pheidias, who was now the closest friend of Pericles since the flight and death of his beloved Anaxagoras. Added to this was his blasphemy in depicting himself and Pericles on the shield of the sacred Athene Parthenos. They well knew that Pericles had insisted that the image of Pheidias be carved on the shield, and they knew that the shy sculptor had refused – unless Pericles, 'for are you not greater than I?' – also permitted his profile on the shield. So Pericles, with a jest, had allowed it for all his reluctance.

The matter of the alleged peculations of Pheidias was somewhat more difficult. Then two of the aristocrats went to the head keeper of the public records of the treasury and under duress and a large bribe – from Callias – he agreed to forge several of the records so that they would reveal that Pheidias had not only received enormous stipends for his work on the acropolis, and the work of his students – stipends that were unbelievable – but had frequently, and arrogantly, demanded even more, saying that the Head of State, himself, had approved of this, and had presented proof in various letters.

'Can we not also prove that Pericles has enriched himself through similar peculations?' asked Callias.

Though the aristocrats and Thucydides had more than hinted of this to the rabble they knew that an open accusation of criminality against Pericles would only rebound on themselves and lay themselves open to punishment. They were well acquainted with the cold and relentless wrath of Pericles.

They knew he was ruthless in pursuit of those who had unpardonably offended him. So they persuaded Callias that this would be impolitic, at least at this time. Attacks on Pericles' friends were one thing; attacks on him personally were quite a dangerous other. 'As yet,' they told Callias, who was disappointed.

They consulted among themselves. The stipends paid to Pheidias and his students had been very small, on his own gentle insistence. How, apart from the forged records, could it be proved that he had literally stolen the people's gold? Where had he hidden it? That was a great problem, for all knew how humbly the sculptor lived.

Callias had another suggestion, which made them catch their breath. They pondered on it, and finally agreed that it had more than a small merit.

So, while the weary Pericles rested in the happy company of his Aspasia and their son, and Paralus, on one of his more remote farms, Pheidias was arrested for peculation and thrown into prison, after the forged records had been presented to the King Archon, who was a cousin to Daedalus, and so a relative of Pericles, himself, the nephew of Daedalus.

Pheidias had been openly arrested in the very midst of his students and assistants, while he had been planning the marble pediments for the statues he was designing. He had gazed silently and incredulously at the police, and then, still stunned, he gave the architectural plans to one of his students and had gone away with the police without uttering a single word, his bald and rosy head suddenly sallow, his face slack with shock, his broad old shoulders sagging. His sandalled feet had been dusted, as with flour, with the dust of marble, and his rough clothing also, and crowds stood aside, wondering, and staring at each other questioningly. Theft? Peculations? Never had anyone possessed less of the aspect of a thief.

One of the students, who was a young man with considerable money of his own, selected a horse from his fine stable and rode away at once to Pericles' farm, though it was sunset and the hot night was approaching without a moon. It was almost the first dawn when he reached the farm, but he awoke the slaves and insisted on seeing Pericles at once, and even the soldiers who guarded the villa were impressed by his despair and his urgent pleas.

Pericles, awakened and pale, his face lined with chronic worry, threw on a tunic, rose from Aspasia's bed where she was sleeping peacefully, and went into the small atrium of the house. The student, overcome, fell on his knees before Pericles, whom he adored, and burst into tears and could hardly speak. It was some moments before Pericles could understand, and when he did, he was disbelieving.

'I was standing beside my master, Pheidias, when they arrested him,' cried the young man, seizing the hem of Pericles' tunic. 'Before God, I tell you the truth!'

Pericles turned aside, his pallid face twitching. Who could be guilty of this enormity? He rubbed his eyes, still incapable of accepting this dire news. Anaxagoras' case had been bad enough. This was much worse, for Pheidias had not thrown any doubt privately or publicly on any dogma. In truth, he was the most pious and devoted of men, the least controversial, the least apt to provoke hostility. He was most shy and retiring, and never been known to utter an impatient word. All his ways were gentle, and compassionate. He could not pass even the most scurvy of beggars without giving him a coin from his little purse. The beggars had known it and he had only to appear to have them crowd about him, whining, thrusting out their hands. That such a man, such a stupendous genius, could be accused of blasphemy and theft was not to be believed. It was accepted widely that he was the glory of Athens, above all others, and multitudes openly reverenced him and foreign and distinguished visitors insisted on meeting him and speaking with him. All had been impressed by his modesty, his tenderness of character, his shining and gleaming eyes in which there was no malevolence but only charity.

I am a calamity to those I love, thought Pericles. He said to

Iphis, who almost always accompanied him these days, 'If blasphemy has indeed been committed, it has been committed by those who have accused Pheidias. I will go to him at once, and arrange to defend him.' He added, with a grimness even Iphis had never seen before, 'This time the vile accusers will be dealt with, and I swear this, before God, and I will never rest until they are brought to justice.'

He rode away with Iphis and two of his soldiers and the student, just as the dawn was throwing pale purple shadows on the quiet countryside. He had a premonition of disaster beyond anything he had ever felt before, and so he uttered not a word, not even when the company entered Athens. He went to his house and bathed, for he was silvery with dust, and he was sweating, and dressed himself in his official robes, forced himself to eat a small breakfast and then went at once to his offices.

There he summoned his cousin, the King Archon, Polybius, to him. His head was throbbing under the heated helmet; it seemed to him that his heart would burst from his chest. He had no doubt that he could save Pheidias and have him exonerated; all but the rabble and a few aristocrats loved him for the virtue not only of his genius but for his kindness and lack of ostentation.

The crime, to Pericles, was in the accusations and the calumnies and not in the actual imprisonment of his friend. Pheidias was in no danger. Tomorrow his accusers would be the laughter of Athens. They would also suffer the vengeance of the Head of State for the insult to Pheidias.

The old King Archon had been over ninety-five years old when he had died. The present King Archon, Polybius, was less than sixty, a small slight man with a parched pale face, small dull eyes, a large nose and a tight wide mouth and thin grey hair. His hands were dry and cold, his manner precise and formal and unbending. He shook hands with Pericles who courteously invited him to sit down and asked him if he desired wine and refreshments. 'No,' said the King Archon shortly.

'You summoned me, Pericles, son of Xanthippus. What is your wish?'

Pericles said, 'I have been informed that my friend, the artist, Pheidias, has been arrested on charges so absurd that the very dogs on the streets laugh in wonderment.'

Polybius drew a rasping breath and he fixed Pericles with a granite stare. 'The charges, lord, are not absurd. They are based on evidence.'

Pericles leaned back in his chair with a negligent smile while he raged inwardly. 'What evidence, Polybius?'

The older man shook his head. 'You, of a certainty, know the law, Pericles. Evidence is not shown or revealed until the criminal appears before the judge and jury. So, I cannot tell you. I can tell you this, however, I am convinced of the truth of the charges. I have seen the evidence myself.'

Polybius might be unlovable as a person, at least to Pericles, but he was known for his integrity, and if his judgement was severe it was at least just. Pericles' incredulity was not pretended.

'You truly believe that Pheidias is guilty of peculation and blasphemy?'

'I do, lord.'

Pericles said, 'I know exactly how ridiculously modest were the fees Pheidias received. He set them, himself, though I urged him to accept more. Many of his students and associates accepted nothing at all. It was enough for them to be helping the master.' He tried to control his wrath.

'I have seen the evidence, myself,' Polybius insisted.

'Then it was forged evidence, and the scoundrels who did it will be discovered and punished. I can promise you that.'

Even the King Archon was intimidated by the daunting blind look directed at him, and he moved uneasily in his chair. 'Are you threatening me, Pericles?'

'No, not you. I know your character too well. But, you have been appallingly deceived by fraudulent evidence, presented by men of no scruples. This, I shall prove, and let them beware for nothing will halt me in bringing them to justice.'

'If you can prove it I shall give the matter my closest attention.'

'I have no doubt of that, Polybius. The only amazing thing to me is that you could believe, on forged evidence, that Pheidias is guilty of anything but possessing the sweetest of natures. You are an intelligent and educated man; you are not a fool who can be persuaded by inconceivable lies. Hence my amazement.'

Polybius carefully examined his grey hands, and did not speak for a moment or two. Then he said, with obvious reluctance, 'If I had not seen the evidence for myself, and listened to the oath of the man who best knew that the evidence was true, I should not have believed it myself. I confess I was aghast until finally convinced. I have no love for your Pheidias, I confess, but the evidence is against him and I was forced to order his imprisonment. There is also the matter of his blasphemy.'

'Of what does that consist?'

Polybius regarded Pericles with open animosity. 'He put his face, and yours, on the shield of Athene Parthenos.'

Pericles smiled. 'At my insistence.' He paused. 'Are you accusing me of blasphemy also, Polybius?'

'I am not sitting in judgement on you, lord.'

'Ah, you are evasive. Judges are famous for that so I will not reproach you. But does not such an artist as Pheidias deserve to have his face or name in an inconspicuous place on the shield? It is there for future ages to reverence.'

'Your face is also there.'

Now, in spite of his emotions, Pericles laughed. 'Pheidias insisted. If you think it best I will have it obliterated, for future ages will not remember me but they will remember Pheidias and give him honour.'

When Polybius did not speak, Pericles continued: 'You must admit that the statue is the most exalted and prodigious creation.'

'It was very expensive.' The older man's tone was obstinate.

Pericles remembered that Polybius was as penurious, if not more, than had been his cousin, Daedalus. He said, in a soft voice, 'My dear Polybius, is not our patron goddess worthy of any cost?'

The desiccated face of Polybius flushed. 'She would not wish Athens to bankrupt herself.'

'The cost of the statue was like a mean copper in comparison with what we have spent, and are spending, on these dreary little wars and skirmishes with Sparta and her allies.'

The King Archon had heard much of the rumour that Pericles had created diversions with those wars, in order to direct attention of the market rabble and others from his own derelictions. This, the King Archon did not believe, though he would have liked to do so. Moreover, there was the honour of their mutual house to consider. 'Still,' he said, 'in these dolorous and costly times it was folly to spend so much on the statue – even if it is in honour of our patron goddess. The gods do not like extravagance in men.'

'If Athene is aware of the statue raised to her, which,' said Pericles very soberly, 'no doubt she is, she will be so gratified that we have sacrificed so much for her that she will bring us peace, or at least chastise Sparta.'

'That is a sophistry to excuse extravagance, of which you, yourself, Pericles, are guilty.' Now the small dull eyes glittered under their lids.

'Oh, I am a very reckless man!' said Pericles. 'I desire only the best and the most beautiful for our goddess! So, indeed, I plead guilty to too much piety.'

'If so, I have not heard of that piety,' said the King Archon, with a tight little smile, and Pericles smiled also.

The King Archon said, 'There is no love between us, Pericles, but I can assure you that Pheidias will be given a just trial before me.'

'You need not have said that, Polybius. I know it without any declaration from you. I do not fear the jury. My anger is not based on anxiety or apprehension for Pheidias. It is based on the cruel absurdity of the charges against him, the monstrous calumnies.'

The King Archon was silent. Pericles refilled his own goblet.

'You will not tell me who brought the charges?'

'No. That will be revealed at the trial.'

Pericles studied him thoughtfully. 'You know who the men are?'

The King Archon did not reply. Pericles' eyes narrowed. 'Can you tell me, at least, if they are honourable men?'

'Of that I can assure you.'

For the first time Pericles felt a thrill of alarm. The men, then, were his powerful enemies and they would stop at nothing to injure him through his friends. He ran their names through his mind. Then, all at once, for no reason he could discern, his thoughts stopped at the name of Callias, the despicable, the swinelike, the brutish. He told himself that Callias, though malign, did not possess the intelligence to deceive such as Polybius, whom Polybius disdained, himself. Whatever else Polybius was, and Pericles disliked him intensely, he could never have been suborned, though he would not flinch at causing Pericles pain under unimpeachable circumstances. Therefore, he had been, without his knowledge, completely deceived, not only by the men who had brought charges against Pheidias but by their lofty station, which, in the mind of Polybius, would render them incapable of lies and perjury.

Pericles did not know what made him say, 'Is Dejanira's son, Callias, part of the plot against Pheidias?'

'I have not seen Callias since his return from exile.'

'You have not answered my question, Polybius,' said Pericles with much sternness.

'Do you think honourable men would associate with Callias?' asked the King Archon, and his voice was indignant. 'Do you believe that I, though his kinsman, would believe a word that rascal said?' His indignation increased and he pushed himself to his feet and his face was as angry as Pericles' own. It was as if he had been mortally insulted.

Pericles said, 'No, you would never believe him. But still, there is something nebulous that flutters in my mind about him, in this matter.'

'No man of integrity or family would receive Callias.'

'With that, I agree. But a man will pick up even the dirtiest stone to hurl, if it serves his purpose.'

The King Archon bowed stiffly. 'If you will permit me, lord, I shall leave, for there are three cases waiting to be tried before me this morning, and I am late.'

Pericles dismissed him. Then he called for his guard and rode with them to the prison, where he found Pheidias in a reasonably clean cell. The sculptor received him with affection but said, 'You have endangered yourself in coming here, my best of friends.'

'Nonsense. I am going to defend you, and make your enemies, and mine, the hilarity of all of Greece.'

Pheidias was not afraid. He only wrinkled his brow and mused, 'There are moments when I laugh, myself, but better men than I have been murdered by lies, Pericles. How have I offended the people of Athens?' His look was ingenuous and bewildered, and Pericles was much moved and again powerfully angered.

'You have done nothing but devote your life to Athens. So do not fear, Pheidias.'

'I do not fear.' Pheidias sat down on his bench and bent his head. 'I do not understand. There is some error.'

'Which I will rectify.'

Pheidias looked up and smiled. 'Of that I have no doubt. But I am wounded in my heart that anyone should suspect me of evil.'

Pericles touched him on the shoulder. 'To ease that wound I have brought you two bottles of my very best wine and some of my more distinguished cheeses and a cold but delectable roasted fowl. I will order that you be tried tomorrow, at the very latest – when I will defend you – so that you may return to your work on the acropolis, to the applause of all of Athens.'

The face of Pheidias became radiant. 'Ah, yes. We must order the marble for the pediments. I was engaged in consultations for their exact dimensions when I was arrested.'

The prison guards looked inquisitively through the bars of the cell while Pericles laid the excellent provisions on Pheidias' bare table. He had also brought fine cutlery and linen from his own house. Pheidias looked with that candid childlikeness of his at the array. 'It comes to me,' he said in surprise, 'that I have not eaten this day, and now my appetite is aroused.'

Pericles, pressed by other business, left him to enjoy the meal, after embracing him.

That night he spent a long hour in his library, thinking, and preparing his case to defend Pheidias. At intervals he rose and paced the floor, shaking his head. Now he was truly afraid, not for Pheidias, but for his city, for if such things could happen to a man like the sculptor then no man was safe, and there was no real justice, but only chaotic emotions and falsehoods, and the worst of venalities.

CHAPTER XIV

Pericles arrived at his offices very early the next morning. The Agora, never empty at any time, had only a few men hurrying along the street, carrying lanterns which they had not as yet extinguished. The clatter of the hoofs of Pericles' horse and the horses of his soldiers on stone startled them. A few raised a shout of acclamation. He saluted them absently. He entered his offices and began at once to search his dossiers. But the King Archon had intimated that Pheidias would be tried only before him and the jury, so grave were his alleged crimes.

For, if proved guilty, he would be sentenced to death, and not to mere exile.

If only I knew the names of his accusers, thought Pericles. He fumed, sitting at his table. But he would soon know. He studied many of the dossiers, slowly drinking wine and eating brined olives and cheese. He had slept little; his mind had been in a turmoil whipped to the utmost intensity by his anger. He had informed Aspasia the night before that he would bring Pheidias to his house for dinner, and that she should send slaves to invite others of their friends also, to rejoice with Pheidias and to laugh with him over his trial and his exoneration.

The case of Pheidias, because it was so important, would be brought before the King Archon and the jury just before noon, when it would be the hottest. Minor cases would be heard first. In the meantime there were many scrolls and papers on Pericles' table, tedious but necessary, written meticulously by bureaucrats, and Pericles must attend to them. He was already sweating. He took off his helmet and laid it near his hand, for rarely was he seen without it outside his house, and after all these years he was still sensitive about the towering height of his brow and skull. His thick tawny hair was grey at the temples and there was a furrow of grey rising above his forehead, sharp and defined, so that he appeared more leonine than in his youth and young manhood, and more formidable. This was accented by his face, which had become haggard and lined in recent years and grimmer, and had lost all its smoothness.

Less than two hours before noon one of the bureaucrats came in to announce that the King Archon was without and prayed an immediate audience with Pericles. Ah, he thought in exultation, he has come to tell me that Pheidias will not be tried at all, that all charges against him had been withdrawn, and that he was free! Smiling, he rose to greet Polybius, who was ceremoniously ushered in, and took a step towards him. Then he saw the older man's face, and stopped short and a great plunging ran through his heart.

For the face of the King Archon was greyer than ever, and he seemed much agitated, and his lips moved soundlessly. For one of the few times in his life Pericles began to tremble. He seized the Archon by the arm and forced him into a chair, and exclaimed, 'What is it? Why have you come?'

Polybius sagged in the chair. He put his hands over his face and rubbed all his features, while Pericles loomed over him, crying, 'Tell me! You must tell me!'

Polybius panted. He rubbed his eyes with the ends of his fingers. Then he dropped his hands and Pericles saw that his eyelids were scarlet and dry, as if burned. He had suddenly become very old, and weak.

'Wine, in the name of the gods,' he croaked. With hands that shook violently Pericles poured him wine and held it to his lips, racked with a terrible impatience and foreboding. The King Archon drank, coughed, almost strangled, then let the still half-filled goblet drop nervelessly to the table, where it rolled and poured out its contents in an acrid stream. It then fell to the floor with a crash. The wine filled the office with a pungent odour.

'Speak,' commanded Pericles. His dread had become unbearable.

'Pheidias,' said Polybius in so faint a voice that Pericles could hardly hear him and had to bend forward. 'He is dead.'

'Dead,' repeated Pericles, and the word had no meaning for him, for he was stricken with an icy coldness in all that heat, and his chilled sweat rolled down his face and body and legs and arms.

'Poisoned,' said Polybius.

Now Pericles could not stand any longer. He fell into his chair and stared numbly at his kinsman. 'Poisoned,' he repeated. 'When? By whom?'

He was taken by a total incredulity. It was not possible. He was uttering mad words, words given to him by an elderly madman. Pheidias, the glory of Athens, could not be dead.

He could not have been – murdered. No, it was not possible. It was all insanity.

Pericles, losing all his control, reached across the table and seized the brittle wrist of Polybius and shook the wrist and the hand so ferociously that Polybius' entire arm was flailed like the arm of a puppet. The ferocity even caused his body to move limply, so that he slid on the seat of his chair. Only Pericles' iron grasp kept him from falling to the floor. Polybius saw Pericles' face as in a nightmare, and he shrank from its aspect.

Polybius' voice, as frail as the crackling of a fallen leaf underfoot, issued from his lips. 'He was found dead just after dawn, by the special guards. There was some wine before him, and remnants of food.' Polybius paused and regarded Pericles with appalled eyes. 'The guards said that you, Pericles, had given them to him. The food was set before – a dog – and he died of it. It contained hemlock.'

The room darkened and swayed about Pericles. Whirling within it he said over and over to himself, No, I am dreaming, or dying. As from an enormous distance he heard Polybius say, 'I was brought the news but an hour ago, and when I could order myself I came to you.'

Murdered, thought Pericles. There was a frightful ache between his temples, rushing over his forehead in intolerable waves of anguish. He did not know that he had closed his eyes and was shuddering.

'I am a just man,' Polybius said. 'I know that you did not do this thing, for did you not love Pheidias and had you not come to his rescue? You are incapable of such an act. You are also – my kinsman. But who placed the poison in that unfortunate man's food? I have questioned the guards.'

Pericles opened eyes so weighted that he could scarce lift his eyelids. His face was the face of a man near death. His throat was so arid that he had to swallow over and over to moisten it with viscid spittle. He said, 'I ate of that food, myself, in my own house, and my old cook filled a basket with it.

It was not poisoned, either the wine or the cheese or the fowl.'
The anguish in his head was in his throat now and stabbing
down into his heart. The face of Polybius advanced and
retreated before him in a mist.

He felt rather than saw Polybius start. 'Wine? Cheese?
Fowl? But what of the broiled fish and pastries you also sent
him just before dawn, today, for his breakfast?' The older
man's voice was bewildered yet stronger.

'I sent nothing,' Pericles whispered. 'I did not send those. I
brought him, yesterday, but wine and cheese and fowl, for his
supper. With my own hands, I brought them.'

Polybius stared. He thought Pericles had become calmer.
'But one of your slaves brought the fish and pastries, saying to
the guards that you had commanded that he do so! That you
wished the illustrious Pheidias to be refreshed and strong for
his ordeal!'

Pericles began to shake his head, helplessly, and could not
stop. 'I sent no one. My slaves have been in my house for
many years, and I trust them all. None would have reason
to murder Pheidias.'

Then he struck the table with a loud crack of his palm upon
it, and when a scribe rushed in Pericles commanded that his
soldiers be brought into the office. The scribe bowed, after first
gazing at Pericles with astonishment. Then he ran off. The two
men sat in silence, and Pericles' great shuddering did not
cease.

The soldiers entered in haste, and Pericles said to them,
'Did anyone leave my house at any time in the night or the
morning?'

Iphis said to him, 'No, lord, none left the house. I myself,
patrolled long before dawn, and my men reported that no one
had even approached your house, and none had departed. Not
even a mouse could have come or gone without our knowledge.'

The other soldiers nodded emphatically, and saluted. Iphis
looked at Pericles and was alarmed at his colour and expres-

sion. 'You must believe me, lord. Has there been some calamity?'

Polybius spoke, for Pericles seemed beyond speaking now. 'Do you trust the slaves in the house of Pericles, Captain?'

'Yes, of a certainty. I know them all; I have known them many years. There is no newcomer among them, male or female.'

'There is no young man of a pleasing aspect, and of a good height with an engaging voice and an agreeable manner, as if he had had considerable education?'

'No, lord. The youngest man is over thirty years of age, and he is partly crippled. The master wished to set him free, with a lifelong stipend, but the slave pleaded not to be sent from the house and refused his freedom.'

Pericles could now speak, with short gasps. 'Pheidias, Iphis, was found poisoned this morning, by food someone brought him, saying it was at my command and from my house. The stranger declared he was my slave, of my household.'

Iphis uttered a strangled word that was a hardly disguised oath. 'That is impossible!' he cried in a raised voice. His brown eyes bulged upon Pericles. 'I do not believe it.'

'It is true,' said Polybius. 'The guards described him, to me, when I sent for them. They were as aghast as myself. They are not regular guards of the prison, Captain. They are soldiers of your own company. I have no reason to believe they are lying. They were sent to me by your superior officer, at my orders, for I had come to believe' – he paused and glanced at Pericles – 'I had come to believe that Pheidias was innocent of the charges brought against him, and I wished him well protected.'

Pericles roused himself. 'Why did you fear, Polybius, that someone might desire him to die before his trial, so that you ordered those soldiers?'

Polybius hesitated. 'Call it an old man's intuition, an old man's doubt, after I talked with you yesterday, Pericles. I have never done this before, for any prisoner. I told myself it was folly, and I am not a foolish man as a rule. But still, there was uneasiness within me and I have no name for it.'

'But why should Pheidias be murdered, lord?' asked Iphis, and he moved closer, protectingly, to Pericles. 'The charges against him were grave. I have heard it in the city, and from Pericles, himself. He might have been condemned to death, or exiled. Therefore, why was he murdered?'

Again Polybius hesitated. 'I have no proof. But I say this: Someone was afraid he would be exonerated and freed. Or someone hated Pericles enough to strike at him in this manner, so he made certain that Pheidias would die. Or – '

'Or what, lord?'

Polybius averted his face. 'Or, someone wished to spread the rumour that Pericles, himself, wished Pheidias dead.'

'But why?' cried Iphis. 'It is known that they were the closest of friends, closer than brothers!' His strong soldier's face was astounded.

'Yes,' said Polybius. He thought for a moment, passing his hand over his face. 'They killed, as Aesop would say, two birds with one stone. They deprived Pericles of his best friend, and so wounded him almost to the death. They may also have prepared a rumour that Pericles had poisoned Pheidias, so as to make him accursed in the eyes of all Athens.'

Iphis himself shuddered. His thoughts were now only for his general, Pericles, so that he almost forgot Pheidias. 'But it will be easy to prove that no such slave is in Pericles' house, such as came to the prison.'

'They will then say the stranger, the murderer, was a hired assassin. If they can convince Athens of that, then the disaster of what happened to Pheidias will be less than the disaster they will be able to inflict on Pericles.'

'Gods,' Iphis whispered. He poured some wine for Pericles and forced him to swallow it. He put down the goblet and clenched his fists. His eyes glowed with fire. 'I would I had them before me, now!'

'I have another thought,' said Polybius. 'It is possible that now many will believe that had Pheidias been brought to trial he would have implicated Pericles in peculation and heresy.'

'But the people will not believe any of these things!'

Polybius sighed. 'I am an old man and I have never confessed this before: There is nothing the people will not believe of one such as Pericles.'

Pericles now roused himself. He fixed Polybius with a deadly look.

'Tell me now, Polybius, my kinsman. Who were the men who brought charges against Pheidias?'

Polybius threw up his hands. 'As Pheidias is dead, there is no harm in telling you, for the evidence is useless. Thucydides, the money-lender, came to me with Polycrates, the head keeper of the treasury in Athens, saying that Polycrates had come to him, as an old friend, to show him records that Pheidias had received enormous sums for his work on the acropolis, sums of unbelievable amounts, and that on several occasions Pheidias had said this was your command. Pheidias had shown him letters purported to be from you, letters which he took away with him. I made Polycrates swear the most solemn of oaths that this was so, and he repeated his charges and expressed his distress, for was he not a friend of yours and had you not appointed him keeper of the treasury? He implored me not to speak of this to you, for fear of your grief, but his conscience had been tormenting him, he declared. He had come to believe that you gave no such letters to Pheidias. Yet, if the sums became public property he would have to speak, in defence of himself.'

Polybius paused. 'Again, he repeated to me that he did not believe that you, Pericles, knew of this robbery, this peculation, and once more implored me not to tell you. I, alas, had no doubt of his sincerity. His distress, it appeared to me, was genuine.'

He added, almost piteously, 'Is not Polycrates of a great and noble family? Why should I have doubted his word?'

'Or the word, Polybius, of the old usurer, Thucydides?'

Polybius spread out his old hands. 'Yes, I know he has always hated you and complained of your extravagance, among many other things. But he is a friend of Polycrates.'

Pericles stood up suddenly, and then to keep himself from falling grasped the back of his chair. He went to his cabinet and then brought out a scroll. He sat down and began to read it to himself, and his face, white as death, burst into fresh sweat. Then he said, 'Polycrates, son of Arrian. Yes, of a great and noble family. But they have become impoverished, through unwise investments and certain fires which destroyed much of their property, fires lit by the Persians. They have never recovered from that calamity, for they are proud. It was to assist Polycrates that I appointed him to the treasury, so that he would have a considerable income. No doubt but that made him hate me.'

He looked at Polybius. 'He has been bribed, and bribed well. Moreover, his wife is not of Athenian birth, though only I knew that. In some manner, years ago, the record-keepers were induced to inscribe her name, though a humble one, in the archives of our city as an Athenian. She was very beautiful. How I came upon the knowledge is not pertinent. I have kept my silence out of compassion.' He flung the scroll from him. 'Apparently my own silence was not enough. Others learned of the forgery, and used it against Polycrates.'

Polybius, whose hetaira was an Ionian, and whom he loved passionately for all his age, felt one of the first impulses of pity he had ever known. 'Alas,' he said, 'Polycrates was under great duress. His wife – and money. Love – and greed. They are not to be underestimated. It is not that I exonerate him. I can only understand why he did this.'

Pericles said to Iphis, 'Take some of your men and bring Polycrates to me at once. And Thucydides.'

CHAPTER XV

Polycrates, a man near Pericles' own age, was tall and athletic and patrician of appearance, with a long pale face and large brown eyes and an aesthetic expression. He dressed soberly, as befitted the position he held.

Thucydides, not to be confused with the historian of the same name, was, in the eyes of Polycrates a man to be respected, for all he was a money-lender and therefore pernicious in his dealings. He was rich, and despite his own aristocratic lineage Polycrates held some deference for the old man, though the latter had no ancestors of which he could boast. He was short of stature, broad of shoulders and thin of body, with a mane of white hair and a thick white beard, which was like gleaming silk. It was his only physical asset, for he had little sharp eyes and a nose like a vulture, to which many of those who owed him money likened him.

The two men had been kept separated by the soldiers, so that neither could speak to the other, though this did not prevent them from exchanging glances of fear and dread while they were being conducted to the presence of Pericles. Neither had yet heard of the death of Pheidias, for neither had been in the plot to kill him, for their companions in conspiracy to arrest and try Pheidias had thought it wise not to mention that part of the scheme to them.

Both Polycrates and Thucydides believed they were to be brought to Pericles because in some fashion Pericles had heard of the plot to imprison Pheidias, and to bring him to trial and eventual exile or, in the last extremity, to be condemned to death by the proper and legal authorities.

Polycrates, being more intelligent than Thucydides, had brought himself to the thought, just before entering the presence of Pericles: Of a surety Pheidias has blasphemed

Athene Parthenos, and doubtless was given large sums from the treasury by Pericles, and this will be proved at the trial; Pericles intends to intimidate me – but I have friends almost as powerful as he, and they will not desert me. Thucydides was less trusting in his terrified thoughts, and he said to himself, If our friends betray us then I shall embroil them to the utmost. So they composed themselves as well as they could and when conducted into the offices of Pericles they had lost some of their terror.

They were astonished to see the King Archon there, for was he not to preside at the trial of Pheidias, which would be held despite the delay in the appearance of the chief witness, Polycrates? Even Pericles, himself, could not stop the trial and would be forced to release Polycrates, despite any of his accusations, which he could not prove. One has only to be valiant, said the most unvaliant of men, Polycrates. But could it be that the King Archon, before the trial, wished to hear his testimony to ascertain if it were valid? Polycrates, at this, gave the King Archon a faint smile, and was dismayed when Polybius averted his head. As for Thucydides, he could only gape, for his mind was not as agile as that of Polycrates, and he was an old man.

The two culprits then dared to look at Pericles who was sitting tall and stiffly in his chair, and they shrank when they saw his face and again began to tremble with terror. He studied their countenances. He knew both well, particularly Polycrates, whom he had assisted so generously. As he was a most perceptive and astute man, and understood human nature in all its varieties and venalities, he had his first doubts. Polycrates was quite capable of bending under harsh pressure, but he was not a violent man. Thucydides was an avaricious usurer and swindler and a vulgarian on his mother's side. Therefore, he was also a coward. He might be party to libel and slander and covert attacks, and he was notoriously malicious. He loved money as a man loves his mistress; he would not endanger that money – however he might jeopardize his life in the pursuit of it – by engaging in murder. It was not in the character of either man, and Pericles wondered if they knew that murder had been plotted by their fellow conspirators. He doubted it. It was more likely that they had never been informed by their more malignant companions.

Nevertheless, he said to them in a quiet and frightening voice, 'What have you two murderers to say for yourselves?'

He saw that both of them were instantly stunned. He had spoken to them while they were bowing to him, and they stood paralysed, half-bent, and their faces were grotesque with shock, their mouths dropping open, their eyes bulging. They stared at him, unblinking, as at a basilisk. Thucydides' ophidian eyes did not waver; those of Polycrates were dazed.

'Why did you murder Pheidias, that great artist?' he asked, for they were unable to speak, and seemed not to breathe.

Polycrates, the man more likely by breeding to find his voice first, gasped, ' "Murder," lord? Surely you are jesting!'

'Jesting,' repeated Thucydides, wavering on his feet.

Pericles said in that dreadfully quiet voice, 'I am not jesting. He was poisoned early this morning, in his cell.' Now he raised his voice so that it cracked in the room, 'What had he done to you that you plotted against him and killed him?'

'Gods,' groaned Polycrates, and he turned feebly to the King Archon and held out his hands as if for succour. But the King Archon's countenance was as pitiless as Pericles'. Polycrates then turned to Pericles and cried out in anguish, 'If he was murdered I knew it not, and had no part in it! Before the gods, lord, I swear it!'

'Before the gods, I swear it also!' Thucydides quavered, and his eyelids fluttered as if he were about to faint. He began half to retch, half to sob. He looked at Polycrates, then he caught the younger man's arm to keep from falling. His white hair rose like a mane in the worst fright he had ever felt in his life. 'Why should anyone – ' He could not continue for a moment. 'Why should anyone murder Pheidias?'

'I do not know,' said Pericles, in the most terrible voice

anyone had ever heard him use. 'But as you two were part of the plot to destroy him you are also capable of murder, if that will serve your purpose.'

He had accomplished what he had desired: He had shaken them to their very marrow and rendered them feeble and petrified and helpless. Perjury and bribery were one thing; assassination was another. Before they could recover their sense of self-protection and seek to lie to him, he said, 'You see my captain and my soldiers. It is lawful to execute murderers on the spot, if they confess. Why do you then not confess and die easily, and not face trial, public ignominy and public death? You, Polycrates, are a man of a noble house. You would prefer private execution to exposure to the eyes of the populace when you die. Iphis!'

Iphis stepped forward. Polycrates regarded him with ghastly terror, and retreated a step. Pericles lifted his hand as if to restrain his captain.

'And before you die, Polycrates, it will be revealed openly that you had your wife's name forged on the public records as an Athenian. Therefore, she is not your wife; she is your concubine, and your sons are illegitimate. They will inherit nothing from you, and your family will shun them forever afterwards.'

Then all Polycrates' last resistance disappeared, and he fell to his knees before Pericles and clasped his hands beseechingly and wept and said, 'Lord, have mercy on the helpless, if not on me – who am innocent of murder and knew nothing of it! I will die gladly to spare those I love from infamy and shame – '

'You did not spare Pheidias, whom I loved. Why, then, should I spare you, who killed Pheidias?'

Polycrates groaned over and over. He bent, still on his knees, and beat his head on the stone floor until it suddenly bled. Pericles gave a signal to Iphis, and the soldier seized Polycrates by the neck and dragged him to his feet. Tears and his blood ran down his face. He repeated, 'I am innocent of murder! Do with me what you will, but spare my wife and children! I am not afraid to die; I fear only the destiny of my family. You have sons, lord, and so you are not insensible to their fate – '

Thucydides stood shaking and whimpering and wringing his hands. Pericles gave him a glance of awful loathing, but he spoke only to Polycrates.

'It may be that you did not murder Pheidias, or give orders for him to die and that you did not know that his death was plotted. I will accept that for a moment. But you did forge the public records of the treasury that Pheidias was a thief, that he had received boundless sums for the glorious work he has done. You did accept a bribe for that evil work. You were threatened with exposure concerning your wife and sons.'

Polycrates wiped the blood and sweat and tears from his face with the back of a palsied hand.

He said in a despairing tone, 'Yes, that is true. I would have resisted the bribe, however I lusted for the money. I confess that in the end I even convinced myself that it was indeed true, that Pheidias had looted the treasury with your consent, lord. Yes, I confess that, for were the sums not enormous which were poured out on the acropolis? I had my conscience to overcome first, before I could accede to pressure. The bribe alone – yes, I might have resisted that. But I was threatened by exposure of my illegal marriage to my beloved wife, and that I could not resist.'

Pericles' pale lips tightened. The man's obvious agony was beginning to affect him. So he turned to Thucydides.

'What part did you play in this most monstrous plot, you senile old wretch?'

Thucydides whimpered, 'I never knew. Mercy, lord. I was maddened by your extravagance. I confess that. I hated you, I confess that. So I joined in the conspiracy against you, to strike at you through Pheidias. But, murder! Gods, not murder!'

Pericles leaned back in his chair and considered him with intense hatred.

'Had Pheidias been found guilty, through the force of Polycrates' forgery, and your accusations and conspiracy, he would have been executed. And that would have been murder, would it not?'

Thucydides wagged his head and whimpered louder. 'No. I would not have thought it murder. It would have been execution. But, I was assured that almost the most that would happen to Pheidias would be exile, or imprisonment, and public disgrace. I had nothing against Pheidias as a man or an artist. There was only your extravagance. Again, yes, I hated you. You had me prosecuted as a usurer – ' He had become incoherent and now he could only utter whining and incoherent sounds.

'I, then, of a surety, was intended to be your victim. That is so?'

The silence of the two men was more of a confession than words.

The King Archon spoke for the first time to the culprits. 'You, Polycrates, of an aristocratic family, would have sworn most solemnly before me today that Pheidias was guilty of peculations. You, Thucydides, would have declared that Pheidias was also guilty of sacrilege, though even the market rabble has not yet reached that conclusion. Neither of you dared to attempt the assassination of your Head of State openly, or to defame his character openly. But you plotted to do that through Pheidias. This, in my opinion, is worse than murder. Alas, that there is no adequate punishment for both of you!'

Now he rose in the full dignity of his official robes and said to them with bitter sternness: 'I am your judge, before the gods. Before me, Polycrates, you would have committed perjury against an innocent man, for his destruction. You are more guilty than your companion, Thucydides, who is very old and considers money sacred, and is of a lowly house through his mother. Therefore, I now put you both under arrest and confine you to prison to await a public trial, where all will be exposed and nothing hidden.'

404

'A moment,' said Pericles. 'I need the names of your fellow conspirators, for they shall not escape my own judgement. Speak, Polycrates. You have nothing to lose now.'

But Polycrates hesitated, for he was of an aristocratic house. It was Thucydides who took a trembling step towards Pericles and cried out, 'I will name them, lord, if you will have mercy on me! I am an old man, white of hair and beard, and I would die in prison. Have mercy!'

Pericles said, 'I will promise you nothing, but I will take into consideration that you have made a full confession of your guilt, and that you have not withheld the names of your guilty companions.'

He lifted his pen and drew parchment towards him. 'Well?' he said. Thucydides glanced swiftly at Polycrates, who could only stand, the blood trickling down his face.

So Thucydides named them. The King Archon listened in silent horror, for several were his friends and one was married to his niece. Once or twice he made a gesture of despair and sickness. Pericles wrote down each name as Thucydides mumbled it, still wringing his hands. When Thucydides stopped speaking, Pericles contemplated the names he had written and his eyes had the blank look of a statue staring at the sun.

He said, most quietly, 'Polycrates, I thought that I, and I alone, knew of your illicit marriage. I never told you I knew. I had pity, as you did not have pity, or gratitude for my appointing you keeper of the treasury. If you remain alive and are tried, that marriage will become public knowledge. I assure you of that. If you are not tried, your companions will keep their own silence, for they are of your class. They will also believe that you never betrayed them, and so will not speak.'

He then turned to Thucydides. 'I do not wish you tried, either, for you might blurt out the pathetic concealment of Polycrates. Yes, I call it pathetic, for do I not, myself, love a foreign woman? You are not to be trusted in open court,

Thucydides. So, you must leave Athens at once, for self-appointed exile, for life. And,' again his voice rose dauntingly, 'if you speak of Polycrates, and his family, then even in exile you will be sought out and you will die.'

Thucydides, overcome with feverish joy, clasped his hands and beat them against his bearded chin. 'Lord, may the gods bless you for your mercy! I will leave, today, today, with no word to anyone, not even my kindred!' Tears of both exhaustion and relief spurted from his eyes.

Pericles made a mouth of total disgust. He said, 'You have not told me which man it was who bribed Polycrates.'

Now Thucydides himself hesitated, for he had withheld the name of Callias out of fear of Pericles, himself, for was not Callias the son of Pericles' rejected wife? Callias might hate Pericles, and Pericles detest Callias, but he was the brother of Pericles' sons. He was in a dilemma, and again he darted a glance at Polycrates. But Polycrates had bent his head and appeared to be meditating.

'Was it you, Thucydides?' said Pericles.

Terrified again, fearful that the mercy offered him would be withdrawn if Pericles believed him guilty, the old man exclaimed, 'Lord, you must not be angry, for have I not confessed and given you the names of the others? Lord, the man who bribed Polycrates and threatened him was – was – Callias, brother to your sons.'

There was a prolonged silence in the room, while all stood as statues, even Iphis and the soldiers. Then Pericles said, without any emotion apparent at all, 'I should have guessed it. Yes, I should have known.'

He laid the pen down on the table with a steady hand. He began to roll the parchment as if he was not aware of those about him.

Finally he looked at Polycrates and now Polycrates looked at him steadfastly. The blood was clotting on his forehead.

'You are a brave man, for all your venality, Polycrates, and all your crimes against a good and innocent and illustrious man.

'Yes, you might have resisted bribery, but not the shame of your family. You see that I am merciful, after all.'

Polycrates bowed in silence, and his face was the face of a dead man.

'You understand entirely, Polycrates?'

'Yes, lord,' Polycrates replied. His smile was heart-broken but unshaken. Thucydides stared. Polycrates was more guilty than himself, yet Pericles had spared him and he gaped and frowned. Polycrates was not even condemned to exile!

'You may both leave now,' said Pericles and turned in his chair away from them. Then he said to Polycrates, 'Go in peace. Embrace your family.'

When they had left the King Archon said in a wondering and tremulous voice, 'I have deeply wronged you, myself, Pericles, and I beg your forgiveness, for you are a noble man.' He stopped and smiled a little. 'For all you are also recklessly extravagant!'

But Pericles said nothing, and after a compassionate glance at him the King Archon departed also.

Polycrates did indeed embrace his beloved family that night, then retired to his chamber, alone. Then with a firm hand he plunged his dagger into his heart and quietly died. His suicide was never explained.

Callias was followed a few nights later when he went to one of his disreputable haunts near the sea, wrapped as always in a cloak and hood. He was murdered in an alley. His murderers were never found, but it was said that he had been slain by robbers, who had taken his purse.

The other conspirators were deluded that Polycrates had died rather than implicate them, so in gratitude they did not betray him in his death. As for Thucydides – where was that old vulgarian? No one ever saw him again. He had fled, they concluded, when he had heard of Polycrates' suicide. Therefore, the only two witnesses who could have brought them to trial had vanished. But when Callias was murdered, ostensibly by thieves, they guessed a little of the truth, if only a little. As for the stranger who had poisoned Pheidias, he was to remain undiscovered.

One by one they silently left Athens for prolonged absences, and a number of them did not return. But the rumour they had begun, that Pericles had had Pheidias poisoned, was believed by the market rabble.

CHAPTER XVI

Paralus requested permission, through a slave, to speak to his father in Pericles' library. When the permission was given Paralus entered the library where Pericles, his face like grey marble, was studying some war maps and plans of strategy. His heavy and white-streaked mane gave him an implacable look as it fell over his brow and ears, and he was no longer Head of State in his appearance but again an indomitable soldier, for the war with Sparta and her sister city-states had suddenly broken out in tragic thunder and fire. Athens had never been so ominously threatened since the Persian wars.

He looked up at Paralus almost as if he did not see him, then motioned to a chair. He returned to his maps. He wore a thick robe of crimson wool and a brazier burned warmly near him, for it was winter, and snow already lay heavily on the far Macedonian mountains and the air in Athens was as sharp as a sword to the flesh and a dull sky overlay her blasted hills. Pericles' feet were encased in fur-lined high boots, and his hands were chill and he rubbed them for a moment, absently, not taking his pale eyes from the maps.

Since last summer, when Pheidias and Callias had both been murdered, something had changed in Paralus. He had never been garrulous like his antic brother, now in command of a huge garrison of soldiers guarding the approach to Athens.

Paralus was not subject to abrupt changes of moods, as was Xanthippus, and his humour was more ponderous, for all it was telling. He was steadfast and somewhat slow, in comparison with Xanthippus' volatile and witty nature. He was never noisy and he spoke only when he had something to say. Still, he had become more and more quiet since last summer, and his natural gravity had increased and often he appeared abstracted. Pericles, despite his awful problems, had finally become aware of this, though he had not remarked on it. Like Paralus, he never invaded the secret thoughts of others, except Aspasia's, for to him she was a second heart, a second mind, a second spirit. Even his loved sons never approached him as closely as she did; she was, to him, his own flesh.

Now he looked up at Paralus and said, 'You asked to see me, my son. I must beg of you that what you have to say will be short, for it is very late and I have more maps to study.'

Paralus said in the voice of Pericles' youth, firm and resonant, 'I should like your permission to visit my mother for a time, until her grief subsides. She is all alone, except for her very aged mother, who cannot leave her bed any longer.'

Pericles looked at him intently. Then he said, 'You are not a child, or even a youth, Paralus. You are a young man. It is for you to decide.'

Paralus bowed a little. Then their eyes fused together for several long moments. Finally Pericles sighed, and said, 'I know there is something troubling you. I do not ask you to tell me, for you are a man and have the problems of a man, and it would be wrong for me to intrude on your thoughts. I have the fate of Athens in my hands; even my family must not supersede my duty there, or my strength.'

'I understand,' said Paralus. 'I am not a petulant woman, demanding attention when weightier matters must be considered. I am the son of a soldier, the brother of a soldier. I would I were a soldier, myself. No matter. I thought, in all courtesy, that I should ask your permission to visit my lonely mother for a time, for I am still under your roof.'

Pericles' hand tapped the maps slowly. Still holding Paralus' eye he said, and his voice had changed and become hard and slow:

'My son, Athens will never recover the glory she had in my dear friend, Pheidias, so heinously murdered. Part of the soul of Athens died when he died. He was of a stature of a god. When men die their families and friends mourn them. When a god dies the very heavens are shattered.'

A small spasm passed over the face of Paralus, but he remained silent. For a moment his eye shifted; then it returned to the countenance of his father.

'Pheidias,' said Pericles, 'was, as you know, murdered not because he was hated – for who could have hated such a soul as was Pheidias'? He was murdered in order to render me desolate. There was also a plot against me, your father, to depose or exile me.'

Paralus said very quietly, 'Yes. I know. I have heard rumours in the city. Athens is the very well of gossip.'

Suddenly Pericles became almost wildly impatient. 'Enough! I am glad that you have shown filial devotion to your mother, who indeed is alone. Return if and when you wish.'

Then he softened somewhat towards Paralus, and held out his hand to him. 'Is it farewell, my son?'

Paralus took his father's hand; his own fingers were very cold. He said, 'No, it is not farewell, my father, but it may be for a long time.'

Pericles tried to smile. He held his son's hand and said, 'There are many things you do not understand, Paralus, which must remain a secret to me. There are others who need my silence, and their needs are greater than your own, or even mine. Go, then. Console your mother, who grieves for her dead son. She has, in you and Xanthippus, deeper consolations than she knows, unfortunate woman.'

Paralus bowed again to his father, then left the room with Pericles' own stateliness, and Pericles watched him go and his heart was heavy. He returned to his maps and scrolls and pen.

Suddenly he felt exhausted and sorrowful. Pheidias' death never left his mind; all at once his pain was as acute and as unbearable as if Pheidias had just been murdered, and his old incredulity returned that Pheidias was dead. Savagely, he flung a scroll from him and it dropped to the marble floor, which was so cold that even the thick Persian rug and his boots could feel the penetration of it. He shivered. He blinked his tired eyes, for a film had formed over them, which dimmed his vision.

He blew out the lamp and went to his large chamber. Aspasia was not yet asleep, though it was very late. She seemed to know when he was disturbed and ill at ease, even if she never spoke of it. She held out her arms to him and he dropped on his knees beside the bed and rested his head on her breast, and she held him close to her. Her flesh was warm and sweet and fragrant; her hair fell over her shoulders and far down her back. Her touch was one of comfort and tenderness. Her eyes quivered with many sparkling lights, like brown wine in the sun.

He said, revelling in the clasp of her arms, 'Paralus asked me for permission to leave my house and visit his mother – for a long time.'

'I thought he would do that. I have thought he would for several months.'

Pericles was astonished. 'But you never told me.'

'No. Were you not anxious enough, and distressed enough, at the outbreak of this great war which has been smouldering for many years? Until the hour came when Paralus had finally come to a decision was time, alas, for you to know. Before that, the added burden would have been too much.'

He clung to her. He said, 'Did I ever tell you that I love you, my darling?'

She rested her cheek on the top of his head, and laughed so that she would not weep. 'No! Never did you tell me!'

His body was cold, and he shivered again, and he threw aside his robe and went under the blankets to her, and they

411

made love as if this were their wedding night and they were young and ardent lovers, exultant and cleaving together, one flesh, one soul, consumed with passion and rejoicing in it, and it was a reprieve.

Among the associates of Xanthippus was a dissolute and very rich young man of considerable brilliance of mind, and a general in the army. He was also a relative of the family of Pericles, for he was of the house of the Alcmaeonidae. He was notable for his extreme handsomeness and his love for fine horses, and was infamous for his dissipation. His name was Alcibiades, and he was considerably younger than Xanthippus. When he chose to display it – which was not very often – his intelligence was extraordinary. He was somewhat of the character of Xanthippus and a great favourite among his men and the populace, for unlike Xanthippus in this regard he had a suave tongue and rarely offended anyone by a joke touched with the urbane cruelty Xanthippus could smilingly display. His men jested with him, but they knew they could not go too far in this respect, and loved him as they did not love Xanthippus, who, on occasion, could reveal a sudden flash of his father's cold hauteur and ruthless command. Alcibiades and Xanthippus were not friends, even if courteous to each other as fellow officers, for they were too close in character to be congenial.

Xanthippus held some resentment against Pericles, his father, because Pericles was fond of his young relative and esteemed his qualities as a soldier and as an incipient and potent politician, who could charm, Pericles often said, the marble peplos off a Vestal Virgin statue, and cause her immediately to lie supine, warm flesh and blood. At all times, even in the field, he was immaculate in appearance and even perfumed, and languid of manner and effeminate in gesture, though he was completely masculine of personality. It vexed Xanthippus that Pericles admired the young exquisite, for Xanthippus held a secret jealousy of his father and often had been annoyed when Pericles showed too overt an affection even for Paralus, whom Xanthippus himself loved dearly. So Xanthippus often surprised his father with complaints of Alcibiades in his letters, complaints not always justified.

This puzzled Pericles, and added to his woes, for he was ever susceptible to the members of his family and too sensitive concerning them. Callias' father had been married to another woman before he had married Dejanira and she had borne him a daughter, and before Callias had been murdered he had given his sister in marriage to Alcibiades. Xanthippus now began to refer to this fact in his goading letters to Pericles, and he would show those letters to Aspasia. She said to him, 'Xanthippus is jealous of you, my love, and would have you love no other so strongly as you love him. He was, at times, even jealous of your affection for me.'

'Nonsense,' Pericles would reply in irritation. 'That is a womanish interpretation.' So his perplexity was not assuaged. Aspasia would tell him, 'When writing to Xanthippus, do not refer to Alcibiades very often,' sage advice which he ignored. So Xanthippus' complaints of his kinsman, who was already a general, took on a bitter edge, though the complaints were not entirely explicit. Once he wrote, 'No doubt your affection, my father, for Alcibiades rises from the fact that at one time he saved the life of your friend, Socrates, on the field of war. But Socrates,' he added, 'returned the favour, if you will remember.'

It was at that point that unknown to Pericles Aspasia wrote to Xanthippus: 'Your father feels grateful to Alcibiades in that he saved the life of Socrates. Alcibiades is also very amusing, and your father needs all the amusement he can encounter in these direful days.' To which Xanthippus replied, 'I am subtle enough, my dearest friend, Aspasia, to understand that you wish to soothe my natural resentment against Alcibiades, who is corrupting the morale of our men. He often drinks with them, and gets drunk with them, and their bawdy laughter and shouts are not in the military tradition.' Aspasia smiled at the last, for Xanthippus could be very bawdy indeed, even when speaking to her and his wife. She answered him, 'Your father speaks of you constantly, for though a long time has passed Paralus has not returned home and rarely visits your father's house. You are Pericles' surrogate in the field, and his pride in you is overwhelming.'

For a time Xanthippus was placated and did not mention his kinsman, but as Pericles inquired of him more and more Xanthippus' dangerous temper grew stronger, and his resentment. His letters became fewer and more formal, and again Pericles was distressed. Aspasia could only sigh. It was bad enough that the great war was raging and Athens endangered, and Athenians, long ago wearied by skirmishes and small battles that were incessant, regarded the rising conflict not only with alarm but with increasing anger. The treasury had been drained by the intermittent wars and was now being impoverished to a huge extent in the larger struggle, and young Athenians were dying in enormous numbers. The Peloponnesian War had reached a perilous climax, and many said that even the Persian wars had not been so frightful and so devastating. Moreover, Athens' ally, Aegina, reluctant member of the Athenian empire, protested that Athens was taxing her too heavily for this war, and that Pericles had refused to grant her the Home Rule established by treaty. It was no secret that her revolt both against the government of Athens and the war itself was very probable and soon. She had not too secretly been engaged, lately, with overtures to the enemy, Sparta and her allies. Sparta, though a city-state of warriors, had preferred in the past to let her allies skirmish with Athens, and had contented herself with raids into Attica. Now she was only too eager to fight Athens to a finish and break up the Athenian empire and its maritime supremacy and its formidable navies. Moreover, Potidaea, another ally of Athens, or rather a subject ally, was showing alarming signs of betraying Athens, and some of her people had taken up the war-cry of Sparta, 'Liberate the Hellenes from the rule of the despot, Pericles!' 'Liberty or death!' cried young men in the streets of Potidaea, and often they fled rather than fight Sparta.

All this, darkened by the disaffection of many Athenians, notably the young, was a heavy burden to Pericles. 'Do they not understand, our people, and our allies, that we are fighting for our very existence?' he would exclaim. 'Sparta, if victorious, will not only make us a subject state but will enslave our people and impose on them her gloomy and barbarian philosophy, and make of Athens one vast prison camp, where all will labour and no song ever be sung again.'

'The lion is at bay at last,' Pericles' enemies said. They exulted in this, though their own lives would be forfeit if Athens were conquered. Many of the rich aristocrats scoffed at Pericles' alarm and his grim determination to save his city no matter the cost. These particular aristocrats had had no part in the old plot against Pericles, and had been honestly horrified at the murder of Pheidias, preferring their ease and feasts and the Great Games and the theatre to controversy. But now that their own fortunes were being diminished in taxes in the war they wanted only peace with Sparta, forgetting that Pericles for many years had sought such a peace in vain, for Sparta had never given up her determination to rule all of Greece, and force it to adopt her own way of life. 'Do they not understand, these idle sybarites, these effetes, that if Sparta wins they will be the first to be eliminated?' Pericles would ask his friends. 'Barbarians detest such as these. Yet, our lazy covert traitors would even have us surrender to Sparta, or grant her incredible concessions for what they call "peace and amity".' He would add with icy rage, 'If my city would be able to throw off the rule of Sparta, in the future, I would delight in watching what Sparta would do to these elegant dissidents.'

'They have deluded themselves that Sparta would give the governing of Athens, with all despotism, to them,' Aspasia suggested, and eventually Pericles had to agree with her. 'They not only want to keep their money but they desire power, too. Power,' said Pericles, 'is the final and deepest lust of those who have too much money and too much amusement and too much leisure. They are jaded; they would have absolute authority over our industrious middle class and abolish it, and have a nation of docile and voiceless slaves.'

Now once more the old allegations that Aspasia had urged this war upon Pericles, and that the gods were in a vengeful mood, and that Aspasia was angering them with her impiety, her corruption of the young girls of Athens, and that her house was only a house for courtesans and assignations, began to be heard louder than ever and publicly. The rabble milled and seethed with hatred, inspired by the aristocratic enemies of Pericles and their money. They told each other that Aspasia, as an alien, had no love for Athens and wished to see her downfall.

One day, when Pericles was absent, visiting the garrison of Athens in the company of his son, Xanthippus, Aspasia was arrested 'for her many crimes, this foreign woman, against Athens, including treason'.

CHAPTER XVII

On the pretext that he needed the advice of an excellent physician, Polybius the King Archon granted Helena permission to visit him at his house. He took to his bed, and even his beloved hetaira was not admitted. He was a widower. Helena entered, and he marvelled that time had so little changed her, for though she openly admitted that her once auburn hair was now dyed to its original colour, and though the years had fattened her so that she appeared even more robust and rosy and hearty than ever, her big blue eyes had lost none of their vital hue and she still exuded the enthusiastic and expectant air of youth, and that abounding animal exuberance which men found fascinating.

Once Polybius had been one of her lovers, and when she fondly dismissed him he had wept for many nights. Out of her kindness for her rejected lovers she inevitably found younger and more complaisant hetairai for them, and the King Archon was no exception. His hetaira was young, gentle, intelligent and attentive to all his needs, and for this he owed Helena deep gratitude.

He was eating a light meal of anchovies, sardines, wheaten bread, goat's cheese, fruit, roasted onions with garlic, cold roasted pig, broiled fish, olives and wine in his chamber when Helena arrived with her two female attendants, whom she left outside. She regarded the meal on the table and said, 'I see we are eating very sparingly these days, dear Polybius!'

'Spare me your sarcasm, which I well remember, dear Helena,' said the very slender Polybius. 'After all, I am not really ill; this was your own suggestion. Join me, will you not?'

'And deprive you of your meagre sustenance?' exclaimed Helena, with pretended astonishment. She picked up an anchovy in her fingers and said, 'Too much salt. I have warned you about this, my cherub, but you will not listen. Hippocrates taught that salt is harmful in middle age, and should be used in only slight measure. Do you desire to die suddenly in the arms of Daphne?'

Polybius' friends would have been astounded at his grin and to hear him say with rare humour, 'Would that not be the death best to be desired?'

Helena shrugged as she sat at the table with him and accepted a goblet of excellent wine, Polybius' only real extravagance in the matter of niceties. Though an austere man of prudent conversation, who preferred to listen and not comment, he loved gossip of the city, and Helena obliged him until his laughter was so loud that his distant slaves heard him and were amazed.

At last Polybius became sober and he looked at Helena with his piercing and knowledgeable eyes. 'Now that we have had our hilarity, dear Helena, I must say that I know why you entreated this visit. Aspasia.' His face became very sombre.

'Of a certainty,' said Helena, sipping at her refreshed goblet. Her pink cheeks had turned quite red with the wine. 'Who else? You know the charges against her are ridiculous, Polybius.'

He considered her thoughtfully for a long moment or two. Then he said, 'I have no love for Pericles, as he is extravagant and I do not approve of his war strategy, which is costing too much money and too many Athenian lives. No matter. However, I respect him deeply, and I know him for a just man, who, therefore, attracted enemies. I have never seen a rascal who did not have a legion of devoted friends. A good man, no. As Pericles' enemies struck at him through Pheidias they now strike at him through Aspasia. They thought they could put him to flight through Pheidias, but he was stronger than that. They know Aspasia is his most vulnerable Achilles' heel. To save her, they believe, he will agree to be deposed, or banished.'

'You think he will agree to that?'

'You know he will not, Helena. It would not even occur to him. Athens is dearer to him than all else, Aspasia, his sons, his friends, his life.'

When Helena was considering this, which she knew to be true, the King Archon said, 'This is a grave matter. Charges have been brought against Aspasia through not only the Eponymous Archon, who tries civil suits, the Polemarchos Archon, who presides over metics [foreigners], but through the Thesmothetai Archon, who protects the city's material interests. Also, alas, through me, on the charge of impiety.' He added drily, 'But not through me, on the charge of murder! That would have been absurd.'

'You know she is not guilty of any of these things, Polybius.'

Prudence came once more to the King Archon. He pursed his lips.

'What you and I or any other may believe, Helena, is not

pertinent. The charges have been brought before me. They must be resolved in open court, before a jury also. I have no other choice.'

'You cannot give me the names of those who have brought these comically monstrous charges against Aspasia?'

He looked at her rebukingly. 'Helena, you know I cannot, not before the trial.' He hesitated. 'Have you sent for Pericles – I know his own government would not inform him, alas.'

'Instantly, on learning of Aspasia's arrest.'

The King Archon turned the goblet around in his fingers and stared at the wine. 'It is the desire of his enemies that Aspasia be tried, and convicted, and disposed of, before Pericles has the opportunity to be here in time. Sad for them, is it not, that the King Archon, the chief magistrate, is so stricken at this time that he cannot preside, as he alone must? I am an old man; I have such palpitations of the heart, and such indigestion, that I am completely indisposed, and no one can take my place – for mine is not a mortal illness.'

Helena stood then, threw her arms about his neck, and, with tears in her eyes, she kissed him soundly over and over. He deftly slipped his hand under her peplos and she leaned against him. 'I know it is not for your magnanimity that you dare to caress me, lord, and that I permit it. It is your justice, and so my pulses bound towards you.'

She then slid the bolt on the door and blew out the lamp and they repaired to his bed. He would remember that night for the rest of his life, for Helena had given him once more the passion of youth, which he had thought he had lost forever. Even his young hetaira had been clumsy and inexperienced compared with this delightful wise woman, whom he had never forgotten.

Helena, as she did daily, visited Aspasia, carrying with her a basket of dainties and fine wine. She had already noticed, before, that special military guards were in attendance and not the usual prison police, and that the guards compelled her to eat of the food she brought for Aspasia before releasing it for Aspasia's consumption. They had told Helena, 'It is the orders of the King Archon, Lady.' At each admonition Helena felt her heart swell with tenderness for Polybius and she promised herself that she would occasionally give him her favours whenever he desired. She almost loved him. A just man, she would reflect, is a rare jewel among politicians, or even among other men, and he should be cherished as the adornment of his country. However, he is more frequently despised, rejected and murdered, or, at the least, defamed. Mankind, at the last, cannot endure justice and honour and integrity.

Aspasia's cell was really a comfortable chamber; at whose instigation Helena could only guess. She had with her her favourite furniture and books and ornaments, and there was a large window which admitted light and air, though it was barred. Moreover, one of her slave women was permitted to attend her, a woman she could trust.

Helena laid down the basket, which also contained plates, a jewelled goblet, silver cutlery and linen napkins, and she prepared the table for Aspasia. She said, robustly, 'You must eat every morsel of this. Do you think Pericles, on his return, will be disposed to rescue a hag?'

Aspasia had been confined but a week; her face was already white and thin. Her wonderful hair was now more deeply mixed with silver so that light alternately picked out golden gleams or pallid ones. 'I have, here, my favourite cosmetic,' said Helena, 'a mixture of pounded almonds and honey, which you must use several times a day around those despicable wrinkles which you have insisted on acquiring. There is also here a jar of milk of almonds and lemons, perfumed with oils, which you must daily rub on your arms and body and hands. There is, too, a pot of attar of roses, Pericles' favourite scent. How dared you neglect yourself, you darling fool? Do you think a man loves a woman only for her mind and her solicitude for him? No, being a man, he desires physical assets also. Have you forgotten?'

'Alas,' said Aspasia, 'I have ruined him.'

Helena was disgusted. 'So, then, did Pheidias and Anaxagoras and Socrates and a multitude other of his friends. So did I. So did the old King Archon; so did the middle class Pericles is desperately trying to save. So did Zeno of Elea. Shall we, still on earth, and the others in the Blessed Isles – I hope – then cover our heads with ashes and moan our guilt?'

Aspasia, despite her terror and despair and anguish over Pericles, laughed involuntarily. She said, with pretended meekness, 'Physician, I shall obey your orders.' She forced herself to eat of the repast. She said, 'How is my son, Pericles?'

'As you know, he is in my house, and has an imperative disposition like his father. He commands my slaves, in a regal manner, for which I must occasionally slap him. I must remind him, ever, that he is a guest in my house, and a youth, and that he must defer to me. He has taken, mockingly, to calling me "Mama", I, who never bore a child, thank the gods. Children are no blessing, as the farmers once believed. They can become your most mortal enemies, worse than any other foe.'

Aspasia, eating of the repast Helena had brought, considered. 'I have heard, from Eastern philosophers, that when the Unknown God is born to us His most terrible enemies will be of His own house.'

'Of a certainty,' said Helena, chewing on a citron. 'Who else can be so malign as a brother or a child or even a parent, if a man attains eminence? "Who is he," they will say, "who dares to be above us, our kinsman? Is he not of my blood? Therefore, he is not superior to me."'

Aspasia said, 'The gods choose among men, for their holy purposes, and their kindred have no part in it.'

Helena said, with cynicism, 'That is a matter which should be brought to the attention of envious relatives.'

'Helena, dearest friend, I do not wish Pericles to jeopardize his position in defending me.'

Helena threw up her hands. 'Dear fool! I must say again that you are but one little shaft in the hands of his enemies! Why do you persist in your belief that if you die they will stop their attacks on him? Their goal is despotism. They use the mindless rabble to that end. In defending you, sweet idiot, he will be defending the dignity of men, the workers, the middle class, the artists and scientists, freedom of speech, the laws of Solon, civilization itself, the glory of Greece, law and order, national security – all of which the rich and powerful and lusters for authority hate. They are, in their souls, tyrants, and have nothing but loathing for those who toil and love their country.'

Aspasia never forgot the words of her friend. She was never to see Helena again. For, on the way to her house in her litter, the ebullient physician was killed by an unknown congregation of the whimpering rabble and those overpowered by opium, which had been distributed to them by the plotting aristocrats, who knew that drugs were the best way of controlling potential rebels and rendering them impotent among impossible dreams. Her litter was attacked, her slave women slaughtered. Helena, who had loved life, for all the monsters who claimed to be men, was done to death because she was a compassionate woman who regarded humanity, despite its terrible errors, worthy of living. She, who had cherished the world, and who had believed in the dignity of men, was disproved at last, at least to the satisfaction of those who craved despotism, and had ordered her murder.

The King Archon, on hearing of the murder of his loved Helena, clenched his fists, wept alone, and said to himself, 'At the end, my lustrous pomegranate, you have been the victor. For, if the gods are just, they will honour those who have died in the defence of freedom. But only God can give them complete honour.'

He, being a prudent man, made up his mind and grimly resolved that, for once, justice must prevail, despite the rabble.

When Aspasia and Pericles met in her cell they were both

stunned at the appearance of the other, for, in the short time of their separation, they had aged. Pericles was aghast at Aspasia's emaciation, the lost brilliance of her complexion, her sunken eyes, and she, in turn, was stricken by his air of utter exhaustion and despondency and pallor. Deep clefts were in his cheeks, on his brow. There was much more white in his hair, and his lips were purplish.

She wept in his arms and said, 'I have brought you nothing but calamity,' to which he replied, smoothing her hair, 'You have brought me my life. If I had never known you I would still be in my present situation. Only you have given me comfort.'

He did not speak of the estrangement of his sons, nor of the mysterious plague which was beginning to seep through Athens from the east, and was already decimating his soldiers in the field. He sat with Aspasia on her bed and held her hands tightly and tried to smile in her devastated face, while she searched his own despairingly.

'Helena has been murdered,' she said, sobbing, 'and only because she was my friend.'

'I know of her murder,' said Pericles. 'I have posted an enormous reward for the apprehension of her assassins. No, it was not because of you, sweet. Do not be so egotistic,' and he attempted to laugh. 'Helena has long been hated in the city because of her philanthropy, her enlightenment, her lack of sentimentality and mawkish speech, her courage, her refusal to lie charmingly, her open support of liberty and her friendship for me. She was hated and derided before you came to Athens. Her ultimate fate was certain. None of the multitude she has saved and delivered from suffering has uttered a single word of reproach for her murder, nor has cried out against it.' The bitterness in his voice was lethal and full of hate.

'I would that I were dead, too,' said Aspasia miserably.

'Nonsense. Would you leave me alone among my enemies, with none to console me? That is selfish of you.'

'You must not defend me,' she pleaded, clinging to him.

'You would ask me not to defend my very life?'

They spoke of their future together when all this was over, and they spoke of their son, Pericles, who was now home in his father's house. 'He declared to me today, the impudent lad, that his name will be greater than his father's,' said Pericles and his face became affectionate and even a little humorous. 'I told him he need not strive. I would not be famous in history.' They spoke of Aspasia's school, which was under the stern guidance of her well-trained and loyal teachers. Then Pericles' face changed subtly and became darker. 'What would this world of savages be without teachers? And how do we repay them? With miserable stipends, if any, with contempt. Yet, they hold the future of men in their selfless hands.' He paused. 'Do you recall, my treasure, one of your young ladies, named Iona, daughter of Glaucus, who is a minor magistrate?'

Aspasia, wondering why he should speak of trivialities in the midst of their sorrows and anxieties, said, 'I know the girl. Her mother was a woman of mind, and before she died of the flux she forced her husband to promise to send Iona to my school. Unfortunately, the girl did not possess her mother's intelligence and self-control. I dismissed her. That was a year ago. Why do you ask?'

But Pericles said, 'Tell me of the girl's character, not her lack of intelligence.'

More and more wondering, Aspasia replied, 'She was, in addition to being remarkably sly and malicious, a trouble-maker. Discovering that she could not compete with her companions, and resentful of her teachers' reproaches, she concocted scandals concerning both her teachers and companions. Strange to say, they were clever scandals, elaborately conceived, so that even I once believed one of her tales, so detailed were they and spoken with the utmost sincerity. She has the face of a nymph, the soul of a demon, and is soft-spoken, gentle in manner, apparently meek and earnest, and has a demure way of licking her lips. She deceived many for a considerable time. That is the high art of the wicked.'

'When you dismissed her, what did you say to her, Aspasia?'

She stared at him, greatly puzzled. 'Why do you speak of the little wretch at all? I said to her, "You are unfit to be among my maidens, about many of whom you have spread calumnies. Moreover, your mind is not extraordinary, except in the manner of evil. Therefore, you must leave us and return to your father's house." ' She thought for a moment, then frowned. 'Her father, Glaucus, whom she resembles, came to me in a great anger and demanded the reason for her dismissal. As I had been a friend of the girl's dead mother I wished to spare her memory. I told Glaucus that I did not believe his daughter to possess the gifts necessary for her to become distinguished. Still angered, he left me.' Aspasia concentrated her gaze on Pericles. 'I do not understand. What is this girl to you, or her father?'

Pericles glanced away from her, evasively. 'I have heard that Glaucus is seeking higher office. I wished to know if he were worthy to be presented to the voters.'

'Oh,' said Aspasia, 'he has integrity enough – for a bureaucrat – if they have any integrity at all. He is very careful of himself and has a not inconsiderable intelligence.'

'A bad man with intelligence is only a little less dangerous than a bad man who is stupid,' said Pericles. He continued with an artless manner, 'I think I will oppose his nomination.'

One of the military guards entered the cell with Aspasia's dinner, which was well prepared and appetizing, for Pericles had brought it and it had been in an oven to keep it warm. The guard saluted Pericles respectfully, hesitated, then said, 'It is the command of the King Archon, lord, that whosoever brings the Lady Aspasia food must first partake of some of it before she dines.'

Pericles smiled with gratitude at this care of his mistress, and said, 'I cannot thank the King Archon enough.' He took a morsel of each of the dishes and the guard watched him with a sheepish expression of apology. Pericles winked at Aspasia who smiled for the first time since he had come to her. 'Would it not be of interest to the great poets, Aspasia, if we died together of poison?'

She did not consider this amusing, nor did the guard. To please Pericles she forced herself to eat and to drink. Though it was now advanced spring, and the air outside was hot, the cell was pleasantly cool. At least, thought Pericles, my darling is safe in this guarded place, thanks to the King Archon. She is in no danger of being murdered as was Helena.

Aspasia asked of the war between Athens and her allies and Sparta and her allies. Again, to spare her worry, he was evasive. 'We are doing well enough,' he said. 'Xanthippus is optimistic, but when was he ever not? I wish, however, he was not so hostile towards our kinsman, that beautiful reprobate, Alcibiades, who, himself, is a notable soldier. Paralus?' Pericles hesitated. 'He believes his mother's grief has not yet diminished enough so that he can leave her.'

He did not tell Aspasia that his military guard had been more than trebled, for the market rabble was becoming perilously inimical, and unusually vocal when seeing him in the Agora or on the streets. While he detested them he knew that they were not to blame. They were being incited by his enemies to the point of violence against his person.

When he left Aspasia, after sternly admonishing her that he would defend her despite her protests and tears, he found his soldiers perturbed. Iphis said, 'General and lord, the rabble seems very restive today, since your return this morning. I have reports that many of them are armed, and threatening.'

Pericles was not a man to take threats lightly, even from rabble. So he pulled his hood over his face and kept his sword in his hand while his guard rode tightly about him. He had removed his helmet, the harder for his appearance to be recognized. But he was indeed recognized, for all the shade over his features, for a vast crowd was awaiting him near the prison, and bloodthirsty shouts roared to his ears from hundreds of voices.

'Tyrant! Despot! War-bringer! Robber of the treasury! Malefactor! Poisoner! Deceiver! Liar! Thief! Pervert! Defamer of the gods! Heretic! Shame of Athens! Traitor! Resign!'

And higher voices, 'Impeach him! Exile him!'

'Aye!' screamed the crowd.

Iphis said, 'Give the word, my general, and we will charge them.'

'No,' said Pericles. 'It is not they who shout. It is the soft safe others who hide in their luxurious houses and meet in secret, and plot against Athens. Who dares accuse them, touch them? They are too rich, too powerful.'

But now, above all, was his terror for Aspasia and he could think of nothing else.

He felt a momentary refreshment when he raised his eyes to the acropolis, that forest of statues and columns, of temples and gardens and fountains, and to the Parthenon where the enormous gold and ivory image of Athene Parthenos glittered in the sun. Her great face seemed to glow down on him, and he said to himself, 'Above all things, protect my city and my people.' It seemed to him that she had the face of Helena, and his eyes moistened.

CHAPTER XVIII

The King Archon had miraculously recovered. It was true that when he appeared in court, before the whole Assembly and the Archons, they noted that he seemed somewhat distraught and absent, and that the rims of his eyes were sore and reddened, as if he had been weeping in the night. Otherwise, he was composed and compact as always and, for all he was a small man, he had immense dignity. It had been rumoured for a few days that he had been stricken by the plague, which had already

427

reached Athens, though it had not as yet been of considerable alarm to the physicians, who kept it from the people that their military had been widely afflicted.

The day was hot, the hall steaming, and every face was avid except the faces of Pericles' friends. They had lined themselves against the wall and they gazed at him with deep distress. But he walked confidently in his robes of office, carrying his ivory wand of authority, his helmeted head higher than the heads of any of the others, his ravaged face noble and restrained, his eyes unmoved. He had refused the presence of a single guard, except those at the doors which were not his. However, he wore his sword under his cloak.

'Once let them see that I am afraid and they will be gleefully at my throat,' he had told the anxious Iphis. 'One never flinches before mad dogs. It is too inciting.'

He now stood before the King Archon, whose grey face twitched involuntarily, but whose eyes met his with a steadfast gaze. They greeted each other formally. The King Archon said to the guards, 'Bring in the prisoner, Aspasia of Miletus.'

Before Aspasia arrived Pericles studied the faces of the Archons who had brought charges against her of treason, vice, corruption, impiety and various minor crimes against Athens and her people. They stared at him, impassively. None were his friends. He did not believe that any of them was essentially corrupt or had been bribed; they had been compelled, by law, to have Aspasia arrested 'on information'. He then studied the jury, that large body of men. They would do their duty, one way or another, after receiving dispassionate instruction from the King Archon.

Everyone was sweating in the smouldering heat except Pericles. He was cold with fear and dread. The charges against Aspasia were formidable, far more grave than the charges brought against Anaxagoras and Pheidias, for she was a foreign woman, and the metics were always suspect.

Pericles had warned Aspasia before he had left her on his last visit that she must appear tranquil and serene before this assemblage, that she must attend to her neglected appearance, that she must assume pride and fearlessness. He turned towards the door through which she would enter, and when she did enter he felt a weak surge of relief. For she seemed as a queen, tall and slender, clad gracefully but discreetly in a lilac tunic and a robe of white linen, her face calm and pure, her hair raised and bound in the Athenian fashion with white ribbons, her feet in light leather slippers, her manner distant. She had not reddened her cheeks or her lips, and they were as smooth and still as marble, and she had not used kohl on her eyes. She wore no jewels, at Pericles' behest. 'There is nothing so maddening to anyone, who cannot afford it, as jewellery on another.' Envy, he knew, was the most powerful emotion of men, and the most deadly.

When Aspasia was beside him it was as if she were merely an acquaintance of his, and she looked at him as if he were only her appointed defender. She bowed to him in silence, then folded her hands before her, and waited. All watched this encounter, the majority with enmity, the few with compassion and anger.

Pericles said to the King Archon, 'Let the accusers of this woman speak, lord.'

The Eponymous Archon, who tried civil suits, stood up portentously, and addressed the King Archon. 'The woman is accused of the corruption of young women in her house which she alleges is a school, of procuring them for unspeakable purposes for gain. The witness, the father of one girl who resisted pollution and so was dismissed from the house of Aspasia of Miletus, is here to testify. It was to me that he pressed charges. He desires redress, three thousand gold talents, for his daughter had been forcibly taken by three men in the house of Aspasia of Miletus, and has been ill in her father's house ever since, overcome by shame.'

A subdued roar of anger came from the assemblage, and the King Archon raised his neutral voice and said, 'There will be no demonstrations before me. This is a court of justice.' He turned to the Archon and said, 'Produce your witness, the father of the girl, one Glaucus, a magistrate of the city.'

The Archon beckoned to one among the crowd and he stood up and shambled towards the King Archon's seat. But he stood at a distance from both Pericles and Aspasia, and his face was malign. He was a lean and nervous man with a countenance too mobile even for an Athenian, and his features were narrow and restless, his head bald.

The King Archon looked at him with no expression at all. 'Repeat to me the words of your daughter, under oath.'

Glaucus was duly sworn. He never took his malignant eyes from Aspasia, except to give a flickering glance at Pericles, who was faintly smiling. As for Aspasia she seemed to be stunned. But only her hands visibly trembled.

Glaucus said, 'My daughter was dismissed from the school of the foreign woman. She had been sent there at the request of my beloved dying wife. I could not deny my wife, though I objected. My daughter returned to my house in tears, obviously suffering. She took to her bed without speaking at that time, for she was to ashamed at what she had endured in that infamous house. Puzzled, I visited the foreign woman who stands before you this day, lord, and she gazed at me with contempt and informed me that my daughter had been dismissed because she was not suited to her studies and the school. Though I was glad that my daughter was returned to my house – for I do not approve of the education of women – I observed that Iona's illness became more obvious, and then I questioned her more closely.' He shut his eyes as if he could not bear the disgrace of his daughter. After a moment he said in a weaker voice, 'She then informed me that she had been taken by force, by unknown men, in the house of Aspasia of Miletus, and that now she wished to die. I have warned her slave woman never to leave her for a moment; I fear her suicide. She is a virtuous girl. In her smirched name, I demand redress, not only in money – I am not a rich man – but in the punishment of this depraved woman.'

It was rare that a woman was permitted to speak in her own defence before an assemblage of men, but Pericles broke precedent. He said to Aspasia in a cool voice, 'Speak, Aspasia of Miletus, and tell us of this matter of which you are accused.' His eyes admonished her to compose herself.

But for a moment she could not speak. Then she could do so, in her clear sweet voice, which only faintly shook. 'The accusation, lord, is false and malicious and untrue. I had doubts about admitting Iona to my school, for I already knew that she was not suited to it. However, her mother had been my friend, and she had been a kind and gracious soul and a woman of intelligence. So, I admitted Iona.'

Aspasia drew a deep and audible breath, but she gazed at the King Archon and he saw the vivid brown of her eyes, like jewels. 'Iona was not only mentally incapable of absorbing her studies, she lied, she slandered, she caused great trouble in my school and among my teachers and pupils. She had an innocent appearance, which deceived many for nearly a year, among them, I must confess, myself. I investigated her calumnies thoroughly and was finally convinced she was a liar. I then dismissed her. I did not tell her father of her crimes against her companions and teachers, for I respected the dear memory of her mother.'

Again there was a faint roar of indignation against Aspasia in the hall and the King Archon protested. He said to Aspasia, 'There is no truth to the accusation that you procured men to rape this girl?'

'None, lord.' She hesitated, then added, 'If the girl is not a virgin she did not suffer the loss of her virginity in my house.'

Glaucus cried, 'She lies against my child! I demand – '

But Pericles interposed. 'Iona is not a child. She is fourteen years old and of an age to marry. Tell me, Glaucus. Have you had your daughter examined by a competent physician, who can discern her lack of virginity or her possession of it?'

'No!' he almost screamed. 'Has my child not suffered

enough that she must endure the harsh examination of a physician? She is modest, also.'

The King Archon pursed his lips.

Aspasia said, 'Iona was not too modest to attribute the vilest of perversions and other unspeakable acts to her companions and teachers. Where she learned of these I do not know, unless it was from the female slaves in the women's quarters of her father's house.'

The King Archon frowned at Aspasia, for it was unseemly of a woman to speak without being first addressed by a man. He looked at Glaucus. 'It is my command that a physician be sent immediately to your house to examine your daughter. I will choose the physician, so he will not be suborned. You do not consent, Glaucus? Well, then, your charges against Aspasia of Miletus will be summarily dismissed.'

Glaucus said at once, ' I agree to your edict, lord. Choose the physician and let him be sent at once to my house.'

So, thought Pericles, the father has also been deceived by his wretched daughter, and in spite of everything Pericles felt some pity for him. The King Archon summoned a guard and whispered in his ear and the guard departed at a trot. Pericles then had another thought: What if the vicious wench had indeed been deprived of her virginity by someone unknown? Yet, she had been sedulously guarded in the school of Aspasia, and no doubt in her father's house also. However, it was well known that lust had a thousand entries, even to a prison.

'The next witness against Aspasia of Miletus,' said the King Archon, and the Thesmothetai Archon, who protected the city's interests, rose and said, 'Aspasia of Miletus has been accused of treason, that she has been giving aid and comfort to our enemies, to the danger of our existence.'

'Produce the accuser,' said the King Archon. The Thesmothetai Archon beckoned and the accuser came forward, a fat little old man with an eager face. Aspasia started at the sight of him, for he had been a teacher of history in her school. She

432

had been compelled to dismiss him, for he had made obscene advances to several of her pupils.

'What have you to say before the King Archon?' asked the Thesmothetai Archon.

For a fat man he had an unusually thin and insistent voice.

'I taught in the supposed school of this woman,' and he pointed at Aspasia, 'until a year ago. I am a teacher of history, and am a patriot. One day she entered my schoolroom – it was her wont to do this with other teachers, also, on occasion – and she heard my fervid eulogies about our history. She listened, with a contemptuous smirk on her face, and then interrupted. She said, "It is not enough to utter eulogies. It is also necessary to utter the truth." I then asked her what was truth and she shrugged and said, "Only God knows. Certainly not historians."

'And that is not all,' he continued rapidly. 'I confess that I was shocked, but she was always enigmatic. Then one day I was passing through a colonnade and heard her speaking in a low voice to an evident stranger, of a foreign appearance. She put a large purse in his hand and said, "Give my kinsman, the Spartan, this purse from me and tell him I wish him victory." That was just before I was dismissed.'

The King Archon looked down at Aspasia, whose stunned appearance made her seem unconscious though she did not waver on her feet. He waited a moment or two then said, almost gently, 'What have you to say to this, Aspasia of Miletus?'

She spoke, just audibly: 'I did dismiss this man, for he had made lewd overtures to some of my serious innocent girls, and they complained to me. I did say to him once, "It is also necessary to utter the truth." I am not charging that this man lies in entirety. But too many historians have coloured history with personal prejudices, and I wished my pupils to know facts and not fables. Of what use is learning if it is based on mere opinion, lord, and not verity? It is not truth at all.'

Now she turned the restored brilliance of her eyes upon her

433

accuser. 'He lies, and deliberately so, when he says that I gave a purse of gold to any stranger, and that I said the words he alleges to that non-existent stranger. I am an Ionian, and have no love for the Spartans. I was born in Miletus, lived in Persia and then in Athens. I have no relatives in Sparta; I have never met a Spartan and I devoutly wish never to meet one!'

At this a dim surge of amusement ran through the hall, and even the King Archon smiled. He said, 'Lady, I also wish never to meet one.' He paused then looked at the teacher. 'There is but your word against this woman's, though she is only a woman and you are a man. She has accused you of lewdness against innocent girls, and for that she dismissed you. If you still insist she lies then it will be my most distasteful duty to summon the girls who brought the accusations against you, to Aspasia of Miletus. Here, before you, I will ask them the truth. Lewdness against the young and defenceless is a very grave crime, as you know.'

The teacher's face quivered. Then he threw out his hands and bowed to the King Archon. 'Lord,' he said, 'it is not my desire to subject those young things to public gaze and public questions. I revere the young; they have my tenderest regard. Therefore, though it is true, I withdraw my charges against this woman.'

'You withdraw your charges of treason?'

The teacher bowed meekly. 'Yes, lord. I must protect the young females, at whatever cost to myself and my honour.'

'You are a liar!' exclaimed the King Archon with a rare display of emotion. 'You have been caught in a trap. You have lied under the most solemn of oaths. You have accused this woman of treason, and then when the iron jaws of the trap threatened you you dexterously attempted to escape them. I, therefore, exonerate Aspasia of Miletus of treason, but I do not exonerate you for lying to me under oath. I sentence you to a year in prison.'

The little fat man, stricken with terror, turned as if to flee but guards seized him and bore him away, yelling incoherently, his legs kicking the air. It was then that the physician appointed by the King Archon appeared in the hall and the King Archon beckoned to him. He bent his head and the physician whispered in his ear. The face of the King Archon became tight. He summoned Glaucus who came to him, shambling rapidly, his face expectant.

The King Archon leaned over his bench and said to Glaucus in so low a tone that only Pericles and Aspasia could hear: 'The physician declares that your daughter has never known a man, but he did find evidences of perverted activity. He questioned your daughter very closely on this matter and she confessed that she had not only submitted to the sexual advances of her female slaves but that she instigated them, herself. As this physician is not your physician, nor your daughter's, but was appointed by me to inquire into the truth, he has not violated any confidence, and he is famous for his skill and his probity.'

Glaucus' face turned yellow both with shame and fear, and there was a flicker of rage in his eyes.

The King Archon continued in his low voice, 'If it is your desire I will put this physician under oath, and demand his testimony.'

Glaucus covered his face for a moment with trembling hands. When he dropped them his eyes were now filled with tears. 'It is not my desire, lord.'

The King Archon, who also felt some pity for this deceived father, said in a louder voice, 'We will proceed with this matter. Glaucus, do you still wish to press for alleged redress in money and punishment against Aspasia of Miletus?'

Glaucus gulped. He stared at Aspasia, still with hatred, as if she had brought him to this pass. But he said loudly enough, 'I withdraw my charges, in the interests of my daughter's modesty.'

It was not enough, however, for the King Archon. He said, 'Answer me: Do you completely withdraw your charges that your daughter had been forced to engage in lewd actions with three men in the house of Aspasia of Miletus?'

Glaucus struggled with himself. The hall was totally silent. He clenched and unclenched his hands at his sides; he looked at Aspasia as if he desired to strangle her.

Then he said, 'I completely withdraw my charges.' He gasped. 'As my daughter is an innocent child she has most probably used her imagination, as do all the women in the women's quarters, for want of better employment.'

The King Archon inclined his head. 'It is well known that salacity flourishes in the women's quarters.'

He looked at the jury. 'Aspasia of Miletus is exonerated of the charges brought by Glaucus in behalf of his daughter.' Then he became stern. 'However, there is another matter, Aspasia. You did not report your teacher of history for obscene overtures to the young ladies in your care. Your silence is reprehensible. Therefore, I hereby fine you six talents in gold.'

Aspasia bowed her head and said nothing, and the King Archon stared down at her in genuine rebuke. In the meantime the unfortunate Glaucus left the hall, his head bent. So he escaped the scornful glances of Pericles' friends.

Now a heavy silence fell on the hall for the gravest charge of all was to be brought against Aspasia. Polybius regarded her with intensity, and Pericles moved closer to her as if in protection. The King Archon's face lost all expression except for his eyes which studied Aspasia as if to read her soul. Socrates, near the wall, leaned forward, holding his breath, his radiant eyes fixed on the face of Polybius, as though he felt a foreboding about his own future. The heat of the hall increased. The sun which came through the high windows was an intense flaming light, too hurtful for any gaze, and many blinked in it and averted their heads.

'Aspasia of Miletus,' said the King Archon at last, 'you have been exonerated of the charges brought to you heretofore in this court and before this jury and Assembly. However, there

436

is the most horrible of all – that you are guilty of impiety and I must judge you, for I am the King Archon, and in my hands lies the power of life or death for heresy, the greatest crime against the gods and the people of Athens.'

Aspasia lifted her head and she stood very tall and straight and her eyes were open and serious and the shifting lights in them were like liquid mercury.

'Lord,' she said, 'I do not know what you have heard, what calumnies, what falsehoods. You have asked me concerning my heresy. I can only answer that from my earliest youth I have felt the Presence of the Godhead in all things, that my soul has been shaken as a lily in the field at the thought of Him, that I have gazed on all He has created with wonder and awe and delight and reverence, and that, to the measure of my poor power, I have served Him. His Law has been sweeter to my spirit than honey; His graciousness has caused me to weep with joy. I see His shadow on the mountains, His reflection in the water, His heralds in the skies, His majesty in the smallest flower in a crevice. Because He is in everything that lives there is no ugliness except in the perverted eyes of men. The very stones proclaim Him; the stars sing of His might; the rains whisper of His mercy. What is seemingly dead breaks into blossoms at His gaze; the winds shout of Him at midnight. Before Him there is no despair, there is only bliss and hope. I hear His voice, I see His grandeur in the morning, at noon, in the evening. When I am sad He comforts me. When I laugh I hear His laughter also. When I see a lamb leaping in the spring, my heart leaps also, for the lamb in his dance celebrates God and I celebrate with him. The world teems with the effulgence of God, and only men see darkness.

'Lord, if someone with all authority convinced me that there is no God then I should die, for what is life without Him, and pleasure without His grace? There is only death, and in this death I could not live. He is all, and there is none else.'

She paused, then said with simplicity, 'If that is heresy, lord, condemn me. God, alone then, shall be my Judge.'

The King Archon bent his head as if meditating, and all waited for his next words. After a long minute or two he raised his head and said to the jury, 'This woman is not guilty of heresy. If you believe she is, after hearing her words, speak now or never speak again.'

The silence that followed his speech was even more ponderous and weighty than before. The men of the jury looked at each other furtively, peering over each other's shoulders. Some nodded; some shook their heads; some were gloomy; some were threatening in their glances, some sullen, some moved, some angry, some resentful, some impatient, some with tears on their cheeks. Pericles watched them closely. He had begun to tremble. The life of Aspasia lay with them for all of the King Archon's grave remarks.

Now he could not restrain himself. He swung about and faced the jury and his face changed and became passionate, as none had ever seen it before.

'My countrymen!' he cried. 'I am Pericles, son of Xanthippus, the great warrior whose name is honoured among you! I am your Head of State, because it was the will of our people, despite the efforts of my enemies, and yours. It is not Aspasia of Miletus who stands waiting your judgement. It is I. For, I have been condemned by the vile and the envious and the lusters of power, those who desire to enslave you. Because of the strength of you, my fellow countrymen, they dared not attack me directly, or kill me.

'But they have attacked, killed or exiled those I have loved. They sought to kill my son, Paralus, because he is my son. They slew Helena, the physician. They murdered Pheidias, though he was the glory of Greece. They drove a mighty scientist, a gentle man, Anaxagoras, into flight with their persecutions. My son, Xanthippus, is fighting to save our beloved city, and is prepared to give his life. He is fighting as I fought, and as my fathers fought, not for money, not for elevation, not for power, not for shouts of honour. We fight and we have fought, for the love we hold in our souls for our country. If a man does not love his country then he is not a man. He is not even a traitor, for to be a traitor a man must first have loved, then turned aside. He is a beast who does not know that he is a beast. One trough anywhere is only a trough to him, for his feeding. One master, to him, is no different from another. He asks only to live in his animal living.

'For what does a true man live? He lives for his God, his country, his family, or he does not live at all. He lives for truth, for the liberty which God has bestowed on him on his birth. But our enemies, yours and mine, hate all these blessed things, for so long as you adhere to them they cannot reduce you to slavery, or force you to your knees, or compel you to bow before them as your lords, nor strangle you with chains, nor take from you your holy manhood, nor make you less than the beasts of the field.

'Many of you here know their abominable names, but they are not present! They lie among their sleek women, and dine in luxury and count their money and bejewel themselves and breed fine horses for the Games, and build palaces for their pleasure. They tell you that their hearts bleed for you, that they would have you kings among men, that with their help you will ride in chariots and walk on marble and never know hunger or pain again. They lie! A man is born to labour and to rejoice in his labour, for he who does not serve is condemned to death, not by men, but by God and nature. To serve God and country, in whatever fashion God ordains, is the highest servitude and the highest freedom.

'Men of Athens! Sons of the laws of Solon! We Greeks, for the first time in known history, have brought a dream to mankind, the dream of liberty, of law which all men, rulers and the ruled, must obey, of just rewards for just service, of freedom of speech and freedom to write, of judges and juries, of punishments to fit the crime, of order not imposed but self-imposed, of the power to vote and the power to seek redress under a dispassionate government, even against that very government, of equal taxation instead of the tribute other

439

rulers exact of their helpless people, of the right to protest and dissent, of the right to demand justice if oppressed or reviled or harmed or defamed, and, above all, to be free in your person, your property, your houses, your opinions.

'Of all these your enemies would deprive you and me. They would silence our voices. They would drive justice from her altars. They would make of our country but a vast prison camp where all would labour and none would be rewarded and none, ever again, be men!'

No one shifted or stirred and now only a few revealed malignant and cunning faces. Before that countenance turned upon them, before that eloquence, the majority were deeply moved.

Then Pericles took the hand of Aspasia and looked at her, and suddenly he was weeping and the tears ran down his face, and never had they seen this before and a great sigh rose from the assemblage.

Pericles drew Aspasia to his side and put his arm about her.

'Behold this woman, whom I love, as you know I love her. She is a symbol to you, in the vicious accusations brought against her, of what awaits us if our enemies prevail. They sought her death, not because she has done any wrong, but because she is innocent and fearless and will not bend before tyranny and lies. But more than that, they would kill her because I love her. They would take from me – as they would take from you – all that we hold dear, out of their hatred for us. They would set the rabble on us, the avaricious rabble who would seize the fruits of our labours, who would stain the glory of our fathers with their envious spittle, the envious rabble which has no honour and no soul and no manhood but only greed and spite and malice and bottomless bellies. They would do this in order to crush you and silence you and overcome you with terror, for a rabble armed is more frightful than an army with banners and bloody spears. They would give the rabble arms for your destruction, to subjugate you.

'It is your choice: to stand on your feet as men, or crouch

on your knees as slaves. The dream of Solon can endure, or it can die. It is your choice, for now you appear at the bar of history and God is your Judge.'

The silence remained, even though the white walls seemed still to vibrate with the power of Pericles' voice. Every man looked at him, and looked at Aspasia at his side, and saw his tears and the resolute set of his mouth and the force of his eyes, which challenged them, not with rage or contempt, but with their mutual brotherhood.

At last the King Archon spoke. 'Before this jury of equal men, I exonerate Aspasia of Miletus of all the accusations brought against her. Speak then, if any man wishes to speak.'

But the jury did not speak and the King Archon appeared to examine each face and though a number were still malignant their tongues were silent. The King Archon then said to Aspasia, 'Go, then, in peace, absolved of any charges.'

Pericles bowed to the King Archon and Aspasia bent her head. Pericles took Aspasia's hand and walked through the voiceless assemblage with her and the guards opened the bronze door wide so that the sun burst in and covered the two with light.

PROLOGUE

'The past is only prologue.' Socrates

The Great Plague came to Athens and overwhelmed the already demoralized citizens. It struck down in particular the women of child-bearing age and the young, and equally decimated the middle-aged and old. A multitude of voices rose that the gods were avenging the insult to their dignity imposed on them by Pericles and his friends, and 'that infamous harlot, Aspasia of Miletus.' Few paid heed to the fact that Pericles' two sons, Paralus and Xanthippus, died of it, without being fully reconciled to their father, that his friends were well one day and conversing with him, and dead the next.

The clamour against him rose even higher when, from the walls of Athens, the Athenians could see their enemies pillaging their countryside. The best of the navy had been destroyed. It did no good for Pericles to recall to the government that they had permitted Sparta to grow so strong that they had been able to attack, with her allies, and gain tremendous victories. 'Did I not warn you that we must increase our armaments?' he demanded of the Assembly. 'But you talked of "peace" and a more benevolent attitude towards Sparta, who has always hated us. Can you come to terms with a nation which is determined to destroy you and rule the whole of Greece? We were a prosperous people, we of Athens, and became fat and complacent and scorned those who warned us of the approaching conflict. There is no substitute for the military and the navy in this dangerous world filled with ambitious men. There is no substitute for liberty, which so many of you have ridiculed. Human nature never changes. Therefore, those who desire peace must resolutely prepare for war, horrifying though war is. Only a strong man can resist his enemy. Placating that enemy, assuring him that your intentions are peaceful and that you desire only trade, is a signal to him to attack.

'But when I warned you, endlessly, you shouted to me that I wished to be a king, have absolute power over you, that I was a dictator and a tyrant and a despot. I did not want a strong army and navy, you said, because I feared for Athens. No, you said, I wish to have a powerful military so I could turn it on you!'

'We want peace!' the people cried. 'Our sons are dying in the prison camps and the quarries of Syracuse!'

Pericles was himself stricken by the plague, but recovered under the devoted care of Aspasia. But despite his recovery his spirit seemed to have been overcome by sombreness and his physical condition never became stalwart again. It was as if something had died in him, as it had died in Athens: the will to resist. Athens' great navies were almost totally destroyed, her armies put to flight, while the Spartans, a disciplined and gloomy and warlike people, proclaimed that they had driven Athens from the sea and from the land. It was no matter to Sparta that she had, herself, suffered huge losses of men and arms and ships. Only victory had been her dream, and power, whereas Athens had desired only prosperity and trade and commerce. Now Persia, never forgetting her defeat by Athens, allied herself with Sparta. The internal enemies of Pericles suddenly rose triumphantly in Athens and betrayed her, saying that 'the experiment in general freedom has failed', and that it was now time for an oligarchy to seize power. They opened negotiations with Sparta, particularly the rich haters of liberty, Antiphon, Peisander and Phrynichus. That they were defeated later and crushed by Alcibiades and Theramenes, who established the Constitution of Five Thousand, and continued the struggle with Sparta, meant nothing to Pericles then.

For he had died of exhaustion and the debility brought on him by the plague, and of, said his devoted kinsman Alcibiades with bitterness, a broken heart 'inflicted on him by an ungrateful people'.

444

Alcibiades said, 'The glory of Greece was not the glory of the whole city-state. It was the glory of a handful of great men, though their fellows were sleeplessly at war with those heroes and murdered or exiled them. Athens heaped infamy upon Pericles, and only at the very last was he permitted to inscribe the name of his son, Pericles, in the public records of fraternity. If the name of Athens survives the ages it will not be because all Athenians were men of grandeur, patriotic men, artists and scientists and philosophers, and men of extraordinary stature. Only a few laboured and loved, and were hated for these qualities. They were not of us. They were visitations of the gods. And we did them to death.'

An immense numbness came to Aspasia, mercifully, when Pericles had died, sighing, in her arms, one hot midnight. It did not lift. She gave up her school and immured herself in her house, with her son, Pericles, until he was called to active service in the war. Then she was alone, seeing few if any of her friends.

It is only the foolish who say that one can live on happy memories, she would mourn to herself, dry-eyed because she could not weep and had not wept even when Pericles had died. Her grief was too deep, too immutable.

It is better to have lived a life of sadness and pain, unalleviated by joy or peace or happiness, she would think. For then one approaches death with relief and gratitude. But joyful memories of a love that has gone, of arms once filled, of gardens which no longer bloom, is a torment worse than any torments in Hades. Ah, if I could have the memory of my love blotted from my mind it might be possible for me to endure with some measure of equanimity, and think of tomorrow. But now I am desolate and memory is the curse of Hecate. Would that I had never lived!

Her only dim consolation – and it did not always console her – was when she looked up at the white and gold glory of the acropolis at sunset or dawn and could contemplate the ineffable majesty of temples and terraces and friezes and columns and colonnades. It was the crown of Athens and it seemed to her that it was deathless and that men would always remember what stood there and bow their heads in wonder and reverence.

Pericles had been entombed near the Academia. But to Aspasia he walked under sun and moon with his friends in the colonnades, Pheidias, Anaxagoras, and all the others who had made Athens glorious, and they were eternally young and their faces eternally illuminated, and, as they walked and conversed they would sometimes pause to look down upon their city and bless her and love her again.

'Ah, my beloved, my dearest one, my love and my god,' she would murmur aloud, lifting her arms to the glory above her. 'Wait for me. Forget me not.'

There were occasions when she felt a gentle comfort, and promise.